FIVE STAR REVIEWS FOR AUTHOR'S FIRST BOOK

RESCUE FLIGHT

ACTION-PACKED THRILLER

God, country, honor. If you don't believe in these, you probably won't enjoy this book. But if you do believe, then you have just found a dandy of a book. Non-stop action tale about the rescue of the President's daughter and her fellow Peace Corps mates from the hands of kidnapper terrorists in the jungles of Guatemala. Follow the McWain cousins along with their Gov't accomplices as they make their way through back country roads with unknown enemies potentially awaiting around every corner. Never a dull moment, no story-stalling 'relationship' sidebars, just the constant nail-biting action of our unlikely team of heroes. Can't wait to read the sequel, Operation Firestorm!

GREAT BOOK

I am a great Baldacci , Childs, Grisham, Patterson and Jance fan. Sparks is right up there with them. I have known Carl since 1975 and was very anxious to read his book, but didn't expect it to be so good. Great Job and looking forward to the next one.

RESCUE FLIGHT

Finished reading "Rescue Flight" by Carl A. Sparks, and I can highly recommend this book on many levels. It has an engaging story line that is well developed and believable. The plot builds steadily from start to finish keeping the reader engaged in the action. The character development is through and credible. The story line is full of twists and turns that keep the reader on the edge of their seat. Matt, the lead character, is a no holds barred guy that will go to every limit possible to get the hostages safely back on American soil. If you like adventure and action packed stories this is a book for you.

ACTION-PACKED AND SUSPENSE-FILLED

This is a new author that's been put on my radar screen. It only took me a few days to read the 407 pages because the story line is tight and very engrossing. The author has made the characters come alive with detailed descriptions so you can get a good visual in your mind as you read about them. I liked the action, the plot and the suspense, which really builds at the end (so allow time to read the last few chapters all at once). A good author will write what he knows about, and Mr. Sparks' knowledge about planes and fire fighting comes through clearly. This is a book worth your time and money if you like action-packed, suspense-filled novels that reads like today's news headlines!

EXCELLENT

It was very hard to put the book down. I keep looking for every excuse to read and see what was going to happen next. Job well done.

ASOLUTELY FABULOUS READING

From the first page to the last was an incredible adventure. This author has no reason to feel less than a seasoned author. As a reader I would never have known the difference. I can hardly wait for his next book to be released. He has the ability and imagination to keep the reader on the edge of his chair throughout the entire book.

I have read many novels but I can say without hesitation, this one peaked my interest like no other.

FIVE STARS AND TWO THUMBS UP

This book pulls you in from the start and keeps your interest all the way to the finish. I hope there is a follow up book for this one. Would recommend this book for everyone to read. I had trouble putting it down.

OFF THE CHART

I love action books and regularly read Thor, Baldacci, Clancy, Grisham, Flynn, etc. This book was right there with them and better in many ways. It started a little slow but the plot and action were paced very well and did an incredible job building, so much so you won't put it down(just ask my wife...) Most action books always make mike little mistakes here and there and being a gun guy, I'm critical in that regard, but the details were nailed down, used ideas and enhancements to the story that were very original, and gave the story a very realistic feel, keeping the players human. While many books in this genre don't have a lot of hope, Carl Sparks did an awesome job keeping it quality, clean, and honoring. Ended up reading the whole book in two sitting, it was off the chart and am impatiently waiting for the next one.

GOOD BOOK

This book is very well written. It keeps you on your toes . It has a lot of turns to keep you guessing . Mr. Sparks writes without using swear words. That is hard to find in this day. I love it. It is a very good read.

RESCUE FLIGHT

Very enjoyable reading! I like the characters and the development of their motivations. It had action and adventure; a page turner. I like the president and others in the story who have faith in Jesus with prayer.

OUTSTANDING

I am reminded of Tom Clancy but with more refined characters and crisper dialogue. Very much looking forward to the sequel, Operation Firestorm.

GREAT READ

This book kept my attention and I didn't want to put it down. Was easy to read and follow and was very entertaining. I would recommend this book to anyone who enjoys reading about chasing the terrorist. I can't wait for the sequel.

To Maurice,

Operation
Firestorm

Carl A. Sparks

*Trusted friend and
fellow pilot!
God's Blessings
Carl*

OPERATION FIRESTORM is a work of fiction. Names, characters, businesses, organizations, places, events, and incidents either are the product of the author's imagination or are used fictitiously. Any resemblance to actual persons, living or dead, events, or locales is entirely coincidental.

Copyright © by Carl A. Sparks

First Edition: January 2016

Operation Firestorm

Cover Art by Joshua Medling

ISBN-13: 978-1519119711

This Book Is Dedicated

To the men and women who risk their lives every day
in the war against terrorism!

God Bless each of you
for your dedication and commitment!

Acknowledgements

I am greatly indebted to the following people who helped make *Operation Firestorm* possible: First and foremost, to Sue, my beautiful wife, for her never ending support, encouragement, and inspiration, and for putting up with my quiet moodiness during those periods of creative brain flashes, and suffering alone through long hours and days while I stayed sequestered in the privacy of the "blue room." To Paul Alexander, an extraordinary author and editor who graciously—and patiently— guided me through the painful process of ridding me of chronic verbosity and making the manuscript flow. To Jan Main and Margaret Worthington for the time you spent proofreading the manuscript and offering valuable corrections. To Josh Medling for another outstanding job with the cover art. Most importantly, to God, our Creator, for blessing me with what meager talent I may have and giving me an imagination rivaled only by the late Hugh Dill.

Prologue

Juan Alvarez nervously checked his watch for the third time in the past few minutes. He tried not to be too obvious so JD, the rookie officer he had requested today, would not take notice.

Two minutes, fifteen seconds …

Alvarez was a wreck. He was only thirty-eight, but the lines etched in his face made him look ten years older. His once glossy black hair was dull and hints of gray lined his temples. He was at least thirty pounds overweight and developing a noticeable paunch around the midsection. His olive complexion had an almost gray pallor. Alvarez promised himself that if he lived through this ordeal, he would start eating right and working out again.

He was sweating beneath his winter uniform and he prayed to *Allah* that the perspiration would not show on his face. That would be a dead give-away of his nervousness. He looked up and caught his subordinate watching him. He smiled and then glanced again at his watch.

One minute, forty-five seconds ...

Alvarez glanced across the marble floor in time to see another tour come through the large glass doors from the Capitol Visitors Center east entrance. The group would funnel through the security lane staffed by Alvarez and JD and pass by the metal detector before placing briefcases and other carry-in items onto the X-Ray conveyor. Alvarez managed to turn the alarm function to the security system off without JD noticing.

Thirty seconds...

This was going to work out great, he hoped! Alvarez pushed back his rising anxiety, offered a smile to the approaching tour group, and began delivering the required greeting that visitors to the U.S. Capitol expected from the Capitol Police.

Zero time!

The noise behind him was right on schedule and Alvarez smiled to himself. The raucous teenagers coming down the cordoned section next to the east wall created the perfect distraction, which caused JD to focus on those coming into the Capitol, not those exiting the building, all according to plan. As the large school group spilled out of the rotunda into the Visitors Center and on to the line of yellow buses waiting alongside the curb at the east entrance, JD failed to notice several of the departing visitors were a lot less bulky under their down-filled coats than when they entered the Capitol two hours before.

Not all in the noisy group were high school students. The field trip had been infiltrated as they entered the Visitors Center by seven young men who could easily pass as teenagers. With their dark hair color and skin and learned mannerisms, they also passed for Hispanics, like Alvarez had been doing for a really long time.

It would be very unlikely that Juan Alvarez would have become a 12-year veteran of the U.S. Capitol Police should anyone have discovered his real name, Rahimi Musa. Even more unlikely would he have been promoted to the rank of sergeant, in charge of south wing security for the Capitol, and setting the day-shift staffing schedule.

Alvarez had purposely scheduled the rookie, JD, to be on the entrance security checkpoint with him today. He also purposely scheduled Adolofo Mena, aka Saeed Jalil, to the security checkpoint on the second floor, south wing, at the House Chamber gallery.

No one had a clue that Alvarez and Mena were sleeper agents.

As Alvarez watched the young men leave, he noted how well they intermingled with the large group of students, ignoring his scrutiny as they were trained to do. Alvarez allowed himself another smile and let his nervous jitters melt away.

Today was dress rehearsal. Alvarez and Mena would collect the left-behind items when they went on break. But in two weeks it would be for real. They would have no need to retrieve the left-behind items. In two weeks only four of the young terrorists would be leaving with the school group, instead of all seven.

~~~~~~~

Mall of America
Bloomington, Minnesota

One of the largest indoor shopping malls in the United States is the Mall of America, located in Bloomington, Minnesota. The shopping mega-giant is visited by nearly 40 million shoppers annually and contains over 4 million square feet of retail space on 4 floors; plus an incredible 7-acre amusement park on the bottom floor known as Nickelodeon Universe, a 300 foot curved tube known as the Sea Life Aquarium, and a themed food court. The second floor was principally noted for hundreds of shops of every variety, while the third and fourth floors boasted several more large food courts, a number of elegant restaurants for fine dining, and a few nightclubs for dancing and informal activities.

The place was virtually a city within a city.

It was also a target.

Mustafa Kalil set the timer on his stopwatch as he entered through the main door at a brisk pace. Close on his heels were four more team members, all carrying backpacks, all laughing and cutting up. To the aging security guard standing near the railing inside the main lobby they were just another group of young hooligans playing grab-ass and acting stupid.

Without being too obvious, Kalil sized up the guard. He knew there were approximately thirty-five guards in and around the mall this time of day, employees of the private security company contracted by the mall. Each guard was armed with a Glock handgun, taser, mace, radio and handcuffs. Undoubtedly, a few would consider themselves to be super cops and carried a second gun strapped to an ankle. Earlier visits confirmed the guards were neither extra vigilant nor overly suspicious. They were obviously instructed to smile a lot and be helpful ambassadors to mall visitors. Dealing with shoplifting pretty much summed up their police powers. As far as Kalil knew, none wore protective body armor. That might pay huge dividends on the next visit.

Kalil and his group headed straight for the escalators, laughing and pointing excitedly as they descended to the lower level. Once there, they split up, each proceeding to his designated location within the amusement park complex and, of course, a predetermined place to deposit their backpacks for maximum affect.

Today the backpacks were filled only with books and each man would carry his pack out as he left the premises. When they return the backpacks would be extremely lethal, and would be left behind as the men departed individually by a different escalator.

Kalil knew his team was not alone. They had discussed and rehearsed the operation with two other groups, over and over again, pouring through volumes of building plans and blueprints. A total of fifteen terrorists were inside the Mall of America at that precise moment. The other groups entered using separate side entrances and had their own specific level within the gigantic structure in which to leave their deadly cargo. And just like Kalil and his team, they too were part of today's dress rehearsal.

The operation went smoothly, efficiently, and exactly as Kalil and the other team leaders had been told it would. In precisely 17 minutes, Kalil saw the last member of his team exit the main entrance and dash toward the parking lot. Kalil smiled as he pressed the button on his stopwatch and his cell phone vibrated. Each team was reporting in.

They would celebrate tonight. In two weeks they would return for the live performance.

~~~~~~~~

Grand Palace
Branson, Missouri

Local entertainers and business leaders branded it *America as it should be*! Branson, Missouri, the heartland of America. The live music capital of the United States; located, most assuredly, in the heart of the Bible Belt. A vacation Mecca where visitors were assured of wholesome family entertainment and where the name of God and Jesus Christ were spoken reverently and unashamedly. Where the Red, White and, Blue waved proudly as each of the nearly 100 live daily shows celebrated America's veterans during every performance.

Branson, a town of 10,000 residents and upwards of 60,000 daily visitors, continued to be one of the top ten destinations in America year after year. Seven million visitors annually traveled to the modern marvel located in the rich Ozark Mountains in southwest Missouri to see the diverse and modern entertainment venues. It was a place to totally relax, to be inexorably detached from the pressures of life, and feel completely safe.

The Grand Palace was the largest of the live entertainment theaters with over 4,000 seats. The Palace, located on the main strip known as Country Music Boulevard, was a huge, white colonnaded structure, with a wide covered veranda. The enormous lobby with twin spiral staircases and exquisite golden chandeliers elicited an initial impression of an old southern plantation, but inside the large auditorium was state-of-the-art theater technology.

The theater had fallen on hard times some years back and the beautiful chandeliers had remained dark for many seasons. A few attempts had failed to rekindle the grand dame of Branson, but lady luck finally smiled favorably on the great icon. A complete restoration was nearing completion. In two short weeks the theater would come alive with lights and laughter. Harmonious strains of music would drift out to the refurbished lobby where the polished lighted chandeliers would once again welcome guests and visitors.

Work inside the theater was at fever pitch as the grand opening grew closer. Rehearsal for entertainers collided with stagehands hustling to learn set changes. Musicians attempting the first round of sound checks struggled to overcome the cacophony of power saws, pounding hammers, and clamoring construction workers.

High on the catwalks directly above the stage, Antonio Morales finalized the continuity tests on the wiring looms. The thirty-two year-old lighting technician worked alone in the tight space, coordinating his progress via handheld radio with the technical supervisor in the control booth located at the rear of the theater. Little did the supervisor know that Tony Morales' real name was Hashim Sarhan. He also did not know Morales/Sarhan was stringing an additional set of wires and a series of limit switches to the wiring loom that controlled the cluster of moveable wash lights affixed to a single bar.

During dress rehearsal, scheduled in just two short weeks, Sarhan would once again be on the catwalk. This time he would be installing a separate apparatus to each of the ten canned LED lights for simultaneous operation.

Sarhan leaned back to admire his handiwork and gazed down at the chaos on the lighted stage as he fumbled for a pack of cigarettes in his shirt pocket.

"I'm gonna take my break up here," he spoke into the walkie-talkie. He had learned to fake his accent perfectly.

"Okay, but no smoking up there," the supervisor replied harshly.

"Yeah, right." The owners were adamant about no smoking inside the theater, but forty feet up on the catwalk who would be the wiser? He lit up and sucked in a lung full of smoke while picturing ten simultaneous explosions bouncing off the acoustic inner walls of the theater. He could almost hear the horrified screams and wailing. He envisioned the panic and hysteria as people trampled one another while fighting blindly for exits in the darkened, smoke filled theater. The image brought a sinister smile to his lips. He would show them *America as it should be*!

Sarhan took another drag from the cigarette and reflected on his four roommates. Today they would be acting like tourists while quietly scouting their specific individual target areas. It is best he had not allowed himself to become too close to them. Odds were, they would not survive beyond the first hour of the initial attack.

He stubbed out his cigarette on the metal grating and bent over the wiring loom with one last thought of his companions. No, they were not technically savvy like him. They were foot soldiers. Highly trained, to be sure, very good marksmen, but still just foot soldiers. They would be locked into a pivotal battle at ground zero with maybe a dozen law enforcement agencies breathing down their necks while he would be miles from Branson when the event started.

One

South Texas International Airport
Edinburg, Texas

Flying into the jaws of a mammoth storm in the middle of the night was not exactly his idea of fun. Even though he handled it extremely well, the sooner he could get this bucking bronco on the ground the sooner he would breathe a sigh of relief.

"Corpus Approach, King Air Zero Two Romeo Golf approaching JIME, out of eight thousand with information India."

"King Air Zero Two Romeo Golf, Corpus Approach! Cleared for GPS approach runway Three-Two, South Texas International."

"Roger, Romeo Golf cleared for GPS approach, runway three-two."

The Rio Grande Flying Service twin turbo prop bumped through the night sky. A large cold front was sweeping down from the northwest, pushing a band of heavy rain showers out in front of the main storm. The unstable air mass was building quickly with moderate turbulence already prevalent at lower altitudes.

The weather had turned sour as the day wore on, rapidly cranking up into a raging storm. The race was on to get into Edinburg before the airfield went below minimums.

Right now that wasn't looking very promising. "Information India" contained current conditions for their destination, with startling news that the ceiling and visibility were already close to marginal.

An exhaustingly full day of flying had involved several long legs, the last of which was an emergency Air Medic run into San Antonio. The ground ambulance that picked up their critical heart patient had been delayed and now the flight was dead-heading home to Edinburg in deteriorating conditions. Only the pilot and copilot were onboard.

Matthew McWain was in the left seat, a former United States Marine Corps aviator, co-owner of Rio Grande Flying Service. The thirty-four year old decorated war hero stood six feet, broad shoulders and a well-defined muscular build. He wore his dark brown hair a half-inch longer than a Marine Corps buzz. His prominent bright emerald "McWain family eyes" lit up a ruggedly handsome face. His long-sleeve white shirt with the four-stripe black and gold epaulets was stained with sweat despite the fact the outside air temperature was below freezing.

The copilot was Chase McWain, Matt's cousin, also a former United States Marine Corps aviator and owner of the other half of the fledgling flying service. The two were less than a month apart in age, but the only similarity was the McWain eyes. Chase was a lean six-foot-three and his sandy colored hair was a tad longer than Matt's. His humorous personality could pretty much take the edge out of the most perilous situation, although in the cockpit he was serious and focused like Matt.

The two men were like twin brothers, practically inseparable, had been since they were babies. They grew up on the immense McWain ranch located a few miles northwest of McAllen. Their fathers were twins, but equally different as night and day, in looks and character. In fact, the only thing they had in common, besides emerald eyes of course, was exceeding wealth and an unquenchable desire to make even more money.

McWain Industries stretched across the entire Rio Grande valley and much of south Texas. Technically, on paper anyway, Matt and Chase's Grandma McWain was sole owner of the empire, but the twin brothers co-chaired the business and controlled it with an iron hand.

The desire to stay out of McWain politics and infighting between a half dozen siblings, each shrewdly plotting to stake a larger claim to their inheritance, was the exact reason the cousins jumped ship by going into Marine Corps aviation, and eventually launching their flying service, totally autonomous of McWain Industries.

The GPS instrument approach for Edinburg started at waypoint JIME and continued exactly 26.5 miles to the Initial Approach Fix (IAP). From the waypoint the King Air would follow a series of published descents and turns before coming up on final approach to runway three-two.

Matt pulled back on the throttles as they crossed the waypoint at 220 knots and set the autopilot to the pre-programmed approach mode.

"Approach Checklist," Matt commanded. His face was cast in the faint red, amber, and green panel lights in the darkened cockpit. The two powerful PT6A-60A turboprops droned in perfect harmony, adding a sense of security to the quiet cockpit.

"Roger that! Slow to one-eighty, flaps one, radios tuned and set, auto-ice…"

Chase read the approach checklist aloud from the multi-function display on his side of the cockpit and physically touched each item on the list to verify completion, while at the same time scanning through the windscreen and side windows.

Angry thick clouds swirled around the aircraft and heavy rain blasted the windscreen, reducing night visibility to less than the wingspan of the aircraft. Even so, it was the copilot's responsibility to maintain outside contact while the pilot concentrated exclusively on his instrument panel while blind flying the airplane. It was the orderly sequence of cockpit crew management, which Matt insisted on prior to each flight.

Despite torturous winds and unrelenting turbulence, the big King Air streaked down the approach course as though it were attached to a giant invisible string. Matt's hands lightly caressed the controls while maintaining a continuous vigil over the two flat screens of the "glass panel" on his side of the cockpit: the primary flight display (PFD) and the multi-function display, which could call up any type of data involving the aircraft and the flight.

In the short time that Rio Grande Flying Service leased the King Air, Matt had become confident in its autopilot and other systems. Even so, he sat prepared to take control of the airplane at the first hint of an electronic glitch. It would not be the first time an errant circuit breaker went offline or an alternator unexpectedly crashed; instantly shutting down the autopilot, along with the entire electronic glass panel. Which was a good reason for backup "round gauges" on the panel.

The King Air 350 was an easy airplane to fly once you had the procedures nailed down, which was something Matt and Chase had struggled with at first. Their neophyte flying service began operations two and a half years before in a well-used Cessna 421 Golden Eagle, so all of their civilian flight time was in reciprocating engines. Transitioning back into turbo props required calling upon their considerable experience in turbine aircraft owned by the United States Marine Corps.

"Approach checklist complete. Descendin' to nineteen hundred, speed one-eighty," Chase announced in his South Texas drawl. Something he practiced to a fine art. "Initial approach fix in, ah, six-point-seven minutes."

"Check McAllen for current ceiling and visibility," Matt directed. A single bead of sweat rolled down his cheek. He didn't do this kind of flying often enough to feel totally relaxed. At least not as relaxed as he would have been in their twin Cessna. The Golden Eagle, on the other hand, would not be able to handle these conditions with the same confidence, nor the same comfort.

A brilliant flash of lightning lit the sky and the airplane shuttered and rolled in the turbulence. The autopilot instantly righted the aircraft while Matt's eyes shot to the stormscope in the center of the panel. The colored bands shaded in red and purple indicated the intensity of the storm was much closer. Lightning dotted the northwest horizon, rapidly closing on their flight path.

"Storm's movin' faster than predicted," Chase observed, reading Matt's expression.

"Yup! Gonna be close." Another blast of lightning, this one much closer, jolted the airplane as though it had been swatted by a giant invisible hand, driving them 300 feet below their assigned altitude.

"I'm thinkin' we probably shouldn't be tryin' this." The humor drained from Chase's voice.

"Yeah well, we'll take a look. We can always divert. Out run the storm to Corpus."

"Okay … McAllen's lookin' good right now. Couple hundred feet above minimums, visibility two miles."

That sounded good, but McAllen was only 20 miles south of Edinburg and the approaching storm. *Maybe we should divert to McAllen while we still have time,* Matt thought. *On the other hand, what would it hurt to take a look?*

He knew that was flawed logic. Aviation publications were filled with horror stories of incidents where pilots failed to turn to an alternate when faced with deteriorating conditions.

"Turn to final approach fix comin' in fifteen seconds," Chase stated matter-of-factly. "Descend to one thousand-eight hundred."

The ninety-degree turn toward the final approach fix would point them directly into the approaching storm and exactly ten-point-two miles from touchdown at South Texas International. Ten-point-two miles directly into the jaws of the storm.

"South Texas International, King Air Zero Two Romeo Golf, ten miles northeast for landing." Chase made the call on the common traffic advisory frequency, CTAF, out of habit. The airport office was closed, the weather really sucked, and it was unlikely another airplane would attempt a landing under these conditions.

No one was going to hear—

"King Air Zero Two Romeo Golf, South Texas International ..."

Matt and Chase looked at one another in surprise as the feminine voice continued to call out conditions on the field.

"What's Marie doing there this late," Chase asked.

"Worried, I imagine. We're gonna get a scoldin' when we land!"

In two minutes the autopilot approach mode would return full control authority over to Matt. His fingers tightened ever so gently on the control yoke.

"Crank up the A/C just a tad," Matt said without taking his eyes from the instrument panel.

"Like grandma McWain always said, 'Ifen y'all cain't take the heat, stay outta the kitchen.'"

"Bite me, Cuz," Matt replied sternly. "Before Landing Checklist!"

"Roger that! Props autofeather, flaps two, landing gear down, speed one-twenty.

"I'm leaving the landing lights off 'til we pop out of the goo ..." Chase had also shut down the strobe lights because the brilliant flashes bounced off large raindrops like a psychedelic kaleidoscope, destroying their night vision and causing spatial disorientation.

Just as the autopilot kicked off a sudden gust of wind slammed into the plane, shoving them sideways like a giant sledgehammer. Matt gently eased the controls to the right, barely correcting their flight path before a powerful downdraft pounded the airplane like the sky was caving in on top of them. Once again, he eased the airplane back on glidepath.

Three miles from Missed Approach Point, lightning covered the horizon like a battlefield barrage. The aircraft buffeted side to side, slammed up and down like a toy in a hurricane. If the high-intensity runway lights were not visible when they reached the minimum descent altitude of 660 feet MSL, Matt would have to abort the landing. They were a little over a minute before calling a missed approach and hitting the TOGO on the control yoke. The take off-go around button would automatically reconfigure the airplane into a climb and set a course to the missed approach fix, which was ten miles directly into the teeth of the storm. *Unacceptable*! Matt was contemplating an immediate 180-degree climbing turn and beat-feet to McAllen.

"Five hundred feet," Chase said barely above a whisper.

"Five hundred," Matt responded. The aircraft shuddered and bounced in the storm, but still it responded to his gentle touch on the controls.

"Four hundred!"

"Roger, four hundred," Matt's eyes darted to the stormscope. The giant bow echo leading the front of the storm, only 15 miles north of the airport, was a harbinger of powerful straight line winds, blinding rain, and the very real likelihood of hail.

"Three hundred!" Chase stared intently over the nose of the King Air. Searching the gloomy darkness for the faint images of runway lights was like staring down into a bottomless abyss. Only scarier.

"Two hundred … One hundred … Missed approach, go around!"

Matt knew that if he busted the minimums by a hundred feet that would still give him more than 450 feet above the ground. Still a good margin of safety where the only obstructions were no higher than a mesquite tree or the hump of a steer's back. *Besides, Edinburg ain't a controlled field, so who the heck's gonna know!*

"I called missed approach, Matt! Go—"

"Hold it."

"I said go … Wait! There, five degrees left! I see 'em! Runway lights!"

The parallel string of yellow lights glimmering faintly in the torrential deluge spread out like a welcome mat, only much prettier. Moments later the Beech King Air bounced safely on the ground, sending up a spray of rainwater as it streaked down the flooded runway …

… and a collective sigh in the cockpit.

Matt glanced over at Chase and grinned. "If Uncle Billy finds out about this he'll have a hemorrhage of green paint!"

The excitement was not over yet, however. The storm front was less than ten miles away and coming on fast. Matt knew they only had minutes to get the big twin inside the hangar before it was pummeled with hail. The airport office had closed hours ago, so it was a task that would require him and Chase to dash out into the pouring rain to fetch the tug, connect to the aircraft, and shove the airplane inside. That could not be done inside five or ten minutes, and they did not have that much time.

They splashed through the pouring rain past the new terminal and FBO office building, readily visible in the halo of bright apron lights. Matt gazed admiringly at the two-story modern structure. He recalled the difficulty they went through getting elected officials to uncork the municipal budget and construct a facility that had been on the planning table for over two years. He had no delusions thinking the two of them had ultimately worn down the bureaucrats. No, that kind of juice came from higher up the chain. Much higher.

"Whoa!" Chase said. "Would you check that out?"

In the thunderous downpour a lone figure perched atop an open-cab tug looked positively miserable, dressed in a two-piece yellow rain suit, as he squirted out of the open doors of the large aircraft hangar into the pounding rain.

"Are you kiddin' me?" A smile tugged at the corners of Matt's mouth. "Twelve-freakin'-thirty in the morning, pourin' down monsoon, and there's Uncle Billy?"

"Crazy old fart," Chase laughed.

"I won't tell him you said that."

Matt shut down the engines and Uncle Billy immediately connected the tug to the nosewheel and pushed the aircraft into the hangar. The tug no sooner cleared the door when the heavy gauge metal building was lashed with a barrage of lightning and a clattering of hailstones like a dozen machineguns. The hangar shuttered under the impact of 70 mile-per-hour winds.

Matt McWain lowered the airstair door and stared down at the tired, weathered face and emerald green eyes looking back him.

"Hey there!" Matt grinned. "Didn't Grandma McWain teach you to come in out of the rain when you were a little boy?"

"You should talk, pissant! Didn't I teach you two yay-hoos not to fly in this kinda crud? I swear, you two dim-lights don't have a brain 'tween y'all!"

"Aw c'mon, Uncle Billy, we've seen you fly in a whole lot worse than this."

"That's cuz I'm a whole lot better 'n you two mental midgets." Uncle Billy's eyes twinkled as he waved the two cousins down the airstair. "C'mon inside, Maria has a message fer y'all."

"Why are y'all still here?" Chase asked in amazement as he followed Matt down the stairs.

"Some of us do worry over the mentally challenged."

"Aw, Uncle Billy—" Matt began. Uncle Billy quieted him with a growl.

William McWain, younger brother to the McWain twins and more or less the black sheep when it came to the family empire. The fact that the Vietnam era U.S. Marine Corps fighter pilot was a genuine war hero didn't seem to impress the older McWain's, but it made him both mentor and hero to Matt and Chase. It was his remarkable influence that created the cousins' passion for flying when they were still in high school and that same influence caused them to follow his footsteps in Marine Corps aviation.

They waited a few minutes for the storm to ease up before dashing fifty yards to the lighted terminal building.

~~~~~~~

Maria Connors had the patience of Job; tolerant well beyond her thirty-four years, at least where the McWain cousins were concerned, despite their unpredictable behavior. That is what made her the ideal office manager for Rio Grande Flying Service. But in that moment her Hispanic blood was boiling, her dark eyes blazed with worry-induced anger.

The attractive single parent had known Matt and Chase since grade school. Grew up with the two boys on the sprawling McWain ranch, in one of the guest houses, where her mother had been head housekeeper for as long as anyone could remember. Truth be known, Maria had had a crush on both of the cousins before Nick Connors swept her off her feet. When her husband was killed in Iraq the McWain family had wholeheartedly taken her and her daughter Carmen under their wing.

The flight through an impossible storm caused Maria to be relieved, frightened, and more than a little hostile when the McWain's burst through the terminal door soaked to the skin. Their navy blue slacks and white uniform shirts clung to their skin and two growing puddles of rain water spread across the tile entryway of her sanctuary. If that was not bad enough, Uncle Billy shucked out of his rain suit and dropped the soggy mess in a pile just inside the door. Dirty water inched along the colorful ceramic tile floor, which Maria had proudly picked out, along with all the other interior furnishings, hence claiming as her own.

Angrily, she tossed a handful of towels at the McWain's and yelled, "Don't you uncouth barbarians take another step! Look at the mess you guys are making!"

"Look, Maria—" Matt began.

"Don't 'look Maria' me, you mollycoddling twerp! Who do you think has to clean up your mess?"

"Well if you're worried about—"

"Shut up and get out of those wet clothes before y'all catch your death!" With that she turned on her heels and stalked angrily toward her private office located behind the customer reception counter. "And be quick about it," she called over her shoulder. "You have an urgent message."

"A message from who?" Matt asked, throwing his arms up in frustration.

"*From whom*, you ungrateful dirt clod! The message is from that nice man back in D.C., Carter Manning."

Matt glanced at Chase and Uncle Billy. He shook his head and let out a sigh.

"I think she still loves you," Chase said softly.

Two

The C-20 VIP flight dropped Matt into Joint Base Andrews. Less than four hours after it had magically appeared behind the remnants of the fierce storm that pounded South Texas International. The U.S. Air Force flight crew, including Staff Sgt. Carrie Childress, a stunningly beautiful auburn-haired flight attendant, had enthusiastically welcomed Matt aboard, before the aircraft made an immediate takeoff. He was the only passenger aboard the luxurious Gulfstream 450.

He had changed out of his wet uniform and was now dressed comfortably in tan Dockers, brown ankle-high lace-up boots, a light blue long-sleeve button-down shirt and a muted orange and black windbreaker with Rio Grande Flying Service embroidered on the back. *Never hurts to do a little advertising*. He carried an overnight bag with a change of undies, toiletries, and his nine-millimeter Berretta.

Matt stood in bright, chilly sunshine at the door of the aircraft, staring down at Carter Manning waiting at the bottom of the airstair. He shook his head and grinned at the irony. If someone had told him six months ago that he would be working again with Manning, he might just bust them in the face. The very idea was downright repugnant.

Grandma McWain always told Matt that he wore his emotions on his sleeve, that people who knew him could read him like a book. Because of that he had learned to keep his feelings neutral or even apathetic. With Carter Manning he had not bothered to disguise anything.

~~~~~~~~

Matt's dislike for Manning began about two days after he first met the man. Or maybe it was two minutes; he really didn't care to think back on those early days during his first combat tour in Iraq. He had deployed with 1st Force Recon Company and had promptly made a name for himself flying black ops snatch and grab missions, the specialty of the 5th Platoon.

Carter Manning ran black ops for the CIA in the same AO, area of operations, as Marine Recon. It was only a matter of time before Manning discovered the reputation carved out by the 5th Platoon; he had somehow managed to get the entire platoon "temporarily" assigned as his own personal strike force.

Over the course of three combat tours there were numerous ops that ended tragically. Matt blamed Manning for flawed intel and horrible timing that resulted in a handful of dead Marines. As far as he was concerned, the CIA operative was either crazy or incompetent, or both.

Chase had come onboard with 1st Force Recon at the beginning of Matt's third combat tour. The two cousins commiserated over the inevitable fact that their mutual dream of a career in Marine Corps aviation was in serious jeopardy. The thought of bailing on their buddies in the 5th

Platoon was a tough decision, but both agreed that if they could not wrangle a transfer into another combat unit, they would likely not re-up when their current enlistment ended.

The problem, however, was the classified nature of the work they were doing and the security clearance necessary for them to be part of the team. The CIA convinced the Marine Corps that it would not be in best interest of all parties to break up a well-coordinated team.

In the end, the Corps turned down Matt's and Chase's request for transfer, thus setting in motion the reality of Rio Grande Flying Service. It was a traumatic decision to make at the time, but it turned out well. Far back in their high school days, when they had jumped on bikes and rode out to the McAllen Airport for flying lessons, they dreamed and schemed of someday owning their own flying service. Even after joining the Marine Corps they would remind each other of that dream, but by mutual consent they agreed that the flying service would have to come after first following Uncle Billy's footsteps pursuing a career as U.S. Marine Corps aviators.

Circumstances changed, and after ten years of flying some of the finest aircraft in the world and serving with the proudest bunch of guys found anywhere in the world, they pooled their resources and hung out their shingle at the South Texas International Airport, just ten miles from where they were raised.

It had been a premature move filled with struggles and considerable obstacles, which neither had thought to consider. For Matt, leaving the Marine Corps before he was truly ready brought a huge load of disappointment. It also created enormous contempt aimed at the man he considered responsible. Carter Manning.

Deep down, where it really counted, Matthew McWain was fulfilled, made complete as a Marine Corps aviator. Nothing could totally take its place. So, yeah, Manning was the target of his frustration. For the first two years, every time Rio Grande Flying Service bumped into another hurdle, faced another obstacle, and once even teetered on the brink of bankruptcy, Matt cursed the name of Carter Manning. He promised he would never again look at the despicable creature, let alone work for him. Yet, here he was, amicably meeting with the source of his frustration.

Carter Manning no longer worked for CIA. He was now director of the National Counterterrorism Center, NCTC. And for the past six months Manning changed from being the man who stole Matt's dreams to the man who had given everything back, and then some.

Someone much further up the chain of command convinced Matt that Carter Manning was not solely responsible for failed decisions and busted missions. He was not responsible for a bunch of dead Marines. He was not even responsible for Force Recon being inducted into black ops. Manning just did not want them getting in his way.

Carter Manning did, however, remember the unique talents and skills that Matt and Chase possessed, and six months before had pulled the reluctant cousins into an extremely sensitive and complex rescue operation. The successful outcome of that rescue led to a working relationship that seemed to grow a little stronger with each successive visit.

It was the turning point in the life of Rio Grande Flying Service as well. Business was booming, employees were added. Now they were turning business away because they simply could not handle everything coming their way. Suddenly life was good.

Weird! Matt thought. *Ten years of channeled anger reversed in six short months.*

~~~~~~~

The director of NCTC turned sixty just last month. His gift to himself was getting his head shaved slicker than a billiard ball. Matt thought it made him look even more intimidating than before. He was a tall man, maybe six-four. He had deep-set eyes, brooding forehead, and square-cut jaw. It was apparent the man thrived on Washington politics because he still looked a good ten years younger. He was dressed in charcoal gray slacks and yellow short-sleeve shirt that revealed well-defined biceps nearly as large as Matt's. His black patent leather loafers were so bright you could shave yourself in them. All in all, pretty dapper for a man who had once made his living slinking in dark shadows.

Manning smiled and stuck out his hand as Matt came off the stairs. His perfect white teeth contrasted against a dark tan. *Hard to get one of those this time of year, 'less it's store bought*; Matt smiled at the thought of Manning's apparent vanity.

"Matthew, good to see you again." Manning steered Matt toward the black Lincoln Town Car parked a short distance away.

"You too." Matt nodded toward the car. "Nice wheels."

"Yeah well, a little comfort is one of the perks." Manning climbed in behind the wheel.

"I figured you'd have a chauffeur like the other big shots," Matt baited him.

"Too obtrusive. That's not for me."

In fact, being the director of the NCTC was too high profile for Manning. He worked best behind the scenes, not out front leading the charge. For the President of the United Sates to be satisfied with the job Manning was doing meant he was one heck of an organizer … and had learned to be satisfied riding a desk.

Matt shuddered at the thought of having to face that someday. Flying was all he ever wanted to do. Sitting in the cockpit, hands on the controls was more satisfaction than he dreamed possible. Flying a desk? No way! Scheduling and dispatching and managing others to do the flying was so foreign he did not want to think about it. Not now, not ever.

"Looks like you've been hitting the weights since I last saw you."

"Yeah, a little," Matt offered. In the past six months he had substantially increased his workout regimen, adding a couple inches to his chest and arms.

"Looks good on you. Makes you look even younger than when you were in the Corps. How's Chase doing?"

"Flyin' less, if you can believe it. Hung up on gettin' the McAllen Bulldogs ready for the coming season." Chase put in time as a volunteer pitching coach at their alma mater, McAllen High School. "He's gonna pitch at the annual alumni game over in Corpus next week. Unless you plan on throwin' a monkey wrench into his plans?"

Chase had been a record-setting All-Star pitcher in high school and at Texas A&M. The A&M alumni played an annual fundraiser game against the Corpus Christi Hooks, one of the major events in the minor league team's spring training schedule. It was no coincidence that the Hooks were still trying to woo Chase onto their permanent roster. Matt knew his cousin was giving the prospect careful consideration now that Rio Grande Flying Service had turned the corner financially, making it possible for them to bring on some competent backup pilots. Chase was quick to deny such allegations.

Manning shrugged. "A little long in the tooth for a career in professional baseball, isn't he?"

"I wouldn't tell him that if I were you. He says growin' up ain't mandatory. Besides, he can still throw that smokin' hot fastball all day long without gettin' tired; and still nails it inside a three inch square every time. The guy truly is an amazing ballplayer."

Manning noted the pride in Matt's voice and smiled. "What about you? You're just as good. Aren't you going to play too?"

Matt laughed at that. "Catching is tough on the knees. I wouldn't last an inning against those guys. Thanks anyway."

Manning nodded at Matt's modesty. He knew better. He remembered standing in awe just six months ago seeing Matt, through the benefit of real time satellite perform a near impossible feat requiring super human strength, endurance, dogged determination, and pure guts. He knew Matt's physical ability surpassed anyone he had ever known, but he decided to leave it alone for now.

"Well, I'm sure Chase will do fine. I'd like very much to make it down for the game ..." Manning let that trail off.

The two men stared at one another. The sound of passing traffic and horns honking interrupted the silence.

After a long moment Matt finally said, "You didn't bring me all the way out here to make small talk, Manning. What's this all about?"

"We have a situation, Matt," the NCTC director spoke softly. "One that is going to get very ugly, very quickly."

Matt glanced outside at the bright sunshine. Some of the cherry trees lining the street were already beginning to bud. "Go on."

"Ahmad Hassam has raised his ugly head again."

The mention of that name sent a shiver up Matt's spine. He had come away the loser in a bitterly fought hand-to-hand battle the only time they met, though in reality it would have been ruled a draw. He would love to get his hands on that slime ball terrorist again. The next time he would be better prepared.

"Where? How?"

"We're on our way to a meeting," Manning answered, glancing at his watch. "We'll go over the details there.

There is supporting evidence indicating an imminent attack on the United States. The reason I drove out to pick you up is that I wanted you to hear this from me. We think Hassam is targeting the Cortez family before he comes to the states."

Matt's face blanched white and his fists clinched in anger.

Three

Liberty Crossing
McLean, Virginia

The black Town Car turned onto Tysons McLean Drive in McLean, Virginia. Through the bare oak trees Matt could see the twin six-story modern structures. This was Liberty Crossing, home of the National Counterterrorism Center. The building directly behind NCTC was the offices of the National Intelligence Director and a few hundred analysts and technicians providing for the security of the United States.

It was only the second time Matt had been here. The first was about three months before when he and Chase picked up their Cessna 421 Golden Eagle following a complete restoration at Joint Base Andrews. He recalled that the interior of the building was equally impressive, lots of glass and plenty of ornate furnishings.

The swearing in ceremony inducting Matt and Chase as agents of the NCTC had been conducted in Manning's office, a large, richly appointed headquarters with an enormous cherry wood desk set in front of a floor-to-ceiling window. What struck Matt as being odd was that the light colored wood paneled walls were not decorated with the usual *Hero Wall* things like plaques and picture frames associating him with famous people. Instead, there were a few nicely chosen and appropriately framed art pieces, a large picture of an old dilapidated barn in the middle of a farmyard, reminiscent of a boyhood memory. His desk contained only a laptop and a dual picture frame containing photos of his five grandchildren: three by his son, two from his daughter. Funny, Matt had never considered Manning as a family man.

They reached the sixth floor office by private elevator off the side entrance. Manning whisked Matt through a door located on the back wall of his office. The door opened into a modestly decorated, windowless conference room about 15 by 20 feet. There was a sturdy conference table made of the same fine cherry wood as Manning's desk and eight black leather, high-back swivel chairs: three on either side and one on each end. On the table were two coffee carafes and a pitcher of ice water set on small white linen cloth. An assortment of mugs and glasses were assembled close by, along with a tray of condiments.

A grouping of color photographs of military aircraft and ships were clustered along one wall, one of which immediately caught Matt's eye. It contained the members of Force Recon, 1st Company, 5th Platoon, Able Team. Matt was on one end of the lineup, Manning on the other. The background showed the super-structure of the USS *Tarawa* (LHA-1) and an MV-22 Osprey. On the opposite wall was a bank of flat screen monitors, all dark at the moment. A furled Stars and Stripes stood in the left corner; on the right was a blue flag with the NCTC emblem.

At the head of the table, smiling at Matt's astonished face was the President of the United States. He rose from his chair and came forward.

"Hello Matthew. It's good to see you again," the president said, grasping Matt's hand and then pulling him into a bear hug.

"You ... too, Mr. President," Matt stuttered, looking up into his smiling face.

The fifty-five year old president was dressed casually, dark brown slacks, powder blue long-sleeve shirt with a dark blue tie, and a button down beige sweater left open. He stood an imposing six-foot-six, with broad straight shoulders and narrow waist. He was a powerfully built man who kept himself in excellent condition and did not look a day over forty. He had the aquiline nose, high cheekbones, and bronze skin that was prominent to his Navajo ancestry. A full head of black hair neatly parted on the left side framed his most prominent feature: clear light blue eyes the color of ice water, soft and caring.

Matt first saw those amazing eyes six months ago on the president's daughter when he and Chase rescued her from the grasp of terrorist abductors in the jungles of Guatemala. He thought at the time that she had the most amazing eyes he had ever seen. He had been equally surprised that her father had the same incredible eyes and fine chiseled features.

"How are Chase and your family?" The president inquired.

"Chase is fine, sir. Busy as usual. The rest of the family are doing very well, thank you."

"Sorry I was not able to come to your swearing-in ceremony in January, Matt. I would liked to have been present if for nothing other than to thank you again for agreeing to my request to join the NCTC."

"That's okay, sir. We know how busy you are."

"Well, it's good men like you and your cousin who will make a difference in the war on terrorism and I just want you to know how much I appreciate you boys for coming onboard." The president released Matt's hand and motioned for him to take a seat. "Actually, it was more a matter of listening to my chief of staff that day than being busy, as you were obviously told."

"I don't follow, sir," Matt responded.

"James suggested it would be best that the press not know we were here that day. Could create undo curiosity and we are not quite ready for that yet. *I* am not ready for Carley to have that kind of exposure."

"I understand, sir." Matt was amazed. After six months the news media was still unaware that Carley Downs— Secret Service code name *Caduceus*—had been abducted and held hostage by the master terrorist, Ahmad Hassan. So of course they were not aware of the dramatic rescue that Matt and Chase had pulled off to get her back virtually unscathed. Incredible in this era of enlightenment, transparency, and unlimited access by the public media. The mindset with the newsies was such that everyone wanted to know about everything all the time, which was a patently foolish concept, but go figure.

Matt just assumed the reason the media had not picked up on the harrowing escape was because someone in the administration was doing a darn good job keeping the story contained. In addition, the newsies were so keenly focused on the president's remarkable success with the economic recovery and unprecedented foreign policies, there was no reason for them to go sniffing around in search of behind-the-scenes-deals.

President Downs still enjoyed an unprecedented eighty-three percent approval rating after more than a year in office. The media played a big part in that, largely based on his philosophy that trust, like any other relationship, was a two-way street. He operated with compete and open honesty and his policies and decisions resonated with the American public. He did not withhold the truth, but there were times when he was not forthcoming with certain information. He let the media know his ground rules up front and for the most part they accepted. As long as he maintained an honest, open relationship and continued with successful policies, he would have them eating out of his hand.

The president leaned back and rested his hands on the table. "So Matt, I've been anxious to hear how the King Air is working out for you, and did the folks at Andrews do a good job rebuilding your twin Cessna?"

"The King Air is great, sir. It's an incredible workhorse, especially with the business that's suddenly come our way—" Matt saw the quick wink President Downs tossed at Carter Manning. *Guess that pretty much confirms who the sudden benefactors for Rio Grande Flying Service are*, Matt thought.

"The 421 looks very professional, sir. No one could have done a finer job ... Mr. President, Chase and I can't thank you enough for everything you have done for us."

President Downs raised his palm and nodded.

"Sir, I don't pretend to know how this works," Matt continued with a little guilt in his voice, "but I'm pretty sure that everything you've done for us would be a pretty hard sell to the American taxpayers."

That brought a chuckle from the others.

The president's eyes twinkled behind an open grin. "I appreciate your concern for my political career, Matt. You're right, public funds cannot be used for this sort of thing. Asset seizure laws basically allow all property seized during illegal activity to be confiscated and turned over to the arresting agency to be used within their own budget. The Senate Select Intelligence Committee authorized all assets confiscated from terrorist organizations to be used to fund the war on terror. That's how we financed the expansion of NCTC beyond an analytical think tank into a fully functional organization with operational capabilities. Including that brand-new MV-22 Osprey with all the bells and whistles and high-tech gadgets that you and Chase like to play with every time you come out this way."

Matt nodded silently. The Cessna Golden Eagle he and Chase used in Carley's rescue got shot up during the attempt and not airworthy to continue service in Rio Grande Flying Service. The president showed his deepest appreciation to the cousins by giving them a fully reconditioned U.S. Army King Air 350 for a $1 per year lease. He also authorized U.S. Air Force maintenance staff to refurbish the damaged twin Cessna.

"How's Carley doing, Mr. President?"

"Splendidly Matt, thanks for asking. She is back at the University of Arizona Medical Center for her residency in neurosurgery. That was her chosen field of medicine from the day of her mother's accident. I'm happy she's pursuing her dream."

Matt grinned. "The streets of Tucson are a little safer than Guatemala, right?"

"Yes," the president laughed. "Safer indeed. She manages to get out to our ranch occasionally and keep an eye on things, check on her Grandma Doli, do a little riding."

"What about Jordan?"

Jordan Scott was the Secret Service protection detail assigned to the first daughter. She had been savagely beaten in Guatemala and was one of the victims in the daring rescue.

"Jordan recovered nicely. She's back to work trying to keep Carley out of trouble. During the winter, Carley introduced Jordan to the joys of deer hunting from horseback in the mountains above the ranch." President Downs laughed again. "Don't think she wants a repeat of that adventure. Said something about still walking bow-legged!"

Matt and Manning were laughing at that when the conference room door opened.

"Sounds like I missed a good joke." Alex Strayhorn, Director of National Intelligence entered the room and moved directly to the chair next to Matt. Manning was on the opposite side of the table. "Sorry I'm late, Mr. President."

"Alex," the president nodded. "You remember Matthew McWain."

"Yes, of course. Matthew, good to see you again," Strayhorn offered his hand. "Thanks for coming on short notice."

Alex Strayhorn had been the president's first and only choice for DNI. The long-time personal friend to the president was a short, powerful man, built like a fireplug. Thick neck, barrel chest, and a grip like a pipe vice. The Twenty-seven year veteran of law enforcement was serving as chief of police for Cincinnati when President Downs tapped him for the top intelligence job. Strayhorn was a consummate professional and as anticipated, he instilled a high degree of credibility, efficiency, and cooperation like never before within the ranks of the intelligence community. The man was not loved by many, but he was well respected by colleagues, as well as elected officials on both sides of the aisle.

"Sir," Matt responded, flinching under the DNI's powerful grip.

"I was just telling Matt about Jordan Scott's introduction to hunting from horseback in the snow-covered mountains."

"Oh, yes." The DNI chuckled. "Doing that again is surely on Jordan's bucket list."

The president glanced at his watch. "Gentlemen, I apologize for being brusque, but we need to move on. Alex, would you bring Matt up to speed?"

"Yes, sir, Mr. President," Strayhorn began. "In the interest of time, I'll be blunt. Carter, feel free to jump in if I miss anything."

Manning silently nodded.

"A massive terrorist attack on the United Sates is imminent," Strayhorn let that hang in the air for a moment. "We've speculated for years that it was only a matter of time before major terrorist organizations or some rogue nation would bring their jihad to our shores. We now have supporting evidence suggesting that a major attack—or series of attacks— is in the final preparation phase. Much of the evidence we owe to you, Matt, and to the terrorist you captured at the hunting lodge in Guatemala. Naval Intelligence and CIA gave him a pretty thorough and exhaustive interrogation."

Matt subconsciously moved to the edge of his chair. "Do we know how soon?"

His eyes darted from Strayhorn to the president, to Manning, and then back to The DNI.

"Not down to the hour," Manning answered. "Could be a few days, probably not more than a couple of weeks."

"Maybe you oughta shoot that raghead's other ear off to get at the real intel."

"We considered it," Manning volunteered with a smile. "But decided we wouldn't be lucky enough to get away with it as you were." They were well aware of the drastic actions Matt had taken to make a captured terrorist tell where they had taken *Caduceus*.

Matt leaned back, blowing out a big sigh through his steepled fingers. "So why now? What's going on that's raised the threat level?"

"Several sources of intel point to the same conclusion," Strayhorn answered. "FBI surveillance at Puerto Barrios and Puerto Santo Tomás started prior to you going to Guatemala and is still ongoing; CIA, along with Naval Intelligence has closely monitored transshipping activity in and out of Guatemala and the United States—"

"Wait a minute," Matt interrupted. "Are you saying Ahmad Hassam is back in business in Guatemala?"

"Not only is his business still in operation, we expect Hassam to arrive there within the next few days," Manning responded.

Matt shook his head. "You gotta be kiddin' me! The master of all terrorists is allowed to continue workin' right under our nose?"

The president held up his hand to silence the others and smiled. "Keep your friends close and your enemies closer, Matt."

"The president is right, Matt," Strayhorn added. "We need to keep eyeballs on these guys to obtain more intel."

Ahmad Hassam—aka *as-Syf*—*The Sword*—because of the 14th century Persian sword he used to behead captured Israeli soldiers years before. Not just *Sword,* but *The Sword*, partly out of fear, but mostly as a way for his loyal followers to express profound admiration and respect for his savagery and overwhelming victories. Hassam had soared through the ranks of Hezbollah before being recruited by Iran to train an army of terrorists.

It was believed that Hassam's Army, as it came to be known, was for exclusive use along the Afghanistan border to create chaos and interdiction raids on coalition forces. It was common knowledge that a number of terrorists trained by Hassam at the large camp located in eastern Iran had indeed crossed over into Afghanistan and waged their own kind of *selective* war against sworn enemies.

Intelligence sources discovered that over the past several months a large number of specially trained terrorists had slipped out of Iran and resurfaced in Latin America. A few had slipped into the United States before being detained, while others had been identified and were under continuous surveillance. However, Matt was now informed there could be a hundred or more unidentified terrorists inside the U.S. borders for every individual they knew of.

"Border patrol, harbor patrol, customs, FBI, local law enforcement … every agency we can utilize has been ordered to be extra vigilant and at a high state of alert," Strayhorn continued. "Hassam's people stayed out of Guatemala for five months after you snatched Carley and Jordan away from them. In the past month they have begun to filter back. Small groups at first, but in the past week or so that number has increased dramatically. Confidence is high that Hakeem Larijani is already there, waiting for Hassam to make an appearance."

Larijani was Hassam's top lieutenant, friend, and faithful servant. Their relationship had bonded over years of working together. As far as anyone knew, Larijani was the only person Hassam trusted … and that wasn't very much.

"We think they slipped in to clean up loose ends and finalize last minute logistical support," Manning offered. "That in itself tells us something big is about to pop."

"Their message traffic," Strayhorn added, "which was fairly regular up to about two weeks ago, has all but dried up—another indicator that something is imminent. A few intercepts made reference to *Mylh A'Sifh,* Operation Firestorm; you heard that phrase when you were in Guatemala." Matt nodded, indicating he was familiar with it.

"We are confident that *Firestorm* is their operational plan of attack on the United States. Don't know at this point if Israel or the UK—or maybe even a few other western countries—will be included in *Firestorm*, or if we have the distinction of being their sole target.

"We need to know where and how, Matt. Almost as badly as we need to know when," the president said grimly.

"Okay. Where do Chase and I fit in?" Matt asked.

"We need you down there, Matt," Strayhorn responded. "Our friends, the Cortez family, are in danger. Hassam doesn't leave unfinished business. You drove him away for a spell and you terminated his support from Manuel Cortez.

"You left a hole in his operation and now his return to Guatemala suggests he intends to settle up with the Cortez family before he jump starts *Firestorm*."

Matt nodded and started to say something before Manning cut him off. "Yesterday, the dock manager at Santo Tomás was found floating in the bay. He had been beheaded. We expect his head to turn up on Samuel Cortez's front door."

Matt shook his head slowly and clinched his teeth. Images of the Cortez family being massacred flashed through his mind. All nine adults and fifteen children living at the mountain top hacienda. His eyes burned with anger. He knew these people, had supper in their home, and sampled the love and happiness that lived inside the adobe walls of their compound located in the foothills above the town of El Achiotal.

President Harlan Downs saw the pained expression on Matt's face. "Matt, I've established a Crisis Response Team with Marine Force Recon to meet the imminent threat to the United States. Right now that team is standing guard on the Cortez hacienda. I want you to take command of the team. Stop Hassam and this *Firestorm* operation before he has time to hit the Cortez family."

"I understand. Thank you, sir." Relief spread across Matt's face when he heard that protection was already afforded to the Cortez family.

"Matt, we need you to hit Hassam's headquarters. Confiscate all the data you can lay hands on," Strayhorn jumped in. "Computer terminals, thumb drives, maps … everything.

"We've learned that Hassam has been inserting people and resources into the U.S. for two years. We need to know where these ragheads are hiding and what's going to trigger them into action. Moreover, we now have documented evidence that Iran started putting sleepers in America as far back as 1980. For what purpose? How many? Where are they?

"We trust the answers to these questions will be on Hassam's attack plans.

"We're counting on you to snatch the data from him."

Matt pulled his chair forward, placed both hands on the table, and interlocked his fingers. "Do we know how many troops Hassam has in Guatemala and where they keep the data I'm looking for?"

"Carter can provide those details before you leave." President Downs answered and glanced at his watch. "Do you have any further questions of us, Matt," President Downs asked.

"Just one, sir," Matt responded. "If we have all this proof about Iran, ain't it about high time we bloodied their nose?"

The president smiled. "It's coming, Matt. It's coming!" President Downs rose to his feet and moved to shake hands with Matt. "Godspeed, Matthew. We're counting on you."

"Thank you, sir."

Carter Manning led Matt back to his office and pulled a Top Secret folder from his desk drawer. "This is woefully small, and will probably generate more questions than it answers," he smiled," but I've put together everything I think you'll need … at least to get you started."

Matt took the folder and nodded grimly. "When do I leave?"

"The Gulfstream is waiting at Andrews to take you back home. A COD Osprey from USS *Iwo Jima* will pick up you and Chase at O-five thirty tomorrow morning. Your special ops aircraft is already aboard the ship."

When Matt raised an inquiring eyebrow, Manning continued. "The president intercepted *Iwo*'s return to port from their combat tour in the Arabian Sea. They've been operating in the Caribbean for three days."

"That's how you're gonna know when Hassam arrives?"

"You got it!" Manning walked Matt to the elevator. "Speaking of the Osprey, I'm thinking about staging it in Edinburg at some point. What are the chances your city council would approve another large hangar, long as it doesn't cost them anything?"

"Don't know! I'll ask … When this is all over."

"Not necessary! It'll be a done deal before you get back." Manning ignored Matt's questioning look. "Be safe, my friend. Bring me back some good intel … and Hassam's head on a stick!"

Four

USS *Iwo Jima*
30 Miles Off
Coast of Belize
Western Caribbean

Lt. Cmdr. Clayton Downs entered the GCS compartment balancing a tray loaded with egg salad sandwiches and two iced-down cokes while wrestling with the heavy steel hatch and gentle rolling motion of the ship. The ground control station was dark, illuminated only by the soft lighting of computer screens and the amber and green display lights from a myriad of aircraft sensors. Transitioning from a lighted passageway into the darkness added to Clayton's unsteady footing.

Lt. (jg) Todd Clarkson occupied the aircrew station at the far console.

Clayton set the tray down on the electronics bench directly behind the aircrew stations and turned toward Clarkson. He laughed inwardly. Clarkson reminded him of a giant toad from the way he hunched over the control panel, hands folded in his lap, lost in oblivious concentration. Clarkson's faint humming was barely audible over the silent buzz of the small fans in each corner of the compartment, but Clayton could not make out the tune.

Clayton stepped forward to stand over the lieutenant's shoulder and silently studied a screen revealing a mostly clear real-time image of Puerto Santo Tomás less than a hundred miles away. Tied to the dock were the two freighters Clayton had been keeping a wary eye on. The 9000-ton *Alaed*—registered under a Liberian flag of convenience even though the whole world knew the vessel was Russian—was moored adjacent to two giant dockside cranes. Directly behind the *Alaed* was the North Korean merchant ship, *Chong Jin*. The 13,000-ton vessel also operated under the Liberian flag of convenience.

The optics screen on the control panel focused mostly on the knot of people moving between the ships and large warehouses. Every few minutes, Clarkson zoomed in on the deck railings of each ship, hoping to catch a fleeting image of their primary target, then he would zoom out, panning the wide area of the waterfront.

"Any sign of him yet?" Clayton asked.

Clarkson nearly jumped out of the crew chair. "Geez, Commander! You nearly scared me to death!"

"You need to relax, mister," Clayton laughed. "This can be fun if you'd just loosen your grip a little bit."

"Aye, aye, sir," Clarkson smiled. It was not the first time he had been told to relax.

Todd Clarkson was a twenty-five year old technical guru in every sense of the word. The Annapolis graduate wanted to be a naval aviator as long as he could remember, but eyes hiding behind coke bottle glasses kept him out of the cockpit. Instead, Clarkson became an aeronautical engineering genius. He personally developed many of the programs implemented by Clayton's team, including redesigning multiple components of the MQ-9 Reaper, a specialized unmanned aerial vehicle project successfully flown from *Iwo*'s flight deck for over six months. Two thousand and twenty-eight flawless flight hours shared between two airframes.

Though not as thrilling as zipping through the sky in an F-18 Super Hornet at 1,000 miles per hour with your hair on fire and high G forces pulling your face into your lap, Clarkson still found a measure of satisfaction in flying the Reaper and was proud to be one of the back-up pilots on the team.

Today, however, Lt. (jg) Clarkson was hunched over the control panel of the much smaller, catapult launched ScanEagle, guiding the tiny UAV in lazy circles above Puerto Santo Tomás.

They were ten hours into the current surveillance flight. Clayton had relieved the remainder of his six-person project team to keep them rested. He assigned port and starboard watch rotation to provide 24/7 surveillance until the primary targets were sighted. Once that occurred, he suspected the challenge would ratchet up and become a little more complicated.

The advanced high resolution Synthetic Aperture Radar (SAR) on the ScanEagle was providing quality real-time ground images. From 12,000 feet above the surface the advanced optics delivered close-up identification of people milling around the dock when Clarkson zoomed in.

Clayton leaned closer and studied each face. "Anything yet?"

"Negative, sir," Clarkson responded.

"Keep a close eye, Todd. Navy Intelligence says it could be anytime."

"Aye, aye, sir!"

"I brought you some sandwiches and a coke. I'll be down on the hangar deck. Page me if anything comes up."

"Thank you sir. You'll be the first person I call."

Clayton slapped the young UAV pilot on the back, grabbed one of the egg salad sandwiches and a coke, and headed out.

~~~~~~~~

Clayton stood near the large opening on the hangar deck, staring out at a perfectly clear afternoon sky. The thirty-one year old son of President Harlan Downs was in a pensive mood as he studied the peaceful Caribbean.

USS *Iwo Jima* (LHD-7) sailed across calm, sun-dappled waters thirty miles off the coast of Belize. The massive *Wasp*-class amphibious assault ship was joined by her two escorts. Two miles on point for the small flotilla was USS *Vandegrift* (FFG-48), a *Perry*-class frigate and one mile off *Iwo*'s port beam was the aegis guided missile cruiser USS *Bunker Hill* (CG-52). The three ships, along with the 26th Marine Expeditionary Unit (MEU) embarked aboard the assault ship made up the *Iwo Jima* amphibious assault force.

For the past six months the assault force had been part of a multi-national joint task force patrolling the Arabian Sea and Persian Gulf in response to threats coming from the Iranian president, telling the whole world he was going to shut down the Persian Gulf over thinly veiled threats from the United States and Israel regarding Iran's undisclosed nuclear program. The Iranian's bluster was thought to be a diversion, but on the whole had to be taken seriously. Shutting down the Persian Gulf would bring world oil imports to its knees, ringing the death knell for an already exhausted economy.

Then, following Iran's presidential elections three months before, nothing but complete silence had come out of Tehran and a weary world welcomed the halt to all the bluster and threats, if even only temporarily.

Every intelligence agency in the western world was scrambling to figure on which side of the coin the new Iranian leadership would come down. No one was taking the silence as good news, but the joint task force commanders did ease up on the urgency of their patrol profile.

The *Iwo* assault force was eventually released from the joint task force and allowed to return to port—although that was more a matter of the end of their duty cycle than it was an easing of tension. Most everyone knew hostilities with Iran were merely a matter of time.

Three days before arriving at their homeport in Norfolk, Virginia, the *Iwo Jima* assault force was ordered into the Caribbean at top speed. Nearly a week ago they arrived at this very same spot where they had been six months earlier, rendering critical assistance in the dramatic rescue of Clayton's sister.

Clayton reflected on the performance of his team during their deployment and his chest swelled with pride. Man and machines operated to perfection. Best of all, the team proved the operational concept of flying the modified Reaper MQ-9 from the short deck of amphibious assault ships. Even though they had not flown actual combat patrols per se, each mission they flew provided vital intelligence.

The data Clayton had seen streaming through Naval Intelligence, some of which was generated by him and his staff, left him with a feeling of doom niggling at the back of his head.

He remembered standing in this exact spot just six months earlier when *Iwo* sailed these same waters. A time which caused his emotions to race up and down like an out-of-control roller coaster. They were the most terrifying moments of his life when he thought he might never see Carley again. Even now, the mere thought of those stress-filled hours left a lump in his throat and his eyes began to water. Praise God all had ended well, even if it had been touch and go for a few heart-stopping moments.

This time, however, felt different. Something unseen, indescribable, was waiting out there. Something cold and calculating and evil.

Clayton was shaken from his melancholy by the sudden vibration of the deck as *Iwo* went to full power and healed into the wind. He heard the 1MC blare a familiar announcement. "PREPARE TO RECEIVE AIRCRAFT!"

He knew the MV-22 Osprey COD, Carrier Onboard Delivery, was coming in from Texas with the two former U.S. Marines who had rescued Carley. He also knew the purpose of their visit was classified and short-term. They would be flying out in the sinister looking solid black MV-22 within a few minutes of their arrival. The black Osprey sitting majestically on the hangar deck had fueled the rumor mill on *Iwo* since coming aboard the same day the assault force turned away from Norfolk.

Clayton had been looking forward to actually meeting Matthew and Chase McWain face-to-face, even though he knew their clandestine arrival was the source of the sour feeling lying in his gut like a chunk of rusty iron. He made his way to the small conference compartment just aft of the captain's cabin. Since he was part of the Assault Force/MEU intelligence staff, Lt. Cmdr. Clayton Downs was expected to attend the top-secret briefing with the McWain's.

Five

El Achiotal
Guatemala

The black MV-22 Osprey slipped between the rolling forested hills like a giant shadow floating on gossamer wings. The huge 38-foot proprotors thumped the air as the NCTC aircraft lined up on long final to the Cortez airstrip in El Achiotal. The long black ribbon of asphalt centered in Matt's windscreen stood in stark contrast to lush green pastures and thick undergrowth of encroaching forest and foothills on either side of the valley. Just ten miles north lay the Petén rain forest. Out the left side of the aircraft, perched atop the foothills overlooking the town was the expansive Cortez compound; its brown adobe walls reflected a golden light in the late afternoon sun.

"Looks peaceful enough," Chase said, leaning forward to get a better look at the hacienda out Matt's window. "Just like the last time we were here."

"Yep, let's hope we can keep it that way." Matt stole a quick glance, then brought his attention back to landing the aircraft. He pulled the thrust lever back and dialed the knurled wheel at the center of the lever handle aft, which rotated the engine nacelles 78 degrees, converting the tilt-rotor from airplane configuration to a helicopter. "Gear down," Matt ordered.

"Roger that," Chase reached for the handle to lower the landing gear. "You belted in back there, Master Chief?"

"Why, you guys gonna botch another landing?" Master Chief Petty Officer Walter Roberts growled over the intercom. "You wrinkle my bird, I'll wrinkle your face!"

The diminutive master chief looked every bit of his fifty years with thinning red hair and deep lines etched into his leathery tanned face. His pug nose and perpetual scowl made everyone think his bite was worse than his growl. That worked well for him.

Carter Manning hired the thirty-one year U.S. Navy veteran away from Air Test & Evaluation Squadron HX-21 at NAS Patuxent River, Maryland, by promising a little adventure and a lot more pay. The timing had been perfect because Walter Roberts was bored with what he was doing and looking for one more fling with excitement before settling down with his wife of thirty-two years and their two-story Chesapeake Bay home.

Roberts was chief of maintenance for the NCTC and considered every aircraft his own personal responsibility, just as he did in the navy. He figured he could fly the Osprey better than the test pilots at Patuxent River—certainly better than these two former jarheads.

"Relax, Walt," Matt chortled. "We know how wobbly you old people are; we don't want you falling down and smash something in the aircraft."

"I'll show you smashed, smart mouth!" Roberts grinned to himself. He was starting to like these McWains. They knew how to get the job done without being so all-fired uppity, like those pencil-pushers at Patuxent River.

Matt dialed the engine nacelles to 89 degrees vertical and the Osprey slowed to a hover 20 feet above ground.

He eased back on the thrust until the aircraft softly kissed the asphalt, and then rotated the nacelles forward and taxied toward a large metal hangar.

"Man, look at that! These guys are ready for war," Chase said with a whistle.

Pickup trucks with machine guns mounted in their beds appeared on either side of the aircraft. There was a man on each gun, two in every cab, and another armed vehicle was parked near the small wood frame airport office building.

"Yup," Matt responded, looking out both windows. "And that's only what we can see. Probably got two times as many hidin' out in the weeds starin' back at us."

Matt knew their visit six months ago nearly caused disaster for the Cortez family. Ahmad Hassam's troops had attacked the villa out of vengeance when the terrorist suspected Samuel Cortez's nephew, Manuel, had betrayed him by refusing to turn over Carley Downs and Jordan Scott. At the time Manuel thought the two women were working with the DEA. He had notified Hakeem Larijani of his discovery, but before Larijani could arrange to have them picked up, Manuel learned that the women truly were part of a Peace Corps medical team, as they had claimed all along.

That sudden knowledge set in motion a harrowing rescue in which Matt and Chase—along with help from Marine Force Recon and a handful of others—snatched the two women right out of the hands of the terrorists.

Ahmad Hassam had been defeated for the moment and was left with a bitter vendetta against the Cortez family, which Matt now felt responsible for causing.

Matt knew Manuel Cortez's greed and corruption had been the real catalyst fueling Hassam's wrath, but he also knew if he had killed the master terrorist when he had the chance, they wouldn't be in this mess today. He felt as much to blame as Manuel for turning a vengeful, bloodthirsty animal loose on the Cortez family.

Matt's blood chilled at another thought. *Hassam knows who stole Carley Downs away from him. If I don't stop him here, he might very well show up in Texas next … Dear God, please forgive me if I've brought this evil down upon my own family!*

He shut down the two Rolls-Royce turbine engines and engaged the control that automatically folded the rotors and wings, greatly reducing the size of the Osprey. Even so, the big aircraft was a tight fit through the door of Samuel Cortez's large maintenance hangar. Previous arrangements had been made to conceal the Osprey until it was needed.

Matt pulled the M9 Berretta from his flight bag and shoved it in the waistband of his tan cargo pants in the small of his back. His loose-fitting button-down khaki shirt concealed the weapon well enough, but if the security guards just outside the aircraft decided to do a pat-down search all bets was off. Chase, who was dressed same as Matt—with the addition of his purple and gold McAllen Bulldogs ball cap—armed himself similarly with his own Berretta. They gave each other a wary glance and stepped off the airplane.

Matt realized his concerns about a security pat down were needless as he looked into big dark eyes and friendly smile of a familiar face.

"Señor McWain, welcome back to my country." The young man's voice was warm and humble. His pistol was holstered and he used both hands to eagerly grasp Matt's hand, but the guards close by kept their weapons loosely trained on Matt and Chase.

"Ramón," Matt returned the young man's smile. "It's good to see you again, my friend. Especially on your feet and lookin' fit."

"Thanks to you, Señor McWain."

"Chase, this is Ramón Ortega. He's the brave young man who led the counter-attack at the hunting lodge against Hassam's people, one of very few to survive the massacre."

Ramón blushed as he reached for Chase's hand.

"Honored to meet, ya'll," Chase returned the handshake. "I'm this ugly ducklin's favorite cousin!" Chase jerked his head toward Matt. He grinned when Ramón arched an eyebrow in confusion.

"Come," the young man turned, "I am not to keep Señor Cortez waiting."

Matt noticed Ramón's slight limp as he led them toward a red GMC Yukon. The young guard took three bullets on that bloody night when Larijani's men attacked.

~~~~~~~

Twenty minutes later the Yukon pulled into the circular cobblestone driveway at the sprawling Cortez mountaintop compound. A security guard at the bottom of the hill had called ahead and Samuel Cortez was standing out front to greet his guests.

The regal patriarch of Cortez Enterprises was exactly as Matt remembered, tall, thin, and ramrod straight. His dark eyes seemed to dance. He was a handsome man with distinguished salt and pepper hair and nicely trimmed mustache. His energetic pace and amazingly sharp mind belied his seventy-seven years.

"Señor Matt! Señor Chase! Welcome to my humble *casita*!" Samuel's ever-present smile spread across his face as he rushed forward to give each man a warm hug.

The men exchanged pleasantries for moment before Matt said, "Looks like you're pretty well prepared for trouble."

"Oh yes! The Iranian dog will get another beating if he comes here again."

"Is there anything more we can do to help?" Chase asked, looking around. Unlike Matt, he had not been to the Cortez villa when they were here six months before. He was awe struck by the beauty and splendor of large mahogany trees surrounding the sprawling compound, the cobblestone courtyard beyond adobe walls and wrought iron gate, rich green pastures and lush hillsides as far as the eye could see.

"No, Señor Chase, your people have done more than what is necessary. For decades we have defended our homes from a corrupt government and other enemies much stronger than a handful of Islamic fanatics."

"We have no doubt that you can, sir," Matt responded. "It's just that we take this threat seriously and we don't underestimate Ahmad Hassam's resourcefulness. Besides, defending your home is the least we can do to repay you for allowin' us to stage our operation here."

"Nonsense, young man! After all you have done for Manuel and for all of my family, *mi casa es su casa*!" Samuel beamed.

"Thank you, sir. Speaking of Manuel, is he here?" The last time Matt saw the leader of the Guatemala drug cartel, he lay beaten on the floor of the family hunting lodge, barely able to tell Matt that Hassam had abducted Carley.

"No, I am sorry," Samuel answered. "My nephew is away on business, as usual. But come, please. I want you to see the others." With that, Samuel Cortez put an arm around Matt's shoulders and led the men through the courtyard to the back of the expansive hacienda.

Matt remembered the giant covered veranda that ran half the length of the home. Lush bougainvillea vines climbed each support post, cascading down from the header beam in a sea of red and purple blossoms. A myriad of colorful plants hung in clay pots, swaying in the light breeze. On the far side a giant stone barbecue grill put out a pleasant cloud of smoke and delicious,

mouthwatering aroma of sizzling steaks. One of the sons-
in-law oversaw a team of cooks at the grill while Samuel's
wife and daughters proudly prepared an assortment of
dishes brought out from the kitchen to an oversized table
covered with red and white linen. Matt had forgotten how
hungry he was until the wonderful aromas overpowered
his senses.

It could easily be a scene similar to large family
gatherings back home, except for the serious look on each
face and the absence of children usually playing under foot
and in the pool terraced below the veranda. Matt took note
of the armed guards methodically walking patrol at a
discreet distance, many of whom were Manuel's *Sicarios*,
enforcers or elite guards.

But what really caught Matt's eye was the collection of
familiar faces kicked back on elegant handcrafted patio
furniture enjoying the cool shade of late afternoon. On the
flagstone floor centered between the special guests was a
large galvanized tub containing iced-down bottles of
water, Corona, and Dos Equis. A blue haze of cigar smoke
enveloped the veranda, blending with the delicious aroma
of food. The raucous laughter and mixed conversations
stopped abruptly when Matt and Chase stepped up.

"Well looky here at what the cat dragged in!" The
booming voice belonged to a large man struggling to climb
out of a chaise lounge. He had a frosty Dos Equis in one
hand and a fat *Cohiba* in the other. He set his beer on a
small table and wrapped Matt in a bear hug, lifting his feet
six inches off the ground.

"Put me down ya big ape," Matt cried.

"That's *Colonel* Ape to you, lightweight!" The others
laughed hysterically.

"Dang it Butch, you're crushing me. Put me down
before I have to hurt you!"

"Okay, you big sissy!" Butch Larson dropped Matt to
the floor and held him at arms length, looked him up and

down. There was no mistaking the sincerity when Larson continued, "Man, you are a sight for sore eyes."

Lt. Col. Butch Larson, USMC, stood six-foot-six and tipped the scales at over 240 pounds of solid muscle. His arms and legs were like tree trunks. On his right bicep was a tattoo of the U.S. Marine Corps emblem, beneath which a red banner proudly proclaimed "Semper Fi." He wore his dark hair shorter than a Marine Corps buzz. He was wearing baggy knee- length cargo shorts and a khaki short-sleeve cotton shirt unbuttoned to reveal his powerful chest and broad shoulders.

Everything Matt knew about being a Force Recon Marine he had learned from Butch Larson. The colonel often joked that Matt should stick to flying because he was incapable of being more than a half- assed grunt.

"Good to see you too, Colonel," Matt smiled. He then turned serious. "You feelin' okay?"

"Never felt better." The last time Matt saw Butch Larson the big Marine was unconscious and bleeding out. Matt had saved his life in a super-human effort, carrying the big man across his back down a 35-foot ladder. Matt's knees still ached every time he moved after sitting for awhile. "You're looking pretty good too," Larson said. "Looks like you've pumped up a bit."

Second time Matt had been told that in two days. It was true, though. In the past six months he had doubled up on his workouts in the small weight room he and Chase had built at the back of the maintenance hangar at Edinburg.

"Well, I figured if I had to haul your ugly butt down another ladder, I need to be better prepared."

"Which reminds me, Matt," Larson spoke softly, his broad smile replaced by a frown. "I never had a chance to thank you properly."

Matt waved his hand dismissively. "Next time beer's on you!"

"Gladly," Larson laughed, reaching his hand into the iced-down tub. "Here, catch!"

Matt caught the frosty bottle of Dos Equis *cerveza* in mid-air. Larson then tossed a bottle, and then an opener to Chase.

"Oh man! Thought you'd never ask," Chase hooted, snatching the items, one in each hand, with the dexterity of an expert pilot and All-Star ballplayer. He guzzled half of the contents in a single gulp.

"Guys, listen up!" Larson turned to the group who had been looking on in amusement. "Here is *the* Matthew McWain and his screwball cousin Chase."

Two men standing close by tipped their bottles in his direction, smiled, and nodded. Matt did not know either of them, but there was a familiar face rising from the chaise next to Larson's and ambling over.

"Matt, you remember Gunny Stevens," Larson said.

"Of course … Gunny!" Matt extended his hand and immediately wished he hadn't. The barrel-chested gunnery sergeant with shaved head, hawk-shaped nose, and perpetual scowl had a bone-crushing grip. He grinned with delight at seeing Matt wince in pain.

The colorful warrior was a decorated Force Recon Marine from a handful of wars and Matt marveled at the man's invincibility. He knew Gunny had more purple hearts than medals of special commendation, yet the grizzled old veteran of thirty-four years could outrun anyone in the platoon through the thickest jungle ... and come out the other side full of piss and vinegar. Matt had served with the gunny in all three combat tours.

"So you're the boss of this op, huh?" Gunny Stevens pulled a cigar from his mouth and growled.

"Well—"

"Hey, Cowboy!" Another voice shouted from across the veranda. "I thought we ran your butt out of Guatemala." This was Phil Lenox, the outspoken chief of station at the U.S. Embassy in Guatemala City. The fifty-something CIA agent with a short rotund body and grumbling attitude had been an indispensable asset to Matt in rescuing *Caduceus*—Carley's Secret Service code name. Lenox's knowledge of the area and general feel for the political elements involved would make an important asset to the team this time as well.

"Lenox," Matt raised his bottle high. "Good to see you too, 'ol buddy!"

"Matt," Larson pulled Matt toward the two unfamiliar men. "Want you to meet Corporal Ernesto 'EZ' Zavala, expert with the long rifle. Arguably the best sniper in the business."

"Good to meet you, EZ."

"Likewise, sir." Corporal Zavala was a ruggedly handsome man of twenty-two, though he looked like a kid. Not much taller than five foot eight and had a wiry build. Matt could tell from his stance that EZ was agile and quick. His Hispanic accent, olive complexion and dark hair fit well with the locals.

The freckled faced kid with sandy red-hair standing next to EZ had the same wiry build and grim features. He too did not appear much more than a teenager. Larson introduced him as Lance Corporal Laney Stone, "Stoney for short." He was team medic and communications expert.

Larson introduced Matt and Chase to the other Recon Marines: Mullins, Graft, and Vincent. "There's another six team members tramping around out in the bush with Cortez's security people. All together, we make up your newly constituted Crisis Response Team, call sign Watchdog."

Matt looked around at the group of Recon Marines. No doubt they were a pretty formidable team, but Matt knew they would have their work cut out for them.

He turned back to Larson. "You and Lenox are my advisors, correct?" Matt knew Larson had been assigned liaison between the military arm of the team and the civilians who might join the group later on. Lenox was to run interference between team actions in Central America, the U.S. State Department, and local government officials.

"Yup! Where you go, we go. But don't go expecting me to sit in no freaking command shack ten miles from the action," Larson admonished. "So, now that you've called this little soiree, how about filling me in on what the heck we're really doing? Except for looking after the Cortez family, our intel's been pretty sketchy."

"Right. C'mon." Matt caught Lenox's eye and jerked his head for the CIA man to follow. Together, the three men strolled a short distance into the backyard, out of earshot.

Chase mingled with the crowd of Recon Marines and within minutes he had the group regaled with tales of amorous pursuits and legendary exploits of daring-do. The men were rolling with laughter and plying him with a few more bottles of iced-down beer.

The dying sun caressed Matt's shoulders as he gazed upon the idyllic setting. For a brief moment he could believe that all was well. The backyard bordered a lush green pasture slopping several hundred yards down to a thick stand of trees surrounding a creek where hundreds of cattle went to drink. Rolling hills beyond were covered with rows of coffee bean trees and coca plants. In a giant valley half of a mile west stood a never ending sea of poppies—just one of many valleys owned by Cortez, which supplied opium to his pharmaceutical manufacturing company.

Matt turned to his two advisors and spoke in hushed tones.

Six

The Boeing ScanEagle loitered at 40 knots in a wide surveillance pattern 14,000 feet above the docks of Puerto Santo Tomás. The small surveillance drone was auto-flying while Lt. (jg) Todd Clarkson readied its replacement, ScanEagle II, for flight.

From the large wall-mount screen between the two flight consoles, Clarkson watched the team of handlers step back from the UAV after they had loaded it onto the catapult. He moved the control stick side-to-side and from the screen he watched the flight controls respond as he sped through the preflight checklist. Clarkson was satisfied the aircraft was receiving radio signals. A quick check with the optics screen verified all systems ready. He hit the engine start, moved the throttle located on the left side of his console full against the stop, and remotely activated the catapult launch from his console in the GCS.

The two ScanEagles onboard *Iwo Jima* were highly modified models with advanced software packages developed by Lt. Cmdr. Clayton Downs, which would allow Reaper to auto-fly the ScanEagles, coordinating the video feed from the ScanEagles optics and overlaying the images through Reaper's own optics feed. The software made it possible to shift control of the ScanEagles back and forth from Reaper to the GCS.

The system was still in the test phase but every flight thus far revealed greater potential than Clayton's team had envisioned. Presently the two MQ-9 Reaper UAVs were in the hangar deck, ready to fly when needed.

"Whoa, what's this?" Clayton said from the crew seat next to Clarkson.

Clarkson had just stabilized ScanEagle II and put the bird on direct auto-flight to the target area before regaining manual control of ScanEagle I. Instantly the real-time optics screen filled with a clear image of three figures moving briskly from the waterfront toward the warehouses.

"That's him!" Clarkson shouted. "That's the guy I was telling you about. They must have just come off the *Alaed*."

The three men on the screen were dressed casually as if they could easily fit in with the longshoremen busy at work on the docks. Two men walked close together, talking animatedly. Both had caps pulled low over their faces. One was rather small, frail; the other was not that much taller, but appeared to be more solidly built. *Ahmad Hassam!* The man following several paces behind was huge by comparison; his clothes bulged as if they were several sizes too small. The three men kept their heads bent low, as if purposely hiding their identity from overhead surveillance.

Clayton knew Ahmad Hassam was an expert at keeping a low profile and often relied on disguises, allowing him to slip undetected in and out of foreign countries. Other times he would appear quite ordinary, blending in with a crowd. The master terrorist was cautious, seldom repeating his chameleon-like tactics.

The possible giveaway in this instance, however, was not entirely the manner in which he appeared. It was more the fact that in the past six months he was seldom spotted without the presence of his gargantuan bodyguard. The huge, nearly seven foot, built-like-a-tree-trunk, man walking behind made it a ninety percent "probable sighting."

"Yeah, I believe you're right, Mr. Clarkson. Good job!" With that Clayton reached for the ships phone.

"Captain, GCS!"

"Go ahead, Commander Downs." Captain Elway Reynolds sat in his red leather commander's chair on the bridge. He stared silently at the tranquil sea and crystal clear sky while contemplating the message from CINCLANT, ordering them to abort their scheduled port return and sail into the western Caribbean. He had kept a lid on the scuttlebutt and nervous patter throughout the ship, but tension was palatable as the entire crew puzzled over whatever was keeping them from seeing their families after being at sea for nearly seven months.

"Captain, we've got a probable sighting on both primaries," Clayton told him. "I recommend launching Reaper."

The forty-six year old captain pulled the blue *Iwo Jima* ball cap from his head, ran his fingers through thinning blond hair, and let out a sigh. *It's about to start.*

In the short time Matthew McWain had been aboard *Iwo* a Plan of Battle had been hastily drawn up with input provided by the outspoken commander of the 26th Marine Expeditionary Unit, Colonel Tommy G. Kramer, USMC, and *Iwo*'s operations officer, Lt. Cmdr. Charlie (Muddy) Waters.

The plan made the assumption that McWain's Crisis Response Team would be sufficient to subdue enemy forces on Puerto Santo Tomás. Matt asked for the Reaper UAV to patrol the area prior to the attack. He also requested an MV-22 with the remainder of the 5th Platoon Recon orbiting close by, "Just in case."

They hoped to avoid any appearance of an invasion force on Guatemala, but the objective was to contain the terrorist threat here and now, and not let it spread like a cancer into the United States.

"Very well, Commander! Reaper launch approved. Advise when ready."

"Aye, aye, Captain."

Clayton picked up his cell phone and sent a quick text to Lt. Louis Rogers: *Get Reaper One ready to fly*!

~~~~~~~~

**Waterfront,
Puerto Santo Tomás**

Ahmad Hassam entered the warehouse office and tossed his cap on the tattered brown suede sofa against the far wall. The thirty-six year old Lebanese did not like hats of any kind, but his intuitive powers constantly guarded him against the probing eyes of America, the *Great Satan*. The Hezbollah terrorist practiced shielding himself and his activities from spy planes and satellites for many years and it had served him well, making him a successful master of his tradecraft.

Hassam ran a hand through his medium-length curly hair, then stroked his new Van Dyke goatee as if still getting used to it. His black hair, along with the goatee, was sprinkled with gray as part of his new identity. He was a powerfully built man, five foot ten, large broad shoulders, and deep set dark eyes that penetrated to your very soul. He was the agent of evil. The devil himself shuttered when Ahmad Hassam came near. No one, absolutely no one, dared betray him.

His revenge on Manuel Cortez would have been consummate and immediate had it not been for a more important matter. Ahmad Hassam was the mastermind behind *Mylh-A'sifh, Operation Firestorm,* an intricate plot that would finally bring the Great Satan to its knees. A design to annihilate the Americans; rid the world of their corrupt influence once and for all. The action would be swift, the carnage unmerciful. His holy warriors would strike again and again against hundreds of soft targets where men and women and children stood unprotected and vulnerable. Fear would reign; terror would spread across the decadent land of unbelievers. And then, with the infidels cowering from hundreds of vicious attacks, he would unleash the real *Firestorm.* America would be powerless to prevent him from bringing hell on earth.

Once the protective arm of the United States was disabled, Israel would be virtually powerless to defend against his warriors.

Final preparations and coordination for the operation had been building for the past two and a half years and Major General Imad Abu Mughniyeh had ordered Hassam to proceed without further delay, thus sparing the Cortez family for a brief time.

An order from the general could not be taken lightly. The commander of the Iranian Revolutionary Guard had bestowed the honor of taking their jihad to the United States with the understanding Hassam would have absolute command—including all assets already in place within the U.S. He was promised complete autonomy with which to conduct the operation and guaranteed virtually unlimited funds. In recompense for such an esteemed honor, it was made clear to Hassam that he was to confer with the general on certain details. The terrorist was made to understand that the general alone held the authority to commence the operation. Of course, it was not lost on Ahmad Hassam that the purpose in choosing a Lebanese officer of Hezbollah to lead the assault was principally to provide Iran deniability of instigating such an atrocity upon the western world.

It was at their third meeting, very early on in the planning process when Mughniyeh revealed to Hassam that a forward-thinking plan for in-place assets had been initiated by the Grand Ayatollah Ruhollah Khomeini and continued into the late 90's. The general provided a list of each agent, fictitious name, location, and their eventual assignment.

To Hassam's great surprise, he was given complete access and control over each sleeper agent. He had expertly woven each of these agents into the intricate fabric of his plan against America—but as far as he was concerned the holy warriors he had personally trained were the real tip of the spear.

Ahmad Hassam had returned to Guatemala not only to launch *Mylh-A'sifh,* but to quench the fires of revenge raging in his belly like a burning inferno.

"Are they absolutely sure of this?" Ahmad demanded, the moment the office door closed behind them. His fists were clenched and the chords in his neck were bulging. His eyes blazed.

Hakeem Larijani stepped back, fearing the wrath pouring out of his commander like a bubbling volcano. He was the only person Hassam would call friend, but he also knew few had survived the fury of his unforgiving rage.

"Yes, Ahmad, it was surely an American aircraft, like many we saw in Afghanistan. The one they call the Osprey. Only this one is painted black, no identifiable markings." Hakeem gauged the leader's reaction before continuing. "I am afraid the American infidels knew you were coming for the traitor Manuel Cortez and are preparing a trap. We must get you out of here!"

The explosion came just as Larijani had feared. Hassam's balled fist slammed down on the solid oak desk with such force that the *Crraaack!* could be heard from outside. His face clouded over with a mask of fury and his eyes cut through Hakeem's soul like a blazing fire of black death. Even the huge Ali stepped back and cowered in the shadows.

But as fast as the storm of emotion came on, it silently disappeared. In a calm, quiet voice Hassam began issuing orders. "Tell Rahim to begin the attack as soon as his men are in place. They are not to wait for us."

"As you wish, *as-Syf!*" Larijani breathed a sigh of relief, moving closer to Hassam.

The terrorist leader smiled at Larijani's use of his legendary title, *The Sword,* and then continued. "Come, sit with me. The time has come to begin our final preparations." Hassam moved to the padded chair behind the desk as Larijani pulled one of the straight-back chairs closer. Ali kept his protective vigil in the darkened corner of the office.

"Order the captains of the *Alaed* and *Jin* to prepare for immediate departure. Our friends can take you to rejoin the *Alaed* as we planned, but first you must return me to the airport."

Larijani nodded. They were nearly ready. All that remained was a few more messages that would set in motion an irreversible chain of events. Some of which included the assistance needed to assure his timely arrival at their forward command site deep in the heart of the United States.

Hassam did not allow his disappointment to show. For six months he harbored thoughts of personally ripping the heart from Manuel Cortez, *after* forcing the traitor to watch him butcher everyone residing in the Cortez villa. Now that very deed would be carried out by a loyal army of twenty-eight handpicked warriors led by Rahim Musa rather than himself, and the disappointment was great.

Much time and planning and money had gone into the attack. The logistics of just getting trained jihadists and their weapons inside the network of Cortez's faithful employees had been monumental. Hakeem had pulled it off, as he always did. Just as the dependable, ever steadfast Hakeem had pulled together all the needed resources and assets to assure success of their destiny in America.

For the next hour Hakeem Larijani walked Hassam through broad details and timing of *Mylh-A'sifh*, for the hundredth time. When he had finished Hassam glanced at his watch and then back to Hakeem.

"You have done well, my friend."

Larijani beamed. "*Yathaï ilâh! Praise God!* With *his* guidance this will be your finest hour."

"We must not delay the timing. Not even for a moment. If I do not arrive on time, you are to launch the operation without me. We have come too far, you and I. We must not let *anything* stand in our way. Do you understand?"

Larijani caught the meaning in Hassam's words and shook his head violently. "Nothing can prevent you from getting there on schedule, *as-Syf*!"

Seven

El Achiotal
Guatemala

Samuel Cortez stepped out onto the veranda and announced that supper was ready. Six starving Marines managed to somehow beat Chase to the large table with good-natured shoving and tripping. Matt, Larson, and Lenox sauntered over to grab one of the large hand-carved chairs. Being the grateful host, Cortez blessed the meal before ushering in a virtual parade of delicious smelling food on the arms of his servants. The festive occasion came alive with laughter. It was hard to imagine this was a family living under the threat of imminent attack. But then, Matt had to remind himself that the Cortez family lived under an ominous threat of attack for 30-years when Samuel was leader of the URNG—Guatemala National Revolutionary Unity—during the Guatemalan civil war.

Their laughing and bustling around the table somehow made Matt feel like some kind of conquering hero … without doing a single solitary thing. He looked up and saw a small boy squatting in the shadows against the far wall. His tussled long black hair framed a crusted sad face with huge dark eyes staring back; his dirty elbows rested on scuffed bare knees. Matt winked and the little boy grinned, winking back with both eyes tightly clinched. *This is what it's really about. Protecting innocent lives from hate mongers like radical Islamic ragheads!*

Matt then noticed the beautiful young lady standing beside him. She smiled down at him with a face of recognition.

"Señor Matt, you remember my little *nieta,* Katalina?" Samuel said, sitting across from Matt.

"Of course I do, sir. Who could forget the stunning future International Aerobatic Champion?" Matt returned the girl's smile. "Hi there, Katalina. Good to see you again."

Six months had somehow transformed the lively petite teenager into a radiant vision of beauty. Her bronze skin was clear and soft, her dark eyes glistened like deep pools and her wide smile was a brilliant white. She wore her long black hair pulled back in a ponytail that bounced and swayed when she moved. She was dressed in tight jeans, white peasant blouse and brown leather sandals. Matt was amazed how much she had matured in few short months.

"It is good to see you too, Señor Matt," Katalina blushed and curtsied primly.

"If you will remember Matt, you promised to fly with my little *nieta* when you came again." Samuel glanced at the girl and winked.

Matt felt the setup coming and smiled inside. "Actually, Señor Cortez, I clearly remember saying Katalina was so good that she could take *me* flying!"

Katalina blushed deeper. But it was true. Matt had watched from the ground as the girl and her grandpa soared and sliced through a clear August afternoon sky in Samuel's beautifully restored red and cream colored UPF-

7 Waco open-cockpit bi-plane, as if performing an aerial ballet.

"That she can do," Samuel beamed proudly. "Kat soloed last month on her sixteenth birthday. She's already better than I ever hope to be!"

"Congratulations, Katalina," Matt said, bumping fists with the girl.

"Thank you, Señor Matt." The girl lowered her head, embarrassed by the attention. She felt her sisters and cousins eyeing her with envy.

Samuel glanced beyond the veranda. "I believe there is plenty enough daylight … in case you might want to take her up when we have finished eating." He smiled openly. He knew he had put Matt in a delicate situation with Katalina standing right at his elbow.

"How could I possibly refuse an offer like that?" Matt turned to the young girl and winked. "Let's go bore a hole in the sky, kiddo!"

Katalina shrieked with delight and took off on a dead run for the house to get her flight gear.

"Oh man, you made her day," Chase said as he forked a huge bite of steak into his mouth.

"Ya think?" Matt grinned as he watched the girl charge into the house, her ponytail flying.

"Thank you, Matt," Cortez said, but Matt didn't hear. His earbud came alive.

"Quarterback, this is Striker Base, do you copy?"

"Copy Striker Base! Go ahead!"

Chase was the only person in the group with a comm-set tuned to the NCTC channel as Matt, but even so the others looked up when Matt replied. The raucous banter around the table went quiet.

"Quarterback, primaries are at the target site! Repeat, it's a go on primaries!"

"Roger that! I'll get back to you!" Matt sat quietly for a moment. The hair stood up on the back of his neck.

Ahmad Hassam had been sighted at Santo Tomás. He knew they would not have much time to spare. He glanced down the full length of the table and found everyone staring back. The good-natured joking and fun was over, it was time to go to work in the deadly business of hunting terrorists.

"Gentlemen, the bar is closed. It seems tonight very well could be the night." Matt checked his watch. From recent experience, he knew it took about three hours to drive from Puerto Santo Tomás to El Achiotal. If Hassam left right now, he could get here and have his men in place by 2200 hours.

The remaining daylight would give Matt plenty of time to do some aerial reconnaissance. His ulterior motive to fly with Katalina was really an excuse to check out the defensive perimeter. See if the Marines may have overlooked anything.

Matt was mentally running down a checklist of things needing to be done when a rifle shot suddenly split the air, echoing up the valley from the creek.

The Marines bailed away from the table, scrambling for their weapons stacked along the back wall of the veranda, while the women ushered the children back inside the house.

~~~~~~~~~

Rahim Musa swelled with pride and placed the satellite phone back in the web holder on his belt. Hakeem had given him authorization to launch the attack; *as-Syf* himself had placed his trust in him. His eyes watered as he considered the unexpected honor bestowed upon him. He could not fail. He *would* not fail.

Rahim was not the youngest lieutenant in Hassam's organization, nor was he the strongest and most fierce. His boldness and intelligence had propelled the thirty year old

Palestinian terrorist through the ranks. From the first days at the Birjand training camp located in the rugged hills of eastern Iran, Rahim had impressed his superiors to the point of receiving attention from the esteemed commander, Ahmad Hassam, *as-Syf*. When Hassam specifically requested Rahim to handpick a brigade of dependable warriors for service in Central America, he knew he was destined for greatness. The phone call moments ago confirmed that very thought.

Success tonight would assure his hopes to take his brigade to the United States, to stand beside Hassam in their holy war. *Praise be to Allah*!

He would also be reunited with his older brother who was already in the U.S. preparing for the attack to begin. He had not seen Rahimi in nearly ten years.

Rahim lay on the creek bank, concealed in the tall grass as he peered through binoculars from the dense forest. He cursed again over the considerable distance of open pasture between him and the Cortez villa. The RPG-7V2, rocket propelled grenades, had an effective range of 400 yards. His people would need to traverse a couple hundred yards of open ground before getting into position to launch the attack. Without good cover it was impossible to advance on the target before darkness set in. He could see sentries walking the fence line around the compound. The sniper he had placed in the tall tree 150 yards east of the villa reported similar defenses on the front and east sides, and a number of guards on the veranda, which was out of Rahim's line of sight.

He whispered into his walkie-talkie, telling each team to remain in-place until he gave the order to advance. He had dispersed his people in two-man teams; one man to carry the launcher while the other carried an assortment of spare rockets with fragmentation and thermobaric warheads in an over-the-shoulder canvas bag. Each man carried an AK-47 assault rifle slung over his shoulder as well.

The teams had spread out in a pre-assigned pattern based on intel provided by Larijani—Rahim never questioned how Larijani had obtained such detailed information. The twelve rocket teams would pretty well guarantee success in meeting their mission objective: death to every man, woman and child, and total destruction of the Cortez compound.

The short-range radios provided by Larijani were obsolete models, strictly line-of-sight and severely hampered by the trees and hilly terrain. A couple minutes after sending the message a *crack* from a rifle shot echoed down the creek bed and Rahim had a sickening feeling that someone in his brigade did not get the message. One overzealous team had pushed their luck trying to get into position before darkness fell over the valley.

"Teams report! All teams report!" Rahim hissed into the radio.

~~~~~~~

"Watchdog units report!" Larson calmly spoke into his comm-set. Matt and the others waited for the patrol to report on who fired the shot and why? EZ, the expert sniper and firearms specialist instantly verified the shot was one of theirs, an M27 Infantry Automatic Rifle. The patrol had two IARs. That narrowed the identity of the shooter.

"Watchdog One, negative!"…"Two, negative!"…

One by one the team reported in until finally… "Watchdog Eleven, affirmative! One tango down, one hundred-twenty yards east of my position. Second tango spotted same location, negative on clear shot!"

"Roger that, Watchdog Eleven," Larson answered. "Watchdog units maintain your position. Keep your eyes open, Marines. This is it!"

Larson turned to Matt and said, "The tangos probably won't move 'til dark."

"Agreed! Good time to take that flight. Scope out their positions."

Eight

"Reaper One, you are cleared for takeoff," The air controller said as the large amphibious assault ship heaved into a steady 15 knot westerly wind.

"Roger, striker base! Cleared for takeoff," Clayton Downs pushed the throttle wide open, alternating his gaze between his Primary Flight Display, or PFD, and Reaper's optics screen which showed the flight deck racing past, framed in a blue horizon of a crystal clear sky.

Sitting beside Clayton inside the ground control station was Lt. Louis Rogers, Clayton's second-in-command, and arguably the best software designer in the business— second to Clayton, of course, although Louis denied being second to anyone. The twenty-four year old technical engineer was short and wiry and looked the part of a nerdy computer geek with longish red hair and thick glasses with large black frames. He had a nervous tick of pushing his glasses up at the nose bridge with his thumb knuckle, which he was doing now as he ran a quick diagnostics scan on all sensor systems. Louis flew right seat as the sensor operator, or SO. They made a perfect team.

Without taking his eyes from the PFD Clayton said, "Mr. Clarkson, is the deck crew ready to recover ScanEagle I?"

A quick glance at the large wall-mounted screen between the pilot and SO consoles confirmed that the recovery team was on the flight deck erecting a pair of 30-foot masts with a rope stretched between used to snag the "skyhook" retrieval system of the smaller UAV.

"Affirmative, sir!" Lt. jg Todd Clarkson responded from the crew station on Clayton's left. He scanned his own flight console and declared, "ScanEagle I is fifteen miles out, bearing one-niner-zero, descending through eight thousand, two hundred." Clarkson's position report confirmed with Clayton that the ScanEagle was not on a collision course with Reaper.

"Quarterback, this is Reaper! We copied Watchdog's traffic. Can we be of assistance?" Clayton spoke calmly into his headset; his hands caressed the controls of the MQ-9 UAV, making minor corrections as his eyes danced across the four screens on the pilot's console. He licked his dry lips and rolled his shoulders to ward off tension.

~~~~~~~~

El Achiotal
Guatemala

"Your location, Reaper?" Matt responded, immediately recognizing Clayton Downs on the other end. Samuel Cortez was up front with his body guard behind the wheel, while Katalina sat beside Matt in the rear seat as the red Denali approached the airport. She was wide-eyed at the excitement happening all around her. If she was scared, she certainly did not show it!

"*Approximately three-zero minutes out!*"

"Copy thirty out. Can you keep eyes on our primary?"

"*Affirmative! We have another asset over the target.*"

Good news, Matt thought. T*wo UAV's in the hunt.*

"Okay then, continue to my location. Standby for further!"

"*Roger that!*"

Samuel Cortez twisted in his seat and said, "Hassam's not coming is he, Matt?"

"No sir, it doesn't appear that he will." Somehow Hassam received word that reinforcements had arrived to assist the Cortez family. He realized that a successful attack on the family was probably doomed, in which case the Americans would then turn their attention on his port facility as soon as the assault on the Cortez compound had been thwarted.

The illusive master terrorist would have ample time to disappear while the battle raged here in EL Achiotal. But the question was, disappear to where? Back to his base in Venezuela or into the United States to launch *Firestorm*?

Matt could not turn his back on the Cortez family to go chasing after Hassam, but what could he do to delay the terrorist until he could get to the port facility with his response team?

Cortez searched Matt's eyes as if he were reading his mind. "Matt, I want you to go after this madman terrorist who haunts my family."

"Yes sir, I plan to. Just as soon as we take care of the ragheads closing in on your home."

"No, Matt," Cortez continued. He glanced at Katalina, wishing he could spare her from the awful brutality of evil men. "I want you to take your people and go after Hassam. Do not worry about us. We can take care of ourselves. We have managed that quite well for many years."

Katalina's eyes blinked back and forth between the two men. Perhaps the real gravity of the situation was lost on her, but even so she sensed the seriousness of their conversation.

Matt recalled how effortlessly Cortez and his men had dispatched two carloads of terrorists when they came to kill Manuel. Sure, Butch Larson had a full team of Recon Marines here then as well, but the truth was, Cortez and his *Sicarios* made quick work of Larijani's men. They might be able to do it again, but this time Matt had a feeling the enemy force would be a lot bigger and more heavily armed.

"I am sure you can, Señor Cortez, but it's my responsibility to—"

"No, son," Cortez said in a stern voice. "It is *my* responsibility."

Their eyes locked, blazing with intensity; it was a battle of wills. Matt realized the elder Cortez was far too resolute to give in. His intentions were honorable, if not stubborn. The Guatemalan wanted Hassam dead, forever out of his hair; and he knew the terrorist could possibly be making his escape while they sat here arguing. He also knew if Hassam escaped, he would return and they would go through this whole exercise all over again, not knowing which moment the terrorists would attack, or from where.

Cortez was correct in his thinking. Hassam would most certainly return if his men failed tonight, but what Cortez did not know was that the enemy coming tonight would be better organized and better prepared than they were six months ago.

Matt was not convinced the former URNG commander was prepared to take on a well-armed enemy. A formidable enemy with zero regard for human life.

They pulled into the airport with the Denali's tires crunching over the gravel road. The driver wheeled the big SUV to the row of hangars while Matt and Cortez remained locked in a stare-down. Neither had spoken for several minutes.

Finally Matt broke the silence as he opened the car door. "Alright Samuel, you have a good point. I think there may be a way to do both. When Katalina and I get back, we'll sit down with Colonel Larson and kick around a few ideas."

Samuel Cortez smiled and nodded.

~~~~~~~

National Counterterrorism Center
Liberty Crossing
McLean, VA

The Operations Center at the NCTC in Liberty Crossing was located two levels below ground. There was a conference room elevated six feet above the main floor, shielded from noise by a floor-to-ceiling glass wall half an inch thick. There was a long conference table in the room with computer terminals arrayed in front of six padded chairs. The terminals were tied into eight individual workstations down on the main floor. On the opposite wall of the conference room was a bank of TV screens from which to view live news from around the world or for telecommunications with parties outside the facility.

Large flat-screens capable of displaying real-time images or other raw data dominated the wall directly in front of the main floor workstations. The center screen was much larger and generally activated by the duty officer to provide detailed images for people up in the conference room.

Personnel within the Ops Center communicated through headsets so that everyone knew what was going on and could coordinate their activities. The duty officer controlled the flow of communications and kept things operating efficiently and productively. Usually this was not much of a problem. The operations center was activated only in times of major events such as catastrophic disasters having homeland security implications or in rare instances when the terrorist threat level was escalated due to some credible report.

Alex Strayhorn and Carter Manning had convinced the president that the center should be placed on full alert and prepared for 24/7 operations upon receipt of any supporting evidence that would collaborate the threat analysis of an imminent terrorist attack within the United States.

That confirmation went out seventeen minutes ago and Carter Manning was the first to arrive in the ops center conference room. He had been grilling steaks on the back patio when the call came in. It was just a silly habit to leave his phone on the kitchen counter while he cooked outdoors. He never imagined an interruption at this time of evening and was taken by surprise when Pam came out carrying his phone along with a light jacket. There was a chill in the night air and his wife was always doting over him, probably the reason he loved her so much. It took a special woman to put up with his long hours and moody silence, mainly caused from scores of secrets crashing around in his brain.

Two minutes after the call, Manning bolted out the front door of their modest two-story home and tore through the entrance of the secluded gated community near Falls Church. All the way up the Custis Memorial Parkway and then onto the Dulles Toll Road to Liberty Crossing, he ran the list of notifications and protocols through his mind. They had been headed toward this fateful moment for quite some time; he just had not expected it to come with such heart-stopping force.

Manning opened his laptop, then walked to the glass wall to gaze upon the Ops Center floor. Half of the workstations were up and running and two more analysts rushed through the main entrance on the lower level. He saw his own reflection through the glass from the soft overhead lighting and ran a hand over his smooth head. He grinned, realizing he was still dressed in jeans, baggy white pullover long-sleeve thermal shirt, and soft brown leather shoes. Pam refused to allow him to leave the house this way, but tonight he dashed out without her commenting.

He noticed the techs on the floor were mostly dressed casual as well. Everyone had been caught off guard.

The large center screen was blank and only two of the flat-screens were lit. One displayed an overview of the *Alta Verapaz* region in Guatemala; the one Manning focused on, however, was a close-up, real-time video of Puerto Santo Tomás. Slipping his headset on, he directed the analyst on workstation #2 to switch his display to the large center screen. Manning stood at the glass panel gazing down at the crystal clear image of the waterfront on Amatique Bay.

The radio transmissions were just beginning to come through his headset when his administrative assistant entered the conference room and handed him a cup of coffee. Manning smiled and nodded, and then softly asked her if everyone on the notification list had been contacted. Once the assistant left the room, he set the coffee cup on the table and paced nervously back and forth, hands behind his back as he stared at the screens below.

Manning nodded grimly when his boss, Alex Strayhorn, Director of National Intelligence, burst into the room. Strayhorn looked beyond Manning to the activity on the main floor. The DNI put on his own headset just as Manning called Matthew McWain.

"Quarterback, this is Ops Center, do you copy?"

Nine

El Achiotal
Guatemala

The beautifully restored red and cream Waco UPF-7 biplane was immaculate, a treasured piece of art. From the shiny propeller spinner to the chrome wires on the tail, every square inch had been lovingly polished by Samuel Cortez and Katalina on a regular basis, practically after each flight. The care and compassion they shared for this fine flying machine was manifested in the bond between grandfather and granddaughter.

Matt walked down the right side of the fuselage, running his fingers along the taut fabric covering while Katalina pulled a beige flight suit over her jeans and blouse. The young girl quickly completed her preflight inspection, and then scampered up into the rear cockpit. He circled the plane, came around to the left side to stand next Katalina, and grinned. Her eyes radiated with confidence and she smiled back at him as she adjusted a tan colored cloth flying helmet around her ponytail.

The Waco is soloed from the rear seat; hence that's where the main instrument panel and radios are located. Matt remembered the smooth aerial ballet he had witnessed the young girl perform months ago and had no problem with her taking the rear seat now. He settled into the front cockpit and was adjusting his parachute harness, seatbelt and shoulder harness when his wireless comm-set came to life.

"Quarterback, this is Ops Center, do you copy?" There was as a slight hesitation in the voice as it was scrambled and decrypted.

"I copy, Manning. A little busy right now. What's up?" *Geez, that's just great,* Matt thought sarcastically. There were pros and cons to satellite communications. The good outweighed the bad, but someone watching over his shoulder from half-a-world away was one of the downers. There was a time not long ago, when the very sound of Manning's voice caused Matt to bristle. That was behind him now. For the most part the two were getting along well.

"Ops Center is up and running. We're monitoring your traffic with Reaper One. How many tangos are you up against?"

"Figuring that out now. Will advise. Expecting attack after dark." Matt glanced out of the cockpit at long shadows encroaching from the forest.

"Roger that, Matt. Are you hitting Santo Tomás later tonight?"

"That's the plan." His eyes danced over the cockpit and he cinched his seatbelt.

"Alright, I'll have the president contact Ambassador Steward. Hopefully we can keep the Guatemalan authorities off your back this time." The time before they barely avoided a disaster when both the Guatemalan army and local law enforcement crashed down on the waterfront practically in the middle of the rescue attempt.

"Appreciate it. Will advise when ready to go. Quarterback out!"

Matt pulled in a deep breath and reveled in the nostalgic aroma of leather and avgas, and motor oil. His mind raced back to when he and Chase were at Pensacola for Marine Corps flight training. They discovered an old airstrip about twenty miles from the base owned by a grizzled old aviator who rented out a newer version of the venerable Waco, a YMF-5 model. A smile spread across his lips when he remembered how they would thunder through the sky for hours and turned that incredible airplane every way but loose.

He plugged his headset, which was built into the cloth flying helmet he had borrowed from Cortez, into the intercom jacks on the instrument panel just in time to hear Katalina shout, "CLEAR!"

The aircraft shook and trembled as the big Continental W-670 radial engine rumbled to life in a cloud of blue smoke. Katalina bumped the throttle up to 1,000 RPM and the exhaust stacks rumbled while she checked oil pressure and adjusted her flight instruments.

"You ready?" Katalina asked, pulling the control stick back and releasing the brakes.

"You betcha," Matt answered with a grin. *This is gonna be a hoot!*

Taxiing the Waco is an art form. The nose is parked high in the air because of the tailwheel, so in order to have forward visibility the pilot performs a series of S turns all the way to the runway.

"You handle the aircraft very well," Matt said approvingly. He was impressed with the precise symmetry of each S-turn. She had been well taught.

"Thank you, sir."

"C'mon, girl, we're about to defy gravity together, you can call me Matt. Okay?"

"Okay, Matt," she giggled. "My *Papá* calls me Kat!"

"It's an honor to fly with you, Kat!" Matt smiled.

They rolled up to the departure end of the runway and Matt felt the surge of power and blast of air from the propeller as Katalina ran-up the engine. The biplane shuttered and strained against the brakes and Matt checked his shoulder harness snug.

"You want to take her off?" she asked calmly over the intercom.

"No thanks, you better do the first one. Been awhile since I've flown one of these babies."

With that she pulled out on the runway and applied full power. Instantly, Matt felt the rush of air on his face. He laughed like a young boy on a carnival ride, but his laughter was drowned out by the distinctive rumble of the 220 horsepower radial engine.

At several hundred feet above the ground Matt said, "Nice flying, Kat. Let's take her over your house, give the guys a thrill." He didn't say that he really wanted to have a look at the perimeter surrounding the compound.

"Roger that," she responded, immediately rolling the Waco into a climbing turn.

A few minutes later they soared above the Cortez home. Matt searched the tree line in the valley south of the hacienda as Katalina rocked her wings to say hello to her audience waving back. The sun was a big orange ball resting on the western horizon and shadows lengthened across the pasture making it difficult to see into the darkened forest. Matt knew the Recon Marines were scattered across the area on the right side of the airplane. The tangos should be on his left or directly below. In the tangle of the thick forest it would be almost impossible to pick out a man from this altitude.

Katalina circled back to the north, climbing away from the rising terrain of the Sierra De Santa Cruz mountain range. At two thousand feet she pushed the nose into a shallow dive. The Waco picked up speed rapidly, wind singing through the flying wires, and the windscreen filled with the sight of green pastures dotted with hundreds of cattle.

She gently pulled back on the stick until the nose of the airplane climbed through the horizon, up and up, into the dark blue sky. Matt was shoved down into the seat with three times his own weight. Instinctively, he raised his head to catch sight of the ground as they raced deliriously down the backside of a perfectly executed loop. He screamed out a loud "*Woohoo!*"

Katalina nudged the stick forward when they were three-quarters of the way through the loop, pushing the airplane momentarily inverted before snapping it upright into a half roll, continuing downward, regaining the airspeed lost at the top of the loop.

She had brilliantly executed the first half of a Cuban Eight, then hauled the stick back to start the second half …

Matt closed his eyes and smiled. This is what flying was really all about. He caught a breath of exhaust and hot oil as the Waco hung briefly upside down at the top of the loop, the engine laboring to pull the airplane over the top, and then plunging again down the backside.

Flying was his passion, the one thing that brought meaning and focus into the chaos of everyday life. When stress and worry crowded into his daily existence, all he needed to do was jump into an airplane, point it into the glorious blue, and instantly all was well in his world. His very soul would be cleansed, and he would be ready to go back down among mortal beings and start the grind all over.

Grandma McWain told Matt long ago that God had blessed him with extraordinary skills and talents. She had been his very first passenger after he got his Private Pilot's license in the summer between his junior and senior year in high school. He would never forget the joy in her eyes when he banked steeply over the McWain ranch. She gave him a teasing grin and told him this was probably as close to God as he would ever get. Grandma must have conspired with his mother judging from the similar comment mom had made later that very same day when she climbed out of the right front seat as his second passenger.

No doubt in his mind, he was born to fly, and he sensed Katalina felt exactly the same way. To become one with the airplane, lost in the thrill and peace and wonderment of flight.

Rolling out of the Cuban Eight, Katalina tugged the nose above the horizon, shoved the throttle full open, yanked the stick to her chest and kicked the right rudder pedal to the firewall, riding the bi-plane through two perfectly executed snap rolls in the time it takes to draw a deep breath.

"Your turn," Katalina said with maturity beyond her age.

"My airplane," Matt said, wiggling the stick back and forth to signal that he now had the controls.

There was no way Matt could match her precision without an hour or two of practice, but he took the stick confidently and attempted to duplicate Katalina's maneuvers. By the time he finished the routine with a pair of snap rolls, they were back over the Cortez compound.

Matt pulled the Waco straight up into the darkening sky. As the speed quickly dissipated, he shoved the stick full forward and to the right, and at the same time pushed full left rudder pedal. The nose pivoted slowly left until it pointed straight down in a well executed hammerhead stall. It was a classic way to reverse direction to remain inside the "box" required for competition aerobatics. Still in a dive the aircraft quickly gained airspeed. The ground rushed up, the hacienda grew larger and larger in the windscreen until Matt pulled hard on the stick, the nose climbed above the horizon. He yanked the stick hard left, rolling the airplane ninety degrees into knife-edge flight, then he slammed the stick neutral and in a split second they rolled inverted, paused, rolled another ninety, paused, then upright, straight on course away from the compound back toward the mountains.

Matt grinned to himself. A pretty decent four-point roll even if he did have to say so himself. He heard Katalina scream with delight.

"Okay, Kat, your airplane."

"My airplane," she responded, taking the controls. She rolled the airplane inverted, pushed the nose up to bleed off a little airspeed. They hung upside down on their shoulder harnesses for a moment before she hauled back on the stick and chopped the throttle. The airplane plummeted into a split S.

~~~~~~~

"Rahim, do you see the two-winged airplane above?" Rahim Musa's walkie-talkie crackled to life. Through openings in the tree limbs he watched the amazing antics of the red and cream bi-plane in the fading light, covering his ears against the thunderous roar of the radial engine each time the airplane came screaming down in another dive.

"Of course you idiot," Rahim hissed in reply. "How could you not know the aircraft is up there?" He recognized Saeed's voice

"I think it is the airplane used by the old man! I have a clear shot!"

"Standby …" Rahim glanced up the ravine to the point where Saeed lay near the creek bank. He was only 30 yards away but with the fading light and thick forest it was practically impossible to see him, so Rahim wasn't concerned that the crazy pilot tumbling through the sky could possibly pick Saeed out in the shadows. He did not want to prematurely tip his hand, but still, what a crippling blow to the Cortez family if he could turn the old man into a giant fireball right in front of the entire clan.

Saeed was the best gunner he had when it came to firing the RPG-7V2 rocket propelled grenade. In actual combat situations in Afghanistan, Rahim had personally witnessed the diminutive soldier fire a 105 mm HEAT anti-tank grenade through the window of a moving vehicle at 200 yards like he had been doing it all his life. On several occasions, Saeed had been praised for his accuracy when no other gunner could come close to their intended target.

The 40 millimeter fragmentation grenade Saeed was carrying today had an accurate range of 300 yards—probably more like 400 yards with Saeed behind the trigger. If anyone could score a direct hit on the red biplane it would be Saeed. Daylight was fading fast, so perhaps people up at the villa would not see the telltale plume of white smoke trailing behind the rocket grenade. A quick glance at the gunner's position and then back through the trees at the airplane made his decision.

The airplane was heading toward their position, climbing steeply into the sky just as it had moments earlier. Higher and higher it climbed. If it repeated the same maneuver from earlier it would come screaming back toward the earth almost directly toward Saeed's position; well within range for the expert gunner.

The Waco pushed over, heading straight for the ground. "Saeed, take the shot when the plane pulls up from the dive."

"Allahu Akbar!" Saeed eased out from under the trees, knelt on one knee, steadied the rocket launcher on his shoulder, and lined up his optic sight on the biplane. Just as he had done on the battlefield a hundred times, he led the target by its estimated speed, so that the biplane would fly directly into his RPG round. Saeed held his breath and squeezed the trigger.

Ten

El Achiotal
Guatemala

What's that? Matt caught a bright flash out of the corner of his eye. Katalina had just rolled the Waco straight and level from a diving Split S when the flash came zipping out of the trees near the creek. The hairs on the back of his neck stood up, a quick shiver ran up his spine. Instinctively, he grabbed the control stick.

"My airplane," he shouted through the intercom. He shoved the throttle to full power and pushed the nose down while bending the airplane hard to the right. His instincts where screaming *DANGER*! The perfect gemlike evening was instantly pitched into a frantic life or death struggle as Matt pulled the nose of the airplane toward the threat and allowed the airspeed to build. The faster the airplane flew the more maneuverable it became. It was an automatic reaction honed by hundreds of air combat hours … and it saved their lives!

The rocket missed the Waco's tail by less than three feet and continued climbing into the empty sky until running out of fuel. It then plummeted back to earth, exploding harmlessly in the pasture some 200 yards short of the crowd of Recon Marines.

Matt eased the stick back to level flight and pointed the airplane toward Cortez's airfield, away from the tree-lined creek. He glanced back over his shoulder to see if he could spot the gunner, but the shadows were too dark. On the other side of the aircraft he saw Marines scrambling to defensive positions.

"Sorry about that," Matt said into the intercom. "Your airplane!"

"My airplane," Katalina gasped.

The whole thing happened so fast, he was pretty sure she did not see the danger. From the moment he first saw the flash and the rocket zipped past them was only a few seconds.

"Hey Cuz, that's an interestin' way you have for flushin' out the bad guys! Y'all need a fresh change of undies?"

Matt pulled the airplane microphone away from his mouth and took a few deep breaths. He was not surprised to find his hands trembling. It had been that close. He answered Chase through his wireless comm-set. "Affirmative on the undies!…You didn't happen to see the direction that thing came from did you?"

"Roger that. Watchdog One reported seeing the rocket come out of the trees but no shooter yet. They're lookin'!"

"Okay, keep 'em on their toes. Won't be long now." Matt paused to look around, updating his situational awareness. The big radial engine rumbled comfortingly, the sun was well below the horizon and dark shadows covered the ground. Over the engine cowling, he could barely make out the airfield, a long black strip on the velvety green carpet. In the distance he could see the beginning of the Petén region of thick jungle and rain forests. He took another deep breath to calm himself while taking in the natural beauty, enjoying the peace and serenity that once again surrounded them, as if holding them in a soft, comforting embrace. Even though he had not seen them before, Matt was now aware that the terrorists were closing in on the family compound and danger stalked the peaceful night air.

Matt figured the terrorists had learned from their mistake several months before when they came charging blindly down the road into El Achiotal thinking they could take the Guatemalans by surprise. Instead, the surprise was on them. The firestorm of lead waiting for them was worse than running headlong into a meat grinder. This time they effectively came creeping through the woods with stealth and cunning.

This time there could be a lot more of them, Matt feared. He needed to get a clearer picture of what they were up against, and he needed it quickly.

"Reaper, Quarterback! Location?"

"Five minutes out!" Clayton's voice clearly came through Matt's earbud.

"Okay! Got an urgent mission for y'all. Ready to copy?"

"Go, Quarterback!"

Katalina reduced power and descended toward the airstrip. Matt scoured the area, his head on a swivel, searching for enemy troops sneaking from the woods toward the small airport. It was unlikely that the terrorists would make the airstrip a target, but even so, the Waco would be a sitting duck on final approach and taxiing to the Cortez hangar.

"Reaper, we're taking enemy fire from a narrow tree line running west to east, following a creek, seven hundred yards south of the Cortez compound. You will see a bend in the tree line. We have friendlies in the trees west of the bend. Enemy positions are east of the bend. Can you plot them with your infrared?"

"Affirmative, Quarterback. Standby!"

"Quarterback standing by! … Master Chief, are y'all with me?" Matt hoped the aircraft crew chief was still monitoring the communications net.

Katalina dropped the aircraft over the foothills and lined up on short final.

"Affirmative, college boy! what's up?" Walter Roberts fired back.

"I need you to pull the Osprey out and get her ready to fly, ASAP!"

"Roger that!" Matt detected an air of excitement in the master chief's voice and was frankly surprised there were no questions. It was not an easy task folding the stubby wings and prop/rotors and shoving the big aircraft into the hangar. Fact was, the grizzled old master chief had barely completed the task, and now Matt wanted it brought out again. Roberts had every reason to be fired up and hopping mad, but he didn't let on.

Matt knew Reaper was quite capable of identifying hostile targets in the closing darkness with its infrared optics, but the Osprey had equal capability, plus the means to take the fight out of the terrorists rather quickly. And time was something they were running out of.

~~~~~~~

Matt climbed out of the front cockpit while Katalina shut down the engine. He extended a hand to assist the girl out of the airplane. He was doing everything possible to make things seem normal in her world while his mind raced through the myriad of tasks to meet the urgency crashing down around them.

"Great job, Kat!" Matt bumped fists with Katalina and smiled down at her blushing face.

"Thank you, Señor Matt—"

"Uh huh, it's Matt, remember?" She turned away with a demure grin.

Samuel Cortez strode quickly toward them. Matt saw the concern in the old man's eyes and knew he had been in radio contact with his *Sicarios* and was very much aware that the threat against his family had gone live. But like Matt, Samuel Cortez masked his fear to shield his granddaughter from the horror of terrorist gunmen.

"So tell me, Matt," Cortez began, placing an arm around Katalina's shoulders, proudly pulling her to his side, "is my little *nieta* ready to take on international competition?" A smile spread across his face, but Matt could see worry behind his tired eyes. Darkness would bring the attack on his home and it was only minutes away.

"Pretty close, I would say." *Only about a thousand more hours of practice*, he didn't say. She was more than good. She was a natural. A great stick! But what she really needed—

"I know, we need a better airplane for her to become truly competitive." Samuel finished Matt's thought as if reading his mind. The Waco was graceful, maneuverable, and powerful, and Katalina had learned to pull the maximum performance out of the venerable machine. But the truth was the old biplane was a cumbersome pig compared to the high performance aircraft used in competition aerobatics.

"Correct, Samuel. Katalina has the potential to be the next Patty Wagstaff, but we need to get her into a plane that will challenge her far beyond anything she ever dreamed."

"We?" Samuel Cortez asked with an arched eyebrow.

"Sure," Matt nodded. "I would be happy to help train her, if you still want. I'd also be glad to help you find an aircraft she'll feel comfortable flying."

Katalina's head was on a swivel moving back and forth as the two men continued to talk about her. She felt herself becoming more excited at the prospect of actually competing on an international level. Up to now such thoughts seemed like an impossible aspiration, rekindled each time her *abuelo* encouraged her to pursue her dream, reach for the stars. How could a teenage girl from a remote village in Guatemala ever hope to become recognized as a serious aerobatic competitor? She felt her skin tingle with anticipation.

Samuel pulled his granddaughter close and kissed the top of her head. "Kat, I want you to help Victorio put the Waco away while Matt and I talk over some things. Okay, Sweetie?"

"Oh *Papá*," Katalina said with a look of disappointment. "You just want me out of the way so you and Señor Matt can discuss killing the bad men attacking our home!"

Samuel chuckled. "My little *nieta* is much too perceptive. Now please, go help with the airplane so we can get back home, quickly."

They watched as Katalina turned dutifully and trudged off with her head down.

From the larger hangar beyond, they saw the sinister black MV-22 Osprey pulled outside. Electric motors slowly rotated the wing and extended the large prop/rotors into position like a giant bird of prey stretching as it awakened from its slumber.

Samuel Cortez turned back to Matt. "There is little time to spare. The *terroristas* are already moving on my family. Hurry, you must take your men and go after Hassam."

"Yes, I know." Matt did not want to argue with his host, but there was no way he was leaving this beautiful family to defend themselves. "Look Samuel, I have an idea that will save us a little time. You go on with Kat. Master Chief Roberts and I will meet you at the villa."

"But—"

"No, please Samuel, trust me on this. We'll be along in a few minutes and then I'll pick up my people and head out for Santo Tomás."

Samuel glanced toward the Osprey and then back to Matt. He shook his head as if in doubt, shrugged, and then chased after Katalina.

Eleven

El Achiotal
Guatemala

"Reaper, Quarterback! Airborne in Dark Horse One. Your location?" Matt thumbed the knurled wheel on the thrust lever, rotating the engine nacelles into the airplane mode. The large black tilt-rotor aircraft picked up speed quickly and was soon soaring toward the hilltop compound.

"Reaper is two-point-three miles west of the Cortez compound, heading zero-eight-five, at one-five thousand. I have you in sight!"

"Master Chief, I want you on the Gatling gun," Matt said.

"Aye, aye, Cap!" Master Chief Roberts answered as he strapped himself in to the copilot seat.

The NCTC Osprey was specially armed with a retractable, belly-mounted M197 3-barreled Gatling Gun. The 20 millimeter cannon had a firing rate of 1500 rounds per minute. The gun was slaved to the forward looking infrared, FLIR, pod located separately from the gun. The multi-function screen on the copilot's panel could display real time images with a targeting reticle in the center much like a rifle telescope. The system provided both offensive and defensive firepower in just about all weather and lighting conditions. A joystick located next to the copilot's right knee rotated direction and deflection of the FLIR and a red trigger engaged the gun.

"Talk to me Reaper. Give me locations and head count on the tangos."

"I got thirty ... make that thirty-one tangos. They are east of that dogleg in the trees. They're advancing out into the open. Friendlies identified west of the bend!"

"Roger that, Reaper. I'm five-hundred AGL, swinging west of the compound, lining up on targets." Matt passed directly over the hacienda and banked the Osprey hard left to check activity around the compound. On the infrared screen he saw the Marines fanned out in a semi-circle with over-lapping fields of fire. They would be ready when the terrorists reached the summit and charged the compound. But Matt was not going to let the terrorists get close enough for that.

"Hey Chase, that wasn't a very friendly wave," Matt chuckled through the comm-set as he flew over the hacienda and saw his cousin flip him the finger on the FLIR screen.

"Seriously? Dude?" Chase groused. *"You leave me with these ground-pounding snake eaters?"*

"Relax buddy, I will be right down to—"

"BREAK RIGHT! BREAK RIGHT! ..." Reaper screamed.

A brilliant flash came from somewhere behind the Osprey, arching across the night sky trailing fire for 200 yards before impacting the ground less than 100 feet short of the veranda. Matt was already in a sharp bank before realizing the Osprey was not the intended target.

The battle had begun. Within seconds two more rocket grenades joined the night air. Then another ... and another.

Explosions erupted across the back perimeter of the compound. Most fell well short of their intended target. Screams pierced the darkness as several Cortez men went down in the initial rocket barrage. They were farther out on the perimeter than the Marines, closer to the terrorists rushing up the hill.

The radio came alive with chatter, adding to the confusion of the battle. Matt tuned out the frantic voices, half-listening for his own call sign while focusing on flying the big Osprey. He needed a few more seconds before turning into the terrorists to deliver a solid offensive punch.

~~~~~~~~

"Watchdog Eight's been hit! Sniper in the tree east of the garage! RPG same location, on the ground below the sniper."

"Watchdog Eight, this is Linebacker! Your location?" Lt. Col. Butch Larson turned to his left, searching the darkness through his night vision goggles. He had two men guarding the left flank, Watchdog Eight and Nine. The flank was now compromised and he would need to patch that hole quickly.

Shots rang out, automatic rifle fire and single shots filled the air from both sides of the battlefield, adding to the confusion and degrading communications.

Larson had warned Cortez to keep his men back from the line-of-sight between his Marines and the enemy troops, but dark figures darting haphazardly left and right told him the *Sicarios* had other ideas. Their communications net was separate from his, leaving a disjointed effort from the very beginning—just as Gunny Stevens had predicted. A recipe for a disaster if he couldn't get a handle on the situation soon.

"Linebacker, Watchdog Niner! Sniper terminated ... RPG gunner too!"

"Roger that, Watchdog Niner! Good shooting!"

Watchdog Nine was Corporal Ernie, EZ, Zavala. Larson had assigned EZ to an overwatch position atop the garage roof. The terrorist sniper made the fatal mistake of not looking high before taking his first and only shot. It had not occurred to him that the Americans would have their own sniper.

"Watchdog Eight, say your situation!" Larson commanded.

"Linebacker, Watchdog Niner! Eight is hunkered down inside the gazebo!"

The small, octagon-shaped open structure was maybe 30 yards to Larson's left, but even with night vision goggles, he could not see into the black shadows inside.

"Watchdog Eight ... I'm ... still in... the fight!" Watchdog Eight, Corporal Billy Graft, gasped for breath. His left arm was numb, dangling useless at his side. He felt a sticky wetness trickling down his sleeve and dripping off his finger tips.

"Stoney, Eight's been hit! He's in the gazebo, tend to it!" Larson commanded.

"Twelve copies! Moving!" Watchdog Twelve was Lance Corporal Laney (Stoney) Stone. The wiry twenty year-old from Milwaukee was team medic and comms expert.

The advancing terrorists were 500 yards out, still below the crest and out of sight for Larson and his defensive perimeter. He would not be able to engage them until they were 300 yards. But EZ had a clear, unobstructed view of the black silhouettes from his vantage point on the garage roof. They were crouched low, moving steadily up the hill in pairs; many of whom had stopped to take aim with another barrage of RPGs.

EZ's personal choice for a multi-purpose sniper rifle was the AR-10B. The Night Force mil dot scope provided consistent, deadly accuracy to the point that he could put a bullet in the center of a quarter at 500 yards every single time, and the 20-round box mag with .308 Winchester ammo gave him plenty of firepower. He zeroed in on a rocket team that appeared ready to launch. He lined up the cross-hairs on the gunner's chest and slowly squeezed the trigger.

EZ didn't wait to verify the hit—he didn't need to. He moved the gunsight to the loader crouched behind and slightly to the right of the gunner. EZ saw the bewildered look on the terrorist's face as he watched the body of his comrade fling back. He never felt his comrade's warm blood splatter his face before EZ's second round tore through his chest, exiting out his back. The .308 boat-tail hollow point took half of his heart with it.

~~~~~~~~

Rahim Musa moved out from the tree line and crouched in the knee-high grass. He raised the night vision binoculars and smiled inwardly. His men were advancing quickly and apparently undetected; so far there was no opposition. Even though he had warned his people over the walkie-talkie to not fire their rockets until at least halfway up the hill and even then not until they had targets in sight, but some of his over-zealous warriors were already stopping to take aim. They were lobbing grenades over the crest of the hill in hope of destroying something.

Their lack of discipline was costing valuable ammunition and giving away their positions, but Rahim took comfort in numbers. He knew they would still over-run their enemies and lay waste to the great Cortez villa. The lead units were less than a hundred yards from having prime targets in sight. Less than a minute.

His chest swelled with pride as he thought of being congratulated by Ahmad Hassam himself. Honor and praise would be heaped upon him by the great *as-Syf*!

"Allahu Akbar!" He shouted. He jumped to his feet and charged up the hill behind his warriors.

~~~~~~~~

Matt brought the MV-22 Osprey screaming down to treetop level at 300 knots. Less than a mile from his targets he dialed the knurled wheel back, rotating the engine nacelles to 75 degrees vertical. The aircraft slowed so quickly it appeared as if it stopped in midair.

The Osprey had transformed into helicopter mode, its nose pointed low, moving forward at 40 knots. In the FLIR screen, Matt could see the enemy troops as fuzzy white images on green background. They were scattered across the hill in groups of two, one kneeling with a rocket launcher on his shoulder, the other standing close ready to reload. He knew Master Chief Roberts had the same image on his screen and was already designating targets.

"All ground units, live-fire run commencing now!" Matt spoke softly through the comm-set. "Anytime you're ready, Chief!"

Master Chief Walter Roberts delivered his answer with a short burst from the Gatling cannon and the Osprey shuddered from the recoil. In the screen Matt saw the closest two-man terrorist team disappear in a cloud of dust and chunks of flesh. Seconds later Chief Roberts again stroked the trigger of the multi-barreled gun and another team disappeared under a shower of fifty 20-millimeter rounds.

Then another … and another. Within ten seconds of the initial engagement, Roberts had obliterated four rocket teams, eight tangos. Just then another barrage of rockets arched high into the dark sky, trailing streams of yellow fire before terminating around the backyard and fence perimeter. With a look of horror Matt saw a grenade explode on the rear corner of the house. Chunks of terra cotta roof tiles lifted into the night air as if in slow motion. *Please dear God, don't let that beautiful family get hurt!*

"*QUARTERBACK LOOK OUT!*" Reaper boomed through Matt's earbud. *"Rocket team, far end!"*

Matt jinked to the right and slammed the aircraft down fifty feet just as Roberts fired another burst, which went harmlessly into the trees. He searched the screen for the terrorist gunner, but all targets were off the screen because of his evasive maneuver. The hair on the back of Matt's neck stood out and sweat rolled down his face as he fought to bring the nose of the aircraft back to the field of fire. He glanced quickly out the right window. He actually felt the trees dangerously close.

"*Rifle! Rifle!*" Reaper called the missile shot and a bright flash streaked overhead.

For a moment Matt thought it was a terrorist rocket. But then he saw the explosion on the horizon to his left and knew a Hellfire missile just took out his threat.

"Nice shooting, Reaper. Thanks!" Matt said, shifting the Osprey to the left, climbing fifty feet.

"My pleasure, Quarterback! ... Looks like you have the tangos on the run."

"Copy that!" Matt checked his screen. The terrorists were in full retreat, high tailing it toward the tree line. He nudged the stick forward and bumped up the throttle, gaining a little speed. The tangos were more than a hundred yards from reaching the safety of the trees and he intended to thin the odds as much as possible.

The Osprey trembled again as Chief Roberts ripped another burst into the fleeing targets. Just as quickly he swiveled the big gun and stroked the trigger again.

It seemed surreal for Matt, sitting comfortably in the cockpit watching ghostly images of men on a dead run, then disappearing in a cloud of white and green fuzz. Less than half of the enemy force managed to disappear into the trees along the creek. Their fate was not looking very promising, though. Matt could see the images of the Watchdog team moving east from their positions toward the area where the terrorists entered the tree line.

"Hold your fire, Master Chief," Matt ordered just as another burst pumped sixty rounds into faint images moving through the trees, destroying timber and flesh and anything else in the line of fire. Without question they could probably search out and destroy a few more tangos before they managed to hide from the infrared sensor, but Matt didn't want to risk firing close to the Watchdog force.

"Copy that!" A gruff voice returned.

"Good shooting, Chief!"

Twelve

Ahmad Hassam's face grew darker by the minute. Hakeem Larijani was on his satellite phone and Hassam knew from the one-sided conversation, it was not good news. He could barely control his anger as he felt the heat rising on his skin, creeping up from his neck until his face flushed crimson.

He glanced at his bodyguard and slowly shook his head. Ali gave an understanding nod. Hassam allowed himself to consider the huge man for a moment while Larijani was screaming into the phone.

The giant stood close to seven feet and weighed over 280 pounds of solid muscle. He had a broad barrel chest and a head the size of a pumpkin sitting on no neck. His smashed nose was fat and crooked, thanks to an infidel woman getting in a lucky kick, which Ali had been too slow to dodge. His hands and forearms were massive. He could easily snap a man's neck one-handed. Hassam had seen him do it.

Hassam had known Ali for only six months. The giant had met him at the airport terminal when he came to Guatemala to pick up a captured American female DEA agent who, as it turned out, happened to also be friends with Carley Downs, daughter of the President of the United States. In a very short time the hulking giant had proven to be trustworthy and loyal. A man who would gladly lay down his life to protect Hassam and for the glory of *Allah!* So Hassam had taken the big man away from Larijani to be his own bodyguard.

Larijani switched off the phone, angrily stuffed it into the pocket of his loose fitting pants, and turned to face his very angry boss. "Bad news," Larijani's face flushed with anger. "That was Rahim. His force has been driven back. He said the large black aircraft appeared out of nowhere, firing missiles and machine guns. The few surviving the attack have retreated—"

"RETREATED?" Hassam snatched a small ornamental clock off the desk and hurled it against the wall, shattering into a dozen pieces. His dark eyes blazed, his nostrils flared. Muscles in his neck and shoulders bulged as he clinched his fists. Even Ali took a step back.

"Our warriors do not RETREAT!" Hassam looked around the room as if searching for something else to throw.

Larijani glanced at Ali and knew his own eyes reflected the same fear as that in the big man's eyes. They both had witnessed fits of rage in their leader that often ended with extreme violence. With that in mind, Larijani trembled, his eyes traveled to Hassam's hands and to the shoulder rig holding his favorite Makarov PM 9-millimeter with blood-red wooden pistol grips. The weapon was a gift by none other than Major General Imad Abu Mughniyeh of the Iranian Revolutionary Guard. If Rahim Musa walked through the door right now, Ahmad would shoot him and put his head on a stick outside the warehouse door for all to see what happens when you fail *as-Syf*.

But almost as fast as the rage came, it was gone. Hassam slowly shook his head and sighed. His voice softened. "Had Rahim launched his own attack prior to the aircraft arriving?"

"Yes Ahmad, he did." Larijani took a couple steps toward Hassam. "Each of Rahim's rocket teams launched several grenades. He was unclear how many hit their target, but he saw multiple explosions on the house and heard many screams—"

"Did he see Cortez?"

"No, Ahmad. They did not get close enough to see faces before they were attacked." When Larijani saw a dark cloud come over Hassam's face he quickly added, "But Rahim's sniper reported getting off several successful shots before being silenced. We can hope that—"

"No! We will not *hope!* We will come back and finish the job. Later! Our enemies must know we never fail." Hassam's eyes blazed again. "Do you understand?"

"Yes, Ahmad, I understand." Larijani answered softly. He reached out and lightly grabbed Hassam by the arm. "We must get you out of here, *as-Syf*. Our enemies are coming for you."

The three men headed for the large warehouse door, but then Hassam stopped in mid-stride. "It was the same man, Hakeem!"

"Sir?"

"The black aircraft, the American force. It was the same man we saw here six months ago. The same infidel who stole our hostages from us and set fire to our warehouse." The dark cloud was back. His face contorted with rage.

"But Ahmad, how can you know that?"

Hassam closed his eyes. The face of the American infidel lurked in the shadows of his mind, taunting, mocking, as if challenging him to reengage their hand-to-hand struggle fought on this very waterfront. Had it not been for the raging fire and the warehouse collapsing on them it would have been a fight to the death. Never before had he seen such fierce determination, such conviction, as in the bright green eyes of the American.

Hassam broke off the battle that day, forcing himself to focus on the bigger picture. Focusing on his responsibility to lead the greatest attack in history against the Great Satan. He knew the moment he had slipped into the darkening shadows of super-heated smoke that there would be another opportunity to finish what the two warriors had started. Today was not that day, but it was coming. Soon.

Hassam opened his eyes and looked at Larijani. "Because, Hakeem, I can feel his presence."

They continued out into the evening air and Hassam looked up at the star-studded sky. He could feel the eyes of the cocky American upon him. It made him smile.

"Hakeem, my good and faithful friend. I want to know everything there is to know about this American infidel. I want to know where his family lives. Do you understand?"

~~~~~~~~~

USS *Iwo Jima*
30 Miles Off
Coast of Belize
Western Caribbean

Captain Elway Reynolds strode into the darkened CIC ramrod straight, his mouth set, blue eyes taking in the hushed activity. The forty year-old captain of the USS *Iwo Jima* was a tall and lanky man with thick blond hair cut short. The '94 Annapolis grad from Modesto, California had climbed through the ranks like a skyrocket, aided by an uncanny ability to instantly analyze any situation and make accurate snap decisions. Tonight the man who usually had a warm smile for everyone was all business.

Every chair in the combat information center was occupied and each person sat up straight when Captain Reynolds entered the compartment.

"As you were gentlemen … and LADIES!" The twenty-year Navy veteran made a point to the males in his command that the women aboard *Iwo* had served with distinction on their recent combat tour in the Middle East—much to the disbelief from certain male officers and enlisted personnel.

"Gimme a SitRep, Muddy," Reynolds said quietly as he settled into the red leather command chair to the left of his operations officer, Lt. Cmdr. Charlie "Muddy" Waters.

"Captain, the Cortez villa has been attacked by an unconfirmed number of terrorist combatants." Lt. Cmdr. Waters nodded toward one of four large tactical screens mounted on the forward bulkhead. The real-time infrared image on the flat screen transmitted from Reaper One displayed the entire battleground from the villa down to the tree-lined creek. "The Dark Horse Osprey repelled the attackers with its Gatling canon and Reaper One launched a single Hellfire.

"Watchdog units have now engaged the tangos here inside this stand of trees."

Waters circled the eastern creek area with a red laser pointer.

At that moment Col. Tommy Kramer, USMC, Commander of 26th Marine Expeditionary Unit, MEU, embarked on USS *Iwo Jima,* appeared at Captain Elway Reynolds side. Kramer was a short, stocky man with pudgy cheeks, reddish complexion, and a severe short Marine Corps crew cut. The forty-four year old Marine Corps Colonel possessed an incredibly strong command presence and was known to be extremely protective of what he considered to be *his* turf.

Kramer took one look at the screen and turned to the operations officer. "Any report on casualties?"

"No report, Colonel. It's a little early into the skirmish." Kramer glared at the operations officer.

~~~~~~~

The ground control station, GCS, for *Iwo*'s UAV operations was located in a compartment adjacent to the aft bulkhead from CIC, with whom they maintained continuous communications during all flight operations.

All three flight crew chairs in GCS were presently occupied with Lt (jg) Todd Clarkson flying ScanEagle II from the left seat, Lt. Cmdr. Clayton Downs in the center chair piloting Reaper I, and Lt. Louis Rogers on the right as the sensor operator, or SO, for Reaper.

The twenty-five year old Rogers was hunched over his console. He pushed his glasses back with his thumb as he concentrated on the infrared imaging. Like Clayton, Rogers owned a very successful private software company and didn't really need to be "patrolling the high seas in Uncle Sam's canoe crew, but did so only for kicks and grins," as he so coarsely put it from time to time.

Clayton asked Rogers to put the tactical data up on the large screen located on the gray bulkhead between their consoles in four separate frames. A quick scan of the eye would provide complete situational awareness of the mission operations. The upper right corner of the screen displayed satellite weather conditions for the entire region; two other squares displayed the Cortez villa and surrounding area, one showing a night vision optics feed, the other with infrared synthetic aperture radar, SAR. The lower right corner of the large screen contained a night optics view from ScanEagle II circling Puerto Santo Tomás.

Clayton switched Reaper's autopilot on and flexed his fingers. He let out a weary sigh and leaned back in his crew chair. He had been holding his breath during the short engagement with the terrorists and sweat trickled down his back, forming stains under his arms. He pushed his blue *Iwo Jima* ball cap back and ran a hand across his forehead as he watched the PFD, or primary flight display. He then glanced up at the large screen.

Clayton quickly sat up. "Whoa! Todd get a lock on that vehicle and zoom in?"

Optics on the ScanEagle were not nearly the capability of Reaper's, especially night vision, but Clayton's trained eye caught a brief sliver of light at the warehouse door followed by three dark figures moving through the shadows toward a vehicle parked adjacent to the warehouse.

"Yes, sir … got it!" Lt. (jg) Clarkson caught the movement a second behind Clayton and was already nudging the controls on the small UAV, tightening the small aircraft's turn radius to keep the dark-colored vehicle in the center of the screen. He bumped the command key for zoom control, and was instantly rewarded with a distorted view.

"No, too much," Clayton commanded. "Back it out a smidge."

"Okay … there!" Clarkson responded a second later.

The grainy image was as good as they were going to get. They could see three people getting into the vehicle and when the dome light came on they could definitely tell that the man climbing into the back seat was a whopper. Even though facial recognition was impossible, Clayton's intuition told him this was something important. He wished he had Reaper's high-powered sensors over the target to validate his suspicions.

"Alright, take one more look at the freighters and then follow this guy."

The ScanEagle made a wider circle over the docks and then returned to the warehouse. Clarkson picked up the red taillights of the vehicle as it pulled away from the warehouse and drove out the main gate.

"Quarterback, Reaper One! Primary target is on the move! I say again, target is on the move!" Clayton spoke into his comm-set. He then switched his headset to the ships intercom into CIC.

"Captain, GCS! Did you copy target is on the move?"

"We got it, Commander." Captain Elway Reynolds was watching the split-screen tactical data provided by GCS while also monitoring comm-set traffic.

"Captain, *Alaed* and *Jin* have cast away from the dock and are heading into the harbor."

"Copy that, Commander. I want their direction of travel once they clear Amatique Bay and hit the open sea."

Thirteen

Carter Manning poured the remaining coffee from the carafe, took a sip, and set the mug down with a grimace. The coffee was cold.

"Want another cup?" He asked Director of National Intelligence, Alex Strayhorn.

"Or two," Strayhorn responded with a smile. He held the phone receiver away from his ear and covered the mouth piece. He then continued to talk with the man on the other end.

Manning went to the door, stuck his head out, and softly called, "Nadie, we need another pot." He smiled as he handed her the empty carafe. "Please!"

"Of course, Mr. Manning. It will only take a moment. I'll bring it right in." Nadine Hollingsworth had been administrative assistant to the director of the National Counterterrorism Center since the inception of Liberty Crossing in 2003. Her only son was killed in Iraq by an

IED less than a year before her husband died. The grief had been too much for his breaking heart. So the NCTC was her entire life now. She figured she had a score to settle with Islamic terrorists.

Manning returned to his leather chair at the conference table. leaned back, and vigorously rubbed his weary eyes with both hands. It was a few minutes past midnight and he had been awake for almost twenty hours—and he had not slept all that soundly the night before. He blew a big sigh and swiveled his chair to face the DNI, who had just hung up the phone.

"Duty officer at NSA confirms phone intercepts on Hakeem Larijani's sat phone," Strayhorn said. "Larijani placed the first call. The recipient was pinpointed south of El Achiotal, close to the Cortez villa. Second call, same recipient, this time he called Larijani. They're running voice records to identify the unknown male. Definitely was not Ahmad Hassam."

"Based on our chronology, the first intercept was Larijani telling one of his lieutenants to launch the attack," Manning theorized.

"Correct. And the second was the lieutenant telling his boss that he'd just had his butt handed to him in a basket, compliments of Matthew McWain," Strayhorn laughed. "NSA says the guy was screaming like he was scared spitless. They should have the intercepts decrypted shortly."

The National Security Agency at Fort Meade had been picking intercepts off the Russian RORSAT for six months or more. The NSA was assisting NCTC with developing credible evidence that *Firestorm* clearly indicated an imminent terrorist attack inside the United States.

The Russians had parked their newest multi-function radar ocean reconnaissance satellite in geosynchronous orbit over the western Caribbean more than six months before, ostensibly in support of a joint naval exercise between Russia, Iran and Venezuela. The satellite happened to be in perfect continuum, which provided a direct communications relay for Hassam and Larijani in the planned abduction of first daughter Carley Downs.

President of the United States Harlan Downs wanted the satellite destroyed when he was first made aware of these facts, but his staff talked him out of it arguing that the Russians would most likely remove it from the area at the conclusion of their naval exercise.

The fact that the advanced communication/surveillance satellite remained in geosynchronous orbit off the coast of Honduras rather than being flown to a location more beneficial to Russian interests raised the likelihood of possible malicious activity.

Especially after President Downs directed Secretary of State Zachary Ringhold to inform the Russians that the United States had irrefutable evidence that they were in direct contravention of the International Terrorist Act by providing communication capabilities to known international terrorists; and to further suggest that failure to remove the satellite from Central America's coastline would jeopardize diplomatic relations.

The Russian ambassador to the United States basically told SecState Ringhold where he could put his suggestion.

"You know, of course, when the president hears about these recent intercepts from that RORSAT he's going to say he told us so."

"Yup!"

"And then President Downs will most likely get on the horn to Admiral J.B. Turner and order that thing blown into a gazillion pieces of space junk."

"Yup!"

"At which time Secretary of State Zachary Ringhold will inform President Downs that such action will certainly constitute an act of war."

"Yup, again!"

"So what are you going to do?" Manning asked with a raised eyebrow.

"I'm getting the president on the horn. Time to bring him up to speed."

"I unders—"

"*Hey guys, are you catching this?*" The Ops Center duty officer boomed over the intercom. He was on his feet, half-turned away from the workstations, looking up at the conference room.

Manning and Strayhorn stood and moved to the glass wall, caught the duty officer's eye, and stared at the large center screen.

"*Quarterback, Reaper One! Primary target is on the move! I say again, target is on the move!*"

Manning watched the greenish image of a dark-colored vehicle speeding through the security gate at the Santo Tomás docks. His pulse quickened and he realized he was holding his breath. *No! We cannot let Hassam slip through our fingers again!* He wanted to jump in and start barking orders, but he forced himself to wait for Matt's response.

~~~~~~

El Achiotal
Guatemala

"Copy Reaper One. Can you keep eyes on him?" Matt answered. He eased the big tilt-rotor aircraft to a soft landing in the backyard of the Cortez villa in a roaring tornado of dust and grass clippings.

"*Negative, Quarterback! ScanEagle does not have target laser capability. We will lose the target in traffic the moment he gets on the highway.*"

"Can you see which direction he turns once he gets to the highway?"

There was little doubt in Matt's mind that Hassam was heading for the airport in Puerto Barrios. He knew from recent experience that the drive to the airport would not take more than ten to fifteen minutes, depending on the evening traffic. There was no way he could stop Hassam if the master terrorist had an airplane waiting on the ramp.

"Reaper One, when you finish spotting the tangos for Watchdog, I want you to zip over to the Puerto Barrios airport and see if you can resume surveillance on the target."

"Roger that, Quarterback!"

Matt bounded out the side door of the Osprey. Just as his boots hit the ground his earbud came alive again.

"Quarterback, Ops Center! Is there any way you can intercept our primary target? Matt could hear the urgency in Manning's voice.

"We're gonna try, but odds are against us," Matt's voice was anxious as he stepped out to meet Chase and Butch Larson. They were moving briskly toward him.

"Try harder, Matt!" There was a short pause as if Manning was consulting with someone. *"How about having Reaper close on him and blast a Hellfire up his tailpipe."*

Matt visualized the highway leading into Puerto Barrios, the homes and businesses directly abutting the road, and traffic congestion. He remembered the high-speed chase with Hassam on his tail as they raced toward the airport when Carley Downs' life hung in the balance. There were kids playing in the streets that day and they had to swerve several times to miss them. Of course there probably wouldn't be any children playing out there tonight in the dark. But still—

"Negative, Manning, bad idea. Too congested!"

There was another pause before Manning came back. By then Butch Larson and Chase gathered silently around Matt. Both had comm-sets on and monitored the exchanges between Matt, Reaper I, and Ops Center.

"Okay, Matt, I understand." There was resignation in Manning's voice. *"We defer to your judgment. If you can't take him, we need to know where he's going. ... What are your plans for the waterfront?"*

"We're gonna take it out just as soon as we get saddled up here. Quarterback out!"

Matt turned to Chase and Larson. He immediately noticed Larson had changed into jungle cammies, boots, and Kevlar vest. "You guys heard it; we need to load and go! How many troops can we take, Butch?"

"There'll be eleven of us Matt. Seven Recon, us three, and Lenox." Larson responded. "Billy Graft is out, took a round in the shoulder. I'm bringing up two from patrol. They should be here in a few."

Matt considered this before speaking. "That leaves only four Recon Marines out in the bush searching for remaining tangos. That gonna be enough?"

"That, along with a dozen or so *sicarios* should be plenty. Watchdog One reports seven remaining tangos on the run. Reaper found their vehicles hidden in deep cover about four clicks east of here. Lt. Beemer is breaking off pursuit. He's letting the *sicarios* hunt down the ragheads while he pulls his unit into a flanking action."

"Alright! Chase, you get everyone loaded up." Matt turned back to Butch Larson. "Let's go see Señor Cortez about a little mission planning. Just a sec!" With that Matt disappeared inside the aircraft.

When he emerged two minutes later he had changed into navy blue cargo pants, tactical long sleeve pullover, and a navy blue Kevlar vest with NCTC stenciled in white across the back. He wore a thigh-mount holster for his M9 Beretta. A pouch beside the pistol contained two spare mags, and two additional magazines were in pouches on his belt. On his left hip was a Marine Corps Ka-Bar combat knife.

Matt and Lt. Col. Larson found Samuel Cortez on the veranda along with his wife, Alicia, their four daughters, and Katalina fussing over a half dozen wounded sicarios and one Recon Marine lying on the concrete floor. The younger grandchildren were inside with their faces pressed to the glass.

Matt watched the women bring out pots of boiling water while others cut strips from cotton sheets for bandages. They were taking direction from Lance Corporal Laney Stone as he quickly moved among the victims. Blood covered the patio and agonizing cries and moans carried in the night air. It appeared to Matt that several victims were in serious condition.

Matt moved close to Cortez and asked quietly, "What's the situation, Samuel?"

"Could be worse, Matt," Cortez met his gaze. "Without your men it could have been much worse. Words can never thank you enough."

"Not a problem," Matt said grimly. He paused, glancing down at the wounded. "Can Lt. Col. Larson and I have a few words with you, sir?"

Cortez sensed their desire for privacy. "Surely. Let's go inside, out of their way."

Stepping around the carnage, Cortez led them into the house to his office located at the far end of a very large family room. It was Matt's second time inside the Cortez home and he looked around at the familiar surroundings. Wood paneled walls and high ceiling with hand-carved open beams gave a sense of warmth and richness. Wrought iron chandeliers hung at each end of the room provided a soft yellow light. A pair of large, slow-turning ceiling fans stirred the evening air. On one wall was a giant fireplace made of rock. A large mantel above the fireplace looked like it had been hewn from an old oak tree by a bunch of boys using hatchets. The mantel was adorned with numerous photos of grandchildren, including one of

Katalina standing beside the red and cream Waco; her smile was as big as the airplane. Above the mantel hung a Winchester model 1892 .44 caliber, lever action rifle. Matt remembered Samuel Cortez saying the rifle was the first weapon he had carried into battle back in the early '60's, leading the Guatemala National Revolutionary Unity, URNG.

Samuel's office consisted of a very large, polished mahogany desk with matching credenza, several file cabinets, a high-back red leather desk chair, and a pair of matching upholstered arm chairs.

Cortez leaned against his desk, crossed his legs, and nodded for Matt and Larson to take a chair. They declined his offer, preferring to stand.

"...You both remember the layout of the waterfront?" Cortez asked.

"Vividly," Larson answered grimly before Matt had a chance.

"Okay, the warehouse you asked about is on the opposite side of the road from the one you burned to the ground— thank you very much, by the way." Cortez grinned, his eyes sparkled. He went to one of the file cabinets and pulled out a one page document, which provided a detailed layout of the Puerto Santo Tomás waterfront. "I can make more copies if you wish."

Matt nodded. "Several if you don't mind, sir."

The layout was all too familiar to Matt and Butch Larson. A single wide, paved road separated two rows of large warehouses, three on the right side, two on the left.

The warehouse closest to the waterfront on the right side no longer existed. It had burned to the ground during the frantic rescue of Carley Downs and her Secret Service protection detail, Jordan Scott. Cortez made a dramatic gesture of drawing a red "X" through the symbol for that structure, and then looked up at Matt with another grin before tapping his ink pen on a warehouse on the left side of the road, one back from the waterfront. It was surrounded at the rear and one side by rows of stacked forty-foot shipping containers.

"I lease this facility to Acuario Fruit Distributors out of Honduras; our largest competitor in the banana and coffee bean industries."

"Hassam enlisted them after his run-in with your nephew?" Matt asked.

"Yes. They showed up about four months ago. They have been very active."

"Tell us about the building itself," Larson said.

"All wood. Similar to the others in construction," Cortez responded. "A little smaller than the one where they held Carley and Jordan. Everything is at floor level, including the office. No loft. Office is located here, at the far left corner from the main doors. I understand the building was full of large containers stacked to the ceiling just days ago, but most of the containers have since been loaded on the two freighters presently dockside."

"Were dockside," Matt corrected. "The freighters pulled out a little while ago. Did they take on any cargo from your warehouses?"

"None. Everything they have taken on is from Acuario."

"Thanks, Samuel, you've been a great help."

"You are preparing to attack Hassam?"

"As swiftly as we possibly can, sir."

"This is my fight too, gentlemen. I want to send some of my men with you."

"That won't be necessary, Samuel," Matt smiled, "but thanks. Besides, the fighting here may not be finished, so you might still need all the men you have."

"We have four Watchdog units still deployed in the bush with your men, sir," Larson added. "We're leaving them here to assist you. We'll also leave our medic. You need his services to get your wounded down to the El Achiotal hospital."

"That is very kind," Samuel nodded. "One more thing, Matt."

"Sir?" Matt turned.

"Please try not to burn down another warehouse." Samuel's eyes twinkled.

Fourteen

USS *Iwo Jima*
30 Miles Off
Coast of Belize
Western Caribbean

"Captain, the freighters have cleared the harbor," Lt Cmdr Clayton Downs spoke into the ship's phone. "*Alaed* is northbound, sir, and … looks like *Jin* is steaming southeast."

"Very well, Commander," Captain Reynolds responded, "we'll take it from here. Continue your surveillance of Santo Tomás."

"Aye, aye, sir!"

The captain punched another button on the phone mounted on his chair and began to speak. "Communications, this is the Captain. I want a message sent to AMOC; advise them that the Russian freighter *Alaed* is northbound from Amatique Bay, probable destination U.S. gulf ports, suspicious cargo. Read that back to me."

The Air and Marine Operations Center, AMOC, was operated by the U.S. Customs and Border Patrol. The sprawling complex with its massive computer banks and giant 8-by-45-foot, high-definition video screen mounted across the front wall, was located at March Air Reserve Base near Riverside, California. The radar and intelligence center was capable of tracking nearly every aircraft flying over the continental United States at any given moment and providing around-the-clock maritime surveillance of all vessels operating off each U.S. coastline, including beyond the Gulf of Mexico into the Caribbean.

Initially, AMOC was tasked by the Department of Homeland Security, parent organization for Customs and Border Protection, CBP, to supply information to a host of law enforcement and intelligence agencies, particularly illegal cross-border flights and drug trafficking. In recent years, however, the center expanded its focus to human trafficking and terrorist activities.

Over time the center had earned considerable notoriety for providing early notification to appropriate maritime authorities leading to arrest and seizure of illegal contraband, both at sea and in port. In the case of illegal aircraft, AMOC had placed law enforcement personnel on location at landing sites as much as thirty-minutes prior to the aircraft's actual arrival.

New equipment installations currently taking place would enhance the center's capability even more. Within a few months AMOC personnel would be able to monitor real-time video feed of hot spots along the U.S./Mexico border via the UAV program. This would provide an extra layer of safety for law enforcement response, as well as better coordination for interdiction operations.

Within minutes of receiving message traffic from *Iwo Jima*, the AMOC duty supervisor assigned a workstation to monitor *Alaed*. Fifteen minutes after that, the 9000-ton Russian freighter's itinerary was flagged "vessel of particular interest" and 24/7 surveillance of the ship's progress began.

The freighter was scheduled for a port call at Galveston, Texas. At present course and speed, the ship would enter Galveston Bay in 72-hours. The technician assigned to *Alaed* typed a series of commands into his console, which would order a satellite over-flight within the next 24-hours and UAV over-flight 12-hours from port, following approval by the duty supervisor. Live video feed from the surveillance would provide AMOC with detailed data to share with the Coast Guard, Port Authority, and CBP agents at Galveston. With a little luck, maybe a few faces would pop up on the video screen.

Reynolds dialed up the 26th MEU operations room and spoke into the phone. "Colonel Kramer, you can launch your backup team, then please report to CIC."

Captain Reynolds then notified Carter Manning at NCTC that *Alaed* and *Jin* were under way and that AMOC had the *Alaed* under surveillance. He pushed his ball cap back and absentmindedly scratched his scalp. *Whatever cargo the Russian has onboard sure is drawing a lot of attention from the heavy hitters.*

~~~~~~~

El Achiotal
Guatemala

"Chase, you take right seat. Tell Chief Roberts he'll be flyin' us into Santo Tomás." That drew a quizzical look before Matt continued. "I want you to guide him into position and then be ready to disembark with us. You're part of the assault team."

"HALLELUJAH!" Chase shouted. He had bugged Matt incessantly to let him be part of the action and was more than a little annoyed at being left behind in the support role. Things were about to change.

"Calm down, Chase," Matt chuckled. "Before you break out in your happy dance, I might not be doing you any favors, you know!"

Truth of the matter, since Corporal Stone was to remain behind to assist with the wounded, the team was one man short for the operation.

"Oh yes you are, Cuz! You know how badly I've wanted a chance to drop-kick that clown into the middle of next week!"

"Well, he's not there, but we should be able to find someone for you to kick around," Matt grinned again. "I'll come forward after we get airborne and show y'all where we're gonna set it down."

"Roger that!" Matt could not help but notice the spring in Chase's step as he sprinted toward the cockpit.

"Man, you've made his day," Lenox laughed when Matt turned and dropped into the empty wall-mounted web seat between the CIA agent and Butch Larson.

"Shoot! Made his whole month," Larson hooted.

The massive thirty-eight foot rotors began to spool up as Master Chief Walter Roberts shoved the thrust lever forward. Seconds later the Osprey lifted off the ground in a cyclone of grass and dust and debris in a hundred-foot radius, blinding anyone within close proximity. The aircraft hovered a few feet off the ground, pivoting slowly to the right as it gained altitude. Chief Roberts rotated the nacelles to horizontal and the black Osprey shot eastward for the twenty-one minute flight to Santo Tomás. The slow-turning rotors made it strangely quiet inside the fuselage, but outside everyone ducked their head and covered their ears against the vibrating roar of the departing aircraft.

Matt spread the map of the Santo Tomás waterfront across his knees and fished a penlight from his Kevlar vest—the muted red cabin lights were much too dim for reading. Lenox and Larson leaned close to have another look. "Best I can remember there should be plenty of room to set the Osprey down in the street between the parking lot and that first row of shipping containers."

"Yeah, plenty of room, Matt," Larson agreed. He studied the map a moment longer and then added, "We could drop an Overwatch here on this roof before we land. Fast-rope him in with a spotter."

Matt glanced at the site Larson was tapping, looked the big man in the eyes, and nodded. The rooftop location brought back a flood of unpleasant memories for both men. It was the exact spot where Larson had been critically wounded while covering the rescue attempt for Carley and Jordan. Matt had saved his life that day single-handedly, carrying the 240-pound Marine across the roof and down an exterior ladder in a remarkable superhuman display of raw determination and intestinal fortitude.

"Yep, perfect place," Matt agreed, and then turned to Lenox. The rotund CIA agent looked like the Pillsbury Dough Boy in blue, trussed up so tightly in his body armor that the veins in his neck bulged and his breathing was labored gasps.

"Lenox, how are we looking on interference this time? Did someone talk to the Guatemalan president about keeping his people out of our way?"

"Taken care of," Lenox nodded. "President Downs called Maggie nearly an hour ago. It's all set. The Guatemalans will stand down."

"Maggie?" Matt arched his eyebrow and smiled.

"Ambassador Margaret Stewart!"

Matt turned to Larson, grinned, and nodded at Lenox. "He calls her Maggie."

"Must be a *special* privilege for the Chief of Station," Larson commented with a chuckle.

"Yeah, you got something going on that you care to share with us, Lenox?"

"That will be enough, you two!" Lenox glared, his face turned scarlet. "Not that it's any of your business; Ambassador Stewart requires informalities with *all* senior staff."

"Well, let's hope their military listens this time … Cops too, for that matter." Matt recalled how the Guatemalan army, law enforcement—even the fire department—came rushing into the firefight during the rescue operation. It was pure chaos! Matt didn't need to remind Lenox and Larson that it was a miracle there were no friendly fire incidents. They wouldn't be that lucky in the darkness if Guatemalan authorities showed up tonight.

"Okay." Matt turned back to Butch Larson and pointed to the map, "Depending on what the real-time video shows, let's put a man at each of these three corners, with two on the roof here, that gives us …" he paused. The man on Larson's left leaned close, quietly listening to their planning session. Matt had not met this one, but he noticed the strange looking fellow as he climbed into the airplane. He was a thickset man, maybe a couple inches shorter than Matt, though it was difficult to tell because of his enormous hunched shoulders.

Larson followed Matt's stare, then said, "Matt, this is Creep."

"Creep?" Matt asked curiously, his eyes darting from Larson, then back to the other man. In the faint red glow of the cabin interior, he was an intimidating looking fellow. Encountered in the dark, he would scare the heck out of you.

"Sergeant Stan Woodley, call sign Creep." Larson grinned proudly and then added, "When the smelly stuff hits the oscillating rotor, Creep is a good man to have around."

Even dressed in cammies and tactical vest, Matt could tell the man was incredibly muscular. His large flat nose, square jaw, and high sloping forehead were framed by thinning brown hair. His deep-set brown eyes seemed a little too close together. Crooked teeth gave away an almost boyish smile when he offered a huge hand to Matt. His face was covered with three shades of green camouflage combat paint, as did the Marines sitting directly across from Matt.

"Sergeant!" Matt said.

"Call me Creep, sir," the man growled, but the smile remained.

Matt glanced at Larson with a questioning look.

Larson read his mind. "It's not disrespectful, Matt. Creep could sneak up on a sleeping jungle cat and slit its throat before it ever knew he was there. Like I said, a good man to have around when things go bad."

Matt nodded "… as I was saying, that gives us four men for the entry team."

"You think four's enough?"

"It'll have to be. Besides, gotta cover our perimeter."

"We can bring in the secondary Recon team coming up from *Iwo*," Larson reminded.

"Let's wait to see what Reaper has to say about enemy strength."

"Roger that! … Answer something else for me if you can," Larson said, lowering his voice.

"Okay, sure."

"What's going on back in the states?"

"What do you mean?" Matt questioned.

"Okay, we know what the ragheads are doing here, and we got pretty good proof Iran is behind the whole crappy business. What's Washington gonna do about it?"

"Don't have a clue, Butch. I talked to President Downs before coming out here and I can tell you his patience has run out. I think he's fixin' to do some serious ass kickin'."

"Okay. That's good to hear. From the intel I've been seeing for the past couple months it's obvious that Russia's hip deep sponsoring this thing. Maybe North Korea too.

That tells me the Alliance between those three countries that you told me about six months ago is for real."

"Good assessment," Matt nodded. In the corner of his eye he saw Lenox nod as well. Of course the CIA agent, aka Chief of Station, Guatemala City, would have direct access to such intel. Probably a lot more than he could share. "All the posturing and saber rattling all three countries have been doing for the past few years are most likely diversionary tactics to keep us off balance while Ahmad Hassam prepares to unleash unspeakable horrors on our homeland."

"Which begs the question," Larson's eyes grew dark, "when we get through stomping Hassam's butt, what are we gonna do about the Alliance—"

"Quarterback, Reaper One! Suspect vehicle is at the airport. I put a laser designator on it so you can follow it from my video feed. Sending it to you now."

"Copy that, Reaper!" Matt unfastened his seat harness and made his way forward to the cockpit. "Reaper, gimme a gomer count at the waterfront, including those inside the warehouse."

"Roger that, Quarterback! Designate which warehouse!"

Matt squatted down between the pilot and copilot seats, putting his hand on Chase's shoulder. The fourteen-inch multi-function display located in the lower center of the aircraft control panel was presently connected to the Joint Tactical Information Distribution System. The JTIDS provided tactical data within the area of operations from a number of sources. In this particular case, a grainy real-time video of the Santo Tomás waterfront relayed through Reaper from ScanEagle II was suddenly replaced with a much sharper image of the Puerto Barrios Airport. There was a twin-engine commuter plane on the ramp close to the terminal and several cars in the parking lot.

Matt's eyes went to a dark colored vehicle with a red spot on its roof, the laser target designator that Reaper had electronically painted. Now anyone watching the Tactical Data Display could easily locate the vehicle and follow its movement. The laser designator could also provide a precise, constant path for a Hellfire missile, if Reaper was directed to launch one.

Matt watched the video feed move away from the airport, heading northwest over the city and out over the bay toward Santo Tomás. Within minutes lights on the waterfront appeared. As Reaper approached the docks, software in the UAV's synthetic aperture radar sensor filtered the artificial lighting and the faint images of men began to appear.

"Reaper One, Quarterback! Your target will be that second warehouse, north side of the road."

"Copy, Quarterback, I got it!"

Fifteen

Airport
Puerto Barrios

Not by accident, Ahmad Hassam and Hakeem Larijani
arrived at the Puerto Barrios airport the same moment a
twin-engine commuter started boarding passengers for the
seventy-eight minute flight to Guatemala City; nor was it
coincidental that a Mexicana Airline's Boeing 737 was
scheduled to depart Guatemala City for Caracas,
Venezuela, within minutes of the commuter's arrival.

Ahmad Hassam had no intention of being on either of
those flights. Because it was also no accident that a local
charter pilot had just finished preflighting a small Piper
Cherokee parked in front of a rust-covered maintenance
hangar directly across the ramp from the terminal.

The single-engine aircraft belonged to the airport
manager and was frequently used for scenic flights
offering tourists a spectacular view of the Caribbean
coastline and picturesque harbor. Night flights were
especially popular because of the extraordinary multi-

colored light display. Tonight's flight, however, would not be a scenic excursion.

An airport service vehicle picked up Hassam and Larijani in the parking lot and skirted around the terminal building and remained in dark shadows as the driver wheeled the two men out to the waiting Piper.

Hassam looked at his trusted friend and ally. It would be several days before he would see Larijani again. Both men would travel many miles and face much danger until then. He pursed his lips and spoke in a grim tone, "You are sure Rashad is ready?"

"Yes, Ahmad. He is ready and awaiting your command—"

"Or yours," Hassam interrupted. Both men knew exactly what he meant by that.

"Allah be praised for he is merciful. He will guide you swiftly and safely to our command post in plenty of time."

"Yes, he will! But just in case ..." Hassam's voice trailed off.

"I understand *as-Syf*!"

~~~~~~~

USS *Iwo Jima*
30 Miles Off Coast of Belize
Western Caribbean

"Copy, Quarterback, I got it!" Clayton said softly, as he engaged the autopilot to fly a programmed surveillance orbit fifteen thousand feet above the waterfront. Louis Rogers had the real-time infrared feed on the large screen above the consoles and was tweaking the zoom and focus to provide a perfect layout for the assault team.

"Todd, take the ScanEagle over the airport. I want continuous surveillance on the target vehicle and the commuter aircraft." Clayton turned to Rogers. "Louis, gimme a corner for the ScanEagle."

"You got it!" Louis Rogers hit two keys on the console and the video sensor from ScanEagle II instantly appeared in the bottom right corner of the large screen. The small square showed the calm black waters of the bay, and then the coastal lights of Puerto Barrios approaching as the small UAV crossed the harbor. The large screen was dominated by a clear image of the docks and warehouses. Rogers filtered the bright lights along the waterfront so that images of the sentries were readily recognizable.

"Okay, good! Now crank up the IR and zoom in on that warehouse." In a few seconds the infrared sensor penetrated into the Acuario warehouse, revealing thermal images of four men clustered near the main door.

"Quarterback, Reaper One! ETA?"

"Quarterback is zero eight!"

"Copy, eight minutes. I'm streaming video feed on the waterfront." Clayton leaned back in the padded crew chair, locking his hands behind his head. The aircraft remained on autopilot and would stay in a tight surveillance orbit until commanded to change.

"We have it! Counting four tangos inside the warehouse ... ten more scattered outside?"

"Roger that, Quarterback. We show ... Standby—" Clayton went off the air for a moment and then came back. "Quarterback, be advised the commuter aircraft is taxiing to depart Puerto Barrios."

~~~~~~~

500 Feet AGL
30 Miles West of
Puerto Santo Tomás

The black Osprey slipped smoothly through the night air. With the terrain following radar set at five hundred feet the aircraft sharply rose and fell as the Sierra De Santa Cruz Mountains undulated through peaks and valleys.

Matt squatted on one knee between the crew seats in the wide cockpit, the red and amber glow from the panel lights cast an eerie reflection on his face. He and Chase studied the real-time feed provided by Reaper. Master Chief Roberts was hands-free on the controls, listening to the chatter between the cousins while automated systems guided the big tilt-rotor on a straight course toward Santo Tomás.

"Reaper can you track the aircraft?" Matt said.

"No problem! For a short distance, anyway." Matt and Chase knew that distance would greatly increase if the commuter engaged his transponder, but that wasn't always a mandatory protocol as it was in the United States. Not in these parts where surface radar was all but non-existent.

A quick computer search of the air traffic schedule for Central America verified this particular flight to be a Saab 340B regional commuter aircraft that ran from Flores to Puerto Barrios to Guatemala City. According to the schedule it was thirty minutes late on departure, but maybe commercial air travel was not as precise here as it is in the U.S.

"Thanks, Reaper! We are zero six point two. On the deck, crossing the bay north to south."

"Quarterback, Ops Center!"

"Go, Ops Center!" Matt's voice was soft in the steady hum of the aircraft.

"We are monitoring the situation on the JTIDS. Your mission has changed, Matt. Your target is now Larijani. Repeat, you are now going for the secondary target. Do you copy?"

"I copy!" Matt answered sourly as he met Chase's eyes. Disappointment over Hassam's escape was an understatement, but Matt figured Carter Manning must have a backup plan to deal with the master terrorist. He had slipped through their hands too many times to not have a contingency. Matt's disappointment was personal.

He would not be the one to capture Hassam. He badly wanted ... no, he *needed* to personally make up for his failure to grab the terrorist in this very place several months before.

It came as no surprise that Larijani became their new primary target. They could capture the number two man and shake detailed information out of him, one way or another. Truth be told, Larijani knew more details on *Firestorm* than did Hassam.

"I get dibs on knocking that scrawny runt whopper-jawed," Chase said with a determined voice.

"That's a deal!" Matt grinned, bumping fists with Chase as he reluctantly recovered from his disappointment. He quickly mapped out the approach he wanted Chase and Master Chief Roberts to fly when they approach the dock area, and then showed Chase where his assignment would be on the perimeter.

"You haul butt out of this airplane as soon as the wheels hit the ground."

"You got it, Cuz!" Chase beamed. He really wanted to be on the entry team, but knew better than to complain. *At least I'm gonna be on the ground with a rifle ... and hopefully a target.*

~~~~~~~~

National Counterterrorism Center
Liberty Crossing
McLean, Virginia

Carter Manning and DNI Alex Strayhorn stared at the large screen down on the main floor of the ops center. The real-time feed from Reaper showed the twin-engine commuter airliner climbing into the night sky, gently turning on a course to Guatemala City.

Manning glanced at his computer on the conference table.

"TACA Airlines flight 713 to Caracas departs Guatemala City within fifteen minutes after the commuter lands," Manning read the screen. "He's heading back to his Venezuela headquarters."

"Yup, looks that way," Strayhorn studied the large screen deep in thought. This was a twist, but not totally unexpected. With luck it suggested that the imminent attack was further away than suspected.

"Is Admiral Turner in the Situation Room?" Manning asked.

Strayhorn checked his watch. "Should be."

Both men returned to their chairs while the DNI placed a call. In less than a minute they were on a secure video link with the Situation Room in the White House.

~~~~~~~~

Situation Room
White House
Washington, DC

Gathered around the conference table with President of the United States was White House Chief of Staff, James Ritchey; Secretary of State, Zachary Ringhold; and Chairman of the Joint Chiefs, Admiral Justin Blair, JB, Turner. The admiral came straight over from a formal dinner meeting and was wearing dress blues, adorned with four stars on the epaulets and a chest full of medals beneath gold naval aviator wings.

DNI Strayhorn was a key player on the Situation Room team and would be moving to the White House at the conclusion of the video conference.

"Alex. Carter." President Downs began. "We are watching real-time from Reaper. Appears our primary target is getting away, again."

"Yes, Mr. President." Strayhorn stared into his computer screen. He sensed the president's frustration and took it personally. "But not for long, sir."

"With this latest turn of events, I assume you gentlemen are requesting authorization to launch *Operation Night Stalker*?" The president wore a grim expression.

"That is affirmative, Mr. President."

"We were talking about that possibility before your call; or I should say we've been arguing about it."

There was no mistaking the sour, perplexed look on SecState's face.

Ringhold had voiced his opposition on *Night Stalker* from day one and would not give up the argument. *Too risky*! He argued vehemently. *Creates an act of war!*

"Proposed timing?" President Downs asked. The DNI checked his watch and then glanced at Carter Manning who was busy punching keys on his computer.

"*Make it four a.m. local,*" the president heard Manning whisper to Strayhorn.

"Did you hear that, Mr. President?" Strayhorn turned back to the screen.

President Downs turned to Admiral JB Turner and raised his eyebrows in question.

The Admiral set intense hazel eyes on the screen and said, "Understand oh-four hundred local." He then turned to President Downs and nodded.

The president stared into each face seated at the table, put steepled fingers to his chin, closed his eyes, and paused for a full minute. It was a weighty decision.

President Downs opened his eyes, nodded to Admiral Turner, and swiveled his chair to face Strayhorn and Manning in the screen. He drew a deep breath and let it our slowly.

"I want this scum! I want him tonight. You have a go for *Operation Night Stalker*."

Sixteen

Puerto Santo Tomás
Guatemala

Amatique Bay stretched several miles north from the docks at Puerto Santo Tomás before splashing against white sandy beaches. Matt wasn't kidding when he said they would be coming in on the deck. The solid black Osprey approached the northwest corner of the bay, screaming across the water so low that it kicked up a spray, bumping the redline at nearly 275 knots. The huge proprotors were cranking 335 RPM, taking giant bites out of the night air. Even so, inside the aircraft it was quiet enough to talk without yelling.

Matt returned to his jump seat in back of the aircraft to prepare for their arrival at the LZ. He knew that before the wheels even touched down there would be so much frantic activity there would be no time to think. He sat quietly, searching each face along the two rows of seats. There was no tension, all eyes were locked straight ahead, each man focused on his own brand of mental preparedness.

Matt cradled the M4A1 rifle in his arms, extracted the 30-round box magazine to make sure it was fully loaded—nervous habit, really, but it busied his hands in the final minutes before combat—slammed the mag back in, and chambered a 5.56 millimeter round. He selected a three-round burst and set the safety.

He caught Larson staring back at him and gave the big Marine a grim smile and a slight nod. He noticed that the Recon team had given Lenox a rifle. "You know how to fire that thing?"

Lenox rolled his eyes and grunted. "Up yours, Cowboy!"

"Just don't let any gomers close to my Osprey or the CIA buys a new one." Matt could tell that the chubby CIA agent was getting fidgety.

"Yeah, right!"

"So, you think Larijani is still here?" Butch Larson asked.

Matt shrugged. "Yeah! Not likely he left with Hassam. They don't normally travel together."

At that moment the loading ramp came down, engine noise roared, and the wind howled inside the aircraft. The fuselage began to shake. Matt felt the aircraft pitch up sharply as Master Chief Roberts dialed the knurled wheel on the thrust lever aft to rotate the engine nacelles 78 degrees vertical. They slipped in over the docks from the north and approached the warehouse rooftop where they would drop EZ and Corporal Cody "Tex" Allen, the Marine with a camo painted face sitting directly across from Matt. He and Stan "Creep" Woodley had been with the Watchdog units on perimeter patrol at the Cortez compound before Larson called them in for this mission. Tex would spot for EZ, as well as cover the sniper's six to make sure a tango didn't sneak up from behind.

The Osprey pivoted sharply to the left 180 degrees, less than 15 feet above the roof top, their forward speed slowed as EZ and Tex walked out on the ramp. The two-man overwatch team would fast-rope simultaneously and land on the rooftop while the aircraft was still in motion.

The approach was smooth and coordinated. It brought a smile to Matt's lips. He knew Chase had snatched the controls away from the Master Chief for this well rehearsed, intricate maneuver. He envisioned Chief Roberts now, glowering across the cockpit at Chase in disbelief. There was no way Chase would let a "glorified grease monkey" have the controls at this pivotal moment in the operation.

The two Recon Marines disappeared into the night air just as the Osprey lowered its nose. The aircraft gained speed as it eased passed the roof parapet and then pivoted left another 90 degrees. Chase chopped the power when the Osprey cleared the building and centered over the street.

It was a matter of perfect timing: slamming the big tilt-rotor into position with the open ramp facing aft toward the waterfront, and off-loading the assault team as expediently and aggressively as possible. There was nothing covert about it. It was a down-and-dirty-in-your-face-get-out-of-the-way-before-you-die maneuver, and the two cousins practiced it dozens of times until it was like a choreographed intricate dance.

~~~~~~~

EZ had the AR-10B sniper rifle strapped to his chest; an M9 Berretta was in his right hand, safety off, while his other hand held tightly to the rappelling rope. He had the rope wound two turns around his left leg to act as a brake while he controlled his rapid descent with the powerful grip of his hand. He pivoted slowly in the downwash of the proprotors. He was less than four feet from the rooftop when he saw a dark shadow rushing toward him. The Recon sniper twisted around to find Tex still several feet above and to his right. He turned back to see the dark shape now directly in front him, lifting an AK-47 assault rifle to his shoulder. The team had suspected the terrorists would put sentries on every rooftop, and EZ was ready.

The terrorist aimed the rifle, his finger closed on the trigger … and EZ shot him in the face just as his boots hit the tar papered roof. The terrorist lay spread-eagle on his back while EZ disentangled himself from the rappelling rope.

"One tango down! Watchdog Niner moving into position!"

Tex hit the rooftop a second later and stood frozen with a wild-eyed stare. He glanced at his partner, who still held the Berretta in his hand, and then at the terrorist with a wrecked face and blood pooling around his head.

"Holy crap!"

EZ shrugged, turned, and ran in a low crouch across the rooftop toward the edge of the building with the pounding of Tex's boots not far behind. He slid to a stop behind the parapet like a runner sliding into second base and peered over the edge into the street. He immediately laid his sniper rifle across the top of the three-foot parapet and began sighting in on the large pole-mounted sodium-vapor lamps that bathed the entire dock in dim yellow light. Out of the corner of his eye he saw the Osprey plunk down on the street below as he took aim and fired, round after round … aim, fire … aim, fire … until all lighting had been destroyed without a single miss and darkness bathed the waterfront.

~~~~~~~~

Staff Sergeant Eddie Mullins was closest to the ramp and first to unbuckle his harness when the Osprey bounced unceremoniously onto the asphalt. Mullins slipped his night vision goggles in place, jumped onto the opened ramp, and grabbed the M240 machine gun mounted in the opening. The sergeant traversed the barrel of the big weapon left and right searching for targets as his comrades piled out of the aircraft.

The quiet operation of the Osprey permitted them to traverse the bay virtually undetected. The aircraft popped up and crossed the dock complex so quickly and unexpectedly that it caught the terrorists off guard. Even after they heard it and saw it pirouetting above the warehouse, they were confused and slow to recognize the threat. But by the time the Osprey landed in the center of the maritime complex and security lighting began exploding under precision gunfire, the terrorists were on full alert and moving into action.

Just one or two muzzle flashes winked in the darkness at first, then multiple locations on both sides of the street lit up the night and rounds pinged off the fuselage of the big Osprey. Mullins pointed the machine gun and stroked the trigger sending a dozen 7.62 millimeter rounds chasing after the first muzzle flash. Every fourth round was a tracer so he could see his stream of fire pouring into dark shadows between two warehouses. The enemy fire was silenced and Mullins trained his gun on another muzzle flash.

The assault team poured out of the Osprey on a dead run, stepping past Mullins on either side, fanning out in a wide arch outside of the machine gun fire. They sprinted for cover toward the warehouses and steel storage containers while Mullins continued sending measured bursts of fire into the darkness.

Tracers laced the night air, gunfire echoed off buildings and huge steel boxes, and the cacophony of two Rolls-Royce turbine engines spooling down turned the peaceful night into surreal chaos.

Matt heard voices chattering on the comm-set as he sprinted low across the open area between the Osprey and the first row of shipping containers on his left. He raised his rifle and pointed it in the general direction of enemy muzzle flashes and squeezed off several three-round bursts. He took cover behind one of the large steel containers, squatted on his knees, and sucked in large gulps of air while scanning the darkness to check on the progress of his team.

Each man had an assigned position on the perimeter of the tactical area. They charged ahead, leapfrogging down their respective side of the street to reach their post.

With the security lighting gone, night vision goggles gave Matt's team full advantage over the terrorists.

Matt glanced across the street from his position and stifled a chuckle when he saw Chase. The long, skinny form of his cousin bent low, knees stepping absurdly high as if he were running high hurdles at a McAllen Bulldogs track meet. In the dark he looked like Ichabod Crane running from the headless horseman. The image caused Matt to chuckle again. Chase held his rifle in both hands, chest high, eyes focused straight ahead, intent upon reaching his assigned position as though it were a matter of life or death.

Matt turned his attention back to the front. Larson was crouched behind the next row of shipping containers, rifle up to his shoulder, popping off rounds down the street. Matt was scanning the direction Larson was shooting when Creep came sliding in beside him, eyes alert, head on a swivel. Only his bright teeth shown through the heavy coat of camouflage paint. Gunny Stevens charged low, settling behind Creep so that he had a good view of the other end of the shipping container in case the gomers tried to flank them.

They were bunched too closely; time to leapfrog down the street toward the target warehouse. The tactic was speed and overwhelming fire. So far, so good.

Creep read Matt's thoughts. "Go for it, sir!"

~~~~~~~

When the final security light exploded under EZ's deadly aim, the Marine sniper switched his night vision scope on and swung the rifle to the closest building, and waited for Tex to spot a target. He didn't have long to wait.

"Ten o'clock, rooftop, forty-two yards!" Tex called while staring through the lens of a laser range finder.

"Got him," EZ responded, zeroing in on the human shape crouched behind the parapet on the warehouse across and slightly down the street. The cross-hairs lined up on the bright green form. A muzzle flash from the terrorist's rifle created a brilliant light in the night scope, but EZ kept his focus..

Boom! EZ's rifle bucked and a .308 Winchester round punched the terrorist in the face, exploding the back of his head. The Recon sniper would have aimed center mass given the chance, but only the tango's head and shoulders were visible above the parapet. The idea was to take the enemy out of the fight in the quickest way possible, not necessarily kill them, but if every single terrorist died here tonight it would not cause EZ to lose any sleep.

"Twelve o'clock, rooftop, eighty-seven yards!"

"See him!" *Boom!* The terrorist made it too easy when he stood up to take aim on Chase McWain running full speed along the buildings on the south side of the street. The single round drilled the terrorist smack-dab in the center of his chest and EZ had already swung his rifle toward another target.

The two-man overwatch team would clear all high targets first, nearest to farthest.

Then they would go after the low targets in reverse order, farthest to closest. That was when it got a little trickier. They would need to slow each shot to verify the target was hostile and not a team member moving into position. Even with night vision goggles and night scopes it wasn't always easy to tell.

"Eleven o'clock, roof top, two hundred ..."

~~~~~~~

The charred remains of the old United Fruit Company warehouse and terrorist headquarters had been cleared away. Stacks of construction materials lay on a fresh concrete slab in preparation for the new warehouse. A stream of muzzle flashes came from behind one of the stacks of lumber. Sergeant Mullins tugged on the trigger of the M240 machine gun, sending a hundred rounds into the stack of lumber, reducing it to a pile of splinters.

Mullins paused and searched the darkness for movement, and then felt a forceful tap on his shoulder. He turned to look into the scowling face of Master Chief Walter Roberts.

"Outta the way, Jarhead! That's my gun," Roberts jerked his thumb.

"With pleasure, Squid," Mullins shrugged. He snatched up his M4A1 rifle and took off toward his assigned post, joining Watchdog 5, Corporal George "Vinnie" Vincent, to cover the waterfront while the entry team hit the target building.

Phil Lenox appeared beside Roberts just as the grizzled old Master Chief settled in behind the machine gun. Lenox glanced cautiously left and right, his face clouded with apprehension.

"Get around to the front of the aircraft," Roberts shouted over the din of battle. "Cover us from there."

Lenox nodded silently and then jumped from the ramp onto the ground. With his rifle in both hands he scooted around to the front, grateful to have the big Osprey between him and the battle raging behind him. He lowered the NVG's to his eyes and scanned the darkness.

Seventeen

Puerto Santo Tomás
Guatemala

"*Chase in position!*" Matt listened as the team members reported in.

"*Watchdog Five!*"

"*Niner and Seven good to go!*" EZ answered for Tex as well as for himself.

"*Watchdog Six ready!*"

Sgt. Mullins was the last to report and with that, Matt leaped from his position, bolted past Larson on a dead run, raced another twenty yards, and dove into the shadows between the final two rows of containers. Gunny Stevens, following on Matt's heels, jumped in beside Larson. Creep stayed behind to cover their advance. He would move into Larson's position as soon as the Lt. Colonel leapfrogged past Matt.

Matt pulled his NVG's down to his chin, wiped his forehead with his sleeve, then shoved the goggles back in place. He peered around the container to glance across at Chase … and got the scare of his life. Chase aimed his rifle directly at him. *He doesn't know who I am!* Matt started to scream into the comm-set, but before he could utter a sound he saw the muzzle flash. In that same instant he heard a scream and the clatter of a gun falling to the concrete surface.

Matt wheeled around to see a terrorist not ten feet from him, holding his chest as he fell forward on his face. Stunned, his heart pounding, Matt turned back and saw Chase with his cheesy thumbs-up signal. This was not the first time Chase had saved his life and probably not the last.

"Thanks, Cuz," he whispered into the comm-set. Chase flashed another thumbs-up. Matt looked back toward the others. "Ready when you are, Butch!"

The tempo of the battle had slowed to the point you could now pick out the distinctive popping of the M4's, EZ's sniper rifle, and Vinnie's M27 Infantry Automatic Rifle. The machine gun on the Osprey was silent while Master Chief Roberts searched for more targets. An occasional three-round burst from a terrorist's AK-47 was quickly answered by a barrage of return fire.

"*Moving up!*" Larson responded. He slipped from behind his storage container and ran full speed. The M4 looked like a little toy rifle in the big Marine's massive paws. Larson skidded in beside Matt while Gunny Stevens, right on Larson's heels, charged past them, and disappeared into the alley between the target warehouse and the final row of shipping containers.

The chatter of an AK on full auto was joined by a three-round burst from an M4 … followed by eerie silence.

"Gunny?" Matt said with a worried voice. He exchanged a troubled glance with Butch Larson. "Gunny!"

What seemed like interminable silence was followed by, "*Watchdog Two good! One tango down!*"

"Copy that, Watchdog Two ... Don't scare us like that!"

"Quarterback, Marine Zero-One-Two! On station at three miles!" The backup Osprey from *Iwo* had arrived with twelve shooters and two medics onboard.

"Copy, Marine Zero-One-Two!" Matt answered. "Gimme five minutes, then I want you to set her down on the waterfront between the rows of warehouses."

"Roger that!"

The lull in combat told Matt they probably would not need reinforcements, but he welcomed their arrival. If nothing else they could help clean up the area so it would not look like a war zone in the daylight when the longshoremen reported for work.

Matt waited for Creep to join up before he jumped to his feet and dashed to their final position at the corner of the target warehouse. From here the four men would form a stack, basically a single file line, in preparation to make entry into the warehouse. Matt stood with his back tight against the corner of the building, venturing a quick glance around the corner into the street in both directions. Gunny Stevens came out of the shadows to stand beside him. The two men nodded silently, their faces masked in grim determination.

"Everyone on your toes," Matt whispered into the comm-set, then motioned to Larson and Creep. He waited until the two men joined up before making his next call.

"Reaper One, Quarterback! IR status?"

Clayton responded immediately with a detailed rundown of the infrared picture provided by Reaper One. The four combatants inside the warehouse had scattered to separate locations—undoubtedly setting up an ambush. He continued with a descriptive picture of the interior layout: rows of stacked containers, aisles, and other obstructions. Each member of the entry team now had a clear vision of what to expect. Matt closed his eyes and visualized nearly the same layout as in the warehouse where he first encountered Ahmad Hassam.

"Quarterback, you have three tangos coming around the rear of the warehouse, moving behind the shipping containers. Looks like a flank attack on your position."

"Okay, roger that! Thanks … Watchdog Niner, do you have eyes on the exterior tangos?"

"Negative! Looking!" EZ answered. He shifted his position on the roof to get a clear view of the alleys between the stacked rows of containers and directed Tex to keep eyes on the street.

"All Watchdog units," Matt called, "entry team is on the move!"

The four men moved quickly to the front of the warehouse with Gunny Stevens in the lead. The building was 200 feet wide and 100 feet deep. Large sliding cargo doors, made of heavy wood construction, covered much of the front. A personnel door was cut into the cargo doors about midway. This was their point of entry.

Reaper One had told them the entry door was obstructed with large crates. The team agreed that the door was most likely booby-trapped as well. Taking no chances, Gunny Stevens quickly placed a quarter-sized block of C-4 on each of the three door hinges and he chained the explosives together with Detcord. The highly explosive detonation cord provided simultaneous ignition of the C-4.

In less than fifteen seconds Gunny had the charges in place and threaded an electrical detonator into the end of the Detcord. The men moved back several yards and pressed their backs tightly against the building. Gunny flipped the switch to energize the detonator.

BOOM! The concussion rattled the cargo doors, followed instantly by a secondary explosion of even greater magnitude. *KABOOM!* The entire warehouse shuttered, dust and debris filled the air, and hundreds of tiny bright flashes went screaming into the night.

"*YEOW! SON OF A—*" Matt heard Chase scream through the comm-set. He immediately jerked his head toward the corner of the warehouse directly across the street from them. He could see Chase holding his arm and dancing around as if he had been stung by a Texas-size hornet. He did not notice several hundred holes that had peppered the front of the wooden structure.

"You okay Chase?" Matt asked. Fear gripped him like a vice. It took all the discipline he could muster not to go charging across the street to his cousin.

"*Yeah, peachy! ... What the heck did you guys blow up?*"

"Not us, Cuz! Booby-trap!"

The terrorist had rigged an improvised Claymore mine, using nails and screws and other bits of metal packed in front of two pounds of Semtex explosive. Gunny's door buster triggered the booby-trap. Smoke still poured from a hole large enough you could drive a truck through.

"Let's do this!" Matt yelled and the team bolted through the gaping hole. Matt was third in the stack with Gunny Stevens leading the charge, Larson second and Creep at the rear, covering their six as they dashed into the darkness.

They went in low, two going left, the other two right. The smoke covered their entrance into the dark, cavernous building. Even so, automatic weapons opened fire immediately and Matt could hear bullets zinging past his head and smacking into the door and walls behind him. Gunshots echoed throughout the building, causing Matt's ears to ring. It seemed to him there were a lot more than four tangos hiding in the dark. Rooting them out might be a bigger chore than he had hoped.

Matt was pinned down behind the wooden crates, splinters danced all around as the fusillade of bullets continued. It appeared he was the focus of their concentrated fire. Perhaps the only one they could pinpoint at the moment. His eyes were stinging and he again took a moment to remove his NVG's to wipe the sweat away. He rolled over on his back and looked up at the arched, open-beam ceiling expecting to see a tango hiding in the joists.

Man, this is like déjà vu, he thought. Same scenario as the gun battle with Hassam and his thugs six months before. *Well, we kicked 'em then, we'll kick 'em now!* With that, he got on his knees and began crawling to a stack of large crates to his right. Safely concealed for the moment, he glanced back to see Creep close behind, moving more gracefully and much stealthier. Now Matt knew what Larson meant about the odd looking man's exceptional abilities.

"Creep," Matt whispered. He pointed toward the aisle a few yards in front of them. The sergeant nodded his understanding, rose up, pointed his weapon in the general direction of one of the enemy shooters, and ripped off a full magazine as Matt bolted toward the dark pathway.

The building echoed with the pounding of automatic weapons as Matt made his move. In midstride, he glanced across the large room. His eyes went wide in horror when he saw Gunny Stevens go down face first.

Eighteen

Puerto Santo Tomás
Guatemala

Hakeem Larijani cautiously pulled off the main road, switched off his headlights, and rolled a short distance down the gravel road leading to the quay. He saw muzzle flashes and heard the clatter of small arms fire blocks away from the dockyard. As he pulled farther down the road, he could see the dark, sinister Osprey sitting in the street between the main gate and warehouses.

He sat quietly in the dark, listening. It sounded like his maritime headquarters had become a war zone. Just then, there was a muffled explosion immediately followed by a much louder blast.

He listened for a few more minutes while the battle raged, then shook his head in anger. He wondered if this was a bad omen. Another setback, to be sure. They lost their headquarters operation and tons of supplies six months before, and now this, another attack, another costly interruption. More warriors lost, more supplies—although the supplies remaining here now were replacement stock, items which could easily be brought up from the Venezuelan training camp—and the money. The money was a big loss, though not catastrophic. That, too, was merely reserve. Besides, there was plenty more at the training camp.

But his computer. *That* was a tragic loss. He knew he should not have left it behind when he had taken Hassam and Ali to the airport, but there should have been plenty of time to close down the operation before the American infidels attacked. Plenty of time to grab his personal effects and laptop, the money, and still catch up to the *Alaed*.

Larijani touched his shirt pocket and smiled. At least he had taken the thumb drive from the laptop. It contained all of the operational details for *Mylh-A'sifh*. That was all he really needed. Besides, Rashad could build and program another computer for him in a matter of hours.

Sure, a great deal of sensitive data remained in the laptop's hard drive, but it would take the American's days to decrypt the information, *if* the computer still existed. He smiled to himself. Arif Alikhan would have already destroyed the laptop along with everything in the office. Those were his orders in the unlikely event of an infidel attack. The explosion he just heard had to have been his office going up in a blaze of smoke and debris.

It was obvious now. The United States knew about *Mylh-A'sifh*, *Operation Firestorm*. How much they knew was still questionable. But now, even that did not matter, Larijani smiled again. The operation was on automatic. Final approval had been authorized and delivered. Confirmation had been received from Rashad, who was already in place at their forward headquarters in the United States.

The sequence of events was programmed to initiate on specific times and dates and holy warriors of Allah would unquestioningly carry out every assignment. Hassam— or in his absence, Hakeem Larijani—was the only one who could stop the completion of the operation.

Yes, the infidel attack was a bump in the road, but that was all it was. Even so, Larijani banged his fist on the steering wheel. He could feel anger welling up inside and vowed that the first thing he would do when he got to the United States would be to gather all the intel available concerning the American infidel leading this attack, just as Hassam demanded.

Larijani put the vehicle in gear and eased away from the dockyard.

~~~~~~~

"How bad is he hit?" Matt asked from across the warehouse. He uttered a quick prayer as he watched Lt. Col. Larson reach down with one arm, snatch a hand full of Gunny's tactical vest, and drag him to cover without breaking stride. One of the tangos, watching the rescue unfold stood to take a shot at Larson. Creep was waiting for the man to show himself and quickly fired a three-round burst. Two rounds caught the tango in the chest; the third splattered his head all over the stack of crates where he had crouched.

"Ain't hit, fly-boy," Gunny answered for himself. "Tripped over some raghead's feet." Matt felt a wave of relief, as if a huge burden had been lifted away at the sound of Gunny's voice. He saw the tango Creep had killed. Only two terrorists remained.

"Quarterback, tango on your right, running toward the office. Linebacker, you have a tango moving toward you on your left."

"Copy that, Reaper One, thanks!" Matt strapped the assault rifle across his chest, pulled his Berretta, and slipped the safety off. He heard the thumping of Marine Zero-One-Two coming in over the waterfront.

"Butch, you and Gunny take the guy on the left. I'm going for the office." With that, Matt bolted from his cover, his pistol out in front as he charged down the aisle between two stacks of shipping crates. He assumed the tango running for the office would be Larijani and he wanted the second-in-command for himself.

Creep moved forward cautiously, continuing to cover Matt's six.

Matt saw a shadow dart past on an intersecting aisle a few feet ahead. He paused at the intersection and peered around the corner. The office door was 30 feet ahead. The dark figure slipped through the opening and the door slammed shut. *Gotta get there before Larijani destroys the files!* Matt turned on the speed and felt the pounding of Creep's heels behind.

~~~~~~~

Arif Alikhan had screwed up. He felt certain that the IED he had rigged to the front door would slow the attackers. The blast might even kill a few of them, but he would not count on that. Instead, he arranged his people inside to provide over-lapping fields of fire that was sure to cut down any surviving infidels.

But the followers of Satan had moved through the darkness like demons, crushing his defenses faster than Alikhan could have imagined. By the time he realized his mistake he could practically feel the infidels breathing down his neck and he made a mad dash for the office. He had to get inside and destroy all of Larijani's records as he had been ordered.

~~~~~~~

Matt paused at the solid wood door, looked in both directions, then put his ear to the door. There was a sudden exchange of gunfire coming from the left and Matt instinctively dropped to one knee.

"Third tango down," Larson's voice came over the comm-set.

Matt did not take time to answer. Instead, he reared back and slammed his foot into the door with enough force to knock the door off its hinges and shatter the lock. Momentum carried him several feet into the large office space, landing on his knees in a painful crunch. He came up on one knee with the Berretta in a two-hand grip, pointed at the chest of the terrorist standing fifteen feet in front of him.

Matt's eyes flicked left and right, instantly taking in the office. The room was about 15 by 20 feet; the windowless walls were covered with faded wood paneling. The tango stood before a battered gray metal desk against the far wall, a broken swivel desk chair leaned awkwardly to one side. Along the opposite wall were floor-to-ceiling metal storage bins. Several cardboard boxes, lids taped closed were on the floor in front of the storage bins. A collection of maps were pinned to the near wall, each map was marked with a collection of colored squiggly lines.

On top of the desk was a small lamp casting dim shadows throughout the room, a black canvas bag, a semi-automatic pistol, and a laptop computer. An AK-47 assault rifle was propped against one corner of the desk.

The terrorist stood frozen, his dark eyes blazed with a combination of fear and defiance.

This was not Larijani. He was larger, harder. He was a warrior; of that Matt was sure. The man was startled and indecisive and Matt knew that made him extremely dangerous. The tango's hand was concealed inside the black canvas bag; his eyes darted from the laptop, to the pistol, and then back to Matt.

Matt slowly rose to his feet, aiming the Berretta at the tango's face. He sensed movement behind him and he froze.

"Creep?" Matt called without turning around.

"Behind you, sir."

Matt took a step toward the terrorist. He kept an eye on the concealed hand.

"Step away from the desk, now!" Matt motioned with his pistol. The terrorist remained frozen. Sweat streaked down his face. You could smell the fear and Matt did not like the strange look in the man's eyes.

"I said step away from the desk!" Matt raised his voice. From the corner of his eye he saw Creep step further into the room and move several feet to his right. The Recon sergeant held his rifle on the terrorist.

Alikhan jumped away from the desk, pulling his hand from the bag. He was holding an RGD-5 hand grenade high above his head, gesturing for Matt to step back. His eyes were wide, tears spilled down his face, and he began to scream.

"Allahu Akbar! Allahu Akbar!" He raised his other hand toward the pin on the hand grenade.

Matt had witnessed firsthand the destructive power of the Russian-made grenades when he was in Iraq and Afghanistan. No one inside the office would survive the blast.

Without hesitation, Matt lowered the Berretta and snapped off two rounds in quick secession. In the blink of an eye Matt shattered both knees and the terrorist crashed to the floor screaming.

The man writhed in agony, thrashing about on the floor with his knees pulled to his chest. Blood poured through the fingers of his free hand as he clutched his knees. He still held tight to the grenade, now covered with blood, momentarily forgotten in his pain.

Moving with the speed of a cat, Creep jumped forward. He stomped down on the hand holding the grenade, grinding the man's wrist into the floor. He bent down and plucked the explosive device from a shattered hand. The Recon sergeant tossed the grenade to Matt and turned back to the terrorist. In one swift motion he flipped the man over onto his stomach, wrenched his arms behind his back, and secured his wrists with plastic ties.

"Good job, boss!" Creep stated when he had finished.

Kneeling beside the wounded terrorist, Matt turned to see Larson with a big grin on his face. Gunny was standing beside him with a look of astonishment. Matt nodded and turned back to the man who was still twisting and crying in agony.

"Where's Larijani?" Matt asked. The man shook his head and grimaced. His eyes were closed tight so he would not have to look at the man who shot him.

"Not gonna ask again!" Matt dug the muzzle of his pistol into one of Alikhan's battered knees. The man screamed louder, shaking his head violently, and then his face turned a ghastly pallor as he sank into shock.

"He's not going to talk, Matt," Larson said.

"Yeah, probably. Maybe they can get something out of him back on *Iwo*. Let's get him loaded on Marine Zero-One-Two, along with the other wounded."

Butch Larson looked at Creep and jerked his head toward the door. The Recon sergeant snatched the wounded terrorist off the floor with one hand and dragged him outside.

"Let's get our guys in here and toss the whole building. The three of us will take this room." Matt picked up the laptop and slipped it into a leather case that was on the floor beside the desk.

"What are we looking for?" Gunny asked.

"Anything useful, I reckon. We'll load it on the Ospreys and carry it back to the ship." Matt surveyed the room again. His eyes settled on the maps pinned to wall. He walked closer to study them in the dim light, and a chill ran up his spine. Each map was a section of the United States. The colored lines looked like grids of some kind. He stared contemplatively, running a hand through his sweat-soaked hair, and then took the maps down from the wall. When he had finished rolling them up, he turned to Larson.

"Larijani might be hidin' someplace. Tell everyone to keep an eye out for him."

"You don't really believe he's still around do you, Matt?" Larson asked.

Matt shrugged, tucked the laptop and rolls of maps under his arm like a prized catch and walked outside.

Nineteen

El Achiotal
Guatemala

Matthew McWain loved early morning solo flights of solitude. The air was cool and smooth and watching the sun chase shadows from the valleys in South Texas was a sight to behold. Sometimes a damp fog hugged the ground and climbing through the wispy shroud was like watching God peel back the curtains, beckoning a new day to spring forth. Matt could look out and capture dozens of tiny rainbows as the sun pierced the morning veil. He called these moments his "Dawn Patrol." He often arrived early for work just to take the Super Decathlon out for his daily dose of tranquility. His time to thank God for the privilege of sharing another glorious sunrise.

Matt eased the stick forward and glanced out the Osprey's windscreen. Darkness had retreated, giving way to gray dawn. Lush green hillsides began to take on color and higher up toward the top of the Santa Cruz Mountains the rising sun cast its first hint of a golden hue.

"Took five stitches," Chase broke the silence, holding his arm up to admire the bandage. "Hope this chicken outfit awards the Purple Heart."

"In your dreams, Cuz," Matt glanced at Chase and grinned. He could do that now. Now that his knees stopped knocking from the fear of seeing Chase go down.

"Danged near tore my arm clean off!"

"Uh Huh! Just think of the tale you'll tell your grandkids some day when you show them your battle scar."

"Yeah, well," Chase discounted Matt's comment, thinking, *that's not gonna happen!* "at least it ain't my pitchin' arm."

The corpsman on Marine Zero-One-Two told Matt it was a simple flesh wound. "Probably caught a ricochet off the pavement." Other than Gunny Steven's scraped knees, Chase was the only friendly casualty. Measured in those terms it was a very successful mission. On the other hand, Larijani slipped through their fingers, and that made it a miserable failure, which cast Matt into a funk.

Both men sat quietly, looking out at the serene beauty of a new day.

"Thanks, Matt," Chase broke the silence. Matt glanced over, saw the serious look on his cousin's face and raised an eyebrow. "Thanks for trusting me back there; for letting me be a part of it."

"Shoot man, I thank you for saving my life … again!"

"Yeah, that was pretty cool, huh?" Chase made a pistol with his thumb and forefinger and pretended to blow smoke off the barrel.

They both laughed.

Marine Zero-One-Two airlifted four wounded terrorists, including Arif Alikhan, back to *Iwo Jima* for treatment. Their interrogation would begin immediately. It had taken most of the night to search the warehouse. Many crates containing weapons and explosives were cataloged and either loaded onto the Marine Corps Osprey or destroyed by dumping them into the bay. Of particular interest were several well insulated crates, each containing three dozen explosive vests for suicide bombers. Photos were taken of markings on the crates and one vest was taken back to *Iwo*. The remaining vests were weighted down with discarded junk and took a deep swim. Items that were considered significant intel were loaded onto Matt's Osprey; along with four black canvas bags stuffed with $100 and $50 bills.

The dock area was sanitized before the two Ospreys departed, removing as much evidence of the battle as possible. With the exception of the heavily damaged Acuario Distributors warehouse and a gazillion pockmarks from shrapnel and bullets, the place looked almost the same as the longshoremen had left it the day before. The dead bodies were on the bottom of the bay along with the weapons and explosives.

As far as anyone could tell, three tangos managed to escape into the bush. Failing to relocate them after the battle, Clayton brought Reaper One back to *Iwo Jima*. The grueling process of analyzing literally thousands of frames of video and hours of radar imagery would begin once the UAV was safely parked inside the hangar bay.

"*Quarterback, Ops Center! You've had a busy night, Matt.*"

"Mornin' Carter, been wonderin' where you were." Matt had grown used to the NCTC director interrupting operations at the most poignant times. The absence of his voice during the eventful evening caused him to wonder. *Maybe he's finally learned we can do our job without his guidance*, Matt thought. *Nah, that ain't it!*

Matt saw the Cortez compound five miles dead ahead. He would set the Osprey down in the back pasture as he had a few hours before. It would be a quick stop, just long enough to pick up the remaining Watchdog members before heading out to *Iwo Jima.*

"Things are busy here, too, as you can imagine. Larijani got away, huh?"

"Again!" Matt lamented. "Just like Hassam, keeps slippin' through our fingers."

"Well, you can scratch Hassam off the list." There was jubilation in Manning's voice. *" Larijani will step in to fill the void. He is now your primary objective."*

"Oh?"Matt and Chase exchanged glances. This was unbelievable news.

"I'll tell you about it when you get back to Iwo. I've sent a team of analysts out to the ship to get a head start on the collected data ... You did capture some useable intel, right?"

"Yes, sir, we got a boat load of intel!"

"As in hard evidence?" Manning sounded excited, as if he had been vindicated.

"In my inexperienced, unpracticed, and humble interpretation, yeah." Matt caught Chase rolling his eyes and gave him a wide grin. "Pretty solid, Manning. They're comin' after us!"

"Great! I need you to get that stuff on Iwo immediately!"

*"*Copy that!" Matt eased the stick forward, pulled back on the thrust lever, and tilted the engine nacelles to configure the Osprey into helicopter mode.

~~~~~~~~~

The sun was peeking over the horizon when the men climbed out of the Osprey. The air was clean and cool ... and smelled great. Matt's plan to *load-and-go* was instantly forgotten as the delicious aroma of bacon, sausage, and fresh coffee filled the air. His mouth watered in anticipation, reminding him that it had been nearly twelve hours since they had eaten. Twelve hours of burning calories at a prodigious rate. The adrenalin high had long since worn off and Matt felt the weariness setting in with each step he took.

Butch Larson came up beside him. He looked as haggard as Matt felt, complete with a two-day beard, dirt crusted face and arms, sweat stained shirt.

"Long night, eh Matt?"

"Very! Did you hear Manning say they got Hassam?" Matt kept his voice low.

"Yeah! How do you suppose they did that?"

Matt shrugged. "Guess we'll find out when we get back to *Iwo*."

He looked up and saw Samuel Cortez, wearing a huge smile and waving his arms, coming forward to greet them. Things appeared peaceful and returning to normal, and that gave Matt reason to smile back. At least this part of the mission was a success.

"We've been waiting for you," Cortez called when he came closer.

"Like one pig waits on another, right?" Matt chuckled. He saw the remaining four Watchdog members lounging on deck chairs or lying in the grass, propped against their combat gear. Each had a plate heaped with eggs, sausage, bacon, potatoes, and toast. They waved and grinned, their mouths stuffed with food. Grimy faces and tired expressions in their eyes told the story of a long night.

"Come, the women are making lots more. You must be starved."

"No second invitation needed here," Chase said as he pushed past the group.

Matt spied Corporal Billy Graft kicked back on a chaise lounge, smiling through his pain. His shirt was off and clean white bandages covered his left shoulder and wrapped around his chest to immobilize his arm. Matt checked on him before joining the others.

~~~~~~~

Matt, Chase, Larson, and Lenox sat with Cortez at a covered patio table close to the pool. They were on their third cup of coffee, empty plates sat before them. Larson leaned back and stretched his legs. He rubbed his belly and said, "Man, if I stayed around here a few more days you'd have to roll me back to the airplane in a wheelbarrow."

"You are welcome to stay as long as you wish, Colonel. We will forever be in debt of Matt and Chase, and the United States Marine Corps."

"So what am I, Samuel, chopped liver?" Phil Lenox waved his arms in feigned indignation.

"You, my friend, do not need an invitation. You are always welcome."

Matt smiled and asked, "Samuel, what about your wounded men?"

The jovial Cortez took on pallor and sadly shook his head. "Two of my men did not make it. Another is in very serious condition. Our doctor said it could have been much worse had it not been for your medic." He turned to Larson, "I do hope you will see that Corporal Stone receives a commendation when you get back to your ship."

"I'll see what I can do." Larson nodded in appreciation.

"Same goes for all of your people," Cortez continued. "They did not stop searching for the terrorist dogs until just a little while ago." Lt. Wally Beemer, platoon leader, had already assured Matt and Larson that the area was clear. Apparently two, possibly three, tangos had escaped in one of several vans the terrorists had come in. The Marines confiscated all the weapons left on the battlefield and handed them over to the Cortez *Sicarios*.

"Thank you, sir!"

Cortez reached across the table and put a hand on Matt's arm. It was an expression of gratitude left unsaid. "Where do you go from here, my young friend?"

"For now, we pack up the whole team and head back to the ship."

"Must you leave immediately? I would like for Manuel to see you. He owes you his personal thanks."

"I would like to see him, Samuel, but we have to get going. I'm afraid we have some very … important business to take care of."

Cortez nodded in understanding. "I wish there was some way I could help you with that ... I still feel responsible in some way. Cortez Enterprises made it possible for the radical terrorists to establish a foothold." He hung his head and sighed.

"That was none of your doing, Samuel," Matt tried to sound assuring, but he could tell the elder Cortez was not buying it.

"Thanks," Cortez made a feeble attempt to smile. "Still, if there is some way that I can be of assistance in resolving this horrible affair, please promise you will call."

"Guaranteed!" Matt squeezed the old man's hand. "Hey, as soon as you can make arrangements, why don't you drop in on the McWain ranch for a few days? I know mom and dad would love it. Maybe you could bring Kat?"

That made Samuel Cortez beam. His strong business relationship with Matt's father had existed for many years and had grown into a mutual friendship.

"You know how to make an old man feel honored, Matt," Samuel's eyes watered. "I would like very much to visit with your folks again. It's been too long. And Kat … We never had a chance for you to tell me what you thought of her flying?"

"Well, she can fly a Waco a whole lot better than I can, that's for sure—"

"That's for *danged* sure!" Chase broke in. "Of course that ain't saying much. Now I, on the other hand—"

"Can you just shut up!" Matt cut him off with a mock scowl and then turned back to Cortez. "Is she really serious about international aerobatic competition?"

"It's all she talks about," Cortez assured Matt. Katalina's passion was to become a professional pilot, including competition aerobatics. Matt knew that opportunities in Guatemala were slim to none. If she were to actively pursue a career in aviation, she would need to relocate. Pretty daunting for a sixteen-year-old girl.

"Okay, talk it over with her and her parents. If she wants a trial run to see how well she manages being away from home, leave her with us for a few weeks. She can live at the ranch with mom and dad, and do odd jobs around the airport between aerobatic lessons."

"I suspect she will manage that pretty well," Cortez smiled. "The question is how well her *Abuelo* and *Papá* can manage without her."

Matt nodded with a grin. "I suspect you are right about that."

"What about an airplane?" Cortez asked.

"We'll start her in our Super Decathlon, but soon she's gonna need a plane with a competitive edge."

"Okay, whatever it takes. You guys be the judge of that." Cortez included Chase, who nodded in agreement. "Cost will not be an object."

"Alright," Matt said. "When that time comes we'll shop around and get back to you."

"Thank you my friends." Cortez rose to his feet. He knew Matt was in a hurry to leave. "Go with God."

Twenty

The USS *Iwo Jima* steamed across the sun dappled Caribbean as Dark Horse One was lowered inside *Iwo*'s hangar deck. A weary group of Marine Recon warriors handed over the last of the confiscated items from Puerto Santo Tomás to Naval Intelligence personnel. The collection was then whisked up to analysts waiting in a cramped air conditioned compartment one deck below the CIC. The Marines grabbed the rest of their gear and headed off to warm showers and a bunk.

Matt and Chase shared a stateroom to freshen up and get a little sleep, but by the time Matt had showered and shaved, he found himself too wired from four cups of coffee he had with Samuel Cortez. He dressed in Wrangler jeans, a faded short sleeve maroon A&M pull over, and a blue *Iwo Jima* ball cap. He slipped out of the stateroom, leaving Chase snoring blissfully in his bunk, and made his way up to the GCS compartment in search of Lt. Cmdr. Clayton Downs.

Matt pounded on the secured hatch before Lt. Louis Rogers cracked the door and peered out from the darkened compartment as if he were the gatekeeper of the inner sanctum.

"Oh, it's you," the short, wiry computer guru said with a hint of annoyance, and held the door open.

Matt stepped inside, shook hands with the two men, and glanced up at the large screen. In that split second of recognition a gasp escaped his lips as he softly murmured, "Ahmad Hassam!"

A single, enhanced frame from the video feed stared back at Matt with a familiar haunting glare. Even with his head turned, sporting a goatee, glasses, and lighter hair coloring, there was no doubt in Matt's mind that he was looking into the face of the master terrorist.

"Okay," Clayton said, glancing at Rogers with a nod, "that's the confirmation we needed."

Matt turned back to the men as if to speak, but Clayton silenced him with an open palm. "Carter Manning asked for you to call as soon as you came up. He assumed you would be sleeping for a few hours."

Clayton saw the surprised look on Matt's face and motioned him toward the headset at the ScanEagle pilot console.

"Use that one. It's set to the command freq."

Matt nodded and slumped down into the soft leather seat. "Carter, its Matt!"

"Been trying to reach you ... You didn't sleep very long."

"No, sir. You sound as tired as I feel. So, tell me how you got Hassam."

"I am sad to report that my earlier announcement was premature ... We missed him."

"Explain."

"You with Lt. Cmdr. Downs now?"

"Yes, sir."

"Good! He can fill you in on the details we have so far. I want you to work with the commander on intel he's received, then get with the analysis team for an early read on that collection of stuff you brought back from Santo Tomás. Get back to me ASAP."

"Roger tha—" He was talking into a dead mic. "He hung up on me," Matt grinned.

"Yeah, I've noticed that about him," Clayton chuckled. "Busy dude!" He slid into the UAV pilot seat next to Matt.

For the next few minutes, Clayton briefed Matt on *Operation Night Stalker*, a covert black op authorized by President Harlan Downs in the event Ahmad Hassam managed to escape Santo Tomás.

In the highlands west of Caracas, Venezuela, Hassam operated what had been identified as his forward training base. Satellite surveillance produced some useable photos on the general layout of the camp, but revealed little on the overall magnitude of the complex. Of significance, however, was that the facility appeared likely to be Hassam's hide-away when he wasn't off taking care of business.

Like coordinating a hit on an innocent Guatemalan family, Matt thought while Clayton continued the briefing.

Logic indicated Hassam would most likely head back to his Venezuelan base once he finished at Santo Tomás, at least for a short time before heading into the United States, if indeed the U.S. was to be his ultimate target— a conclusion of which now appeared an absolute certainty.

Elements of *Night Stalker* had been in place for several days, including a Marine Corps Osprey from *Iwo,* sitting in deep cover at a secret base just over the Venezuelan border in Columbia.

"At 0400 today," Clayton continued, "a Navy SEAL Team was cleared for a HALO jump—high altitude, low opening parachute drop—into the terrorist base once it was determined that Hassam likely dashed home from Guatemala. The SEALs were ordered to terminate the master terrorist and confiscate all intel."

The exit plan called for the SEALs to travel straight west from the training camp to a prearranged LZ where the Osprey would swoop in and pick them up—exactly as Matt had done dozens of times in Iraq and Afghanistan. He could visualize the action now as if he were actually in the cockpit. His stomach tightened with anticipation.

Somehow, a communications snafu led Manning to think they had succeeded in finding Hassam and completed all mission objectives before successfully exfiltrating out of country. In truth, the SEALs pretty much dismantled the camp and snagged just about everything of importance, but Ahmad Hassam was a no show.

"… Marine Zero-One-Four is due back aboard in," Clayton checked his watch, "two hours and forty-two minutes." He paused, his voice softened, "They're bringing home casualties. Sickbay's going to be busy for a while." The amphibious assault ship had one of the finest surgical facilities in the U.S. Navy. Matt recalled their top notch efficiency and expertise as they successfully fought to save the life of Paul Moore, a missionary who was critically wounded in his attempt to defend Carley Downs.

"So, where did he go?" Matt asked, turning back to face the screen. Louis Rogers had taken down the video feed from ScanEagle II and put up Reaper One. It was a stark contrast in resolution quality and caused Matt to blink in appreciation.

"We're still studying footage," Clayton offered. "Got a ways to go, but we want to show you a couple frames that went unnoticed in the heat of battle." Clayton turned to his assistant, "Louis, send out for a plate of sandwiches and some cokes, okay?"

Louis grumbled something about not being a servant and then turned to the ship's phone to place the order. Clayton touched the trackball on the console and raced several frames forward.

Matt saw a portion of the gunfight on the Santo Tomás dock, followed by wide-angle sweeps of the camera as it surveyed the surrounding area for ground traffic and other potential interference. The white images of men dashing across the screen and brilliant muzzle flashes bumped up his adrenalin as he relived the brief, but intense battle.

"There! Did you see that?"

"What?" Matt questioned.

"Here … look again … There! See it?"

"Uh, okay, I think. That dark shadow flitting across the top portion of the screen?"

"Right. That's what caught our eye. Now let's enhance the image." Louis fiddled with the computer controls for a minute.

"And *voila!*" Clayton shouted enthusiastically.

"That's … a little Piper Cherokee? What the heck?"

"That's right. Northwest bound out of Puerto Barrios airport. They do scenic flights for tourists with that thing. We've been searching frame-by-frame for it to come back for landing."

"And so far you haven't found it?"

"Correct. We obviously did not have eyes on the airport during much of the battle, but a review of our surveillance radar does not show the aircraft returning. At least not yet, we'll keep looking. But here's something else you need to see …"

For the next few minutes Clayton and Louis took Matt through a dozen enhanced frames showing a dark colored vehicle pull onto the Quay during the battle. It sat there for a moment, then sped off. Two frames capturing the unmistakable image of Hakeem Larijani. Matt was right, the terrorist lieutenant was not traveling with his boss.

"That's Larijani. Were you able to track him?"

"Negative. Lost him in the horrible traffic jam you created with your little war on the waterfront."

Matt closed his eyes, lifted the ball cap, and ran a hand through his damp hair. Both terrorists escaped and have now disappeared. He was afraid to think where they were going to show up next, but he had a nagging suspicion they would resurface together, someplace inside the United States. With God's grace maybe the answers they need would be discovered in the piles of intel he had brought back from Santo Tomás, or maybe in the stuff the SEAL team was bringing home. *We've got a lot of work to do. Please dear God, we could use a little help here!*

"Where's the intel analysis team hangin' out?" Matt asked.

"Just about directly under our feet," Clayton smiled. "C'mon, I'll take you down ... Louis, get Todd up here to give you a hand digging through the SAR feed. We need to know where that Cherokee went."

Twenty-One

USS *Iwo Jima*
45 Miles East of
Belize City
Western Caribbean

Matt stepped into a brightly lit compartment almost double the size of the GCS. Three people in civilian attire were seated around a table on bench-style seating firmly attached to the steel deck. Each person worked from a computer, their heads hunkered down in intense concentration. An empty chair in front of a computer was at the head of the table indicating perhaps another analyst belonged to the group. A printer/fax machine was positioned in the middle of the table, half buried by a collection of documents scattered haphazardly as if a box had been turned upside down on the table. Matt recognized the material as that coming from Larijani's office in Santo Tomás. Two easels on the far side of the room contained pages and photos linked together in some semblance of chronology or priority, he couldn't tell which.

His eyes trailed over the people diligently at work ... and there she was! Her back was to him so he could not see her face, but the long black shiny pony tail, smooth olive complexion, and the erect way she held herself as if she were a Spanish *condesa*, an aristocrat, caused a smile to cross his lips and his pulse quickened. Matt moved to the table and stood beside her. He breathed in her familiar clean fragrance that reminded him of spring.

"Find anything important," he said softly.

She jumped and turned with a startled look; he had broken her concentration. Then she met his smile and he dissolved into her intense brown eyes.

"Lots of things, Cowboy. Thanks for the treasure trove of intel." She patted the bench motioning for Matt to sit beside her.

Her name was Angelina Juanita Carmen de Hernandez—AJ for short. She was employed by Carter Manning, who had introduced her to Matt six months before when she traveled to Guatemala with he and Chase to rescue Carley Downs. AJ was a personal friend of Carley's protection detail, Jordan Scott, so she had volunteered to be part of the rescue effort. She showed tremendous ability and self-confidence during that extreme time.

The incredibly talented Latin American was just as beautiful as he remembered. Five feet six, slender yet powerful and moved with athletic grace. She had silky smooth skin and her golden smile was accentuated by a single dimple on the right side. Large gold hoops dangled from her ears and light pink lipstick highlighted her full lips and olive complexion. She was dressed nearly the same as the day he first met her, tight black jeans and white blouse. The spiked heels she wore on that initial meeting had been replaced with black sneakers.

Matt straddled the bench so he could look fully into her face. "So you're an analyst as well as black ops?" He asked with a smile. He recalled inquiring on the flight into Guatemala what she did for Carter Manning since her background was Harvard Law.

She was noncommittal when asked, though he was soon impressed by her skills with firearms and hand-to-hand combat. Without her the mission to save Carley and Jordan might not have succeeded. He regretted not telling her that before he and Chase hastily flew out of Washington, D.C. on the night they returned from the mission. She had gone to the hospital in the ambulance with Jordan that night. He had not even told her goodbye.

"Nope," she answered flippantly. "Just pretty handy with a computer."

Still noncommittal, he thought. But it was obvious she was here to supervise these guys or coordinate their efforts to expedite the findings. Carter Manning did not like delays.

AJ introduced Matt to the two men working with her as special analysts for the NSA. They shook hands and she continued, "Harvey Simmons, the fourth person on our team, is below decks with Naval Intelligence. They are interrogating the prisoners you brought in."

Matt loved her voice. Soft, yet filled with authority and confidence. Never needed to raise her voice in order to make a point. *Man,* he suddenly realized, *I'd really like to get to know this lady better!*

"We uploaded data from the laptop hard drive to NSA. Got some of it back already, decrypted and translated."

"That was quick."

"Very quick. But then our people have been working with this stuff ever since Guatemala." She held a distant stare for a moment, then quickly recovered. "While waiting for NSA to do their magic, we pieced together some miscellaneous items you brought back. It's going to be a long process and you are welcome to watch, but you might want to catch some Z's. You look dog tired, and I have it on good authority that you and your team will be wheels up tomorrow morning."

Matt nodded, staring into her eyes. "Yeah, I'm pretty wiped out," he said. He hauled himself up and headed for the door, but then turned back. "Good to see you again, AJ."

"You too." She sounded strictly professionally. Matt had a feeling that if it were not for the two NSA fellows close by, she might have responded differently. *Wishful thinking,* he shrugged and headed back to his stateroom.

~~~~~~~~

Hacienda Rio Vista
Tuxtla Guttiérrez,
Mexico

The afternoon sun beat down on the poolside veranda of the incredibly spacious home owned by Doña Enedina Arellano Félix. The elegant 14,000 square foot, two-story home sat smack dab in the middle of 2,000 prime acres of rich bottom land, overlooking the east bank of the Rio Grijalva, the largest of three rivers near Tuxtla Guttiérrez, Mexico.

Hidden from the main house was a compound of smaller homes and outbuildings, which housed hundreds of laborers who tended the fruit orchards and rolling fields of rich alfalfa, and most importantly, oversaw the breeding and training of award winning Peruvian Pasos. The spirited saddle horses with their characteristic high-stepping circular gait were Luis Fernando Arellano's pride and passion.

A giant umbrella covered the stained glass table where Ahmad Hassam sat in one of the four plush outdoor chairs. He fidgeted nervously as he sipped from a tall glass of iced orange juice. Idol time was counter-productive time and he despised it. Seated across from him with a frosty Dos

Equis in one hand and a Cohiba in the other was Luis
Fernando Arellano.

Squeals of laughter rose from the pool as Arellano's
four children splashed and frolicked in the blue water.
Beyond the pool, beyond two hundred feet of well
manicured lawn and shrubbery and trees was the estate's
private marina. Hassam gazed upon an incredible river
view, hence the name Hacienda Rio Vista.

The master terrorist wasn't interested in the scenic
view. He did, however take note of the fierce looking
sentry patrolling the grounds, an H&K MP5 machine gun
slung across his chest, and a ferocious guard dog straining
against its leash. High on the hill overlooking the main
house was a guard tower occupied 24/7 by two expert
marksmen with firepower larger than MP5's.

Raising prize horses was only a hobby for Luis
Fernando Arellano. The son of Doña Enedina Arellano,
Félix was boss of the largest, most powerful, and most
brutal drug cartel in Mexico. No one, nor anything, was
beyond his reach.

The boundary for the Arellano cartel extended from
Tijuana across the California/Mexican border to Tucson,
Arizona. Arellano's influence, however, went well beyond
boundaries. It was said he owned judges, politicians, and
high ranking law enforcement officials on both sides of the
border. With that kind of power, he commanded respect
from leaders of the other three cartels operating in Mexico.

The drug czar kept his family safe within the confines
of Hacienda Rio Vista while he operated from his main
offices on the outskirts of Tijuana. But when political
pressure beyond his control became too great, he retreated
back here in Tuxtla Guttiérrez for a few weeks.

"You are anxious, my friend," Arellano said, exhaling a
cloud of blue smoke.

"There is much to be done." Hassam stared into the
horizon. He was unrested, yet alert. The pilot flew him into

this remote city, arriving shortly after one a.m., nearly at the end of their fuel range. The Piper Cherokee labored over mountains and up valleys, the pilot aided by a full moon and experience earned by dozens of similar nocturnal flights.

"I understand your urgency, Ahmad. However, your flight doesn't leave until eleven tomorrow morning. Come; let me show you around the grounds." With that, the portly Arellano rose from his chair.

"Seen it all before," Hassam said distantly. His thoughts were miles away. Days away.

"Alright then, let's take the boat out. Maybe go up river, do a little fishing before dinner."

Reluctantly, Hassam got up from his chair and offered a rare smile. "Thank you, my friend. As always you and *Doña* Félix are gracious hosts."

"For you, anything," Arellano reached out and touched Hassam's arm. "*Mi amigo*, promise you will come back to visit when your mission in the U.S. is completed."

"Of course." Both men knew it was an idle promise. Both knew the dangers involved, even the possibility that Hassam would not be coming back. Might not survive his violent crusade against the United States.

For Arellano it was the pinnacle of mutual interest with his friend and business associate. Hassam's war against the Great Satan would create a diversion of unprecedented magnitude, allowing the drug kingpin to slip tons of illegal drugs across the border every single day. Completely unnoticed. He was poised and ready to reap the reward for taking hundreds of Islamic warriors through his border pipeline during the past two and a half years.

~~~~~~~~

Situation Room
White House
Washington, D.C.

"Hold on, Carter. We have some newcomers joining us," President Harlan Downs said.

The conference table inside the Situation Room was getting crowded. In addition to DNI Alex Strayhorn, SecState Zachary Ringhold, White House Chief of Staff James Ritchey, and Chairman of the Joint Chiefs/CNO Admiral Justin B. Turner, the president had summoned other key staff members. The first of the newcomers was Leslie Salmons, the newly appointed, first female director of the FBI. Minutes later Director of Homeland Security Stu Warner arrived simultaneously with FEMA Director Howard Evans.

"Gentlemen ... and lady," President Downs smiled as he nodded to Director Salmons, "thanks for coming right over."

The three new attendees quickly noticed the fatigue etched on the president's face and the serious tone in his voice. Their alert eyes took in the images on the three wall mounted flat screens. They all recognized the grim face of Carter Manning on the first screen, but only the director of the FBI recognized the photo of the man in the middle screen, even with his altered appearance. None of them recognized the video showing ghostly green images of night action on the third screen.

"We do not have a lot of time," the president continued, "so I will get right to it. Please help yourselves to the coffee and sandwiches on the table while I speak.

"You know that ordinarily I encourage questions and interaction as we proceed. Not today. Please hold your questions until the briefing is finished. It is imperative that everyone knows exactly what is going on." President Downs paused to make sure he had their undivided attention.

"Our nation is facing an unprecedented crisis. One which seriously impacts your respective agencies. The screen on your right is a replay of a raid conducted by

Navy SEALS early this morning against a large terrorist training camp in Venezuela." The president paused again, assessing the wide-eyed stares and disbelief from the newcomers.

"The man in the middle screen is Ahmad Hassam. You know the name and the threat he represents. He changes his appearance frequently. This is the latest. The training camp we raided is operated by Hassam.

"Of course you know Carter Manning, director of NCTC. We just began a secure video link with Carter when you people arrived." The president turned to the video screen. "Carter, say again your recommendation before I interrupted you,"

"Yes, sir," Carter Manning began. "I recommend we pass the new photo of Hassam through all intelligence and law enforcement agencies, border patrol, ports of entry, and international airports. Eventually, we might consider increasing the coverage."

"There is no doubt that Hassam is heading for the United States?" President Downs asked, mostly for the benefit of the new arrivals.

"No, sir. No doubt." Manning could see the shocked expressions on the faces of the newcomers and quickly added, "He could already be here, Mr. President."

"Okay then, I concur with your recommendation." The president turned to those at the table. "Leslie, I hate to thrust you into the middle of a crisis in your first month on the job."

"I understand, Mr. President," Salmons replied stoically. She could feel every eye in the room on her.

President Downs jerked a thumb at the middle screen. "Let's get that guy's photo out to all of your people and every law enforcement agency in the country."

"Yes, sir."

"Alex, same goes for getting this clown's mug out to all intelligence agencies … if they don't already have it," the president added with a grin. He suspected that Clayton had already shared the photo with his colleagues in Naval Intelligence. "Stu, I want every port of entry, border guard, airport security and air marshal to be extra vigilant. We need Hassam apprehended *before* he can spread his brand of misery."

"Howard," President Downs turned to FEMA. "Your predecessor was fond of saying, 'let's make every event a non-event.'"

"Yes, sir!" The FEMA director sat straight in his chair.

"Well, this could transcend every imaginable horror, but let's see what we can do to minimize the effects as much as possible."

The president paused, glanced around the table, and directed Strayhorn to have an intelligence summary prepared for each attendee. Only then did he finally open the meeting for discussion.

"Are the Iranians driving this thing?" Admiral Justin B. Turner asked. His intense hazel eyes burned a hole through the screen directly at Manning.

"We have confirmed a direct link to Major General Imad Abu Mughniyeh of the Revolutionary Guard, Admiral."

"Doesn't prove it is state sponsored terrorism," Secretary of State Zachary Ringhold jumped in. "They will feign innocence. Denounce such horrific acts. Claim the general is some rogue agent working on his own. Besides, Ahmad Hassam is Lebanese Hezbollah—"

"Hogwash!" Admiral Turner thundered. His face turned scarlet, as if he was going to explode all over the room. His voice boomed, "I'm telling you—"

"Gentlemen!" President Downs held up his hand and the room quieted. "First things first, people. We deal with the threat coming to our homeland. We catch this contemptible savage if we can. If not, we develop a full state of readiness, extreme vigilance, and prevent as much damage as we can, where we can. Later, after our citizens and our homeland are safe, *then* we will deal with those who have delivered this abomination upon the United States of America."

"Yes, sir," they said in unison, nodding agreement.

"Carter, any idea how long before we know potential targets and timetables?"

"Soon, Mr. President. My people are pouring over the intel Matthew brought out of Santo Tomás. NSA is supporting us with translating and decrypting electronic files. We'll have answers on that pretty quick." Manning stopped to look down at his notes before continuing. "Preliminary communications with Operation *Night Stalker* indicates they are bringing in valuable intel as well. They are less than an hour out from *Iwo Jima*."

"Okay, good job. Anything else before we wrap it up and get to work?"

Manning quickly laid out a tentative plan for staging crisis response teams around the country. President Downs then terminated the meeting.

"You folks need to coordinate your efforts, share your resources so we have overlap. No holes!"

Twenty-Two

USS *Iwo Jima*
65 Miles East Northeast
Yucatan Peninsula
Gulf of Mexico

USS *Iwo Jima* rolled in gentle swells of a calm sea as she entered the Gulf of Mexico. The time was 0500 and a new day was beginning as Matt walked into the officer's wardroom. Being back aboard the *Iwo* gave him a familiar and comfortable feeling. After spending most of yesterday afternoon and evening, visiting with fellow aviators, the rolling motion lulled him sound asleep. Now the wonderful aroma of coffee and breakfast made his mouth water.

The room was filling up, but Matt spotted AJ at one of the tables and moved toward her. One of her fellow analysts sitting across from her had finished his breakfast and rose from the table. Matt took his place on the bench seat and stared into her exhausted face.

"Mornin'," Matt smiled. "You look like you pulled an all nighter."

"Very." AJ made an attempt to smile back. Her eyes were red and puffy and her make-up was worn off. Her clothes were the same from yesterday, wrinkled and smudged. She took a sip of coffee and set the mug down on the empty tray.

"You always this fresh and chipper so early in the morning?" She asked. She fixed her eyes on him and her smile began to warm. Matt was clean shaven and wearing a navy blue flight suit with NCTC stenciled across the back.

"Pretty much. Aviators love to meet the rising sun." Matt saw the sparkle in her eyes returning and hoped he had that effect on her.

"Hmmmm! Maybe I'll try that some time."

"I'd be happy to take you up. Anytime."

AJ nodded slightly, picked up her mug, and took another sip. This time she continued holding the mug delicately in her slender fingers.

"Maybe I'll look you up and take advantage of that offer when this is over … I do not have to come to Texas, do I?"

"Uh, you got somethin' against Texas?"

"Too far."

"Well, maybe we could work on that one," Matt smiled and shoved a fork full of ham and eggs in his mouth. He chewed for about two seconds, washed it down with a gulp of coffee, then continued. "Find any interesting stuff last night?"

She nodded again. "SEALs brought in a gold mine of computer files, along with six more bags of cash. Between the two raids, you guys brought in over $10 million of Hassam's reserve funds."

"Whoa! He's gonna be pissed."

"To say the least." AJ lowered her voice. "But the real treasure is in the intel you and the SEALs brought back." She went on to say that she and Clayton, along with the analysts, completed a video conference with Carter Manning about an hour ago.

"You will be flying out in a few hours." She kept her voice low. "Carter wants you and the Crisis Response Team on American soil today."

"Sounds serious," Matt said after chasing another mouthful of food with hot coffee.

AJ silently wondered how anyone could swallow a piping hot beverage so easily.

"Yes, well—"

"SHOOT-FIRE-AND-SAVE-ON-MATCHES!" Chase McWain shouted across the wardroom, causing every head to turn. "THE LOVE OF MY LIFE HAS RETURNED!" Chase dropped his tray on their table and plopped down beside AJ; so close she had to scootch over a bit.

Everyone in the wardroom laughed. A thunderous applause went up and Chase got a standing ovation. AJ's face turned scarlet. Matt looked down, shaking his head with an amused grin.

"Chase McWain, you are such a goober," AJ scolded when the room finally settled down.

"I've missed you too, doll! Thought about you every hour of every day we've been apart." His face beamed. And then, without another word, he turned to attack a tray mounded high with bacon, sausage, and ham on top of a mountain of scrambled eggs and hash browns. A second plate was stacked with pancakes drowning in syrup, and a third was piled with toast, a tub of butter, and half a dozen packets of jelly. His drinks consisted of coffee, a tall glass of milk, an equally tall glass of juice, and an iced down coke. It was more food than any three men could eat.

AJ stared at the tray with astonishment as Chase continued to shovel it in, pausing only long enough to take a gulp from one of the beverages. She shook her head, glanced over at Matt, and began to chuckle.

"How on earth can someone as skinny as you eat so much? Where do you put it?"

"I burn it off chasin' beautiful girls like you, sweetness!" Chase paused before shoveling in another mouthful.

"You are disgusting. Do you know that?"

"But you still love me, don'cha, sugar lump?" Chase lowered his voice in mock sensuality. "Why else would you chase me clear across the ocean, huh darlin'?"

"I *didn't*—Oh, for heaven's sake. Why do I even dignify your behavior with a response?" She winked at Matt, a grin tugged at the corner of her mouth. "As I was saying before we were so *rudely* interrupted—"

"Whoa! Hold on there, baby girl! Y'all ain't lettin' my ugly cousin beat my time, are ya?" Chase ratcheted up his South Texas drawl.

"Wouldn't dream of it, Romeo," AJ answered, rolling her eyes as she turned back to Matt.

He could not help but chuckle and turned to Chase. "Hurry up and finish your breakfast, Cuz. We need to get the Osprey ready to fly." Matt glanced at AJ. "Do you know where?"

"No I don't, Matt. Carter will be contacting you later this morning. He said something about setting up an in-flight refueling."

"Geez," Chase said. "What's going on?"

"The smelly stuff is about to hit the oscillating rotor, Cuz!"

"Or something like that," AJ laughed.

They talked a few more minutes before Chase pushed his tray back and stood. "Now y'all gone and ruined my appetite." Only crumbs remained in his tray.

"I'll see you before we head out," Matt said to AJ as he rose to leave.

She nodded, and then called as they were walking away. "Hey guys! Seeing the two of you reminded me of a story I read just the other day. It took place near the A&M campus."

"Really?" Chase answered. Matt cringed. He saw it coming.

"Yup! Two Aggie pilots were walking in the woods. One said, 'Look, a dead bird!' The other looked up in the sky and said, 'where?'"

"Oh, good grief! She did it again." Chase stormed off.

Matt shook his head and exchanged winks with AJ.

~~~~~~~

Two hours later Matt, Chase, and Master Chief Walter Roberts finished preflighting and loading their gear aboard Dark Horse One. Matt and Chase were dressed in navy blue flight suits with NCTC stenciled across the back. Lt. Col. Butch Larson walked up with Gunny Stevens in tow. The two looked like poster Marines in their crisp, freshly starched cammies. Each carried a duffle bag slung over one shoulder, assault rifle on the other, and a tactical bag in one hand.

"Scuttlebutt has it that the team is flying back to the states with you," Butch said to Matt.

"Yep!" Matt grinned at the towering Marine as he wiped a little hydraulic fluid off his hands with a shop towel. "For once the scuttlebutt has the right poop."

"Since when does the Marine Corps conduct black ops inside the United States?" Gunny Stevens demanded. "Or has anyone stopped to realize that's against the law?"

"Since the President of the United States placed Marine Recon on temporary duty to the Crisis Response Team." Matt moved closer to Stevens and in his commanding voice said, "You are TDY, Gunny. All mine for the duration. Now, I suggest you get Watchdog team over here with their gear. We are wheels up in one hour."

"Yes, sir! Fly-boy, sir!" Gunny offered a snappy salute, did a crisp about-face, and marched off as if on the parade ground.

"He only does that with people he respects ... which aren't many," Butch said.

~~~~~~~

With time remaining before their departure, Matt went to say goodbye to AJ. He entered the Intelligence compartment and found Clayton Downs briefing AJ and her fellow analysts. They were standing around the table looking over the latest intel.

"Oh, good, you are just in time," AJ said when she saw Matt. "I was just going to call you."

"What's up?" Matt noticed her broad smile as he approached. He nodded to the others.

Clayton was the first to speak. "We might have an idea where Hassam could be, or at least the route he traveled."

Matt's ears perked up. Manning had ordered him back to D.C., but if they had a positive lead on Hassam, he would rather go chasing after him. He stared at the charts and timetables that Louis Rogers had put together. None of it made sense until Clayton explained.

"Taca Airlines Flight 415 departed Puerto Barrios two nights ago, arrived in Guatemala City at 10:57 local. FBI assets indicated that a very large man matching Hassam's body guard was seen walking through the terminal a few minutes later. No mention of Hassam. The bodyguard boarded a Mexicana flight bound for Veracruz International alone—"

"Mexico?" Matt interrupted.

"Yes, and the kicker is Delta and American service Veracruz, both have multiple U.S. destinations. But here's the deal. The little Cherokee we picked up on radar doesn't have the legs for Veracruz—assuming it continued north bound. It does, however, have enough range for another international airport in Southern Mexico: Tuxtla Guttiérrez International, serviced by Delta with twice weekly flights to DFW." Clayton beamed with his own discovery.

"So, Hassam and the bodyguard traveled separately into Dallas/Fort Worth?"

Clayton nodded. "Quite possibly. And from there, anywhere in the U.S. ... But here's another interesting piece of intel. A little after ten hundred yesterday a Cessna Citation bizjet landed at Puerto Barrios and departed immediately with a small, slender man boarding alone. It flew non-stop to Veracruz."

"Hakeem Larijani!" Matt exhaled a soft whistle.

"That's our thinking," Clayton agreed.

"We do not have assets at Veracruz or Tuxtla Guttiérrez," AJ added.

"How far is it from Tuxtla Guttiérrez to Veracruz?" Matt asked, studying a map spread across one end of the table.

"About 107 miles, Matt," Clayton offered.

"It's not likely they're traveling together," AJ touched Matt's arm. She could see the wheels turning in his head. "That would be too high profile for Hassam. We suspect travel plans for Larijani and the body guard have been improvised because of the little disruption you created." She smiled. "But Hassam's arrival at Tuxtla Guttiérrez was all part of his original plan. We know Luis Fernando Arellano, leader of the largest Mexican drug cartel, has a home there and we've learned that Hassam has established an alliance with him. It is quite likely that Hassam is a guest in Tuxtla, maybe waiting for things to quiet down a little."

Matt silently studied the documents for a moment. He felt the hairs standing on the back of his neck. *DFW down to Edinburg is a short 450 miles.* He raised his head to AJ and Clayton. "Your theories sound logical with one exception. Hassam ain't waitin'. When's the next Delta flight out of Tuxtla Guttiérrez to Dallas?"

Clayton glanced at his watch. "Little less than three hours."

Matt nodded. Started to say something, but AJ cut him off.

"Don't even think about it, McWain." Her dark eyes burned into his. "Carter wants you in D.C. as soon as you can get there—"

"But if—"

"No buts! You think you can intercept him in Texas, but how many times have we seen this guy do the exact opposite of what we expected? There needs to be a coordinated effort laid down to capture this butcher *and* his entire network."

Matt shook his head, but AJ continued forcefully. "Matt, listen to me. Carter regards you as the tip-of-the-spear. Please, go to him. He needs you to lay this thing out. Clayton and I … and the others," she swept the room with a wave of her hand, "will back you up from here."

Matt continued to stare at her, then at the intel, then back again. A full minute passed before he begrudgingly gave in. He knew AJ was right, but he could not shake the overwhelming feeling of dread that Hassam was going to Texas for a very specific purpose. *Please dear God. Watch over my family. Keep them safe 'til I get there.*

AJ walked with Matt to the passageway. She touched his arm again and gazed into his eyes. It felt like an electric current ran from her fingertips. She smiled, her single dimple was captivating.

"Carter has assigned an FBI liaison to your team. Her name is Georgia Shayne. She's a very good friend of mine. Extremely bright and very capable. I want you to know you can depend on her, Matt."

Fifteen minutes later Matt spooled up the Rolls Royce engines on Dark Horse One.

Twenty-Three

Dallas/Fort Worth International Airport
Irving, Texas

Department of Homeland Security surveillance cameras picked up a middle age man walking hunch-shouldered out of Gate 3, Terminal E. They followed him down the concourse until he disappeared into the men's restroom. The man had graying hair, Van Dyke goatee, olive complexion, and had thick, dark frame glasses. He wore a wrinkled green windbreaker over a yellow polo and tan trousers.

Ten minutes later the man exited the men's room and shuffled slowly down the concourse. He stopped a couple of times to check flight information kiosks as if he were a confused first-time traveler. Cameras followed him to Gate 12 where he disappeared into the Jetway to a Delta Boeing 757, currently boarding passengers non-stop to New York.

Surveillance cameras failed to observe a young businessman coming out of the same restroom. He walked briskly in the opposite direction. He wore an expensive metallic gray suit, light blue tie, and highly polished leather shoes. He was clean shaven and his curly black hair shone from rinsing out the gray powder. Gold wire-frame glasses magnified his deep-set eyes; their true color hidden behind light blue colored contacts. He carried an expensive black leather briefcase.

The man moved with confidence, a deliberate cadence to his step as he approached the customs counter. From inside his suit coat, he produced a well-worn passport, and slid it across the counter. The name on the passport read Rafael Juan Carlos Dominguez, executive director of Pemex Oil, Mexico City. He was in Texas on a three-day business trip. Several pages in his passport indicated similar visits, all properly documented.

A few minutes later the well-dressed businessman walked out of Terminal E into the bright afternoon sun and disappeared into a waiting limo. The vehicle headed north and merged onto the John W. Carpenter freeway. They skirted east around DFW toward the small fixed base operators, located on the far side of the airport.

A Cessna Citation CJ3 business jet sat on the ramp with its outboard engine running. The pilots had been notified their passenger was on the way and were in the process of receiving departure clearance while the flight attendant—not at all unusual when transporting "well-heeled" business executives—prepared a light meal consisting of roasted meats and slices of fresh fruit. As instructed, she had also prepared an Alfie carafe of hot tea.

The passenger was escorted to the waiting aircraft by the charter agent where he was warmly greeted by a smiling flight attendant who stowed his briefcase while he reclined in a plush leather seat. The tea was like nectar, as he sipped he gave thanks to *Allah* for getting him this far without complications. He was not a devout man. Not like the others. He trusted in good planning and loyal allies to see him through to a successful conclusion … But still, it could not hurt to utter an occasional prayer.

The bizjet's executive club-style seating allowed him to savor his meal in comfort while the aircrew received final clearance to Kansas City, Missouri.

~~~~~~~~

NCTC
Liberty Crossing
McLean, Virginia

It was an early spring snowstorm; the kind with wet floppy flakes the size of softballs battered to the ground by echoing thunder. A snowstorm that dumps a foot today and mostly melts by tomorrow. Hopefully.

Matt stared out at the slushy gray mess from the front passenger seat of the black Yukon. The vehicle and driver had been waiting at Andrews to bring Matt, Chase, and Butch Larson back to the NCTC.

They flew direct from *Iwo Jima* to D.C., over 1,100 nautical miles, in five and a half hours, no thanks to a stinking headwind. With a forecast of foul weather and increasing headwinds by the time they hit the Carolinas, Matt had requested an in-flight refueling just as they went feet dry over the gulf coast.

Matt was pensive; his thoughts drifted uncontrollably to Edinburg, home, family … and the ever present possibility that Ahmad Hassam was headed there—

Heck! He could already be there, wrecking havoc on everyone I love. He shivered and hugged his arms to his chest as if suddenly aware of the cold.

Matt again chided himself for allowing things to get this far. He should have nailed Hassam's hide to the wall during their first encounter. He promised he would not make that mistake again … and prayed he would not be too late. *Please God!*

Slick streets and rush hour traffic delayed their arrival to NCTC, but by late afternoon Nadine Hollingsworth escorted the three men downstairs to the ops center.

Carter Manning was standing by the large glass wall when the door to the conference room opened. A thin smile tugged at the corners of his mouth when the three men entered. He nodded and motioned for them to observe the large screen located on the ops center floor.

Surveillance footage from DFW, Terminal E, followed a man matching Hassam's last-known description *into* the jetway at gate 12. The final frame froze and zoomed in. Matt stared at the life-size image; his anger rose at the sight of the master terrorist. At the same time a wave of relief flooded through him. Hassam apparently was not headed for Edinburg. At least not yet.

Manning put a hand on Matt's shoulder. "Hassam boarded a flight into La Guardia; due to arrive in," he glanced at the wall clock on the operations floor, "twelve minutes."

"You guys are just in time to see the takedown." Manning beamed as the display on the large screen switched to a real time surveillance feed from the Delta arrival gate inside La Guardia International Airport in New York. At least fifty people were gathered close to the gate waiting on the next flight. "The crowd is staged. About half of them are FBI agents."

In the background communication snippets could be heard over the FBI tactical channel as the agents anxiously awaited the arrival of the most wanted terrorist on the Watch List. Most of them could not believe their good fortune to have been chosen for such a high profile assignment.

"Colonel, welcome aboard." Manning turned and offered Larson a hand. "I'm sure Matt has already made it clear that you and your people have been inducted into the newly constituted Crisis Response Team."

"He hinted something like that," Larson growled.

"We'll get you outfitted with some non-military tactical gear later. In the meantime here, catch." Manning flipped a cred pack to the big Marine, and turned back to the screen. The credentials identified Larson as a special agent for the federal government. "Even after we capture Hassam there's still quite a network of operatives roaming around that need neutralized. That's where you guys come in." Manning smiled.

"How many?" Chase asked.

"Won't know that until … Hold on, here we go."

Delta attendants opened the door to the jetway, in a few seconds a line of travelers poured through the opening. On cue, the FBI agents allowed the "citizens" waiting to board to push forward as a distraction for Hassam. He would not know they were agents until he was surrounded and then it would be too late for him to make a break for it, or pull a weapon and take a hostage.

"Get ready, here we go!"

"Roger that!

"Team one, move in closer!"

"Keep it tight! Keep it tight!"

The target was near the end of the line. It seemed like an eternity before his image emerged from the jetway into the brightly lit room, head down, attempting to look inconspicuous as he moved within the crowd.

"There he is!"

"See him!"

Two agents pounced on the terrorist before he cleared the rope barrier. In the scuffle his head turned toward the ceiling-mounted camera and in that split second Matt knew. *That's not Hassam!* He felt a sinking feeling in the pit of his stomach. Hopelessness and desperation began to override logic. His knees went weak, his breathing increased. *That jackass stayed in Texas.* Matt sagged into a chair. The other men turned toward him.

"It ain't him," Matt responded hoarsely to their astonished looks. He felt sick to his stomach.

"What do you mean, *it ain't him?*" Chase pleaded.

"That's not Hassam. Imposter. He gave us the slip, again!"

"No *freaking* way," Larson said, pushing closer to the glass for a better look.

Manning silently turned back to the screen. He had learned to trust Matt's instincts. After all, Matthew McWain was the only person to ever go head-to-head with Ahmad Hassam and live to tell about it. He stared at the dark eyes glaring up at the camera with a blaze of defiance. The man wore a smirk on his twisted face. The FBI agents surrounding the terrorist were now shaking their heads.

In minutes the truth was realized by everyone. Ahmad Hassam was at large inside the United States

Twenty-Four

Carter Manning leaned back in his chair and exhaled a heavy sigh. He ran a hand over his chin stubble, then vigorously rubbed his tired eyes with both hands. His gaze shifted from Matt to Larson and then Chase. They were feeling the pressure as they tried to get a grip on the question handed to them by President Downs: "How on earth have you let a radical terrorist get into the United States, especially when you knew he was coming?"

The uncomfortable videoconference ended, the screen went dark, and no one ventured to speak. The president was frustrated. The disappointment in his voice was unmistakable. Matt stood, poured a glass of water from a pitcher on the table, and moved back to the glass wall. He stared down at the frantic activity on the floor below before taking a sip of water. He then turned back to the group.

"It would sure help if we knew where they plan to strike. Hassam's an egotistical maniac, so he's not gonna be very far from the action." Matt fell back in his chair, discouraged and exhausted.

"We'll have that intel soon, Matt," Manning replied. "Every intelligence agency at our command is fully committed, and the team working under AJ is one of the best. You gave her a lot of material. I suspect the answers will be in there somewhere."

"Anything on that Mexican drug cartel connection?" Chase asked.

Manning shrugged. "We know Manuel Cortez is one of Arellano's suppliers. We think Hassam's connection with Louis Arellano dates back to when Cortez got sucked into the Iranian cesspool. Looks as if Hassam was working both ends. Eventually, when he discovered Arellano was the deep pockets for Manuel's operation, he dealt Manuel out of the picture."

"Honor among thieves and all that stuff!" Larson huffed.

"Exactly. Unfortunately, we do not have assets inside—"

"*Hold up boss!*" Ben Houser, deputy ops center manager, sounded excited when he called from the floor. All four men jumped to their feet and raced to the glass wall. The manager was pointing toward the large screen where grainy surveillance footage from DFW depicted a well-dressed younger man coming out of the same restroom used by Hassam. The manager's voice came over the intercom, saying that facial recognition software gave an 88 percent match to Ahmad Hassam.

When the man on the surveillance tape reached the customs desk the ops center deputy tapped a key on his computer. An insert window on the lower right of the screen showed the open page of the passport in the custom agent's hands.

"... Rafael Juan Carlos Dominguez, oil man. Here on business. Told customs he would be in Dallas for two weeks ... Now watch this!" The ops deputy expanded the screen and they followed the footage as Hassam walked outside to a limo waiting curbside. The airport terminal camera lost the limo as it pulled away, but a street intersection camera picked it up again as it sped onto the freeway looping around to the backside of the airport. Tapping into several more surveillance cameras, they tracked the limo to an FBO located on the east side of the airport.

"FBI says Dominguez boarded a small business jet. The flight plan destination was Kansas City, Missouri." The deputy referred to his computer notes. *"The flight arrived in KC at five-twenty this afternoon. The FBO at Jet Center said the passenger had a limo waiting."*

"Surveillance cameras pick up the limo or get a license plate?" Manning demanded. The excitement in the room was palpable.

"Negative, sir. Camera in the parking lot was not working."

"Wasn't that convenient," Matt said sarcastically. Chase and Larson nodded agreement.

"Ben, see if we can get surveillance footage from cameras around KCI," Manning said. "Hassam might have done the same quick-change stunt he pulled at DFW. Might still be on the airport—"

"Or departed on another airplane," Matt finished Manning's thought. "Are there other general aviation FBOs located at KCI?

"On it, sir!"

Manning led them back to the conference table where they slumped into their chairs. Fatigue was setting in, but even so, Matt felt better now that the threat of Hassam going to Edinburg appeared to no longer be imminent. At least for now.

"So, this was another diversion," Matt said, thinking out loud. "Hassam wanted us to concentrate our attention on the east coast, while he jets off to the middle of the country."

"Could be yet *another* diversion, though," Chase picked up the line of thought. "Might be somewhere else by now."

"You can almost bet on that," Larson said. "We need more pieces to the puzzle."

Everyone nodded agreement.

"This just shows that we have to preposition our strike teams throughout the country," Manning jumped in. "We need to be ready to clobber these guys the moment they raise their heads, no matter where they strike."

"We don't have enough assets for that; besides, with Hassam already in-country, do you really think we have that kind of time?" Larson asked with a look of doubt.

"Couple days, probably. But I'm not talking about taking that long. We have an air force C-5A and a pair of C-17's on standby at Andrews. They can move a lot of stuff across the country in a matter of hours ... Matt, our two other crisis response teams are at your command. We can have them packed and ready to fly in a few hours."

Manning paused, his gaze shifted from face to face. "We have two FBI Hostage Rescue Teams available. They can deploy immediately to D.C. or New York, or any location on the east coast for that matter. We just need to determine staging areas for each of our assets."

Matt nodded, "So, if we scatter our assets and get some timely intel on where Hassam's gonna attack, we could feasibly have a team close enough to strike."

"Exactly—"

"And if there are multiple target locations," Chase interrupted, "we would theoretically have assets nearby."

"That's the theory," Manning responded.

"Well then, I'd keep them fairly hidden. Stage on military bases. One on each coast, north and south border, couple in the middle. Keep it simple," Larson offered. "Identify military installations in each of those regions and move the teams in."

"I agree with Butch," Matt said. "What are the chances of getting a couple SEAL teams? Put one in Southern California and another on the gulf coast; we put the CRTs in the Pacific Northwest and Northeastern seaboard; cover D.C. and New York with HRTs."

"One call to the White House could make that happen," Manning answered.

"Alright then, sounds like we got a preliminary plan until we hear somethin' back from the analysts." Matt looked at the others. "Our team will take the central U.S."

"What's this, a gut feeling?" Manning eyed Matt suspiciously.

"Maybe. Last place he was seen." Matt felt the hair standing up on the back of his neck. *Maybe Hassam left Kansas City ... and maybe he didn't.*

Manning shook his head. "I would really prefer you stay here, Matt. I need you to coordinate team movement when the intel comes in."

"I can do that from the field, Carter. That's why we got all that expensive comm gear, ain't it?" Matt grinned. "Besides, I'm only an airplane ride away."

Manning shrugged. He knew it would do no good to argue. "Alright, agreed." He caught Chase yawning and glanced at his watch. "You guys need some rest. Let's meet back here at 0600 tomorrow. We'll put a fine point on the plan, work up some military installations for staging assignments. By mid-afternoon we should have everything in motion."

"Let's do it now," Matt corrected. "At daylight Dark Horse One will be wheels up for Whiteman Air Force Base, Knob Noster, Missouri."

Manning shook his head and then grinned. "Okay, we can do that. I've assigned an FBI liaison to be on your team. Someone to pave the way for you with other federal and local agencies."

"Get her over here now. Times a wastin'!"

Manning paused for a second, his eyes fixed on Matt. He was dumbfounded. "You know who the agent is?"

"Yeah, AJ told me before we left *Iwo,*" Matt answered.

"Why is it my staff knows everything I do, before I do it?"

They all laughed.

Thirty minutes later there was a single rap on the door. Nadine Hollingsworth entered carrying a tray of sandwiches. The stunning FBI liaison followed close behind with a fresh pot of coffee.

The men jumped to their feet.

Chase leaned close to Matt and mumbled under his breath, "I think I'm in love!"

"You're always in love," Matt whispered.

"No, this time it's for real—"

"Gentlemen," Manning began, "I want you to meet Special Agent Georgia Shayne, FBI."

The woman smiled and greeted each of them with a firm handshake.

Matt guessed Georgia Shayne to be in her mid-thirties, five feet five, slender, and had the same bounce and athletic grace as AJ. She wore her shoulder length, straight blond hair swept behind her ears, revealing two simple diamond studs. There were no rings on her fingers. Her dark brown eyes were clear and alert, her full lips were covered with a neutral lip gloss. Her mouth turned up at the corners and Matt liked the way her freckle-covered nose wrinkled when she smiled. It was a sensuous, engaging smile. He guessed she had a good sense of humor.

She was wearing black denim pants and black sneakers. A green silk blouse accented her blond hair and deep tan. A black lanyard hanging from her neck held her cred pack, which included a security clearance that would gain admission to almost every government facility.

Manning continued. "As I mentioned before, Agent Shayne will be your liaison to all federal, state, and local law enforcement agencies.

"Something especially noteworthy about this young lady. She's the agent who last week discovered a shipping crate containing a dozen suicide vests."

"Where was this?" Matt asked with raised eyebrows.

Georgia turned to face him and spoke in clipped sentences. Her smile was gone.

"Suburb outside Dearborn. It was before the Bureau had received the notice for heightened alert. Following up on a tip on suspicious activity. House owned by a local Islamic cleric. Only one occupant home at the time. He bolted out the back and got away. We tossed the place. Crate was stuffed in the corner of the garage, pretty well hidden."

"Interesting thing about it," Manning jumped in. "The vests were identical to the ones you guys confiscated two nights ago in Puerto Santos. Four blocks of Semtex, 500 ceramic ball bearings the size of double-aught buck. Same remote triggering device. Same booby trap if you tried cutting it off the bomber."

Larson whistled. "That's enough explosives to take out half a city block."

"Or a big open-air event," Matt added.

"Difficult to detect by most security metal detectors," Georgia volunteered.

"Any follow up?" Matt asked, looking at the pretty FBI agent.

She nodded. "Still working on it when I got this change in assignment. The cleric claimed he rented the house to five men who were new to his mosque. He didn't have ID's, no previous addresses. Apparently they just fell off the turnip truck right in front of the mosque. We have him under tight surveillance, house too, of course. So far nothing."

"You are thinking another decoy, aren't you?" Manning asked when he saw the frown on Matt's face.

Matt shrugged. "Maybe, but what I'm really wondering is how many more vests could be out there."

"And all the different locations." Larson added in a low voice.

The sobering possibilities brought silence.

Manning broke the hushed moment. "Special Agent Shayne, we brought you in to help with some strategic planning. Everyone take a seat and grab a sandwich. Gonna be a long night."

Twenty-Five

AJ stared blankly at the computer screen. It was a quarter past two a.m. She had been on the go with only four hours of sleep in the past fifty-six hours. Her eyes burned and felt as if someone had thrown a fistful of salt in her face. She had trouble focusing on words and symbols on the screen. She slouched in her chair, head bobbing, staring at the same paragraph for nearly half an hour. Everything was a blurred mess.

She remembered going to late dinner several hours ago with the rest of her team, even vaguely recalled hearing the ship had been diverted to New Orleans, though she could not remember why. After the meal, she sent her team off to get some much needed sleep and promised she would do likewise after viewing "one more file."

The file she had been working on was from the terrorist training camp in Venezuela. This one was the most informative thus far and she found herself pulled to it from the opening page. It read like some kind of hyperbole proclamation, a manifest destiny. A motivational guide for Hassam's followers, but hinted on strategies becoming more evident with each scrolling page. Nothing substantial, yet, but it was leading toward … *What*?

She yawned and told herself just one more page and then she would head off to bed. *Just one more—Whoa! What the heck!*

AJ bolted upright. Burning eyes, tired and aching muscles, all forgotten in that one astonishing moment. Adrenalin coursed through her body like a wave. Instantly, she was wide awake.

Sprinkled about within the rhetoric and bravado, the file contained snippets of details. She slowed her reading, paused, went back two pages, and began scrolling again. Attack scenarios came alive in her head as they played across the screen.

A few pages later she was aware her mouth had dropped open in horror. Her heart pumped faster and her breathing increased, she bit off her last remaining manicured fingernail. *What brazen arrogance. What unbelievable ruthlessness and brutal disregard for human life.* Her arms were clutched tight against her chest. She was surprised to find herself trembling.

Whoever wrote this is worse than a rabid animal, she thought. She unclenched her fists, reached for the phone and called the ship's communications center.

"Get me a secure line to the National Counterterrorism Center, please." She glanced at her watch. It would be half past four a.m. in Virginia.

"*Duty officer*!" An alert voice came on the line.

"This is AJ. I need Carter."

"He left the building several hours ago."

"Get him on a secure line, now! This is urgent."

Ten minutes later AJ was calling *Iwo Jima*'s bridge. The moment the executive officer picked up the phone, he heard the urgency in her voice. "XO, in a few minutes you will receive an order to fly me back to Andrews, quickest means possible. How soon can I expect to leave?"

"Soon as the captain receives the order and authorizes it, we'll have an AV-8B Harrier II on the flight deck ready to go in ten to fifteen minutes."

~~~~~~~~~

The Farm
15 Miles North of
Mexico, Missouri

Hassam slowly paced the floor, his hands clasped behind his back. The old wooden floor creaked under each step. His people had done a good job refurbishing the eighty-year-old farmhouse. Even the musty odor common in ancient wood frame houses in the Midwest was hardly noticeable. The exterior of the home was right out of Norman Rockwell. The white paint with green shutters and fascia board was peeling, rain gutters rusted and hanging down. Ivy climbed one end of the house, reaching to the top of a crumbling brick chimney. Boards on the rickety front porch were loose, the railing broken and decayed. There were a pair of wooden rockers on either side of the porch; one was occupied by an alert Islamic warrior with an AK-47 resting in his lap.

The interior of the farmhouse was a different matter. The peeling, yellowed wallpaper had been replaced with a fresh coat of paint; the wood floors had been sanded, resealed, and varnished.

The ground floor bedroom at the back of the house had been expanded to accommodate four computer workstations. Two large screen monitors hung on the wall and the windows were blacked out. Low intensity lighting gave a soft glow to the busy room and provided the operators with a clear view of their screens. A weather-proof box attached to the exterior wall of the control room contained a bundle of black cables, which snaked across the backyard to an old ramshackle barn 100 feet from the house.

An essential improvement was the installation of central air conditioning. The farmhouse had been built long before effective insulation had been invented. Winters in central Missouri could be brutal and coping with summer heat and humidity was even worse. The addition of central air had been a welcome relief for the workforce and essential to maintaining a climate-controlled environment for the control room. The additional electrical load necessitated rewiring the entire house, which also provided for high-speed connection and data streaming. No doubt the increased power load raised some eyebrows for officials at the local power company.

At first, local residents wondered who bought the four hundred acre Tucker farm. Only a handful of locals had actually seen the new owners and those that had said the dark hair, olive skin foreigners surely did not look like farmers, but then the land had not been farmed in many years. Grandchildren of the late George Tucker wanted nothing to do with the old homestead.

After two years, the locals had mostly forgotten about the people living on the old Tucker farm. The farmhouse was located a mile off the paved county road. Trees and undergrowth had all but taken over the unused land and no one ever ventured down the gravel road leading to the house. Most people knew the Gargus brothers had taken up residence with the new owners, and no one wanted anything to do with the three anti-government skinhead radicals.

A couple of times a week, one or two Gargus boys would come into town, pick up mail at the post office, shop for groceries, and quietly disappear back to the farm. Occasionally though, the foreigners would venture into town in pairs. Seeing them on the street people would smile, maybe wave. Most people had generally mistaken the foreigners for Hispanics. And since they did not smile or wave back it was easier to ignore them.

Oddly enough, since no more than two of the foreigners had been seen at any given time, no one knew how many actually lived at the farm. No one paid much attention when a vehicle sped down the county road and turned off on the old Tucker farm road—not even the unusual number of vehicles coming and going at night.

Hassam stood behind the four technicians, impressed and intrigued with their work and the rapid clacking on the keyboards. Hakeem Larijani, standing beside him, relaxed when he saw a very rare grin tugging at the corners of his leader's mouth. Ali, the silent giant, stood in the far corner.

"Very well done, Rashad," Hassam said, rocking up on the balls of his feet, hands still locked behind his back. He was speaking to the young man standing at his other side.

"Thank you, *as-Syf.* I am honored by your trust." Rashad Hussain was an ambitious twenty-seven year old wisp of a man, barely five feet four, and weighed little more than a hundred pounds. But what the diminutive man lacked in physical presence, he more than made up for in brilliance.

Hussain graduated with honors from Isfahan University of Technology, Isfahan, Iran, with a number of postgraduate degrees in computer sciences, including a doctorate in computer engineering. Ironically, Hussain's doctorate thesis involved the application of coordinated cyber warfare against military hardware, enemy infrastructure, and soft targets. The subsequent notoriety eventually brought him face-to-face with Major General Imad Abu Mughniyeh of the Iranian Revolutionary Guard.

One week following the completion of his doctoral studies, Rashad Hussain found himself sequestered in an office far more elegant than he could ever imagine, receiving a generous salary beyond his wildest dreams, and given unlimited access and authority over the brightest minds in technology. He was being groomed to be at the forefront of an event of historical proportion. It was heady stuff for such a young man.

Within a year, Hussain was attending meetings far above political and strategic planning levels. It was a bit overwhelming, but at the same time unimaginably exciting, and challenging. He was at the center of power and it was intoxicating. There was nothing he would not do for the General, or for the cause.

Three years ago, General Mughniyeh brought Rashad into the inner circle of *Mylh-A'sifh— Operation Firestorm*. Soon after that, he was one of the first Firestorm Warriors to be smuggled into the United States.

One of the files on the hard drive of the super computer, which Hussain had built himself, contained a short list of locations available for establishing the combination headquarters and control center. He was charged with choosing the best site, based upon criteria, which he himself developed. Once his selection was made, another follower within their expanding network would purchase the property. He would then provide the needed materials and supplies, per Hussain's order. The computer guru was in command until otherwise informed.

Rashad Hussain had full knowledge of all aspects of the operation, and certainly the expectations his superiors had for him. He knew from the onset that he was to be relieved of being in command of *The Farm* and would go back to being the computer genius who had actually designed the myriad elements of *Firestorm*. He had been looking forward to this day, yearned for it. His pride dictated that the facility was prepared, that it would greatly exceed the expectations of *as-Syf*. More importantly, every step, every nuance of the operation would be ready for Hassam to take command.

Today was that day. And when Ahmad Hassam said, "Very well done," Hussain's chest swelled with pride, his eyes watered.

Hassam turned to the computer genius, "Are we on schedule to begin the operation"

"Yes, *'yâ qâd*, my leader." Hussain smiled, stealing a glance at the large digital countdown-clock located on his desk next to the computer screen. Hassam's eyes followed the gesture. "The first attack of phase-one will begin in twenty-eight hours, thirty-two minutes. Activation messages are preloaded and automatic. Only you can stop the sequence, *as-Syf.*"

Hassam walked slowly between the workstations, staring each of Hussain's trusted technicians in the eyes. He came back to the doorway, his hands still clasped behind his back. His grin widened. "Very good."

"*Allahu Akbar*!" Hussain shouted.

"*Allahu Akbar*!" Repeated Larijani.

"Yes, indeed he is," Hassam uttered under his breath.

Inside the spacious kitchen was a long, scarred table made of solid oak, evidence that a very large family once lived under this old roof. Spread across the table was a tattered map of the United States. The map had been prepared by Hussain as a visual display for planning purposes.

The map highlighted cities and other locations that would be attacked and the chronology for each event. Listed next to the dates and times were designated teams and team leaders assigned to the particular event. Each leader was given a code name, essential for maintaining contact through social media and satellite communications.

Hassam spread his hands wide on the edge of the table and leaned in, staring down at the map. He marveled over the magnificent detail provided by his young assistant. The cunning brilliance, the flawlessness, was beyond imagination. Best of all, it was virtually unstoppable. Within two days the American public would be cowering inside their opulent houses. Afraid to come out and face their conqueror. He closed his eyes and drew in a deep breath, then exhaled slowly. His long awaited moment was within reach.

Larijani stood across the table. He waited for Hassam to take in the full appreciation of what he was seeing; to know they were on the precipice of changing the world. When he sensed that his great mentor had fully absorbed the document he said, "Our warriors are ready, Ahmad. They stand beside the great patriots who have lived here for many years, patiently awaiting this day."

Hassam nodded as Larijani continued, "You have trained our men well. They have been preparing for this moment and are fully capable of executing it fully.

"And while our fighters initiate the first crippling blows, the *shaheed* will take to the streets across this land of infidels. Blood will flow in the gutters. Confusion and chaos will rule!" Larijani's chest puffed out with pride. He was practically laughing, but then quickly noticed a look of distaste on the face of his leader.

Hassam trained warriors. He led warriors into battle to be victorious and to live to fight another day, and another. His men would gladly give their lives for the cause if need be, but they were not mindless robots who blindly walked into a crowd and blew themselves into a thousand pieces.

Yes, the *shaheed* suicide bombers served their purpose by striking terror in the hearts and minds of their victims—and that would surely be the case here in the land of the Great Satan. But Hassam had no use for them in his army. He was here to lead a coordinated attack on the United States, with men he knew and trusted to fight, day after day until they had beaten the infidels into submission. As far as he was concerned, the suicide bombers merely provided a savage diversion.

"Come, Ahmad, let me show you a great surprise." Larijani led Hassam outside and across the backyard to the barn. Ali followed dutifully a few steps behind, ever the faithful bodyguard.

Gray, weathered boards left the old decrepit barn in a state of disrepair, leaning to one side as if it might fall over in a strong puff of wind. But inside sat a shiny brand new motorhome. Heavy black cables led from the large vehicle, out through the barn window, to the rear of the farmhouse. More cables fell from the barn ceiling and disappeared inside the motorhome.

"What is this?" Hassam's eyes roamed over the large vehicle.

"This is our mobile control center," Larijani beamed. "Rashad says it will be only a matter of a week or two before the infidels discover our location here. But they will not find us while we are on the move."

Twenty-Six

Whiteman Air Force Base
Knob Noster,
Missouri

The VIP guest quarters at Whiteman AFB were more than adequate. Especially for Matt's planned short stay. The small, duplex style bungalows were designed with a single bedroom, kitchen/dining area, and tiny living room. Whiteman was home of the 509th Bomb Wing. Because of the Wing's strategic mission with the B-2 Stealth bomber, it was common for the base to receive dignitaries. Carter Manning did well to snag comfortable accommodations on short notice.

Chase shared the opposite end of the duplex with Matt. Rather than provide drivers for the group, each bungalow was assigned an electric golf cart to move back and forth to the mess hall and flight ops. To go into town they merely called the duty officer and requested transportation.

Matt dropped his travel bag on the twin bed, went to the bathroom to splash water on his face, and headed out the door to meet the others for lunch at the officer's mess.

Chase was waiting out front, seated behind the wheel of the golf cart, ready to go.

Matt stopped to drink in the cloudless, bright, brisk and windy late morning before zipping his blue flight jacket and climbing into the cart.

"C'mon, Cuz! If we hurry we can beat those jarheads to the chow line before they clean it out."

Matt shuddered at an image of a half dozen golf carts racing down the path like a destruction derby, he chuckled.

"What's so funny?" Chase asked.

"You, speedball! Let's boogey!" Matt pushed back in the seat and held on tight.

Chase leaned over the wheel, gripped it with both hands, stared straight ahead, and punched the pedal to the floor. He took the first turn in the narrow path a little too fast, cranked hard on the wheel, careening the little cart up on two wheels. When the cart bounced back onto all four, Matt noticed Chase rub his arm and wince in pain.

"Arm botherin' you, hot rod?"

"Yeah, a little. Think I need me a Purple Heart."

"I'll give you a Purple Heart," Matt growled.

"Aw, c'mon, man. You already forgettin' I saved your life?" Chase's green eyes twinkled.

"Nah, I didn't forget," Matt smiled. "I'll give you credit for that one.'

"Good! I'll pass on the Purple Heart for a *grand* introduction to Georgia Shayne. And I mean an OUTSTANDING intro, not that little cheapy you threw out there in Manning's office." Chase waved his arms, roaring with laughter.

"We'll see." Matt's face turned serious as he looked over at his cousin. "Chase, I think it would be a good idea for you to go home."

"Home?" Chase shouted. "Well you can think again, Cuz! Why on earth should I go back home? The job's not done and I ain't leavin' 'til it is."

"Chase, I'm not trying to run you off and I'm not trying to keep you from fightin' the terrorists." Matt paused, bit his lip, then continued, "I'm worried about our family. I want you there to protect them."

"I understand that, Matt." Chase nodded and lowered his voice. "I'm gettin' a little concerned too, but I think it's way too early in the game for that raghead to take aim on us personally. I'm thinkin' he's pretty well consumed with whatever this *Firestorm* thing is about. He's busy gettin' that kicked off."

Chased pulled to a stop in front of the officer's mess next to two white golf carts. Two more came racing up from behind. Shouts and laughter sounded like a gang of teenagers as they banged against one another in a dead heat to reach the chow hall.

"Crazing dang fools! Gonna kill each other before we even face the enemy."

"Yeah," Matt agreed.

Chase saw the weight of worry in Matt's visage. He knew it was the threat of an attack on their family and home. "Tell you what, Matt. Let's give it a few days; see what Hassam does. Get an idea what we're up against. If we don't kill the pissant, or it looks like he's gonna make a move south, then I'll gladly head home with a case of ammo. Deal?"

Matt climbed out of the cart and started for the front door. "Yeah, sure. You're probably right. Just somethin' nigglin' the back of my head. Feels like we're forgettin' something. Know what I mean?"

"Yup! Been there before. Maybe we should let Uncle Billy know what's goin' on. Have him keep an eye out."

"Good idea," Matt replied. He put an arm on Chase's shoulder as they entered the officer's mess. "I'll give him a call."

Four Watchdog members piled through the door behind them.

~~~~~~~

They had just finished lunch when an attractive air force sergeant with long blond hair and large breasts delivered an urgent request for Matt to contact Carter Manning. The sergeant's uniform skirt was stretched tight against her backside as she walked away.

Chase muttered under his breath, "Omigosh! I'm in love." Matt could not keep from laughing.

The sergeant had offered the use of a conference room at Base Intelligence where she worked. When they arrived they found the windowless, interior room prepared and waiting. Six comfortable leather chairs surrounded a large oak table at one end of the room. A laptop, along with a half dozen chilled bottles of water, sat on the table. Matt, Georgia, Chase, and Butch Larson made themselves comfortable. The rest of Watchdog Team was taking a 20-mile run/walk excursion of the air base with a full combat load.

Light oak paneled walls were adorned with aerial photos of the B-2 Stealth bomber. Opposite the conference table hung a large monitor. At the bottom of the softly lit blue screen was the 509th's emblem and the words, *Stand By!* The only sound was the quiet hum of the A/C.

"Why here?" Georgia Shayne asked.

"What do you mean?" Matt thought the question odd.

"Why this particular place? Here in the middle of nowhere. There isn't a major city within—"

Matt interrupted her. "Because this is where we last saw him—near here, where he disappeared."

"He didn't disappear!" Everyone turned to the screen at the sound of the voice. Matt quickly recognized the deputy duty officer at NCTC. Behind the man with the rumpled white shirt and loosened necktie was the familiar bank of computers and large display screens. "At least not entirely," the DDO quickly corrected himself.

"Surveillance cameras picked up Hassam entering the GA terminal at KCI. An hour later a twin-engine prop job taxied to the front of the terminal and Hassam reportedly boarded. The aircraft is owned and operated by Central Missouri Air Charter, based out of Midwest National." The face on the screen was replaced by a photo of a red, white, and blue Piper Aztec. The charter company's name and CMAC logo were painted on the tail.

Chase grinned at Matt. They were familiar with the Aztec. The cousins flew one similar for a summer between college semesters for an air-taxi charter operation near San Antonio. It was a flying truck. The models with upgraded engines could fly anything off the ground that would not fall through the floor, but it was old and slow. It made them eager to get into something "sexier" and a whole lot faster.

"Air traffic control tracked the aircraft out of KCI. A VFR flight with no flight plan. The aircraft dropped off radar approximately 85 nautical miles east of KCI. The FAA is forwarding the audio tapes for the flight. I'll shoot a copy to you."

"Matt, we just got off the phone with the operations manager at CMAC." Carter Manning spoke from the conference room. The screen split in half for videoconference mode, displaying the NCTC conference room alongside the ops center. Matt was pleasantly surprised to see AJ seated next to their boss.

Carter continued in an emotionless monotone. "He said the client chartered the flight to St. Louis. Paid cash, including three days standby. I noted concern in his voice when he told me they had not heard from the pilot since yesterday."

"We're in the process of calling all airports in the St. Louis area to locate the aircraft," the DDO added.

Matt nodded, "You may need to expand that call list, in case he's changed his itinerary."

"That's our plan. Either way, we *will* locate that Aztec!"

"What are your thoughts, Matt?" Manning asked.

"I'm thinkin' we're gonna find Hassam settled into a single control location. A command and control bunker, if you will. I'm betting it ain't very far away." Matt glanced at the faces around him and then continued. "From what little I saw of the intel AJ collected out on *Iwo* indicates Hassam has multiple targets. He can't be at every location to command each operation, so it makes sense that he would direct from a single control point. What better place than somewhere close to the center of it all?"

"I think you nailed it, Matt," AJ jumped in. Her smile seemed to light up the screen. "Hassam has a very aggressive agenda. The idea of a centralized command for coordination is right on."

For the next ten minutes AJ shared pieces of intel, clearly indicating a frightening picture of what they could expect.

"So these sleeper agents scattered across the entire country have been here for years?" Chase asked incredulously.

"That is correct, Chase," AJ responded. He let out a soft whistle and moved to the edge of his chair as she continued her briefing. "We have a partial trail on a few of the tangos smuggled into the country over the past couple years. It's sketchy, but it looks like they may have migrated to the same cities as the sleepers."

"Any of those include where we are, AJ?" Matt asked.

"Absolutely Matt! There are numerous references to the 'foundational land of lies' in the captured files. We believe that could mean a reference to the traditional Bible Belt. The Heartland of America that forged our nation's foundation on Godly principles. The backbone of our faith and belief structure remains in large part from the farming and ranching communities across the plains states and the Mississippi and Tennessee Valleys.

"Attacks against government and financial symbols could merely be diversions to keep us focused away from their real target, the soft underbelly of America. Think of it: attacking people during their time of leisure, playing, worshipping, day-to-day routine. Think of the panic and terror—But there is something more in this, guys. Something much more sinister. Don't know what it is, but we have everyone working to figure it out.

"Bottom line, Matt, you need to stop this scum bucket fast."

"Yeah, I'm gettin' the picture." Matt said softly. *"Something much more sinister,"* he mused. *She said that with a troubled voice.*

"AJ, have you been able to tie any of the intel back to the discovery in Michigan?" Georgia queried.

"You bet, Georgi! It all ties together. I will send a complete packet so you guys can integrate it into your game plan. Of course updates will be shipped to you as soon as we can—"

"Carter, AJ? This much activity will generate a ton of communications traffic, no matter where Hassam's parked his control site," Matt stated.

"Already on it, Matt," Manning replied. "NSA, NRO, DIA, every intelligence asset we have is plugged into eavesdropping so tightly the ACLU will be screaming like a Banshee. Problem is, we're talking a massive amount of data that could take hours, if not days, to ferret through. Our top analysts are working on algorithms and trigger words that will cut through the stream of useless data."

"One other thing, AJ. Security on Carley Downs?" Matt suspected Hassam's thirst for revenge went beyond the Cortez family, and probably his own family. The master terrorist lost a prize catch in Carley Downs. Didn't take much imagination to consider he could be going after her at some point.

"Doubled, and doubled again, Matt," AJ answered. "The entire senior staff at University of Arizona Hospital has been alerted as well."

The secure video link continued another few minutes before finally winding down. When the screen went blank, Matt felt exhausted. He grabbed one of the water bottles and leaned back in his chair. The list of things needing to be done seemed overwhelming, but where do you start? *Please Lord Jesus, help us to find this maniac before innocent people are killed.*

"So, your friends call you Georgi, huh?" Matt grinned.

She nodded with a smile,

"Where did you and AJ meet?"

"We've done some classes together through the years," she responded.

"You Harvard law too?" Matt knew AJ went to Harvard.

"No, nothing so prestigious." Georgia answered with a laugh. "AJ's in my martial arts class. We also share an apartment in Georgetown."

"Wow! Impressive. You teach martial arts?"

"Yep!" Georgia glanced at Chase and then back to Matt. "AJ tells me you guys went to Texas A&M? Aggies?"

Matt nodded cautiously. He cringed at what was coming next.

"Tell me something. I've been curious if it's true about the Aggie who got locked out of his car and took two hours to get his wife and kids out?"

The cousins groaned. Chase said, "And to think, I was this close to asking you to be my girl."

Larson and Georgia laughed.

Twenty-Seven

Whiteman Air Force Base
Knob Noster,
Missouri

Matt paced back and forth inside the operations room, stopping occasionally to stare through Venetian blinds at aircraft moving on the flight line. It was four hours with no contact since the videoconference with AJ and Manning. He suspected the folks back east were busier than the proverbial one-armed paperhanger. He did not want to bother them needlessly, but Matt was a man of action and idle time usually made him restless.

He was grateful the base commander had made the ops room available. Every communications and intelligence asset they would need was in the room; plus there was ample seating to bring the entire team together for pre-deployment briefing when the time came. Best of all, there were windows and good lighting. The intelligence office provided earlier felt more like a prison cell.

Matt walked over to the large ice chest brought in by a young airman and pulled out a cold dripping bottle of water. It was his forth since they had taken over the facility. He turned back to the planning table. Butch Larson was studying aeronautical and topography charts while Georgia Shayne worked the keys on a laptop. They were killing time until AJ or Manning called with an update and it was driving Matt nuts. The team was at the hangar cleaning their weapons while Chase and Master Chief Roberts double checked all systems on the Osprey.

"You'll be sleeping in the bathtub tonight if you keep that up," Larson said with a grin.

Matt took a long pull on the bottle and said, "If my pipes don't rust first!"

Georgia glanced up from her computer and chuckled.

"Come here and check this out," Larson said. "If you count private strips there must be at least thirty airfields within a seventy-five mile radius of St. Louis. And I'm counting only those on the Missouri side of the river. At least that many in Illinois."

"But how many of those could land an Aztec?" Georgia asked.

Matt studied the chart for less than a minute. "All of 'em."

"No wonder we haven't heard anything yet."

Matt explained that the number of possible airports was only part of the problem. He knew from experience a large percentage of smaller airports were one-man FBO operations. He or she could be outside fueling an airplane and miss a phone call; they might be out flying, or in a hangar working on their aircraft. They would be doing whatever it takes to stay alive in the aviation world, not sitting around waiting for the phone to ring. Making contact with every airport on Larson's growing list could be measured in hours, perhaps even days. And Matt sensed they didn't have that kind of time.

Georgia looked up from her screen and sighed. "Well, the FBI data base for potential terrorists is equally daunting. Washington is prioritizing a list of possibilities, but even with that it will take weeks to check out each suspect. There simply isn't enough personnel to make it go any faster."

"Big country," Larson volunteered. "Easy to get lost when you want."

"Well, there has to be—" Matt's exasperated voice was interrupted by the secure private line provided by Base Operations. Matt leaned over the table and keyed the speaker phone.

"Hey guys, AJ here. Just checking in. No luck so far on locating the Piper Aztec. The big airports in St. Louis are checking their ramps, but haven't gotten back to us. We sent agents there to speed up the process. Many of the smaller airports aren't picking up." Larson and Georgia met Matt's eyes and gave him a nod.

"Yeah, we've been discussing that little problem. Sure would be nice to have some eyes in the sky out here," said Matt.

"We are working on that as we speak. Won't be much longer."

"Good. In the meantime, we'll pick up some of that load on our end."

"What do you have in mind, Matt?"

Matt paused and looked at the Aeronautical Sectional Chart on the table and said, "We'll take the airfields west of 91' 30" Longitude. Give us a list of contacts already made in that sector."

"Okay, you've got it."

"Anything more on intel analysis?" Georgia asked.

"Yes, two things I need to pass on," AJ responded. "Remember the phrase, *The Farm?* We talked about that from the files you brought back from Santo Tomás, Matt. Well, there are several more references in the files collected by the SEALS. At first we considered it to be referring to the CIA training facility in Virginia as a target."

"Not a viable target, in the scheme of things," Larson offered.

"Exactly," AJ responded. "We are leaning toward a literal designation for something important. Perhaps the location of Hassam's command and control headquarters."

"*The Farm!*" Matt audibly played the words through his mind. "A needle in a haystack when you think about it. There's a gazillion farms out here ."

"Yes, but when you factor everything we've decrypted thus far, it does make a plausible scenario."

"Hmmmmm," Matt rubbed his hand across the stubble on his chin. *The Farm! Almost too simple. Until you figure the thousands of square miles of farmland. And who says the hunt would be confined to just Missouri? Well, you gotta start somewhere!*

"You said two things, AJ?"

"NSA intercepted lengthy satellite communications from Venezuela to a site on the outskirts of Huntsville, Alabama, via the Russian RORSAT. FBI team is enroute, but we suspect this will be bogus. Most likely a remote relay site. I'll get back to you soon as NSA decrypts the message."

"Thanks for the update."

"Sure, you bet, Matt. By the way, we have three C-17's on the way to Whiteman. Lots of high-tech gear and support equipment, including a self-contained field hospital with a full surgical team."

"A field hospital?"

"People back here are taking this very serious, Matt. I'll be in touch." AJ hung up before anyone could ask more questions.

Larson looked up, "What did you mean, 'we will take the airports west of 91' 30"?'"

"I'm tired of waitin'. Let's go make things happen. Assuming the base flying club will loan us an airplane large enough to haul your lard butt off the ground, we're goin' flying."

"Dipwad!" Butch glared at Matt.

Georgia giggled.

"Georgi, when AJ sends that list, I want you to start callin' airports on our side of the line. Contact us on the comm-set when you verify each airport is clear … Monitor the FBI operation in Huntsville too, if you can."

~~~~~~~~

The Farm
15 Miles North
Mexico, Missouri

Hassam turned away from the large screen. Rage coursed through his veins. His fists clinched so tightly that the muscles in his forearms rippled all the way to his neck. His dark eyes narrowed, burning with ferocity, he trembled all over. Never had he wanted to kill someone, anyone, so badly.

The satellite download from Venezuela did not bring good news. One of his lieutenants stood in the foreground reporting on the surprise attack by suspected U.S. military, while behind him smoldering structures were all that remained. Six faithful warriors had been killed, another six severely wounded. The headquarters building had been ransacked and then torched, along with the barracks and several other buildings. The $6 million reserve stash had been taken, along with most of the computer gear.

Larijani stared at the screen, unbelieving at first, but then a smile tugged at his lips. "They are several steps behind, still."

Hassam whirled around, his face inches from Larijani, glaring down with a look of hatred. "YOU THINK THIS

IS A GOOD THING?" He shouted, pointing at the screen, his face a mask of rage. Spittle splattered the little man's face.

"Of course ... not ... *as-Syf,*" Larijani stuttered in a soft voice, taking a step back out of fear as he wiped his face with his shirtsleeve. "I am merely pointing out that we knew the infidels would track our movements. We planned for that to happen. Yet we knew we would always be several steps ahead of them, and this has come to pass." Larijani paused to study the reaction from his leader, then lowered his voice even more, "There is nothing they can do to stop us, Ahmad. You are only hours away from realizing your dream. A few hours from throwing the Great Satan into paralyzing fear and panic." Larijani relaxed when he saw the tension slowly drain away from Hassam's body. "This time tomorrow they will be cowering in their homes while roving bands of their own depraved citizens roam the streets looting and killing one another. *Praise Allah!* It will be glorious to watch."

Hassam stormed out of the control room, back through the house. His crimson face still rigid with fury, but his body seemed less tense. Larijani followed him to the large table and looked on quietly while his leader studied the master plan again. It was several tense minutes before Hassam spoke.

"One man is responsible for these attacks, Hakeem. The American infidel who took Carley Downs from us and destroyed our operation in Guatemala. *Twice!*"

Hassam slowly looked up from the table. "He still hunts us today. I can feel him. He is getting closer."

"We are well hidden here, Ahmad. There is nothing this man—or anyone else— can do to stop what is already in motion. The command code has been launched," Larijani smiled triumphantly.

But Hassam acted as if he was not interested in what Larijani had to say. "Did you get the information on the American infidel?"

"Yes, Ahmad." Larijani reached for another map on the counter behind him and spread it over the table. He pointed to an area in south Texas circled in red. "The man you seek is Matthew McWain from Edinburg, Texas. Here, near McAllen" He glanced at Hassam and smiled. "Quite interesting, his father is Travis McWain."

Hassam shrugged questioningly.

"Travis McWain is listed in *Forbes Fortune 100* wealthiest men in the world. Good friends with President Downs … and Samuel Cortez!"

Hassam's fiery eyes narrowed to slits, his face burned red, muscles in his neck bulged. "All the money in the world will not save this man, or his family."

"Later, *as-Syf.* There will be plenty of time to extract retribution from this infidel." Larijani knew he must keep his friend concentrated on the task at hand. "We must wait until the Great Satan is destroying itself from within."

"I will not wait long for my revenge!" Hassam bared his teeth in an evil sneer.

"I understand, my friend."

The one on the battlefield who reacts out of anger makes the first mistake. Is that not one of the lessons our mighty leader teaches his new recruits on their first day of training? Larijani knew he must somehow remind Hassam of his own words if he was going to keep him focused on jihad.

Twenty-Eight

Whiteman Air Force Base
Knob Noster,
Missouri

"Piper Seven-Zero-Eight-Niner-Papa, Whiteman approach, radar contact eleven miles east. You are cleared to enter left base for runway one-niner."

"Roger Whiteman, Eight-Niner-Papa left base, runway one-niner," Matt repeated back to approach control.

"Eight-Niner-Papa, contact tower, one-three-two-point-four. You are number four to land."

Matt acknowledged the directions as he scanned the sky ahead. The flight of three C-17 Globemaster heavy transports from Andrews had arrived. Two were in line ahead of him by several miles; the lead plane was turning on final approach. The gray, squat-shape airplanes were giants, capable of hauling large numbers of troops and material anyplace in the world. FEMA and DHS were using the large transports to pre-position equipment and supplies in preparation for a siege. Clearly, President

Downs was not going to get caught unprepared by a catastrophic disaster as had previous administrations.

The sky darkened across the horizon toward the southwest. Storms forecast by Whiteman meteorologists appeared to be right on schedule. The prediction was for the heaviest weather to remain along the Missouri and Arkansas border, so getting out early tomorrow morning should be no problem. Matt reserved the club airplane for two days, just in case.

Many military bases offered flying clubs for military personnel who wanted to fly general aviation aircraft. It was an inexpensive way to learn to fly, or an inexpensive aircraft rental for those with their private pilot's license. Generally, base flying clubs were nonprofit and offered several types of aircraft to meet the needs of their members. Whiteman AFB was no exception.

Of the four airplanes owned by the club, Matt settled on the 1989 Piper Arrow for overall best performance for the simple job of airport hopping. The single engine, retractable gear, had been beautifully refurbished with upgraded avionics and partial glass panel, but Matt was not interested in all the bells and whistles. His mission was down in the weeds, taking each airport they came to, generally not more than 30-40 miles apart. They would land if the airfield had hangars in which to store a twin-engine Aztec, or if not, they would just pass overhead checking the airplanes on the tie-down ramp.

The Arrow was quick and efficient, but Larson's massive shoulders took up most of the narrow cockpit, leaving Matt scrunched up against the left-side window with barely enough room to reach the controls.

ATC tapes of the Aztec flight showed it navigating a direct flight from KCI into St. Louis. Matt planned to intercept the airway eighty-five miles east of KCI where the Aztec disappeared from radar. They would check every airfield within twenty miles distance on either side of the airway until they ran out of daylight. Tomorrow they would resume that flight order to Latitude 91'30" and then turn back, expanding the search by forty miles or more. Matt hoped that would not be necessary.

With the late start, they made it to only four airfields before returning to base. Depending on how successful Georgia was with her call list, Matt hoped to complete the surveillance flight tomorrow. However, the absence of communications with the FBI special agent indicated she was not having any better luck than he was.

"Man, those things are huge," Larson observed as he stared out the windscreen at the three giant transports.

"Yup!" Matt eased back on the throttle to slow their approach. "Gotta stay out of their wake turbulence, for sure."

"I wonder what all they brought us?"

"We'll be findin' out soon enough, I reckon." Matt lowered the landing gear and the first notch of flaps. The last C-17 in the flight of three touched down as Matt turned from base to final.

Several minutes later they taxied past the behemoths. The first one to land already had its rear cargo ramp lowered, exposing an assortment of large trailers and cargo pallets inside its cavernous interior. Matt guessed the first trailer to come down the ramp to be a communications unit of some kind. It was about 24-feet long, gray, with U.S. Navy stenciled on both sides. Matt and Larson glanced at one another and shrugged.

~~~~~~~~

Chase begged to tag along on the next surveillance flight, complaining there was nothing for him to do but sit around the base. Matt conceded and immediately put Chase to work preflighting the club plane while he, Larson, and Georgia poured over snippets of intel that had trickled in overnight. There was still no communication out of the St. Louis area as to whether or not the twin-engine Aztec had been located. There simply had not been time for the deployed agents to check every ramp and hangar.

As they geared up to launch the next aerial search there was a general feeling of optimism. By 0800 managers and operators at the smaller airfields would be opening their doors, putting on a pot of coffee, sitting close to their phones. Georgia had the call list beside her on the table.

Thirty minutes later the Piper Arrow climbed into a lavender sky. This time Matt had Chase up front with him.

"You get the back seat today, Goliath," Matt said to Larson with a grin. "Be a lot more comfortable for all of us."

Climbing out over the flat Missouri farmland, Matt turned to look over his shoulder. Larson was spread across the entire back seat, eyes closed, mouth gaped wide. Matt nudged Chase and grinned.

Matt settled back in his seat. It was a beautiful morning. The air was smooth and so clear you could see fifty miles. He leveled off at 2,500 feet and pointed the airplane northeast. They would take up where they left off yesterday, checking every airport and private grass strip along the airway. Chase raised the binoculars to his eyes. Many of the private airstrips could be observed and eliminated at altitude.

Matt glanced at his watch, then checked the aeronautical chart in his lap. They should reach the last airport inside their boundary around noon. Good place to stop for fuel and a bite to eat before turning back to expand the search.

~~~~~~~

Situation Room
White House
Washington. D.C.

Secretary of State, Zachary Ringhold, had a startled look on his face when he stepped into the Situation Room and discovered the meeting he had been summoned to was already well in progress.

President Harlan Downs sat at the head of the oblong conference table. At the opposite end of the table with his usual bank of phones was Chairman of the Joint Chiefs, Admiral Justin B. Turner. Others in attendance included White House Chief of Staff James Ritchey, DNI Alex Strayhorn, DHS Stu Warner, FBI Director Leslie Salmons, and FEMA Director Howard Evans.

Only crumbs remained from a plate of donuts at the center of the table and the two coffee carafes were nearly empty.

"Ah, good morning, Zach," President Downs said with a weary smile.

"Good morning, Mr. President." SecState stepped up to the table, poured a cup of coffee, and took a seat on the president's left. "I see we've already started." Ringhold nodded to the others, and then turned to the president.

"If you aren't early, Zach, you're late," the president casually rebuked. "We've been going over some very frightening stuff. There's little doubt we are only hours away from unprecedented terrorist attacks inside the United States—That's *attacks,* plural! We have pretty much done everything we can do to be prepared. But realistically …" the president sighed, lowered his head, unable to speak.

"Do we know how? Where?" SecState asked.

President Downs shook his head, his voice was soft. "If we had those answers, we could save a lot of lives."

"How can I help, Mr. President?"

"I need you to initiate back-channel communications with our allies."

"Sir?" Ringhold's eyebrows shot up.

"At my request, Admiral Turner has submitted several options for military action against Iran."

"MR. PRESIDENT, YOU CAN'T BE—"

The president held up his hand to stifle SecState's outburst. There was steel in his soft voice. "Listen closely, Zachary. In a few hours there will be hundreds, perhaps thousands, of American lives in danger. Our intelligence sources are ninety-seven percent certain that the leader of the Iranian Revolutionary Guard is responsible for organizing and funding *Operation Firestorm*, an Islamic jihad here on American soil."

Ringhold's face blanched white. He was appalled at what he was hearing, even more appalled at what the president was preparing to do. He spoke calmly, keeping his emotions in check.

"Mr. President, Major General Imad Abu Mughniyeh is a rogue. Clearly, sir, this cannot be state sponsored terrorist activity. They know it would be an act of war. They have nothing to gain—"

"Unless it is to keep us occupied while they attack Israel," Admiral Turner offered.

"Surely, you don't—"

Again the president held up a hand and let out a loud sigh.

"Zach, I have not decided which option I will go with. Suffice to say, we will have several more discussions before that decision is final … You will be part of those discussions, I assure you."

President Downs looked around the table before continuing. "Until we know with absolute certainty that General Mughniyeh is not acting alone, we will hit only military targets. Surgical strikes that will minimize collateral damage."

He turned back to SecState and looked him square in the eyes. "But make no mistake, the very moment Ahmad

Hassam attacks a United States citizen, I will authorize our military to take action inside Iran.

"Now get on the horn and start preparing our allies for the inevitable. I will speak with the Israeli prime minister, personally. "

Twenty-Nine

Mexico Memorial Airport
Mexico, Missouri

Mexico Memorial was the last airport before Longitude 91'30". It was only seven miles north of the direct airway between Kansas City and Saint Louis and four miles east of the town of Mexico, Missouri. Matt approached from the northwest, having just left the airport in the little town of Moberly. The flight had been scenic, even though disappointing. The farmlands in northern Missouri were green with fresh crops sprouting up and trees starting to bud. A long winter had come to an end and the wet spring held promise for local farmers.

Matt turned downwind for runway 24 and slowed the Arrow to approach speed. The long expanse of paved runway and concrete parking ramps were a contrast against lush rows of young corn. Looking out the right side of the airplane, the men saw a number of large hangars.

Plenty of places to hide a twin-engine Piper, Matt thought anxiously.

Georgia contacted the airport manager's son. He verified the Aztec was not on the tie-down ramp, but could not be certain about several hangars leased by out-of-town tenants. The kid's response was vague, which prompted a close inspection.

"Okay, got it! Thanks!" Chase said into his comm-set. Matt nodded that he had copied the new message from Georgia. She had cleared Columbia Regional Airport. No Aztecs on the field there. Two more airfields along their return leg had also been cleared.

"Gear down," Matt said aloud from the *Before Landing Checklist.* "Flaps ten degrees." He reduced power and announced their position on the Unicom frequency. He felt the back of his seat push forward by Larson's knees. The big man needed to stretch.

Matt set the airplane down perfectly on the threshold with only a squeak from the tires and fast taxied to the transient parking area. He was starting to like the little airplane and already regretted promising Chase that he could have the left seat on the return leg.

Matt stepped down off the wing into clear sunshine and nearly 70 degrees. He unlocked the exterior baggage door, pulled the M9 Berretta from his flight bag, and slipped it into his waistband in the small of his back. He wore a beige short-sleeve button-down shirt on the outside of his Wrangler's to conceal his weapon. Chase and Larson grabbed their weapons and all three men walked across the ramp toward the FBO. The only visible activity was a pair of ag planes routinely getting their hoppers refilled. Matt glanced up and saw another ag plane enter the traffic pattern. It was the season when the aerial application business flew practically non-stop.

Slightly off to the left and behind the FBO/terminal sat a long white metal building, considerably larger than any of the aircraft hangars. Its large roll-up doors were open. The parking lot in front was crowded with vehicles. Matt remembered reading there was an aircraft manufacturing company located here, specializing in sport airplane kits.

"Good morning, gentlemen." A sunburned, skinny, pimply-faced kid looked up from behind the counter inside the FBO. A battered red ball cap hid most of his blond crew cut. His orange tank top and faded jeans were covered with grass stains, sweat, and grease. He was wiping grease from his hands. He smiled from ear-to-ear. "Sorry I didn't get out to ya's in time to tie down your airplane. I'm by myself right now, phones won't quit ringing. I'm supposed to be mowing the grass, but the danged tractor is broke … again!"

Matt smiled back at the young man. His story was all too familiar. "That's okay, son, we know what it's like." Matt motioned to Chase. "My cousin and I worked at an airport for flyin' lessons. There was nuthin' around there that we didn't have to do."

"Huh? Oh!" The boy grinned. "Shoot no! I ain't working for flying lessons. My dad owns the joint, he's out flying. We own the ag spraying business and this is a pretty busy time for us. Dad's making me work through spring break to pay my truck insurance ... Gotta work all summer too," he added with a dejected sigh.

Larson howled with laughter, slapping Matt on the shoulder. "Guess he fooled you, fly boy!" He laughed again.

The kid behind the counter merely stared. "What can I do for you guys?"

"What's your name, son?" Matt asked.

"Samuel, Samuel Hogan, but I prefer Sam!"

"Okay, Sam, I understand you have several hangars leased by out-of-towners. We wanna look inside 'em."

The boy stood silent, staring from face to face before speaking. "I can't let you do that. You'll have to wait for my—"

"Sure you can," Matt flashed his cred pack in the boys face. "Federal agents, lookin' for a Piper Aztec. Just need the keys for a quick peek inside every hangar you can't vouch for."

The boys eyes went wide at the sight of Matt's credentials and the stony looks the three men gave him. "We don't have keys to any of the hangars, sir, 'cept for the hangars we use. Customers provide their own locks."

"You have bolt cutters, Sam?" Larson asked.

"Sure, but—"

"Get em!"

"Yes, sir." He moved toward the door leading out to an attached maintenance shop, but then stopped and turned back. "But I really think you need to wait for my dad."

"That's okay, son," Matt said. "We'll take full responsibility."

A minute or so later the boy returned with a pair of bolt cutters. Matt asked him to lead the way to the hangars. The first was on the front row, closest to the FBO building, but from the size of the sliding doors Matt knew that hangars on this row were made for smaller aircraft and would not accommodate a twin-engine.

They snapped the locks on two corrugated metal hangars on the second row, opened, and then promptly closed the doors. No Piper Aztec.

Their luck changed at the last hangar on the third row; the farthest, most remote hangar. Larson popped the lock and slid one of the large doors open. Chase let out a long, soft whistle.

"Bingo!" Matt declared.

Sam followed the three men inside where they discovered the red, white, and blue Piper Aztec with the logo: Central Missouri Air Charter. The boy cocked his head in confusion when Matt started speaking to someone not even there.

"AJ, Georgi! You can stop lookin'. We found the Aztec!"

"Roger that!" AJ answered immediately.

"Copy!" Georgia added.

"I'll get back to y'all in a bit." Matt followed Chase around the right side of the airplane and waited while Chase climbed on the wing.

The entry door remained open. Larson stepped back into the sunlight, glancing in all directions. He developed a sudden uneasiness when realizing they could be close to Ahmad Hassam.

The boy felt tension in the air. Curiosity drove him even closer to the airplane. "This what you're looking for?"

"Think so, son," Matt answered softly. "Think so!" He turned to Sam. "Guess you don't know who the tenant is? How long they've had the lease?"

"No sir," the boy's voice quivered. "But we can check the records in the office. Whoever they are, they get a monthly bill for rent."

Matt looked at the wing and the top of the fuselage. No dust. *Flown recently,* he thought.

"Matt," Chase called from the door of the plane. "You better check this out."

Matt climbed on the wing. His nose wrinkled at the familiar metallic smell. Peering over Chase's shoulder, he saw the dried, rust-colored smear across the top of the beige leather seats and doorframe.

"Blood!" Chase said.

"Uh huh, lots of it," Matt agreed. "Look at the carpet."

Sam stood on tiptoes, trying to see between the two men. *Did they say blood? What the heck?*

Matt stepped down and glanced around the hangar. There were a few drops of dried blood on the concrete floor that he had somehow overlooked. He motioned for Butch to escort the boy out of the hangar.

Matt and Chase poked through piles of old paint cans, tools, a heavy canvas tarp in one corner, and various flotsam of non-aviation junk. They could find no further evidence.

While Sam closed the hangar door, Matt leaned close to Larson. In a low voice he said, "Looks like the CMAC pilot didn't survive his encounter with Hassam."

~~~~~~~~~

"Here it is, sir." Sam handed a 3x5 file card to Matt. "Leased by NetDesign & DataSolutions, LLC, Kansas City.

"Thanks, Sam. Could you make a copy for me?" Matt handed the card back. "We'd also like to use your courtesy car, if it's available.

"Sorry, don't have courtesy cars here." Sam turned to the copy machine at the end of the counter, ran the file card through, and brought back a copy of the information.

"You can borrow my truck if you're not gonna be gone too long."

Sam pulled a set of truck keys from his jeans pocket, held them up, and said, "Careful on the turns, she's got a Hi-Lift Kit—"

Chase snatched the keys from his hands. "Kid, we were drivin' jacked-up trucks before you were even a glimmer in your daddy's eyes."

~~~~~~~~~

U.S. Capitol
Washington, D.C.

Rahimi Musa, aka Sergeant Juan Alvarez, U.S. Capitol Police, glanced up from his post. Coming through the large glass doors leading up from the Visitors Center at the east entrance, a group of college students spilled out into the rotunda. Musa pulled out his cell phone for one last check.

No messages!

The attack was on! After two years of planning and fretting and sweating; two years of praying to *Allah* that this moment would never come, it was really going to happen. Sweat streamed down his face, his white uniform shirt was plastered to his underarms and back, his breathing was labored, his heart pounded so loudly he was sure JD could hear it. He glanced over at JD. Was it just his imagination or was his subordinate eyeing him with overt curiosity?

The group came closer and Musa's knees began to buckle. It was a miserable feeling to discover he might not be able to go through with this. He pulled in a deep breath to steady his nerves and willed himself to calm down. *Allah you are mighty, you are merciful! Give me strength! Give me wisdom to do my duty.*

The seven young men fit well with the college students; no one noticed they were not part of the larger group. Least of all JD. The men were interspersed within two single-file rows preparing to flow through the metal detectors at the security gate.

It was spring break for students, which was part of the plan. Lots of school groups were on tours at the nation's Capitol, lots of noise and distraction. Even better, Musa was relieved to see that the thick coats worn by the seven men also matched many others in the group. The snow had melted, but the spring rain that followed brought a chill in the air that necessitated protection against the elements. No one would suspect what the seven wore beneath their coats. Especially after Musa, in a fluid practiced movement, reached under the table at his station and dialed down sensitivity on the detectors just as the first student stepped into JD's lane.

Musa smiled to himself. The planners thought of every angle. They had projected the American intelligence agencies would get wind of an attack. The government would continue allowing tours of its facilities so as not to create panic, but they had implemented tighter security measures. The conveyors leading to the x-ray were in operation to check briefcases and women's purses, but backpacks were forbidden inside all government facilities. Hence the switch to thick down-filled coats. All but one.

The student imposter wearing a backpack worked his way into Rahimi Musa's lane. The man plastered on a bemused smile, swiveling his head all around as though in awe of the nation's Capitol. *He is a pretty good actor,* Musa thought.

"Young man, you need to hand over the backpack. You may reclaim it when you depart." The man shrugged, shucked off the pack and handed it over with a smile. Musa placed the pack under his table and allowed the *student* to continue on with the group. From the corner if his eye, Musa saw JD's head snap up and turn toward him. *He is being extremely vigilant,* Musa thought. *I must keep an eye on that.*

Everything was going according to plan. Musa took another deep breath as the large group continued into the rotunda.

"Sergeant Alvarez, do you feel okay?" asked JD. "You look a little pale."

"I am fine, JD," Musa managed a tight smile. "Just seems rather stuffy with that big group passing through. I will be okay."

Musa glanced at his watch. *One hour and fifty-three minutes!*

The seven separated from the group in practiced steps. One was already at his assigned position. He shed his coat and shoved the explosive vest between two cabinets located beside a kiosk. He activated the timer, pulled his coat on, shoved his hands in his pockets, and wandered along the magnificent corridor, pretending to enjoy the sights of the grand building. Secretly, his heart filled with pride knowing he was bringing down the symbol of the Great Satan's power.

Each of the vests worn by the seven men contained eight one-pound blocks of Semtex explosive and 500 Teflon coated ball bearings. The same configuration was hidden inside the backpack obscured beneath the table at Rahimi Musa's security gate. All eight bombs were armed and set.

… One hour and thirty-one minutes!

Thirty

Mexico, Missouri

"This is probably bogus, but look for NetDesign & DataSolutions, 1100 Main Street, KC." Matt said into the comm-set.

Two minutes later Georgia Shayne answered.

"Actually there is a listing at that address, Suite 2600. A software design firm owned by Rashad Hussain."

An alarm sounded in Matt's head. "There's no way it can be this simple, Georgi, but you'd better get some of your guys over there to check it out."

Chase wheeled the big Dodge Ram pickup through the narrow streets of Mexico, Missouri with practiced skill. The candy apple metallic red paint job glimmered in the mid-day sun, catching the attention of nearly everyone on the street in this small country town. Most of the locals waved at the step-ladder-high truck with rumbling twin glass-pac exhaust, and then did a double take when they saw it wasn't young Sammy Hogan behind the wheel. Matt rode shotgun with Butch Larson in the backseat, his arms draped across the seatback.

"What's the plan, Cuz?" Chase asked, zipping down Liberty Street, scanning businesses on both sides of the street.

"No plan, actually," Matt answered. "Just wanted to get the feel of the town, see if—*Whoa!*"

Chase whipped the wheel hard left, jumped across the on-coming traffic lane, and bounced into the parking lot of a big red building with a large pink pig next to the door. The sign on the building said Porky's BBQ.

"Good," Chase proclaimed. " Cause I got me a hankerin' for a rack of ribs and an ice cold brew."

"I'll second that," Larson called from the back.

Matt reluctantly agreed, only because they might gather some additional intel from some of the locals inside.

A friendly waitress about Matt and Chase's age seated them at a booth next to a window on the right side of the room. She took their drink orders and promptly retreated to the back. Matt scanned the room and the few occupied tables. There was a short staircase leading down to a slightly larger dining room where a large crowd were having a celebration, or perhaps a luncheon of some kind. Whatever it was, judging from their noise, they were having a good time.

The décor in the two dining rooms was identical. Reddish wood paneling went halfway up the walls with country-scene wallpaper covering the top half. Numerous stuffed animals of all sizes hung from the walls and sat in the corners, including a couple of wild pigs and two Missouri black bears.

Larson leaned across the table and spoke in low tones.

"Check out the skinhead across the room. He's been giving us a going over ever since we walked in. Got a case of the fidgets."

Matt glanced at the small table along the far wall. The man slouched in a chair nursing a bottle of beer stared back with wild bloodshot eyes the size of half dollars. His head was clean-shaven, his teeth were yellow snags. He was a skinny, tall drink of water in his early twenties; though from his crazed look and hardened features it was hard to tell. *That's what being a long-time methhead will do to you.* The man was dressed in stained, ragged cargo pants and long sleeve shirt rolled up to proudly display Swastika tats on both forearms. A large hunting knife was sheathed on his right hip.

"Kinda has that deer-in-the-headlight-look, doesn't he?" Matt grinned.

"Wonder if he'd like to talk?" Chase asked casually.

"Why don't you just mosey over there and ask him, pard," Larson laughed.

"Bite me, jarhead! I'm here to eat!"

After a few minutes the waitress returned. She set three frosty bottles of Budweiser on the table and took their order with a smile. As she turned to leave, Matt called her back.

"Hey, we just pulled into town. Lookin' for a friend of ours." Matt flashed a charming smile at her. "He's about my size, dark complexion. Looks Hispanic, but has a funny accent. He probably got into town two days ago. Heard of anyone with that description?"

"Nope, don't think so," she answered. "But it sounds like the fellas who moved in a while back. Got a place somewhere north of town—"

"Skinhead's on the move!" Larson shouted and bolted out of the booth.

~~~~~~~

Leroy Gargus saw the red Dodge pickup pull into the parking lot from his vantage point inside Porky's. He knew the truck and he knew that the three men did not work at the airport. He also knew that spoiled, jerk face Sammy Hogan would not let just anyone drive his pride and joy.

Nineteen year-old Gargus kept his eyes on the men as they filed through the entrance. *Feds! I can smell 'em,* he thought. There were not many things the Gargus brothers hated more than law enforcement personnel, feds in particular. *Why would those pigs be in town? They couldn't possibly know what went down at the airport already. Even if they did, why would the feds be interested?"*

Leroy saw the men watching him from across the room and he could not resist glaring back. It was his nature. He felt like reaching for his blade and hurling it at the big slob taking up one whole side of the booth. *Could hit 'im right 'tween the eyes from here!*

He listened closely when one of the men began talking to the waitress. *Holy crap! Theys talkin' 'bout them dudes at the Tucker place!* Leroy shot up out of his chair and hit the front door on a run. He had to warn his brothers. Fast!

~~~~~~~~~

Chase peeled out of the parking lot, heading west down Liberty one block behind Leroy's rusted out Ford pickup. The relic swerved through traffic, smoke poured from the tailpipe. He nearly ran two cars into the curb. Chase romped on the gas and the big Dodge shot forward as if it might launch itself into the air. He was gaining quickly, which caused skinhead to drive even more recklessly.

Leroy glanced in his rearview and let out a string of profanity so loudly people a block away heard him. The truck rocked back and forth as he raced down the street. The traffic light ahead was red, but he took the intersection at sixty miles an hour. He saw the black sedan out of the corner of his eye about a half-second before it clipped the right rear bumper of his truck, causing him to fishtail wildly across the on-coming lane of traffic. He overcorrected back to the right, banged into the curb, and blew out the bald front tire on the passenger's side. Smoke and steam poured from under the hood; limping badly at a much slower pace, Leroy foolishly tried to outrun the big Dodge.

Chase shot past Leroy's truck just as the skinhead shoved his arm out the window and flipped them off.

"That peckerwood!" Chase shouted angrily and whipped the big Dodge in front of the smoking truck, forcing skinhead into the First Baptist Church parking lot. Chase stopped directly in front of the broken truck and blocked his exit.

Leroy bounded out his door and made all of three steps before Butch Larson reached out with one mighty arm and yanked him back by his shirt collar. Skinhead spun around, fists doubled, swinging wildly, spitting out a steady string of profanity. The big Marine easily batted away his futile punch. Skinhead reached for his blade. *Gonna carve me up a giant pig!*

Matt was a few steps behind Larson. He saw skinhead reach for his knife and immediately drew the Berretta from his waistband. Before he could shout a warning, the ten inch blade glimmered in the sunlight as it came slashing down. Butch stepped inside the wide arc with lightning speed and grabbed the wrist holding the knife. Skinhead screamed in pain as Butch twisted his arm behind his back, forcing him to drop the knife.

In a continuous blur of motion, Larson wrapped a massive hand around the back of the scrawny man's head, lifted him off the ground with one arm, and slammed skinhead's face into the hood of the Ford truck with enough force to make a head-size dent in the hood.

Matt heard the sickening sound of shattering nose cartilage and two snaggled teeth lay in the blood-smeared concave.

Larson dropped the stunned skinhead on the ground as Matt holstered his pistol. Chase rushed around the front of the Dodge weapon in hand. Larson dropped to one knee, yanked skinhead's arms behind his back, and secured his wrists with plastic flex cuffs.

"Shoot-fire-and-save-on-matches!" Chase exclaimed with a whistle. "You *really* messed that sucker up!"

A crowd gathered as distant sirens blared, drawing closer by the second. People pressed closer, mumbling amongst themselves, pointing at the battered and bloodied skinhead lying dazed on the ground. No one really cared much for Leroy Gargus and his pathetic brothers, but these three strangers had just come into town and beat up one of their local boys.

"We're drawing attention," Matt said stepping closer to Larson and Chase. "Let's toss this trash in the back of the truck and take him someplace where we can … talk."

They moved to yank Leroy on his feet, but it was too late. An unmarked police car slid into the parking lot from a side street, blue grill lights flashing. A plain clothes officer jumped out, his right hand gripped the pistol on his hip, but did not draw the weapon. He was a big man, over six feet, large barrel chest, middle forties. He was dressed in jeans, brown sport jacket and cowboy boots.

"Hands up where I can see 'em," the officer shouted. He stayed beside his car, waiting for backup to arrive. Sirens were getting closer as two patrol cars from the Mexico Department of Public Safety converged from opposite directions. The officer took a step closer, paused with feet spread, pointing with his left hand extended while the right hand remained on his holstered weapon.

"All three of you, on the ground, flat on your face, arms behind you. Do it slowly. *Now!*"

"Federal agents, officer," Matt challenged. "This man is our prisoner."

Two black and white patrol cars arrived simultaneously, bouncing into the parking lot and screeching to a stop. The two uniformed officers were out of their vehicles, guns drawn in classic two-hand stance on either side of Matt's group. The crowd had moved back to the sidewalk, staring with open mouths. They had not seen this much action in their sleepy little town since the brickyard fire.

"Let's see your credentials," the plain-clothes officer ordered, taking another step forward. "Take it out slowly."

Matt pulled his cred pack from his shirt pocket and held it high for the officer to see. Chase and Larson followed suit. Matt saw the two uniforms shifting nervously, their heads darting from the plain-clothes officer back to their suspects. The cred packs had relieved the tension, but the officers remained cautious.

"Okay, you can put your hands down." Plain clothes moved closer to Matt while the uniformed cops holstered their weapons and went to check on skinhead, who was now conscious and thrashing on the street, screaming at the top of his lungs.

"NCTC, huh?" Plain clothes said when he was close enough to study Matt's ID. "Never heard of you, so you've got some explaining to do. Let's start with you telling me why Leroy's under arrest?"

"Alright with you if we move over to your car?" Matt motioned with his head.

The two men stepped away from the scene while screaming profanity belched out of Leroy. They moved behind the officer's car.

"Okay, what's all the secrecy about and what has Leroy got to do with it?" Plain clothes lowered his voice.

"First, let me see your badge and ID."

The officer flashed Matt a *you-got-to-be-kidding-me* look and then begrudgingly pulled his credentials from the inside pocket of his sports coat.

"Scott Brown. *Detective* Scott Brown." He flashed his creds in Matt's face with a glare that said he was running out of patience.

Matt nodded. "Leroy is under investigation for murder—"

"*Murder!* Who did he kill?" Detective Brown's eyes widened.

"I'll explain later. He's also under investigation for harboring international terrorists."

"You've got to be kidding!" Brown's eyes were wide with disbelief.

Matt shook his head. "No doubt your department received the FBI bulletin for a nation-wide terrorist alert?" Brown nodded.

For the next few minutes Matt briefed the detective on what brought NCTC to the town of Mexico, what they discovered at the airport, and Leroy's suspicious behavior.

"Holy cow!" The detective ran a hand through his reddish-brown hair. "Are you saying—"

Matt silenced him with a raised hand while the other automatically touched the earbud in his right ear.

"*Matt, AJ!*" Her voice sounded strained. Instantly Matt knew something was wrong. "*It's started Matt! We need you back at Whiteman, immediately.*"

"Copy that! We're on the move. Can you tell me what's happening?" He could feel the emotion in her voice.

"*We guessed it wrong, Matt. It's happening here. All hell is breaking loose ... Get to Whiteman.*"

Detective Scott Brown stood wide-eyed, head cocked to one side, confused. "Who are you talking to? What the heck is—"

"We have to get back to base," Matt said, pointing to Chase and Larson. "We'll finish this later." Matt turned and walked away with the others.

"So what happens now with Leroy?" Detective Brown demanded, not wishing to be kept in the dark.

"FBI and Homeland Security will want to interrogate him," Matt called over his shoulder. "Hold him 'til they get here. Y'all might wanna get out to the airport and talk with Sam, too."

Thirty-One

Whiteman Air Force Base
Knob Noster,
Missouri

Matt entered the operations ready room and found the place charged with anger, outrage, and disbelief. The entire Watchdog unit huddled around the TV, speechless as they watched the horror unfolding on CNN. Matt moved closer and saw the smoke pouring through gaping holes in the U.S. Capitol. The ribbon playing across the bottom of the screen provided stats on casualties while an off screen commentator offered a number of scenarios and unverified reports of gunfire and high speed chases around the immediate vicinity of the Capitol.

Matt, Chase, and Larson continued to watch as the drama in D.C. resumed. Pundits and Monday morning quarterbacks were already ramping up the finger pointing and proverbial blame game as hysterical speculation ran wild.

Unremarkably, his comm-set remained silent for the time being. Manning and the NCTC staff would have their hands full for the next few hours. The United States was under attack and any hope for rational reaction would be nearly impossible as emotions ran rampant. War had come to the streets of America. Once the shock and panic wore off, anger would take its place. Channeling and directing that anger would not be an easy task. President Downs was not normally prone to knee-jerk reaction. But this time the president and his staff would have their hands full, and Matt did not envy them one little bit.

The image on the TV screen switched suddenly back to the news studio with a grim expression on the face of the anchorman. *"We have just learned another attack as taken place. We take you now live to the Mall of America in Bloomington, Minnesota. with CNN reporter Jerry Adams ... Jerry, what can you tell us so far?"*

The picture switched to a soundless image of a disheveled news reporter yelling at someone off camera. Before the tech crew could get the reporter connected to audio the image changed to the front entrance of Mall of America, taken from an elevated camera set back a distance, well behind police barricades. Smoke poured from shattered windows at several levels of the mall, bright orange flames and a towering column of black smoke belched from the roof. Several fire department ladder trucks arched powerful streams of water over the roof. The scene at the main entrance showed firefighters and EMT's rolling injured victims on gurneys from a thick cloud of gray smoke, through a tangle of fire hose and cascading water.

The image switched back to the news reporter now in the foreground with a live shot of the mall in the distance. *"Here's what we've learned so far, Dan. Within minutes of the attack in Washington, D.C., the Mall of America here in Bloomington, Minnesota was racked with a series of explosions.*

"Local law enforcement officials have verified that multiple bombs exploded simultaneously throughout the mall, including the lower level inside Nickelodeon Universe where hundreds of children played ..."

Matt drifted to the back of the room and collapsed in one of the leather aircrew chairs. He found himself pulled into a state of despair. His mind shut out the drumming TV commentary as he recalled the admonishing words of grandma McWain. Words she would repeat at times of disparaging reports in the news.

Matt pictured grandma now, comfortable in her old rocker in the family room, shaking her head in silent disdain as some travesty committed against mankind unfolded on the screen. The grandkids were seated on a giant oval braided rug, huddled around her as if she were the fount of knowledge, and in his young impressionable mind she was exactly that.

Softly she proclaimed, *"God's justice is comin'! It's just around the corner. We have turned our back on God. We have taken His name out of the school house; we have taken His name out of the court room; we have taken His name out of every public building from the White House to the smallest community.*

"If we don't change our evil ways, ask God for His forgiveness for the way we have treated Him, then I'm afraid He will withdraw his tender mercy and His wrath will pour out on this country in full measure. The persecution of believers in our Lord Jesus Christ is a comin'!"

Matt wondered if his grandmother's proclamation was coming true. *Have we, by our own actions, brought this horrendous tragedy upon ourselves?*

"Matt? Did you hear me?"

"Huh? What?" Georgia Shayne was sitting beside him, shaking his arm.

"The report's back on NetDesign & DataSolutions, LLC. That address in Kansas City is current. The company is huge in software design," she stated. "A very lucrative start-up company owned and operated by Rashad Hussain. Agents found five employees on site, but no Hussain. He's supposedly on vacation, but failed to let anyone know where. At least that's their story."

Matt leaned forward. He saw weariness on her face. Her large, dark brown eyes were red and swollen. The terrorist attacks weighed heavily upon her, but she was all business now and she held his undivided attention. "What about Hussain's records?"

Georgia forced a smile and said, "Confiscated it all. Lock, stock ... and jug, as you Texans like to say. Analysts are poring through it now, but it may be a day or two for results." She frowned before adding, "They suddenly have a few other things to occupy their minds."

"Yeah, bet they do," Matt nodded sadly. "Ask them to report back as soon as they can ... They're here, Georgi, I just know it. Regardless of what's goin' on in D.C. and other places, Hassam's command and control is operating close by."

"I think you are right," she answered. "Agents are on the way to pick up Leroy Gargus as we speak." Georgia stood to return to her computer.

"Good! Any chance they can bring him here? I'd like a few minutes with him."

"Not likely. I've heard about your interrogation methods."

She grinned and walked away. AJ had filled her in on the incident in Guatemala when Matt shot the ear off of a reluctant terrorist to force him into telling where Ahmad Hassam had taken Carley Downs. He certainly was not averse to similar expedient means again if it would bring them one step closer to stopping the siege of terror unleashed by the master terrorist.

Matt's thoughts returned to Grandma McWain. *Dear God, we need your help*, he prayed.

~~~~~~~

50,000 Feet Above
St. Louis, Missouri

"Quarterback, Birddog One*!*" Lt. Cmdr. Clayton Downs called.

Matt bolted upright at the familiar voice in his earbud. *"Go ahead, Birddog One. Where the heck are you?"*

"Just crossed into the Show-Me state, headed your way. Got a few hours extra loiter time, anything you need?"

"As a matter of fact," Matt answered. *"You in the Reaper?"*

"More or less," Clayton shot back. "Reaper's big brother, Sea Avenger."

With the unqualified success in a combat environment earned by the ship-born Reaper, Clayton and his team had been handed a new task: testing the Navy variant of the Predator C, the Sea Avenger, for Carrier-based Surveillance and Strike capability.

The Sea Avenger was a vast improvement over the MQ-9 Reaper. It featured an internal weapons bay to enhance stealth performance of the composite-constructed aircraft, a Pratt & Whitney PW545B turbofan jet engine, which boosted the unmanned aerial combat vehicle to over 460 miles per hour and a ceiling of 60,000 feet. The extra power also allowed for larger fuel capacity, which gave the aircraft 18-hours endurance. There were a number of structural changes as well, differentiating the Sea Avenger from the U.S. Air Force model. Many of which were developed by Clayton and his team. The new generation Sea Avenger was truly a strike aircraft, capable of engaging multiple targets simultaneously while providing unprecedented surveillance.

Because of the aircraft's advanced capabilities and stealth signature, Clayton had personally developed what he called the Advanced Cockpit Ground Control Station, ACGCS. The wrap-around visual display contained multi-dimensional moving maps to increase the pilot's Situational Awareness, while reducing workload.

Sea Avenger trials were scheduled to begin in earnest when *Iwo Jima* returned to sea following their recent deployment, though the prototype had successfully undergone numerous test flights. With the current situation brewing in the United States it took little convincing for Clayton to obtain authorization to deploy the aircraft in limited capacity.

A portable ACGCS had been airlifted to Whiteman AFB. It was currently being made ready to receive Clayton and Chief Petty Officer Maggie Williams, a rated SO, Sensor Operator, and member of Clayton's tech support team. CPO Williams was fully qualified on the complex Sea Avenger systems.

Presently, Clayton and Maggie were flying the Sea Avenger, *Birddog One*—which had launched from Joint Base Andrews—from the Reaper Team ACGCS inside the Pentagon basement.

The rest of Reaper Team remained on *Iwo Jima*—headed for anchorage in New Orleans—to conduct surveillance with the two MQ-9 Reapers along the coast and southern states, and assist the Coast Guard with over-flights of the Russian freighter *Alaed*.

"Birddog One, we could use detailed surveillance and mapping of the area around Mexico, Missouri."

"Roger that, Quarterback, you got it!" Clayton set the autopilot for a direct heading to the little town and reclined back in the comfortable leather pilot seat.

~~~~~~~~

The Farm
15 Miles North
Mexico, Missouri

Hassam and Larijani watched continuous CNN coverage on the big screen in the control room. A thin smile crossed Hassam's lips for the second time today. Initial reports on casualties were better than he had hoped, but that is not what brought the rare show of emotion. What the infidels did not know was that they were getting only a glimpse of the fate awaiting them. It was only the first phase. They could not begin to fathom the horror of what was yet to come. Ruthless barbaric savagery would ratchet up each day, driving them to their knees begging for mercy. But mercy would not come.

Rashad Hussain laughed as news commentators speculated on what had happened and what might come next.

"You haven't a clue!" He shouted, followed by more belly laughter. He swiveled to face Hassam. "Do you wish me to unleash the *Shaheed?*"

Hassam gave a silent nod; Rashad's face glowed with euphoria as he turned back to the computer and sent an instant burst message to a hundred suicide bombers across the country. The first round was under way. Many more would follow.

"It is done, *'yâ qâd,* my leader!" Rashad Hussain crowed.

Hassam turned to Larijani and softly asked, "What was the command?"

The diminutive man looked up at Hassam with twinkling eyes. "The command for the first wave was *as-Syf,* my great friend. The infidel's know you are here. They know why you have come … and now they will know you have summoned demons from hell!"

Ahmad Hassam nodded his head, and smiled for the unprecedented third time in a single day.

Thirty-Two

25 Miles South of
Mexico, Missouri
50,000 Feet

The National Security Agency's newest domestic surveillance program was the Vanguard II Computer Surveillance Network. The complex system was second-generation technology from its forerunner, Guardian. Its use was widely opposed by special interest civil rights groups, namely the ACLU, but so far the project had weathered the storm of criticism and was currently cranked up to maximum efficiency.

A major component of the VCSN consisted of specialized contracts with cell phone and internet social media providers. The VCSN coalesced data from each provider with incredible speed; categorizing and filing information based on any number of specified factors, and then prioritized by criterion and input by NSA analysts. This criterion could range from foreign language, geographical location, message content, even voice recognition.

Daily, literally millions of messages were scanned, then quickly discarded from the system as not noteworthy. Of the thousands remaining in the files, a cursory scan was conducted by an analyst assigned to that particular message criterion. One example of scanned messages was what technicians jokingly referred to as "hate mail" between two or more parties, deriding a government decision at some level of the political apparatus. Tons of these messages were dumped 24/7 as being harmless rantings of disgruntled citizens.

But a few hundred messages demanded a second look, some of which were turned over to the FBI or agents from the Department of Homeland Security. In light of the imminent threat, new Criteria had been established and disseminated in the past 48 hours.

These were the messages targeted by the second component of the VCSN system; ELINT equipped satellites instantly plotted locations of message traffic. These electronic signal intelligence satellites were programmed to focus on the same parameters as internet-based message traffic and social media outlets to provide STI— Simultaneous Tracking and Interception.

The longer the message traffic, the easier it was to intercept through advanced network triangulation and then pinpoint the transmission site using multiple ELINT assets. Even a one or two-word coded command within pre-determined criteria would cue the VCSN system in seconds, tracking origin and destination(s) within a ten-mile radius. The longer the transmission the more precise VCSN, resulting in a smaller location radius.

The electronic suite onboard Sea Avenger was equipped with superior ELINT capability and carried the VCSN system software. The UAV was presently coordinating signals with two ELINT satellites scanning the central Missouri area.

Rashad Hussain's mini-burst transmission lasted less than a tenth of a second, but it rang out with the most dreaded name in the world: *"as-Syf"*, setting off alarms in hundreds of computers world-wide.

The computer-generated alarm in *Birddog One* sounded and activated the sensor system even before CPO Maggie Williams bolted upright in her seat. Just as quickly, the UAV's ELINT hardware interfaced with two satellites on the VCSN network, querying confirmation before automatically triangulating the source. The two satellites sorted through a collection of "ghost" transmissions intricately devised by Hussain to minimize detection.

The net result was disappointing in terms of accuracy, but nonetheless Lt. Cmdr. Clayton Downs was rewarded with a 15-mile radius of accuracy in which to search, and six hours of fuel remaining following his high-speed dash across the country. He pulled the thrust lever back to loiter power setting and set the autopilot for an expanding circle search pattern. He was not sure what they were looking for or if he would even recognize it when he saw it, but now he knew they were close to something and that caused excitement to build inside the ACGCS. He arched his back and stretched, rocking back and forth to get the circulation pumping in his legs.

~~~~~~~

Whiteman Air Force Base
Knob Noster, Missouri

"Carter wants you and your Crisis Response Team back here at once, Matt." AJ was on the comm-set giving Matt and the others a rundown on events unfolding in D.C.

A quick thinking Secret Service agent had apprehended a uniformed Capitol Police sergeant crouched behind a row of trees moments after he had hurled a backpack bomb under a fire truck responding to the nation's Capitol.

Fortunately the manual trigger device failed to detonate the bomb—as had two of the electronic timers on bombs inside the Capitol.

Aggressive interrogation revealed the Hispanic suspect had a dual identity, which further proved intel leading up to this day, especially sleeper agents with origins dating back much further than Ahmad Hassam. The attack on America, which emergency planners had warned about for years, was now a reality.

The casualties continued to climb. It was too early to assess the amount of destruction inside the Capitol building. One bomber had gained access to the public gallery above the in-session House Chamber. A bus load of young school age children were in the gallery observing the political process at the time of the explosion. Nine kids were killed instantly, three more died on the way to the hospital, along with one of the class advisors. Nearly all of the remaining children were injured to varying degrees, while down on the chamber floor two congressmen had been killed and a dozen more seriously injured.

This knowledge, stirred by the horrible events rapidly unfolding, prompted an emergency meeting between the president, full cabinet, crisis management staff, and key members of congressional leadership. The hot topic, According to AJ, was whether to launch an immediate military strike on Iran or hold off until control was gained over the domestic invasion. The vote at the moment was too close to predict.

Manning was locked away in that meeting, leaving AJ responsible for coordinating crisis response teams and other assets. But before rushing to the White House, he made it clear that he wanted Matt there to assist her and he wanted the Watchdog team deployed in D.C. to help defend against anticipated follow-on attacks.

It was knee-jerk reaction to a catastrophic disaster and Matt was doing his best to argue his way out of it.

"Trust me on this, AJ. I understand what you're saying, but the real threat is right here. Someplace close by." Matt continued to watch the action on CNN while pacing in back of the room. He caught the pleading stares from Georgia, Chase, and Butch Larson as they listened in on his conversation with NCTC headquarters.

"Matt, you don't know that for sure. Where's your proof? Give me something I can take to Carter—"

"If I may interject, AJ," Clayton Downs broke into the conversation. *"Quarterback knows what he's talking about"*

"Explain, Clayton."

"We are investigating an intercept on a burst transmission with the VCSN: 'as-Syf!'"

"What? Where are you," Matt demanded.

"That's the good part, old boy! We are triangulating with a pair of ELINT birds on a 15 mile stretch of woods around Mexico, Missouri ... It appears you read it correctly."

"Matt," AJ bounced back, *"you stay there. I'll let Carter—Okay! Confirmation on the intercept is coming in through NSA. My gosh! Is he bragging that he is here? Putting his signature on what is happening?"*

Matt felt the hairs standing on the back of his neck and said with a sobering whisper, "I'm guessing Hassam's sending activation codes."

With that AJ said, *"I'll get back to ya's. Good job guys!"*

Matt asked Clayton if there was any chance of pinpointing Hassam's location.

"Negative, Quarterback. Transmission was too short. But I think if we flood this area with ELINT and other intel assets something will turn up soon."

"Roger that. Shoot me a satellite image of the area you guys are painting!"

~~~~~~

Twilight was settling over Whiteman AFB when Matt and the Crisis Response Team finally decided it was time for supper. Wearily they staggered to their feet as if numbed by the unrelenting barrage of commentary spilling out of CNN. Matt chided himself for watching the same reports repeated dozens of times; hanging on each word as if some positive admonition might timidly confess that the whole thing was a ruse. An Orson Welles fictional tale of doom in the night.

As they opened the door to leave a new report shattered the monotonous drone with excitement. There was an unmistakable crack in the reporter's voice and the team froze in place.

"This just in! We are receiving numerous reports of another bombing ..." The reporter turned away from the camera for a moment while he collected himself. When he turned back to the audience his eyes were watering ... *"The latest attack appears to be a suicide bomber at a rush hour subway station in Manhattan. We'll bring you more as soon as we have news from the scene."*

"And now it starts," Matt announced to no one in particular. He suddenly lost his appetite.

America would be huddled in their homes tonight. Weeping. Praying. Terrified.

Thirty-Three

Grand Palace
Branson, Missouri

Hashim Sarhan, aka Tony Morales, climbed out on the catwalk. Ostensibly, he was making last minute adjustments to the cluster of moveable wash lights affixed to a single motorized rotating bar. But in fact, he was arming the switches to all ten of the devices attached beside each light can. The devices resembled homemade claymore mines: 200 steel ball bearings packed inside a molded plastic container with 2 pounds of Semtex explosive. The container was shaped to spray the projectiles in a 30-degree arc and Sarhan had placed each device to assure an overlapping pattern. A limit switch on each device would trigger a detonator as the rotating wash light bar briskly pivoted backward from center stage to illuminate the first five rows of the audience. The dramatic effect of rotating wash lights was used to connect the entertainers with their crowd. Tonight the effect would take a macabre twist.

Sarhan sweated, his fingers trembled. Opening night jitters filled the air as stagehands and crew worked feverishly on last minute arrangements. Emotions ran high due to the horrific events of the day and Sarhan had worried over speculation that the Opening Night Gala would be postponed while America grieved and huddled in despair. But in the end, it was determined that the American heart needed a little gaiety in the face of atrocity. At least here in Branson, Missouri, hundreds of miles from the harsh reality of terrorism. People here wanted to stand up and say, *"Hey, you don't scare us! You can't defeat us with your cowardly attempts to destroy our way of life! Come down our way, we'll kick your ass!"*

No, the grand opening for the stately theater would herald the beginning of a new tourist season in Branson, and the show would go on.

There was some disappointment for Sarhan, however. The events spiraling across the United States had caused the Missouri governor to cancel his attendance at the gala as did a state senator and two congressmen. Even though high visibility targets were the spearhead of the plan, a brutal strike in the heartland of America was expected to shatter the belief of invincibility. The absence of high level officials was upsetting, but Sarhan knew there would still be a large number of local elected and appointed officials and entertainers sitting in the VIP section.

Sarhan shakily reached out and armed the final switch. The devices were ready. When the lighting tech at the rear of the theater activated the wash lights ten minutes into the show, the first five rows in the auditorium would disappear in a blinding flash of fire and a pink mist of blood and tissue and shredded bodies.

People were already filing into the auditorium, dressed in tuxes and beautiful evening gowns as he made his way down the ladder from the catwalk. The black-tie preshow champagne celebration for the VIPs in the theater lobby was winding down. Sarhan retched at the sight of such contemptuous indulgence. *Infidels!*

He quietly slipped out the back door of the theater. His work was done. His companions could take care of those who survived the blast.

~~~~~~~~

The rain dampened street reflected a million twinkling lights. Lightning flashed in the distant sky, signaling that the thunderstorm had passed and the evening would be enjoyed by thousands of visitors and residents. The stream of vehicles crawled, bumper-to-bumper, tempers in check with the excitement of opening night in Branson. They were subdued by the horrific events playing out elsewhere in America, grateful to be spared from the horror of indescribable brutality.

Patrol officer Tiana Edwards inched down the blinding roadway fondly called the "Strip!" Country Music Boulevard. A living, undulating stretch of humanity. Her window was down, she was awash in the spring night air and the excited shouts from complete strangers waving at one another.

"God Bless America!"

"Praise God!"

"Freedom Forever!"

Flags flew from many of the vehicles. Local businesses proudly displayed the Stars and Stripes and electric billboard signs thanked God for His countless blessings.

Tiana noted the mood of the crowd carried that same bond of patriotism and American pride that had captured this little city in the days following 9/11. People were once again courteous, stopping to allow cars to cut in front, patient. Smiles replaced frowns. They were excited to be on the street with one another and share a common bond.

The five-year veteran police officer loved this part of the job. She grew up in a law enforcement family and learned at a very young age their incredible commitment to honor and duty. Her father was a deputy with the county sheriff and her brother was a career army officer, serving in the military police. As far as she could remember, Tiana wanted to follow their footsteps into law enforcement. The opportunity to get on with Branson PD after college graduation and to serve the community where she grew up was a dream come true. The best decision she had ever made. Her determination, agility, and wiry strength belied her petite build and allowed her to excel over beefy guys in her academy class.

But what made her an admired and respected law enforcement officer was a unique ability to talk her way out of tight situations; disarming thugs and drunken troublemakers with an earnest glare from dark eyes.

Officer Edwards pulled her patrol car into the center lane and cruised between the two rows of cars. A radio call reported assistance needed for traffic congestion at the Grand Palace. The show had started, but people were still trying to find parking. Clearly all 4,000 theater seats would be filled. It was the first time in nearly ten years.

From two blocks away, Tiana saw the giant white colonnaded portico at the Palace; its brightly lit exterior easily overshadowed the myriad of lights descending upon the stately showplace. She saw the clogged traffic trying to file into the front parking lot and was amazed to see there were no blaring horns or shaking fists, which usually accompanied the show time quagmire.

The center lane stacked up within a block from the parking lot and Officer Edwards spied an opening in the solid stream of autos. She cut left across the traffic into the Dairy Queen parking lot. She was only a block from the Palace parking lot and from there she could walk to the clogged intersection. She popped the trunk, grabbed a bright yellow rain jacket and a powerful flashlight.

As she slammed the trunk lid a brilliant flash lit up the night, followed by a powerful blast that nearly knocked the five foot three, one hundred and ten pound police officer across her car. She turned to see the front windows blown across the wide covered porch and out into the parking lot. People screamed and cried out as they tried to dodge jagged pieces of glass. The huge chandelier hanging above the porch shattered, glass and intricate metal works rained down on dozens of bleeding patrons lying or kneeling on the entry steps. Black smoke poured from the smoke hatches above the stage area and strobe alarms sounded from every side of the building.

Officer Edwards immediately abandoned the traffic problem and raced toward the theater. She was cutting across the parking lot when she caught sight of the large exit doors on the east side of the theater burst open with a huge billow of smoke and a hoard of people spilled out into the fresh night air, screaming and shouting. Many were coughing and hanging on to one another in an attempt to escape the smoke-charged atmosphere inside the darkened theater.

The patronizing mood of the crowd had turned to chaos and panic, pushing and shoving in a fight for survival.

Tiana Edwards shouted into the mic hanging from the epaulets of her uniform as she charged forward. "Branson, 221! Explosion and fire at the Grand Palace! Multiple victims! Requesting backup, Fire Rescue, and EMS!"

"Copy 221." The dispatcher's voice echoed with excitement. Tiana heard the 9-1-1 phones ringing in the background and knew the switchboard was lighting up.

Officer Edwards was in the front parking lot near the main entrance when shots rang out. She had never heard an AK47, but she instantly knew that an automatic assault rifle had just ripped through a full magazine. In the distance, coming from the other side of building, another rifle burned through a full mag … and then another, this one much closer, at the side door where people were escaping the building.

People screamed, stumbled, and dropped where they stood. Some ran zigzagging across the parking lot, getting 10, 20 feet before stumbling facedown into the asphalt. Blood and chunks of flesh filled the air as people dropped. The assassins quickly reloaded, firing volley after volley pointblank into the human wave that poured from the smoke-charged theater. Pandemonium replaced disorder, some turned to run back inside to escape the slaughter.

Tiana peeled the yellow jacket off and pulled her duty weapon. Her dark blue uniform blended into the night. She crouched low dashing from car to car, searching the dark for the gunmen. She held the pistol in both hands, safety off, finger on the trigger, muzzle pointed down. She commanded herself to let training override emotion, to block out the human carnage, the screams, crying, and pleas for help, which surrounded her.

She grabbed her epaulet mic and forced her voice not to break while fighting back her emotion packed tears. "Branson, 221! Shots fired! Automatic weapons! Multiple shooters! I need backup, NOW!" Sirens from every direction took on a sudden urgency. It was all too surreal, an unbelievable nightmare. But in the back of her mind, Tiana Edwards knew her town was under a terrorist attack.

My town! She was infuriated.

"Unit 221, this is 213!" The shift supervisor called. His voice firm but urgent. His siren could be heard over the radio. He had directed dispatch to call county sheriff and state troopers for mutual aid, but he knew they would be many minutes away. *"Can you tell where the shooters are?"*

"One in front … One on both sides … Unknown rear," Officer Edwards answered. Her breathing was labored, her hands trembled. The tee shirt beneath her body armor was saturated.

She saw the dark figure off to her left, muzzle flashes poured from his assault rifle. He was less than 50 feet away, turned sideways from her. He fired mercilessly point blank into the crowd. She circled to her left, staying low, keeping out of the shooter's field of vision. The clatter of gunfire and screams from dying people drove her faster. She had to take this guy out. No warning, no offer to surrender. Just take him down before he could reload another mag.

More sirens in the distance. It sounded like a parade of police cars and fire trucks and ambulances coming down the clogged strip. She knew her supervisor would have requested mutual aid by now. Her father would know she was on duty. He always monitored the police scanner; just to hear her voice, to know his baby was safe. Her eyes burned at the thought of what must be going through his mind. He would be burning up the highway to get here. Help would be pouring onto the scene in minutes, but that was too long. People were dying all around her.

Officer Edwards stood, rushed forward several more steps until she had the shooter well within range. She was an expert shot with the Glock Model 22, but she needed to make sure a civilian would not pop up in her line of fire.

The terrorist burned through another 30-round mag and dropped the empty on the ground. In one swift movement, he pulled a fresh mag out of the canvas bag that hanged from his neck. He slammed the mag into the rifle and released the charging handle. In less than ten seconds he was ready to fire.

"HEY!" That was all the warning Tiana was giving. The terrorist paused in mid aim and turned in her direction. She stood straight on, faced her target, feet spread, and fired in a classic two-hand stance.

The first nine-millimeter round punched the terrorist in the forehead, killing him instantly, the second hit him in the throat. Tiana lowered her aim to center mass and kept firing. All 15 rounds found their mark before the terrorist crashed to the ground.

Without hesitation, Tiana Edwards slapped a fresh mag into her Glock and wheeled around. She dashed full speed back across the parking lot toward the front of the theater. Her breathing was ragged, sweat streamed down her face burning her eyes.

"Shooter down, east side," She said into the epaulet mic as calmly as she could on a dead run. "I'm going to the front!"

A pair of police cars wheeled down the street on the west side of the theater. Their red and blue strobes flashing in the night failed to clear the stalled traffic. Upon hearing Officer Edwards' radio traffic the officer in the trailing car slid to a stop, bailed out of his car, and dashed a hundred yards across the parking lot.

The second terrorist was completely exposed and brazenly stood in the light at the front of the theater, not forty feet from the entry steps. Bodies were stacked up in front of him, sprawled across the entry porch at grotesque angles. A wisp of smoke drifted from the muzzle of the AK-47 as he dropped a spent mag on the asphalt and slammed another one home.

Officer Edwards charged toward him at an angle to minimize chances of catching a civilian in a crossfire, but out of the corner of his eye the terrorist saw her rushing forward.

The terrorist spun toward her, holding the trigger down as he turned. The resulting spray of bullets cut down a young couple as they raced down the sidewalk away from the entrance. Tiana caught sight of the girl catapulted off her feet, her white formal evening gown flying above her head, one shoe going end-over-end through the air.

Officer Edwards froze for a split second as the arch of bullets sprayed in her direction. She felt a burning sting in her shoulder, which galvanized her into action. She dove headlong against a parked car, rolled to her right, coming up at the rear of the car with her arms resting on the trunk lid. She lined the iron sights on the target and snapped off two quick rounds just as bullets pinged off the top of the car.

She dropped down behind the vehicle in a sitting position, gasping for breath. *Did I get him?* She thought she saw him stagger when she fired. She rolled on the ground and looked under the car to see if she could spot his body, or at least his feet.

Nothing? Where did he go?

She bolted upright, her back against the cool metal of the car. Fighting back panic, she struggled to catch her breath. *Why am I suddenly so weak?* Her left shoulder burned; pain spread across her chest, making her nauseous. She could not raise her arm. She touched her shoulder and felt the warm sticky ooze between her fingers. *I'm hit*! She realized for the first time. She started to lay her weapon down and reach for her mic, but then sensed danger. The terrorist was coming for her.

It seemed as if time slowed to a crawl. She could hear people screaming and crying and running in all directions, but the sound was remote as if it were a hundred miles away. She shook her head to clear it, then rolled face down to look under the car again. The movement brought a shock of pain so intense she had to stifle a scream.

Tiana was shocked, her eyes went wide with fear. She was staring at the terrorist's feet just on the other side of the car. He was stalking her.

She sat upright again, moving as silently as possible. Slowly, she pulled her heels up against her butt and struggled to raise her left arm but it was limp, lying useless at her side. She steadied her gun hand on her knees. Tiana glanced at the ground ahead of her and saw his shadow coming around the front of the car. He moved slowly with the rifle against his shoulder, ready to fire in a split second.

Maybe he doesn't know I'm here, she hoped. Her breathing was ragged and her heart beat so loudly she was sure he could hear.

He rounded the front fender, rifle poised to fire, his eyes blazed and his teeth glistened in a triumphant, evil sneer.

Officer Tiana Edwards shot him square in the face … five times.

Thirty-Four

Whiteman Air Force Base
Knob Noster,
Missouri

It was four in the morning, dark and chilly on the flight line, when Matt entered the Ready Room. He yawned and stretched and peered around the room with bloodshot eyes. He slept no more than 30 minutes all night. From the looks on the faces staring back none of them had slept much either.

The entire CRT was present, scattered lazily around the room, legs dangled over chair arms, arms folded tightly across their chests as if trying to ward off the chill in the air. The TV was on CNN, still replaying the events from yesterday. The audio was muted because everyone was numb to the unfolding horror. The ribbon scrolling across the bottom ran the casualty tally. More than 1500 American lives snuffed out by radical Islamic terrorists and the number was climbing. More bodies were pulled from rubble, more of the critically wounded died on surgical tables. Occasionally a new report popped up.

Another suicide bombing. Another mall, bus station, hospital lobby …

There had been fifty-seven bombings so far and more were reported each hour.

Six bombers had been gunned down before they could detonate their lethal package in a crowded area. Heightened awareness in the law enforcement community was beginning to pay off.

Matt shook his head as he watched the numbers climb. Monday morning quarterbacks and Pundits alike would come out of the woodwork like water circling the drain, casting blame on the president and the entire administration for failure to issue some kind of specific warning of imminent danger. "*The public had a right to know*," they would be shouting. Blah, blah, blah! Those same naysayers would conveniently overlook the fact that three months ago the Director of National Intelligence, on behalf of the President of the United States, warned of a clear and present danger within our own borders.

Matt stopped at the coffee pot, poured a cup, then joined Georgia who was slumped over her computer, staring blankly at the screen. There was a half eaten donut beside her. Matt picked it up and stuffed it in his mouth before she could grab it. When she looked up in protest, he noticed her eyes looked worse than his own. He washed the donut down with a gulp of rancid coffee and put the cup on the desk.

"Long night, huh?" He said

"Yup." She nodded at the screen. "First images from Birddog One. They've been filtered by Clayton."

Matt stooped to stare at the screen, another image popped up. The photos were high-resolution aerials, color, far better clarity than satellite images. They showed acres of relatively flat farmland, dotted with houses and barns and white gravel roads. Fencerows separated livestock from crops and small creeks fed into a river meandering through the countryside. Tranquil, Norman Rockwell stuff, serene and pleasant. But somewhere down there was a madman. *And I'm gonna find him!* Another photo flashed on the screen, same scene.

"That guy work all night?" Matt asked.

"Without a break, far as I know." Georgia's eyes stayed on the screen.

Lt. Cmdr. Clayton Downs surprised everyone last night when he zipped into Whiteman on the wings of a U.S. Navy C-20, a military variant of the Gulf Stream III. He arrived four hours *after* he had landed Birddog One on the same runway and strolled into the pilot's ready room looking fresh and rested.

The Sea Avenger was presently tucked away, sharing space with a B-2 Stealth Bomber in one of the mammoth high-security hangars while Clayton sat alone in the mobile ACGCS, hunched over a computer workstation, a tepid can of coke in one hand. His practiced eye studied each photograph, deciding on which needed a second look and which to discard. None jumped out with convicting evidence.

"Send him a message. Tell him to put that thing on auto upload and get over here."

"Aw man!" Chase came from behind to peer over their shoulders at the images. "Not a moonshine still in the bunch."

"Now when's the last time you drank moonshine?" Matt asked sarcastically.

Chase looked at the ceiling as if in deep thought. "Back when we were like fifteen. Remember, we stole it from Uncle Billy's stash." He turned to Georgia and said, "Boy, we got our britches tanned but good that day!"

Georgia chuckled, but then her face went serious and she turned back to Matt. "Did you see the update on the attack in Branson?"

Matt nodded solemnly. That attack had staggered them all. It was only 150 miles away by air. Practically in their backyard. Nowhere near what you could call a population center. Strictly a soft target. He had turned away in revulsion after being bombarded with gruesome details for nearly three hours. He stumbled out the door, puked all over a fresh flowerbed, and then jogged all the way back to his bungalow where he spent one of the most restless nights of his life.

Forty-seven people were killed inside the Grand Palace; six times that many had been maimed. One hundred and seventy-eight had been gunned down trying to escape the horror inside the theater; one police officer wounded while heroically saving dozens of lives. Three terrorists had been killed; none were captured, though speculation ran wild that one may have been spotted speeding away from the theater moments *before* the explosion. That was yet to be confirmed.

It wasn't supposed to happen this way. Not in the heartland. Not to innocent lives doing innocent things. Matt clinched his fists, his chest pounded. Sweat ran down his face.

"Matt?" Georgia reached out and touched his arm.

He shook his head, forcing his mind back to the present. "Yeah! …Time to get to work."

~~~~~~~

The Farm
15 Miles North
Mexico, Missouri

For the first time in many nights, Ahmad Hassam slept well. The attack was on schedule, far better than they had hoped. He was back on his feet now, standing just inside the control room. Roosters crowed in the gray dawn. Ali hovered in the shadows. Hassam scanned the news feeds, sensing the tension and fear beneath a thin veneer of stoicism on each news anchor. The infidels were already cracking. They had no taste for war. They would be powerless to defend themselves. Especially when he released *Mylh-A'sifh*. But first his warriors would give the American devils a taste of fear.

On his command, roving bands of Islamic fighters would blaze a fiery swath through public gatherings; they would drop IEDs in the path of mass transit buses, fire trucks, and police cars; they would launch grenades and mortars into police stations, fire stations, churches, and sporting events throughout the United States. They would strike swiftly and brutally, and disappear into the shadows, only to strike again and again.

In two days the infidels would be on their knees, begging for mercy, denouncing their arrogant, self-indulgent ways. But it would be too late, because then he would release *Mylh-A'sifh*.

Hassam's revelry was disturbed by the soft voice of Rashad Hussain.

" *Ya qâd*, are you ready for the next round of *shaheed*?" The computer guru smiled with malice. He enjoyed his first taste of blood.

Hassam nodded, rocking on the balls of his feet, hands clasped behind his back.

The American intelligence network would have realized by now that it was the signal burst yesterday that activated the suicide bombers. He knew another "*as-Syf*" signal would strike fear in his enemies because they would quickly understand another 100 bombers would take to the streets; and there was no way to stop them.

Larijani appeared at his side, motioning him to the front of the house. "We may have a problem," the diminutive second in command said in a low voice.

Hassam followed Larijani into the kitchen and saw the two Gargus brothers, Buck and Cleon, standing inside the screen door.

"These men have informed me that their younger brother did not return last night. They went into town to look for him."

Hassam glared at the two uncouth individuals in dirt covered, tattered overalls. He could smell their body odor from twelve feet away. They appeared not to be intimated by his glare. That would change.

"They discovered Leroy has been arrested by the city police—"

"Afta they's bloodied 'im up a mite," Buck interrupted.

"Yep, took three of them there government fellers to takes ol' Leroy down," Cleon crowed.

"Three *government* people?" Hassam turned his question to Larijani.

"Yeah, tha's what them—"

Larijani silenced Cleon with an upraised palm. He knew Hassam had already dismissed the Gargus brothers from his mind. He explained that friends of the Gargus brothers supposedly observed Leroy's capture by three men claiming to be NCTC agents, then turned him over to the local police after roughing him up a bit.

"So *he* has followed us here already," Hassam frowned. His face grew dark. "This is much sooner than expected. He is very good."

"Perhaps not," Larijani ventured. "They left very quickly after turning Leroy over to the police. I think it odd that they did not take him with them … or question him at the police station."

"They will return," Hassam said with certainty. "We need the one you call Leroy back before he tells—"

"Leroy ain't gonna say nuthin'," Buck Gargus interrupted.

Hassam jerked his head in their direction. "You two! Go after your brother. Bring him back here immediately. Do you understand?"

"Yes, sir," they said in unison and scuttled out the door. They saw the fire in Hassam's eyes and for once in their recalcitrant lives knew better than to talk back.

Hassam motioned to his giant bodyguard after the Gargus brothers left. "Ali, follow them. If they try to flee, or fail to get their brother out of jail, I want you to kill them."

Ali nodded, smiled obediently, and lumbered out the door.

"I want new eyes on the town and the airport, my friend," Hassam said to Larijani. "And we need to expedite our departure from this place."

Thirty-Five

Whiteman Air Force Base
Knob Noster,
Missouri

"Sorry, these aren't going to help us much," Clayton Downs shook his head. He had a thumb drive from the mobile ACGCS loaded with more photos of the target area surrounding the town of Mexico. Clayton had his father's tall frame so Matt, sitting on the computer desk with his feet in one of the straight-back chairs, had to look up at him. Georgia Shayne and Butch Larson crowded around the desk. Chase was with the others in the chow hall for breakfast.

"Any other ideas?" Matt asked. "Hassam ordered up another round of suicide bombers a little while ago. We have to shut him down. Permanently!"

"Well, everything points to him being in the area. We've focused on farms and farm land, based on what AJ said …" Clayton paused, paced around the room. He held his chin in his right thumb and index finger, exactly as the president did when deep in thought. "Hassam would have a fairly large security force surrounding the command bunker, right?"

"Sure will," Butch answered. He moved closer to study the photos.

"Exactly! … My bad for not thinking of this yesterday. Must be fatigue"

"What?" Georgia asked.

"Thermal Imagining! Who else would have sentries hiding in trees and on roof tops? We need to overfly the area with the infrared sensor engaged. Look for warm bodies." Clayton's eyes were wide with excitement.

Matt nodded enthusiastically. "How soon can you get started?"

"Avenger is fueled and ready to fly." Clayton glanced at his watch. "Wheels up in thirty minutes. The route is pre-programmed. I can reset sensor commands in flight. Can't guarantee anything in the heat of the day. Works better at night."

"Alright," Matt said. "Let's get started. If nothing turns up in the first pass, expand the area."

"Roger that!" Clayton scooted out the door, nearly colliding with Chase.

"There goes a man on a mission. What's up?" Chase asked.

"He's gonna lead us to Hassam," Matt smiled. Suddenly the hopelessness he had been carrying on his shoulders seemed lighter.

"So, what are *we* gonna do?" someone asked. All eyes turned to Matt, waiting for an answer.

"We're gonna saddle up and pay another visit to Mexico."

"Aiee Chihuahua mis amigos!" Chase shouted. They all laughed.

"The whole team?" Butch asked.

"The whole danged team!"

"And when we get there?" Georgia asked, expectantly.

Matt grinned. "Gonna kick over an anthill, see what comes crawlin' out! Chase, call down to Master Chief Roberts. Tell him I want the Osprey ready to fly in half an hour."

"Woohoo!"Chase shouted excitedly.

~~~~~~~

Mexico Memorial Airport
Mexico, Missouri

Matt shut down the engines on the big Osprey. He unbuckled his harness, climbed out of his seat, and pulled the M9 from the thigh-mount holster, which he attached to the back of the pilot seat when he flew. He tucked the pistol into the waistband in the small of his back. He wore a button down short-sleeve shirt outside of his Wrangler jeans to conceal the weapon. This would be a soft probe, for now.

Chase mimicked Matt's movements, grateful that he was again included on the frontline of whatever lay ahead.

Sammy Hogan met them on the ramp. His eyes were the size of silver dollars when fourteen men piled out of the Osprey; they went wider still when Georgia Shayne stepped onto the parking ramp. He had read articles on the versatile tilt-rotor aircraft, but never in his wildest dreams did he ever expect to see one close up. Especially sitting here on *his* airport.

"Holy Smokes!" The boy stammered. His eyes went back to the stunning woman accompanying so many armed feds. It was not her blue FBI windbreaker he was staring at.

"Hey, Sammy," Matt greeted the boy from thirty feet away. "Can we borrow your wheels again?"

"Yes, sir. I suppose so." His eyes drifted momentarily to Matt, but immediately returned to Georgia as he spoke.

Matt smiled and whispered to Chase. "Raging hormones,"

"Yup! I can relate. I'm in love too." Chase shot a glance at Georgia.

"You always are."

Several minutes later they climbed into Sammy's candy apple red jacked-up Dodge Ram. Chase was again at the wheel with Matt riding shotgun. Georgia piled into the rear seat along with Butch Larson. The rest of the Watchdog unit stayed with the Osprey. Master Chief Walter Roberts already had his grease rag out, climbing around the aircraft in search of oil leaks or any other gremlin that might be afflicting *his* bird.

"Where we headed first, Cuz?" Chase asked, cranking the wheel hard left to point the pickup down the road between rows of cornfields.

Matt stared at the flag poles near the terminal entrance. The flags were at half mast. He watched the honor guard at Whiteman raising the colors at sunrise this morning. With solemn, traditional etiquette, the flags were taken to full mast, and then reverently lowered back to half. He knew that flags across America would be lowered today, in honor of those innocent citizens who perished in the attacks. They would remain at half mast for many days.

He reached into his shirt pocket and pulled out the business card from Detective Scott Brown. "Take us to the police station, 300 North Coal Street."

"Do you really think Mr. Leroy Gargus spilled his guts before the FBI agents carted him away?" Georgia asked.

"Not likely. I would like to talk more with the detective. Police chief too, if—"

"Good morning, Quarterback." The familiar voice in Matt's earbud sounded uncharacteristically cheerful. *"I see you are back in Mexico already."*

"Hey Carter. You sound cheerful this morning." Matt assumed Manning must be tracking them from the NCTC

Command Center. The comm-sets had GPS units that transmitted their location to an electronic map.

"*Amazing what a little sleep can do for the disposition, isn't it?*"

"Grandma always said things look better in the daylight."

"*Yes, well, let's hope grandma was right. I only have a minute before heading back to the White House, Matt. I wanted you to know that I concur with the data from VCSN and ELINT assets. There is a strong possibility Hassam is near your location … We are pulling out all the stops today, Matthew. Anything you need let AJ know.*"

"Roger that, sir."

"*I see you got the surprise we sent yesterday.*"

Matt knew Manning was talking about Clayton Downs. Live feeds from the Sea Avenger were being transmitted to NCTC and the Situation Room, so Manning knew Birddog One was on station circling the area.

"Yes sir. Appreciate it very much. He will make a difference."

"*Excellent. Good hunting and Godspeed.*"

Thirty-Six

Department of Public Safety
Mexico, Missouri

"No, we didn't have a chance to interrogate him. Talking through a busted face was a bit difficult for him." Detective Scott Brown scowled at Butch and shook his head. "FBI picked him up a couple hours after we brought him in from the hospital."

Detective Brown's small office was crowded with five people. A pair of file cabinets, a scarred oak desk, and two wooden straight back chairs in front of the desk made it even more crowded. Brown apologized to Chase and Butch Larson for having them stand. The single window overlooking the rear parking lot was covered with an open venetian blind. With the door closed it didn't take long for the office to get stuffy.

"The waitress at Porky's mentioned strangers hanging around town," Matt stated. "She said they had brown skin, dark hair, thought they might be Hispanic. Do you see that often around here?" Matt asked.

"Not at all unusual around harvest time. But year round? It caused quite a buzz."

The detective grinned. "Now that you've raised the possibility of Islamic terrorists it all fits."

He leaned back in his chair and ran a hand through his brown hair. "How on earth—"

The phone interrupted. Brown leaned forward, snatched up the receiver and paused. "Okay, thanks. We'll be right down." He looked up at Matt and Georgia. "Chief's back. Let's go!"

They followed Detective Brown to an office at the end of the dark hallway. Brown rapped on the closed door bearing the word "Chief", opened it without waiting for a reply, and led the group inside. The office was huge compared to the detective's. A dark cherry wood desk sat directly across from the door in front of a large window. Two red leather chairs sat directly in front of the desk. In the center of the wood paneled room a small, circular conference table was surrounded by four similar chairs. The chief's hero wall on the left of the desk contained a collection of framed photos and plaques testifying to her popularity and prestige.

Chief of Public Safety Susan Watts came from behind the desk to meet her visitors. She was a short, stocky woman in her late forties. Her smile was warm and genuine and confident. Her short brunette hair was parted on one side and she had a golden tan from spending considerable time in the field with her officers.

Chief Watts greeted each of them with a firm handshake. "Come in please, sit."

She returned to her high-back desk chair while Matt and Georgia took the two chairs closest to the desk. Chase, Butch, and Detective Brown sat at the conference table. A brass desk lamp with an oblong green glass shade was flanked by a model fire engine and patrol car; both with markings of the Mexico Department of Public Safety. She noticed Matt was checking them out.

"I am the director for police and fire," she stated. "Try to spend as much time as I can with the fire guys."

"Bet that keeps you busy," Matt replied with a smile.

"It's a labor of love," she gestured with the flip of a hand. "Let me say, that was quite a bombshell you dropped on my detective yesterday … before you blew out of town." Her smile disappeared.

Lady gets right to the point, Matt thought. *I like that.*

"Yes, ma'am. In retrospect, it probably was and I apologize for that. We got an urgent call to return to base."

"And that 'urgent call' was the reason my flags are at half mast today?" she frowned.

Matt nodded. "Yes, ma'am."

"That adds considerably to your bombshell." She paused for a moment. "And you people seem to think we have Islamic terrorists right here in our community?"

"Yes, ma'am."

Chief Watts cocked her head and studied each face. Her features grew stern. "Okay, how can we help?"

Matt leaned forward. "Leroy Gargus knows something. What can you tell us about him?

Watts turned to Georgia. "FBI couldn't get anything out of him either?"

"Not that we've heard," she answered.

"Where does he live?" Matt asked.

"You gonna ransack his home?" Brown asked with a grin.

"Probably!"

Chief Watts exchanged glances with her detective, then gave a nod.

"Okay," Brown began. "Leroy lives with his two older brothers. Buck, he's the oldest, and Cleon. All three are about as useless as tits on a tomcat. Excuse me, ma'am,"

Brown said to Georgia. She merely shrugged and motioned for him to continue.

"They have a rundown farmhouse about six miles west of town. Parents left them the farm. Used to be a couple hundred acres but they've sold off all but a few acres and squandered away all the money—"

Matt glanced at the others with a raised eyebrow. *Couple hundred acres? Maybe we need to be focusing west of town.*

Chief Watts caught the silent exchange. "Farm's out in the county, so if you're gonna go poking around we'll have a deputy sheriff take you out."

Matt nodded. The chief glanced at Georgia and asked, "Search warrant?"

Georgia inclined her head toward Matt. "He doesn't believe in them."

"I kind of figured that," Watts said, sizing up Matt.

"Might not find them there, though," Detective Brown interjected. "Word on the street is they've been doing some work for the buyers at the old Tucker farm."

"That's the second time we've heard about that place," Georgia said, getting a confirming nod from the others.

"Who are the new owners?" Matt asked.

"Dunno. That's way out in the county. North of here."

"Anyway to find out?" Georgia asked.

"One minute." Chief Watts picked up the phone and dialed the Audrain County Courthouse located in town. "Assessor's office, please."

"While you're at it," Matt said softly, "can you ask who purchased the acreage on the Gargus farm?"

Chief Watts nodded her head, and then spoke into the receiver, "Sheila? … I'm Good, thanks. Hey, I need a favor." She gave the clerk the information. "We're in a bit of a rush for this, Sheila. Okay, thanks."

Chief Watts hung up the phone but kept the receiver in her hand. "She's looking up the info and will get back to us. Leave your cell number. I'll call soon as I hear."

Matt nodded. "Appreciate it!"

"Hold on!" She dialed the phone again. "Glen, Chief Watts. Hey, I have some people in my office in need of one of your deputies." She began explaining the situation, but then stopped. "You know what; you need to hear this from them. Can you come right over?" They talked for a few seconds before she hung up.

"That was Sheriff Glen Daniels. His office is over at the courthouse. He'll be here in five minutes."

"Thanks again," Matt said with sincerity. "You make things happen."

"Well, you people seem to be in a hurry. Besides, there is a cost to all of this."

Chief Watts smiled and winked at Detective Brown.

Matt raised his eyebrows with an inquiring look.

"We want to be in on it when you find the low-life-scum-bucket responsible for these attacks."

Less than half an hour later they walked out of the police station into bright sunshine with Sheriff Daniels in tow. By the time Matt and Georgia finished sharing as much of the intel as they dared with Daniels and Chief Watts, the sheriff readily agreed to have a deputy lead them out to the Gargus farm. By the time the deputy pulled in front of the police station the county assessor's clerk had called with the parcel numbers.

They merged into light traffic heading west behind the deputy's blue Chevy Tahoe. Matt flipped on his comm-set.

"Birddog One, Quarterback."

"*Birddog One, go!*"

"Birddog, I have two county parcel numbers. Can you convert to a GPS fix on both?"

"*Sure can! Shoot 'em to me,*" Clayton's voice sounded enthusiastic.

"Great! How goes the infrared search?"

"Terrible! Should have started earlier. Sun's warming ground surfaces too quickly."

Matt handed the slip of paper containing the parcel numbers back to Georgia. They brought along the satellite laptop and portable three-in-one printer from the Osprey. In two minutes she was transmitting the data to Birddog One.

"So what's your plan, Birddog?"

"Have to wait for dark on the infrared. In the meantime, I am coordinating with two ELINT COMSATS to triangulate his next transmission. Maybe we'll get lucky."

"Matt, AJ here. Do you copy?"

"Gotcha, AJ. What's up?" They had jumped on Highway 54 about two miles out of town and Chase mashed down on the gas to keep the sheriff's deputy in sight.

"Leroy Gargus is a dead end. He is not talking."

"That's because they ain't askin' right," Matt offered.

"Yes, well, we've been over that." AJ paused, then continued. *"We have something going with Rashad Hussain, owner of NetDesign & DataSolutions. FBI had him on the Watch List a few years ago. He was under surveillance but nothing came of it. Eventually he was deemed harmless, but remained in the database.*

"One of the files from his Kansas City office reveals Mr. Hussain might do more than just design software. He taught a course at Isfahan University on writing malware."

"As in cyber warfare?" Matt asked.

"Pretty much. It was a postgraduate class on social engineering—That means hacking to you, Chase."

"How can anyone so beautiful be so downright hateful?" Chase responded with a chuckle.

"Oh, Chase. You know you love me."

"Shush, lady!" Chase lowered his voice. "Georgi is listenin'. Don't want her to know anything about us. Might scare her away."

"Anyway," they could hear AJ laughing through their earbuds. *"There's plenty of data hidden in the files, all of it in code. Coupled with a discovery at NSA that someone has hacked into two commercial satellites and possibly a military comsat as well. Looks like Hussain is one of the sleeper agents working for Ahmad Hassam.*

"The troubling thing is, guys, there's a possibility these attacks may be just a diversion."

"A diversion?" Matt asked. "A diversion for what?"

The thought of something even more terrifying than the unprecedented attacks on soft targets was incomprehensible. What? Steal airplanes and slam them into targets, again? Or maybe—*Oh dear Lord no!*

"Did they bring a nuke into the country?" Matt demanded.

"Matt, we don't know for sure what's going on. Too soon to tell. Right now we have to get a handle on this cyber activity if we are going to stop Hassam's command center from sending out more attack codes, but we are just spinning our wheels here."

"What you need, AJ, is a champion hacker," Clayton broke in.

"Right you are, Clayton. The FBI pulled in some NSA analysts to help. The geeks are digging through the files, but it is slow going. Too slow!"

"Maybe they're starting from the wrong end. Perhaps I can help."

"You a "champion hacker, Clayton?" Matt asked.

"Of course. How else could you build effective firewalls to protect your software without knowing all the ways a cyber attack can be made? Learned that hard lesson back in junior high when some jealous lout hacked my best

game right before it was ready for marketing. I wanted to kill him, but dad said that might be a bit extreme. "

"But is this really necessary?" Matt asked. "After we locate the farm and take it out, won't that kill Hassam's commands to his fighters."

"Not necessarily. If Rashad installed malware in the compromised satellites it's quite likely he has it set up to automatically send commands on a programmed time table. That's how I would do it."

"Good point, but I need you in the UAV. At least 'til we find Hassam's control center."

"This thing practically flies itself. But actually, I was thinking of my assistant on Iwo Jima. Lt. Louis Rogers, is an accomplished hacker in his own right. Let's get him up here to Whiteman. There's plenty of room in the ACGCS and more than enough computer power. We can notionalize the problem together—that's computer lingo for brainstorming, Chase."

"What is this, pick on Chase day?" Chase asked with a grin.

The truck rocked back and forth as they veered off the highway onto a narrow county farm road without slowing. Matt quickly grabbed the handhold on the door post.

Up ahead a cloud of dust shot up as the deputy whipped left onto a gravel road. Seconds later Chase steered the pickup off the pavement and followed the trail of dust. Even with the windows up tight the gray cloud seeped into the cab.

"Sammy ain't gonna have a clean truck for long," Chase said, yanking the truck into a ninety degree turn at the end of a long barbed wire fence. The cloud from the deputy's SUV hung in the still air, reducing visibility to a few feet. They barely avoided splashing into a culvert.

"Back it off a little, Chase." Butch Larson groused. "We can follow that dust trail from a mile away."

Thirty-Seven

Gargus Brothers Farm
Six Miles West of
Mexico, Missouri

A few chickens scratched the dirt in front of the broken down two-story farmhouse. A mangy old dog limped across the yard and slowly climbed the decayed wooden steps leading to the front porch. To the right of the house a tattered gate hung half open from a dilapidated wooden fence in an overgrown pathway which led to a ramshackle barn. The exterior was a faded grayish red. Waist-high weeds testified that livestock had not occupied the barnyard for many years.

The house was quiet, the front door hung partially open on one hinge. Matt did not need a search warrant to look into the ragged, unkempt front room, not that he would have waited for one in the first place. He brushed past the deputy sheriff with his Beretta in a two-hand grip and stormed through the open door with Georgia on his six. Chase and Larson ran around the side of the house to cover the rear.

Matt and Georgia moved quickly from room to room. He charged up the rickety stairs to the second floor while she went through to the kitchen in back of the house. She paused a moment to tell the guys in back to check the outbuildings. In a matter of minutes they had cleared the house. When Matt returned downstairs he found the deputy standing in the front room, hands on his hips with a mixed expression of awe and disbelief on his face.

"What on earth did you expect to find here," he asked.

"Not sure," Matt responded absentmindedly as he glanced around the room. "Somethin' that ties the Gargus brothers to foreign bad guys." The deputy's eyes went wide.

"Nothing," Georgia reported upon coming from the back of the house. "Want to toss the place?"

"You betcha!"

It took several minutes for the three of them to thoroughly search every nook and cranny. Once the deputy got the hang of it, he proved a worthy assistant.

It was obvious the brothers had taken most of their personal items as if they planned an extended stay elsewhere. Even the cupboards were bare and the ancient refrigerator contained only sour milk and some disgusting leftovers growing black mold. They gathered outside, Chase and Larson confirmed the same findings. No one had been there for some time.

"So now what?" The deputy asked with a puzzled frown.

"We hold off 'til we get a little more intel," Larson answered.

Matt nodded in agreement.

"Huh? What about the Tucker farm?"

"Later," was Matt's only response as they returned to the pickup. He did not want another episode like this. *Don't go bustin' in on a possible terrorist hideout ninety miles an hour with your hair on fire!* That is what Matt wanted to yell at the deputy, but he held his temper. Had this been Hassam's command center the deputy would be dead right now, quite possibly all of them. The deputy meant well; leading them to the home of local yahoos like it was an everyday occurrence. Without radio contact with the deputy, they had no way to slow him down or even caution him. Trying to catch up with him merely spurred him to go faster, as if there were a sense of urgency. Matt would not let that happen again.

"Quarterback, Birddog One!"

"Go Birddog!"

"General area is clear."

Matt automatically glanced up at the cloudless sky. "Roger that, Birddog. Give the second site a good look." The deputy followed Matt's gaze with raised eyebrows.

~~~~~~~

The Farm
15 Miles North
Mexico, Missouri

Hassam stood behind Rashad Hussain, watching over the computer tech's shoulder. He rubbed his eyes and stretched. He needed sleep soon or he would be of little use to the jihad, but it was nearly to time to launch *Mylh-A'sifh.* He would have to hold on for a few more hours.

"There! Another one, *sayyid,* master!" Hussain shouted triumphantly. It was bombing number 93 in the second round. This one was inside a movie theater in Pittsburg, 12 dead and twice that many injured.

"That makes 187 bombings thus far." Rashad turned to look at Hassam, his eyes gleamed with pride. "Surely the *Shaheed* is a great success!"

"Yes," Hassam reluctantly agreed. *But wait until you see* my *warriors take the stage, my young friend.* Hassam wanted to say.

"Ahmad!" Larijani called softly from behind. "They have returned."

Hassam turned and followed Larijani into the kitchen where Ali had Buck and Cleon Gargus on their knees. Cleon was crying, Buck glared up at Hassam in defiance.

"This how ya treats people that does ya favors?" The older Gargus asked.

"Depends what 'favors' you have done today, my friend." Hassam smirked. "Where is Leroy?"

"Feds took 'im! Nuthin' we could do 'bout it."

Hassam turned to Larijani. "Do we know if he talked to the locals?"

"Told ya 'afore, Leroy ain't gonna talk—"

"SILENCE!" Hassam shouted in Buck's face, then turned to Larijani.

"That is unknown, *as-Syf.*" The small lieutenant shifted on his feet. He hated delivering bad news to his friend. He lowered his voice, "The man we sent to the airport reports the black Osprey has landed. Many men are gathered around it."

Hassam stared into the distance; his blood went hot, his eyes blazed with fire.

Tense veins stood out on his neck. The American infidel was on his trail. It would not be long before he found the farm.

"How many men?

"Perhaps a dozen, he thinks."

"*Phew*!" Hassam waved is hand dismissively. "A dozen will not be enough for what is waiting for them here."

"I agree, Ahmad. But perhaps we should consider moving to our alternate site."

Hassam paused, deep in thought. "Yes," he said reluctantly. He knew this moment would come. He had planned for it. Still, it was not easy for the warrior inside him to turn tail and retreat in the face of the enemy.

Especially in the face of the infidel who taunted him. "It is time," he whispered.

Hassam moved across the room and silently withdrew the scimitar from the scabbard on Ali's back. The master terrorist moved like a shadow, standing over the Gargus brothers from behind. Buck never heard the large sword scything through the air, never felt it slice through his neck. Cleon had time to scream as he saw his brother's head bounce off the floor, and then everything went black.

Hassam handed the sword to Ali and walked back to the control room. He knew Rashad was not going to be happy about leaving. The computer guru had invested much energy in making this site perfect in every way. But, he too knew the time would come for them to vacate this place. That is why he built the mobile command unit as the real nerve center. It would function even better.

"Rashad?" Hassam laid a hand on the computer wizard's shoulder. "Tell me again how long it will take to break all this down and have the mobile command center in operation."

Hussain looked up with apprehension. "Only a few minutes, Ahmad." It was the first time he dared call the leader by his first name. "We only need to unplug the cables from the motorhome and drive away. If you desire time-delay messages sent from here it will take a moment to enter the commands and connect the system to external antenna."

"Do it now, my friend," Hassam smiled thinly. "Set your equipment to send the *Mylh-A'sifh* command in …" he glanced at his watch … "Four hours."

"It shall be done! *Yathaï ilâh'!* Praise be to Allah!"

The final execution of *Operation Firestorm* centered on Rashad Hussain's prize creation, a Cryptic Hardware Accelerator, which he named *Rostam* after the mythical Persian holy warrior of the 10th Century. Unlike the myth who had supposedly slain his nation's imaginary enemies,

Hussain's device could potentially slay thousands of enemies of Iran. The small portable device attached to his computer contained the encrypted codes necessary to unleash an unprecedented, highly focused, computer virus.

Thirty-Eight

Mexico Memorial Airport
Mexico, Missouri

"We'll need Highway 15 shut down at twenty-two hundred hours, okay?" Matt looked across the planning table at Chief Susan Watts and Sheriff Glen Daniels.

"Why so early if you're not pushing off 'til midnight?" Sheriff Daniels asked.

"We *strike* at midnight," corrected Butch Larson, speaking up for Matt. "This gives us a couple hours to get in place without some citizen wandering into our staging area."

"Gives your deputies time to clear any stragglers out of the area before we land," Georgia added, with a little more subtlety.

Matt made it abundantly clear that neither agency would be allowed inside the assault area. Their presence would create too much confusion once bullets started flying. Instead, he wanted their help in containing the outer perimeter.

They were hunkered over an area map covered with symbols and checkpoints, which Matt and Larson had added throughout the afternoon. A satellite map downloaded from Clayton gave them a better idea of actual topography around the farm. He had identified a good location to land the Osprey on the west side of highway 15, a good two miles from the farm. The terrorists would not be able to hear the silent tilt-rotor from that distance.

Those at the table were joined by Lt. Wally Beemer and Gunny Stevens. They would each take half of the Recon Marines to predetermined locations west of the farm.

The rest of the Crisis Response Team clustered outside of the terminal building, lounging in chairs or lying on the concrete patio, enjoying the cool evening air. They were dressed for battle in navy blue NCTC utilities. Their tactical gear was piled in the open door of the Osprey.

The group had taken over the airport terminal shortly after closing time. Sammy's father saw the black Osprey when he returned from spraying crops. He took one look at the Crisis Response Team cleaning and checking their weapons, passed the keys to the terminal over to Matt, and pushed his son out the door.

~~~~~~~

Chase and EZ slid into the waste-high water and moved slowly upstream. The south fork of the Salt River looped around the Tucker Farm, providing fertile bottom land on two sides. The men would exit the stream about a quarter of a mile from the farm, advancing under the cover of darkness through a patch of thick woods.

The men had a two-hour head start on the others. Their task was to get into position to provide overwatch from which they could observe the target area well before the actual assault. Matt wanted Chase on the mission as an experienced forward observer to communicate with the UAV and himself. Besides, he had a fair working knowledge with the range finder and spotter scope, and that was good enough for Matt to overrule EZ's protests.

The black water was freezing cold and Chase struggled to keep his teeth from chattering. He did not want to give EZ another reason to grouse over his presence. Every noise brought a glare from the Recon Marine; every stumble brought an I-told-you-so shake of the head. Chase was overjoyed with the opportunity to be on the frontline of the action, but knew he had to prove his worth to the expert sniper.

Peep frogs and crickets sang their chorus in the cool night air, drowning out the splashing sounds the two men made pushing upstream. It was a slow current, but the slick rocks on the riverbed slowed their progress. Chase slipped, nearly going under before catching himself. He sputtered with a mouthful of water and found that he'd fallen behind again.

"Keep up, flyboy," EZ growled.

According to the GPS on his wrist, Chase saw they were half way from getting out of the river. *I'll be an ice cube before then,* he thought. He questioned the sanity of his decision to volunteer for this mission.

~~~~~~~

Clayton raised his arms above his head, stretched, and then began rubbing the kinks out of his right shoulder. He flew the Sea Avenger inside the FAA pre-approved block of airspace at 20,000 feet above the Tucker farm, in a loitering orbit. Synthetic Aperture Radar, SAR, and infrared optical cameras plotted the positions of sentries and shooters inside several outbuildings. Chief Petty Officer Maggie Williams monitored the sensors like a hawk, so Clayton gave only cursory attention. EZ and

Chase were not due for a position update for forty-five minutes.

Earlier, Clayton had provided Matt with an "eighty-seven percent confidence" that the old Tucker Farm was the target. He noted very little traffic along Highway 15 while enroute from the Gargus Farm; one sedan, a few pickups and a motorhome, all headed south toward town.

It had taken only two circuits around the Tucker Farm to pique Clayton's suspicions; after two more orbits he called Matt again. A pair of satellite dishes atop the old barn and a large number of people milling around with only a few visible vehicles pretty much sealed the deal. In subsequent orbits, he picked out ten people stationary in the treeline surrounding the farm. Overall, Clayton reported thirty-six individuals on site.

With the surveillance orbit established, Maggie Williams transmitted infrared images to Matt at the Mexico Airport and to AJ at Liberty Crossing. The Sea Avenger crew was in their eighth monotonous hour of surveillance orbiting the same four hundred acres. The radios were quiet, the only sounds in the ACGCS came from the soft hum of the A/C, and the annoying drumming of fingers on the countertop. Clayton swiveled his crew chair toward the irritating sound.

"Do you have to do that, Louis?" In the dim amber and green glow from the monitors and consoles, he could see Louis Rogers hunched over a computer.

"Do what?" Lt. Rogers asked with a confused look, oblivious to his nervous habit.

"Never mind. Find anything yet?"

"That would be the fifth time you've asked in the past hour and twenty-two minutes." Rogers sounded a little exasperated. He turned backed to his computer screen. "Answer's still the same: you'll know when I know."

Upon receiving Clayton's recommendation to bring Lt. Louis Rogers to Whiteman, AJ made one phone call.

Thirty minutes later the U.S. Navy had the computer guru loaded into an AV-8B Harrier II rocketing north across New Orleans Bay on a non-stop flight to Missouri. Rogers was seated at the workbench computer in the ACGCS within minutes of his arrival.

Prior to the lieutenant's arrival, Clayton had managed to peruse the pile of data downloaded from AJ and prioritized a few areas of concern for Rogers to analyze. They searched for congruities between the computer at Rashad's office and the machine found in the suspect's upscale apartment at Chamber Lofts, located a convenient two blocks from his office building.

A major focus would be directed at the activity transpiring with the pirated satellites, and identifying and narrowing the receiver sites. Clayton knew his good friend and assistant would instantly recognize the Iranian hacker's work. They had seen that signature before. The encryption code was a piece of cake. The rest would take a little work.

"For one thing," Louis began, "you can tell the feds they can stop looking at the external hard drive found at the apartment. It's a very well scripted phony. I would say Rashad knew his apartment would be discovered so he planted that thing under his mattress as a decoy." This was Louis' idea of fun and he was having a field day.

"Did you copy that, AJ?" Clayton asked.

"Got it! Good catch Louis. I'll pass it on. Diversions seem to be their MO."

"Helps to know that upfront because nearly all of this code is written in reverse. You might want to pass that along too. In case your people haven't figured it out," Louis added.

"Whoa! Standby—" Clayton swung back to his control panel. "Transmission detection. Short burst. Geez! We're right on top of it!" Clayton glanced at the infrared screen as if he could see the transmission emitting from the farmhouse.

"C'mon, dang it! C'mon," he stared at the ELINT screen, impatiently waiting while the message was decoded. He felt Louis hovering over his shoulder. "There it is! *Mylh-A'sifh?* Not the same command as before."

"Operation Firestorm," Louis mumbled, going back to his computer.

What new horrors would this command signify? The ground control station became silent.

Thirty-Nine

Multiple Locations
United States

The delayed encrypted transmission automatically activated from Rashad Hussain's computer at the farmhouse was aimed at one commercial satellite, where he had planted a virus more than two years before. It had remained dormant until now.

The signal initiated a programmed sequence in Rashad's malware installation and within seconds a series of numbers and commands began scrolling through the satellite's computer. Five minutes later, three hundred and seventy-two encoded signals were delivered across the United States from outer space.

Three hundred and forty-four of these messages were received on laptops or cell phones located in safe houses where teams of Ahmad Hassam's finest warriors anxiously awaited. Their initial targets were predetermined with a single tactical objective: *hit fast, hit hard, and get out*. Each team was given rendezvous locations where members would meet after their first strike; a place where they would reorganize to hit subsequent targets.

They were mobile and on the run. They would spread across the land like wildfire. Safe houses along their route were outfitted with caches of ammunition, explosives, RPGs and Strella 2s, the Russian made shoulder- launched surface to air missiles.

Each team member was highly skilled at building improvised explosive devices—IED's—large enough to take out a fire truck, city bus, or big semi truck. Each team leader had a schedule when to check-in with Hassam's Command and Control facility in order to verify their continuing path of destruction or to be redirected if priorities had changed.

The remaining twenty-eight messages originated from *Rostam* went to very specific, highly secure, locations. The malware secreted away inside the control room at those locations came alive with that single command: *Mylh-A'sifh*

One by one, beginning with Diablo Canyon, Units I&II, in California, it spread quickly across the country. Emergency alarm klaxons sounded at twenty-eight nuclear power stations.

Firestorm had begun.

~~~~~~~~~

The Farm
15 Miles North
Mexico, Missouri

"Watchdog Niner, Birddog One! Good overwatch position, twenty degrees left about two hundred yards. I will guide you in."

"Roger that, Birddog!" EZ responded. It had taken longer to get into place than they originally planned and he knew Quarterback was anxious for an update on the target.

The UAV was doing a good job spotting sentries with its infrared camera, but not quite the same thing as eyes on the ground.

"Use caution going in. There's a sentry near the site, but it looks like he has his back to you."

"Copy!" The woods were loaded with sentries according to Clayton's reports.

Too early in the assault to start taking them out, so he and Chase had altered their track south to avoid contact, hence the reason for running late.

A shallow creek passed through the farm, winding its way to the river. On the north bank of the creek an ageless oak tree stood vigilant. It was mostly open ground from the tree to the farmhouse and barn, obscured only by the hulk of a rusted, discarded tractor, several farm implements overgrown with weeds, and a couple crumbling chicken coops. It was a perfect overwatch position, if they could take the sentry out without alerting the others. Clayton had reported an increase in activity with the sentries, as if they were somehow anticipating an attack.

EZ shucked his pack and AR-10 sniper rifle and handed both over to Chase. He put his finger to his lips and motioned for Chase to stay put. He crossed the creek from the opposite bank as Clayton kept him informed on the sentry's movements. The terrorist was sitting on the ground with his back against the tree.

Clayton left EZ on his own for the final approach while he focused on sentries close enough to have eyeballs on the sniper's target.

Seconds ticked by interminably as EZ inched through the shallow water, careful not to stumble over slippery rocks; careful to keep the thick tree trunk between him and his target.

Through EZ's night vision goggles the tree stood in stark contrast against a fuzzy green background. He could see the sentry's shoulder on one side of the tree and angled his approach to the opposite side. Closer he crept, slowly, crouching lower to the ground with each inch forward. He pulled the razor sharp K-Bar combat knife from its sheath on his tactical vest. EZ paused behind the tree, hauled in a deep breath, and let it out slowly.

Swiftly and silently, the sniper shot a hand out and grabbed the sentry below the chin. He pulled the chin up and snapped the head back with surprising strength. The sentry never had a chance to scream before EZ sliced the combat knife from ear to ear, effectively destroying the man's voice box and severed his carotid arteries.

EZ slipped back into the creek and washed the warm blood off his hands. He did not want the sticky goo and stench on his rifle.

"Scratch one gomer," he whispered in his comm-set.

Leaving the body propped against the tree as life-like as they could make it, EZ and Chase managed to climb up to the first branches in the giant oak. From there they had an excellent view of the southern half of the farm. With NVG's and the spotter scope, the two-man team began prioritizing targets for the assault.

"C'mon, c'mon!" EZ chastised. He had been impressed with Chase's Recon performance, for a pilot, but he wasn't about to tell him that. "We gotta do this right, fly boy!"

"Don't go havin' a hissy fit, EZ, I got this. First target, sniper 30 yards, nine o'clock, tree, 33 feet up. Second target, two o'clock, by that old tractor ... Oh, what have we here? Another sniper, 224 yards, twelve o'clock ..."

~~~~~~~

**Staging Area
15 Miles North of
Mexico, Missouri**

The MV-22 Osprey settled to the ground in a cyclone of dust and dead weeds. Headlights from several cop cars lit the LZ, a flat clearing just north of the bridge where Highway 15 crossed over the Salt River. This was the place Matt had selected for their staging area, approximately two miles west of the farm. The terrain from here was mostly wooded with gently rolling hills for the first mile before opening up to freshly plowed fields. The woods started again about a quarter mile from the farm, offering better cover. Matt had rehearsed the approach to the target in his mind at least a dozen times. His main concern was over the final two hundred yards from the edge of the woods to the farmhouse, which was nearly all open terrain.

Master Chief Walter Roberts, sitting in the copilot seat next to Matt, completed the shutdown checklist while Matt piled out of his seat and strapped on his thigh-mount holster with the M9 Beretta, a Marine K-Bar combat knife was on in his left hip. He had changed into navy blue cargo pants and shirt with NCTC stenciled across the back before leaving the Mexico airport. From a footlocker behind the pilot seat, he pulled a navy blue Kevlar tactical vest with pouches for spare mags for the Beretta and two box mags for his assault rifle. A pouch at the bottom of the vest contained a screw-on silencer for the Beretta.

"What's going on, AJ?" Matt answered his comm-set while snatching up the M4A1 assault rifle, which was slung across the back of the pilot seat.

"Matt, looks like the command Hassam transmitted an hour ago unleashed an army of gunmen." Her voice was firm, tough, as if she would love nothing better than to get her hands around someone's throat right now. Matt knew how she felt.

"We have three confirmed attacks already. They shot down an airliner on final approach to LAX and another at Chicago O'Hare, using shoulder-launched missiles. No

report on casualties, but it's going to be high. In California, gunmen opened fire on a crowd of fans exiting the stadium at a college soccer game. More than a hundred killed, hundreds more wounded. Cops shot and captured one of the gunmen. At least five got away."

Matt caught the master chief staring back at him. The chief's eyes blazed with hatred and his face turned scarlet as he slowly shook his head.

"A new wave of suicide bombers has begun as well," AJ continued. *"You've got to shut this sucker down, now, Matt. Panic and terror is at epidemic portion."*

Forty

The Farm
15 Miles North
Mexico, Missouri

Matt crouched at the tree line surveying the open ground. The farmhouse was less than 200 yards downrange. He had left Chief Watts and Sheriff Daniels at the Osprey to set up a unified command post and organize perimeter control. With a likely potential for casualties, they had called in EMS to establish a triage area. The final notification went to the county medical examiner to set up a temporary morgue.

A media frenzy was sure to light off within minutes of gunfire echoing down the valley and would prove to be their most challenging joint responsibility. Matt had told them they were free to tell the newsies that the firefight was directly related to attacks on America and that an operation was being carried out by "unidentified" federal agencies.

Matt asked AJ to request a 20 mile *Temporary Flight Restriction* from the FAA. The TFR would keep the news helicopters off their backs.

Clayton's infrared sensors identified four persons inside the house, three more in the large barn out back. He continued providing good intel on sentry locations, including one stationed in the woods about a hundred yards back from the clearing. Even with night vision goggles, they would not have spotted him had it not been for Clayton. Gunny Stevens had silently taken care of the unsuspecting terrorist with his K-Bar.

"Overwatch, Quarterback," Matt whispered into his comm-set.

"Overwatch! Go!"

"In place, west side of farm, two groups, tree line. Gimme an update!"

Chase proceeded to give a rundown on everything visible from his vantage point.

Coupled to what Clayton provided, Matt had a pretty good mental picture of the situation.

It did not look good. They were outnumbered three to one, and whoever set the over-lapping field of fire for the terrorists knew what he was doing. It would be next to impossible to get to the farmhouse without taking casualties. But one way or the other, Matt was going to take out Hassam's secret command center and get his revenge on the master terrorist.

Matt had divided his force into two groups. He, Butch, and Georgia, along with five of the Watchdog team members, were at the southwest edge of the trees. Watchdog One, Lt. Wally Beemer, took the remainder of the team to the northwest corner. Everyone held their position waiting for Matt's command.

Screwing the suppressor on the Beretta, Matt pointed at the closest sentry and then handed his rifle to Larson.

"Have Ghost take that guy while I do the gomer farther down," Matt whispered.

Ghost was Watchdog Ten, a muscular, twenty-three year old black from Athens, Georgia, who moved with the night, silent as a ghost. His expertise with a knife was legendary.

Matt planned to take both sentries at the same time, and then the team would be able to move out from the tree line and leapfrog toward their objective foot by foot. If they could eliminate the outer ring of sentries, it might just be possible to sneak past the clusters of guards close to the farmhouse. That was a big *if.*

"Watchdog One, Quarterback," Matt whispered.

"Go for Watchdog One!"

"We're making our move. Stay stealthy long as possible." He knew that command was unnecessary. Larson had informed Matt that Lt. Beemer was an expert at picking his way across the battleground, bringing silent death to night sentries.

Just a soft click of the transmit button told Matt that Beemer understood.

Radio silence was the order of the day.

"Overwatch we're coming your way?"

Click! EZ slowly raised the AR-10 to his shoulder and sighted in on the enemy sniper to his left. With the first detected movement from Matt's group the terrorists would open fire. It would be up to EZ to take out all snipers first, leaving Chase to kill the sentry on his right. The suppressor on EZ's sniper rifle would not prevent the sound of gunfire, but it would mask it sufficiently to keep the terrorists from zeroing in on his location. The moment he opened fire on the snipers, the entire camp would know they were under siege.

There are three sounds that can be associated with a gunshot. The muzzle blast itself; the sonic crack created by the projectile traveling faster than the speed of sound; and the actual mechanical noises each weapon makes as it ejects the bullet casing and chambers another round. Nothing can be done about the latter, but the suppressor can be effective with the former. The only way to defeat the sonic crack is by using subsonic ordnance, but that creates its own set of issues, especially for long range sniper operations.

Matt glanced at Georgia. She squatted beside a tree to his left. She held the MP7 submachine gun confidently, stock extended, ready for action. Her NVGs concealed the apprehension on her face. She flashed him a thumbs up and he crawled forward on his belly.

The chatter of night bugs masked Matt and Ghost's movements. Ghost was in place behind a sentry leaning against a tree, smoking a cigarette. He waited nearly ten minutes for Matt to slip into position behind his target; a small, skinny man standing bravely, feet spread wide, an AK47 cradled in his arms. Each snap of a twig, each scrape across dry ground brought a cringe to his face, worried the tango might hear him drawing closer. Even with the cool night air sweat rolled down Matt's cheeks, streaking the dark camo paint on his face. Silently, he holstered the M9 and eased his K-Bar out of its sheath. The two team members moved in unison, inching closer and closer to their targets.

From the corner of his eye, Matt saw Ghost rise up and grab the sentry across the forehead with one arm, pulling his head back to expose his throat to the razor sharp combat knife, slashing the terrorist from ear to ear without making a sound.

Simultaneously, Matt grabbed his target by the back of his collar and pulled him to the ground from behind. He caught the man by complete surprise. He placed a hand over the small terrorist's mouth and leaned on it with all his weight. In one fluid movement he plunged the combat knife into the man's chest, twisted, and ripped the blade downward.

Ghost had pulled the body of his sentry behind the tree and was moving silently past Matt toward the next sentry on the outer perimeter. Meanwhile, Lt. Beemer's team pushed forward at the same deadly pace.

~~~~~~~~

Matt crouched behind a rust-coated hay rake in the middle of the field and wiped the sweat and grit from his face. He struggled to catch his breath. Georgia was at his side. Larson lay about twenty feet behind, sprawled across a small mound. The five others in their team were spread out on each flank.

Terrorist guards pacing on the front porch were back-lit from inside the farmhouse. The light spilled out onto the front lawn, illuminating two more guards who appeared to be locked in a serious conversation. The Crisis Response Team had crossed more than half the distance from the tree line to the house. In several instances they found it safer and more expedient to by-pass a sentry than attempt to take them out. When the shooting starts, they would need to be mindful of the enemy troops still behind them.

Matt eyeballed the next cover point. Suddenly there was shouting well off to his left followed by a three-round burst from an AK. Instantly the calm night air split apart and the peaceful valley was transformed into a battleground. Bursts of gunfire and flashes of light, interspersed with shouting and excited voices. Their attention had been directed toward Beemer's team and several of the terrorists started in that direction, firing their automatic rifles from the hip as they ran. Others followed as the attention of the entire enemy force shifted in that direction.

A distinctive *pop* came from the right followed by EZ's whisper over the comm-set. *"Sniper down!"* Another *pop,* this one from a silenced M4A1 as Chase took out the guard sitting on the tractor. Simultaneously, EZ swung his sniper rifle 90 degrees in one fluid motion, which he had practiced a dozen times after Chase first spotted the sniper downrange on the north side of the farmhouse. *Pop!* The 175 grain boat-tail hollow point round struck the terrorist sniper in the left ear just as he was lining up a shot on Watchdog One. The right side of sniper's head disappeared in a messy pink cloud.

"*Enemy snipers down*!" EZ whispered confidently in the comm-set. He then methodically began taking out targets between his position and the south side of the farmhouse.

Matt rose up, laid the crosshairs of his night scope on one of the guards on the front porch, and squeezed off a burst from his assault rifle. Three 5.56-millimeter rounds slammed into the terrorist's chest, punching him through the front window into the living room where his lifeless body demolished an antique lamp table. The lamp crashed to the floor with a flash, pitching the room into darkness.

The fight was on. Matt's gunfire opened the door and the Crisis Response Team brought their weapons to bear.

~~~~~~~~

Farhan Alikham screamed at the top of his lungs to no avail. His men continued to run blindly, shooting into the darkness like undisciplined children.

Alikham was sergeant of the guard at the Farm, a title given to him by Rashad Hussain when the guard contingent first arrived. At thirty years of age, he was the most experienced and most regarded among the force. He was given plenty of latitude along with authority commensurate with his position. No one questioned his directives on day-to-day routine, though there was plenty of grumbling when it came to his imaginative training scenarios.

Alikham was a disappointed man, so perhaps the over-reaching training regimen was a manifestation of that disappointment. He wanted desperately to lead one of the cells carrying out attacks on the infidels. He expected to be a part of that action. He deserved it, earned it, having been a top soldier at the Iran training base; he was one of the esteemed who had actually been in combat with Ahmad Hassam. Yet here he was, leading untested men to guard a worthless farm now that Hassam had bugged out.

The men he commanded were all former trainees from Hassam' s renowned camps either in Iran or Venezuela, warriors in every regard ... Except Alikham had his concerns. Unlike the fighters chosen to participate in operations against American targets, these men were untested in actual combat. They had the skills, they had the discipline, but did they have the ability to put the two together under fire?

Alikham was proud of the defensive positions in which he had arranged his force. The overlapping fields of fire were textbook. It would be impossible for anyone to get through that gauntlet undetected, impossible to make it all the way to the farmhouse.

But that was coming apart now. A possible movement in the darkened shadows caused one of his men to open fire, which in turn created a full-scale stampede of adrenalin-laced reaction from his entire force. He knew they were on edge, but this was inexcusable.

Alikham bounded down the steps of the front porch screaming in Farsi, demanding that they cease fire and return to their posts, but his voice was drowned out in a fusillade of gunfire. Men ran past him, shouting and screaming their battle cry as they charged into the darkness.

Suddenly, the air around him was filled with the high-pitched *zing* of bullets as return fire erupted, first from the direction his men were shooting, then from behind, and then coming from the front. *What is this? Where have they come from?*

Alikham saw two of his men go down immediately and he screamed at the top of his lungs for the others to drop and take cover. Two more fell. In the panic and chaos no one was listening to him. He cursed the very idea that Rashad had not provided radios for him and his men.

It was too late to lament that fact now. There was no communication and their lack of experience under fire had turned into a total loss of discipline. More than half of the soldiers stationed around the house had run to join the firefight, like kids playing sandlot ball, racing to catch up with the others for fear they may be left out of the game … racing to die in a hail of gunfire.

From the corner of his eye, he saw one of the men on the porch pitch into the front window with a scream. Alikham drew his automatic pistol and turned back to the steps. There was a sharp sting in his hip and he stumbled into the stair railing. Another sting, this time in the shoulder, his arm went numb, he dropped his pistol. Strange, there was no pain; he just simply lost control of his right side. He tried to take another step and the ground came rushing up to slam him in the face.

Forty-One

The Farm
15 Miles North
Mexico, Missouri

Matt dove headfirst into a dry creek bed 75 feet from the farmhouse then popped up on his elbows to peek over the rim. First Georgia then Larson piled in behind him. Scant grass and dry weeds offered cover from the armed terrorists on the porch.

The gun battle raged at fever pitch. The tangos fired wildly at muzzle flashes and dark shadows. Matt's team returned fire in controlled bursts, scoring hits at a dramatic rate. They had caught the terrorist guards out in the open and with the aid of night vision goggles the result was far better than Matt had predicted. Three of his Watchdog members flanked one side of the porch, taking out several tangos as they drew closer.

Matt saw one of the terrorists on the porch go down as he prepared to charge the house. He was eager to go face-to-face with Ahmad Hassam again. He drew in a deep breath, but just before he pushed off a voice screamed in his earbud.

"*QUARTERBACK, AJ!*" Her voice was excited, filled with urgency.

"AJ, hold on, I've got—"

"*Matt, listen up! No time to explain. We need everyone in the house taken alive. Do you copy?*"

"Yeah, but I—"

"*We need them alive, Matt!*"

"Roger that!" Matt exchanged glances with Georgia and Larson and shrugged. "Well, you heard the lady, let's go snare a few terrorists."

~~~~~~~

Fifteen minutes later Matt crashed through the front door. He moved to the right in a crouched position with his assault rifle pointing the way. Georgia Shayne followed taking the left side of the front room, her MP7 in both hands, locked and ready. Butch Larson remained at the front door for three counts and then charged in. Three of the Watchdog members covered the rear door, while the other two moved around back between the house and barn. Four terrorists lay dead or dying on the front porch.

Occasional gunfire punctuated the cool night air. The battle began to wind down. Matt was amazed they had made it this far without being cut to pieces. Watchdog Seven reported a minor flesh wound to his right bicep. He insisted on staying in the fight.

The trio moved from room to room. In less than three minutes the entire farmhouse was searched. Empty!

They stood in the front room staring at one another. How did Hassam get away this time?

This is really getting old, Matt thought. *Every time we get close—*

"*Barn's clear!*" The report came back from Gunny Stevens following a brief exchange of gunfire.

"Okay!" Matt turned to Larson. "We got three or four people on the run. Have the men fan out and start lookin'." The big Marine nodded and headed out the door.

"Birddog One, Quarterback!" Matt talked into the comm-set as he watched Georgia head toward the back of the house to the control room.

"Quarterback, I'm not seeing any movement outside the perimeter. They are all down."

"Copy. What about the four you had inside the house before the assault?"

"Two went out front, two out the back door. Lost them in the battle."

"Can you recreate?"

"Affirm! Standby!"

"What's happening, Matt?" AJ asked.

"We seemed to have misplaced our targets. They ain't here!" Matt said apologetically.

"Oh dear God! You've got to find them, Matt. Quickly."

"What's going on, AJ?"

"We have a serious problem. Firestorm is an attack on our nuclear power plants. Less than half an hour ago emergency alarms sounded at twenty-eight sites ... This is cyber warfare, Matt. Worst-case nightmare. Don't know how much time we have, but we need to get inside Rashad Hussain's head, fast!"

Matt looked up to see Georgia standing in the doorway to Hussain's control center. She held a armful of scorched electronic parts, shaking her head. Her eyes were big as dollars. She had heard AJ's desperation.

"Matt, Clayton here! Bring in all of the computer equipment you can find."

"Don't think that's gonna help much, Clayton. They sabotaged it before bugging out. Any luck finding them yet?"

"Working on it! Bring what you can, soon as you can!"

Matt sensed the urgency in AJ and Clayton. He shrugged at Georgia.

"On it," she said with a wave of her hand and did a quick about-face back to the control room.

Matt stood in the center of the room gazing around. The ancient farmhouse had a familiar musty smell to it, much like some in Texas where many of Matt's childhood friends had lived. The living room was cast in the dim yellow light of a table lamp. A dead terrorist sprawled inside the front window, one foot hanging in the sill, shattered glass and a broken lamp table lay beneath him.

He glanced at his watch. Less than two hours of darkness remained. They had a lot of cleanup to do before a ton of locals would come creeping out of the woods, sneaking past perimeter checkpoints to discover why the night had opened up in World War III.

"Chase, you with me?" Matt said into his comm-set.

"Loud and clear, your worshipful!" The tension was gone from Chase's voice. He sounded euphoric now that the shooting was over and he had survived.

Matt chuckled. "I'm sending Watchdog Eight to relieve you. I want you to double-time it back to the Osprey. Bring it up here soon as you can."

"Copy that, El Jefe!"

The front screen door slammed as Larson came back inside. "Matt, you might want to check this out." Matt shrugged wearily and followed the big Marine outside.

Farhan Alikham lay propped against the porch stairs. He was lying on a canvas tarp with one of the team medics squatted beside him holding a hypodermic needle poised to jab his arm. Matt stopped, checked out the fresh bandages on the terrorist, and turned to the medic.

"This one okay to travel?" Matt asked. He remembered seeing this man shouting and giving commands before he went down. *One of the leaders*!

"Yes sir, he's ready!"

"Good. We're taking him with us. Any others?"

"Eight still alive, sir. Most are a lot worse than this guy." The medic's face was grim. "Maybe one or two can travel."

"Okay, we'll take 'em. Get 'em over here with this guy, ready to load when the Osprey gets here."

Matt turned back to Larson who then led him to the rear of the house. The lights from inside spilled out onto the lawn, faintly illuminating untended dried roses that bordered the house. A stark reminder of the former lady of the house.

Larson pointed out the thick coax cables and power cord, which ran from a junction box attached to the exterior of the house leading to the control room. Matt followed the cables to where they lay outside an open window at the barn. From scuff marks on the weathered window sill it was obvious the cables had been inside the barn.

"Tire tracks inside," Larson said. "Heavy vehicle, dual wheels judging from the impression."

'Okay, lead the way." Matt followed Larson inside.

The barn was rough-sawn timber with an earth floor and corrugated tin roof. A musty smell competed with aging cow manure and the familiar metal stench of blood. The bodies of two terrorists lay on the straw-covered floor next to an ancient disassembled tractor along the far wall. Behind the tractor a set of stairs led to an empty hay loft. Livestock stalls with feeding troughs covered the back wall and an assortment of farm tools were strewn across a wooden work bench.

There was a large empty area next to the window where the cables had come in, and just like Larson had said, there were deep impressions of tire tracks on the dry dirt floor. Matt walked the length of the tracks.

"I'm guessing motorhome? Maybe a step van?"

Larson nodded agreement. "Big one, judging from the span between the front axle and the dual wheel rear axle. It was parked here for quite awhile."

"Yup! Connected to the computers inside. Probably providing auxiliary power in case of power failure out here in the boonies."

They both looked up at the coax cables descending from the pair of satellite antennas on the roof. The ends lay in the dirt, disconnected as if they had been ripped out of their respective equipment and discarded.

"Birddog One, Quarterback!" Matt called.

"Go for Birddog!"

"I'm looking at large coax cables running from the house out to the barn. They were connected to something inside the barn. Possibly a motorhome. Can you rewind and tell what was here earlier?"

"Standby," Clayton responded. He sounded harried, stressed. The voice of someone balancing an obscene number of tasks. *"By the way, replay on the four tangos fleeing the house, you killed all four."*

~~~~~~~

One hour later, Chase dropped the Osprey down on the front lawn of the farmhouse. Through a settling cloud of dust and debris three cop cars emerged with emergency flashers blazing in the darkness, followed by an ambulance and a white, windowless van.

Lt. Wally Beemer stood beside Matt and Butch Larson, his M4A1 rifle was slung on his right shoulder and only his eyes were visible through the camo-painted face. The wounded Farhan Alikham lay at their feet, bandaged, an IV plugged into his arm. Georgia came out of the house with another armload of scorched computer equipment and dropped the junk beside the first pile.

"Lieutenant, have two men stow this piece of human trash in the Osprey," Matt kicked the terrorist, "and help Agent Shayne get that computer junk onboard."

"Aye, aye, sir. With pleasure."

"Colonel Larson, Agent Shayne, and I are returning to Whiteman," Matt continued. "You are in charge of this scene. No matter what the locals try to tell you, this is *your* scene! Understood?

"Yes, *sir*!" Beemer grinned.

Matt recognized the three local law enforcement vehicles belonging to Chief Watts, Sheriff Daniels, and Detective Scott Brown. He guessed the white van was the medical examiner coming to view the carnage.

"Those three cops are welcome on scene. Absolutely no civilians."

"Yes, sir!"

Forty-Two

"It's an Allegro," Clayton said. "Looks like a thirty-six footer." He swiveled the pilot seat to stare into the video monitor. His face showed the strain from lack of sleep and intense pressure reflected by the tiny amber and green lights on the ACGCS console.

"Birddog One flew over the motorhome enroute to the farm. Few vehicles on Highway 15, didn't think a thing of it at the time." He paused for a moment as if he were checking something on the computer. "Pretty sure this is our target."

"Any chance of finding him again?" Matt asked. He was sitting on the desktop in the pilots briefing room, one leg on the floor, one dangling from the desk. He still wore the NCTC utilities, but had removed his tactical vest. His face was smeared with dark camo paint and he felt grungy. Georgia and Chase were in the room, Larson was handing their prisoners over to base security and would join them in a few minutes.

Matt's screen was divided into two boxes as AJ joined in on the secure video link. She looked even more frazzled than Clayton, but then she was under considerably more pressure. She had Carter Manning pushing for updates every two minutes, while President Downs hammered on Manning. It all rolled downhill.

"We're working on it, Matt. Problem is, Rashad's hacked into the surveillance satellites. Blinded them."

"What can we do, Clayton?" AJ sounded desperate.

"Birddog One is fueled and ready to takeoff. We'll be heading northwest. Records show NetDesign & DataSolutions owns a ranch in Idaho."

"Idaho? You think that's where they're heading?" Matt asked.

"Good a place as any when you're in a rolling, fully functional command center. In the mean time, let's get a BOLO out for the motorhome. They should pass a hundred state troopers between here and there." Clayton gave them a color description of the Allegro motorhome.

"I'll take care of that," Georgia said, edging into view on the video monitor.

"How much time do we have?" Asked Matt.

Clayton looked over his shoulder at something out of view from the camera, mumbled a few words, turned back to the video, and breathed a huge sigh of relief.

"Good news, folks!" Clayton's smile seemed to take away his worry lines. "It looks like we may have a dodged a bullet with the nuclear power plants."

"Explain," Matt demanded.

"Emergency alarms sounded at twenty-eight nuclear sites indicating a malfunction with a coolant valve. The good news is that once the alarms were silenced everything seemed to return to normal. Word from the plant operators and NRC rep at each plant state operations are holding good so far."

"Twenty-eight coolant valves malfunctioned simultaneously?" AJ asked, incredulously.

Louis Rogers stepped into view beside Clayton. Unlike Clayton, his face was stern. He cleared his throat and then began. "Control room techs at each site are searching for the cause. They'll most likely come up with a joint statement: 'computer malfunction.' But, to put it simple, their systems were hacked."

"All of them? Separately? How? When?"

"Yes, ma'am, all of them. The 'how and when' are good questions that will take me and Clayton a little while to determine. Rashad's transmission was definitely the trigger for malware he's somehow slipped into the operations computer at each site. He's developed an algorithm assigning a series of four-digit numbers representing addresses for message recipients.

"We've been able to identify most of those locations. Just sent an email to each of you containing data discovered thus far. We'll nail down the remainder shortly, but you will note twenty-eight addresses clearly indicate locations for nuclear power plants where the alarms sounded."

"Why just twenty-eight?" Matt asked. "Isn't there over a hundred nuclear power plants?"

"One hundred and forty-four, to be exact. Four of which are decommissioned." Clayton answered. "Could have been a matter of timing. Keep in mind the enormous security firewalls built into nuclear power plants. Takes time to break down those walls, if it could even be done by expert hackers like Rashad Hussain. More likely there's a logistical explanation, a common bond if you will, that may point us to the how and when. My money is on social engineering."

"What do you mean by 'social engineering'?"

"There are multiple vectors for accessing a computer," Clayton said. "One way is hackers constantly pinging the firewalls, searching for a way in. Social engineering is gaining access by way of the network."

Matt looked at the two computer geeks and scratched his head. He did not understand a word Clayton and Louis said, but he was mighty glad the pair was on the side of the good guys. His knowledge of computer technology was limited to programming an aircraft flight director and GPS, maybe an occasional glimpse into the internet.

"We're generating a list of commonalities as we speak," Louis put in.

"So this whole deal with ringing alarms was merely a scare tactic?" Chase asked.

"Hopefully."

"You guys get the rest of those locations to us as soon as you can," AJ said, bringing the conference to a close. "Maybe we can prevent a few attacks, Matt."

~~~~~~~~

Interstate 29
52 miles South of
Sioux City, Iowa

Ahmad Hassam leaned back in the plush leather recliner and groused about the opulent features of the new motorhome. Across from his chair was the kitchen; a large stainless steel refrigerator set between polished light oak cabinet doors and drawers. The fridge and cabinets were packed with enough food for the three day drive to Rashad's ranch in Idaho. The gas range, oven, microwave, and kitchen sink were left of the fridge, and on the right was a large flat screen TV. The walls were covered with vinyl wallpaper in modern grays and beige accents. The narrow hallway led to a full-size bathroom complete with tub and shower. The large master bedroom was at the rear of the coach. The floor was covered with beige carpet in the living areas and polished vinyl tile in the kitchen and bathroom.

Between Hassam and the driver's seat, Rashad Hussain sat hunched over an oak desk tucked inside a compact nook set up as a mobile command center. The unit was functional in travel mode, but expanded, along with the living area where Hassam was sitting, into a large operational headquarters when the home-on-wheels was parked for any length of time.

Ali had the cruise control set on 69 miles per hour and the big Allegro Open Road purred down the interstate like floating on air. Larijani rode shotgun next to Ali. His head bobbed as he kept drifting off to sleep, then snapping awake with every thump of uneven pavement or blast of wind from a passing semi.

Hassam glanced up at the clock above the sink. He fidgeted again. He hated being inactive, unable to move freely, although he reluctantly admitted the motorhome was a great idea.

"What are they doing now?" He asked.

"An email from their command center at Whiteman Air Force Base just went out listing locations for the recipients of the *Mylh-A'sifh* message." Rashad replied smugly. Being several steps ahead of the infidels proved he was better, smarter.

"So they know about the nuclear power stations?"

"Oh yes, they have known for a couple of hours. By now the misguided fools are resting easy, believing they were merely false alarms. They have no idea of the disaster coming. "

"I see," Hassam contained his smile inwardly. "When will the next phase begin?"

"It already has, *'yâ qâd.* It started automatically. The moment the plant operator in each control room touched the emergency alarm reset, it initiated the sequence."

"And no way to stop it?" It was the third time Hassam had asked that question in as many days.

"Not from their location. It can only be stopped from right here," he tapped the *Rostam* device attached to his laptop. "The sequence can only be interrupted at your command, *as-Syf.*"

This caused the smile to tug at the corners of Hassam's mouth. "And what of the farm?"

"The man you know as Matthew McWain is presently at Whiteman, so that must mean the farm has been destroyed. We have no intel on survivors."

"Just as we anticipated. That means they are far behind us?"

"Very far indeed. No way can they find us or your field commanders. I continue to block their electronic surveillance satellites." Rashad turned to check his computer screen again. "But it is requiring all the capability of this single computer to do so. There is a truck stop north of Sioux City. We can stop there to send the next attack command and collect updates from your field commanders."

"Very well," Hassam nodded absently. That familiar feeling of pending danger crept into his subconscious again, kicking his survival instinct into high gear. He pulled an Atlas from the small magazine rack beside his recliner and scanned the highway ahead.

He spoke without looking up from the map. "We have friends in Sioux Falls, South Dakota, if I am not mistaken?"

Rashad quickly opened a page on his computer, scanned the document, then said, "Yes, we have a family sympathetic to the cause living on the outskirts of the city."

Hassam turned and stared out the windshield at the road ahead as if in deep thought. After a couple minutes he spoke. "Ali and I will get off there. Larijani can drive you on to Idaho."

"As you wish, *'yâ sayyid*, my master." Rashad flashed Larijani a questioning look and found the diminutive lieutenant staring blankly at his boss.

Forty-Three

Nuclear Power Plant Sites
Eight Specific Locations
United States

Power plant operators and technicians breathed a collective sigh of relief. It was a pretty scary ordeal when the emergency alarm was activated. The night had been quiet and the systems on automatic when the room erupted with an ear piercing alarm. Kind of like a firefighter blasted out of bed from a sound sleep by the klaxon horn and the dorm room lights blazing.

But the sighs of relief were premature for eight of the affected power plants scattered across the country. Malware dormant for nearly two years within its own protective cocoon awakened with the simple act of throwing the switch to shutdown the alarm system. Silently, the virus began taking over certain functions deep within the control room data center. The control room staff was gradually losing control of plant operations.

The virus spread throughout the operations software unabated, surrounding itself with new firewalls as it continued to infiltrate the system. Just as Rashad Hussain designed, each infected layer of the software became inaccessible to plant technicians, rendering it impossible for them to stop the silent and devastating sequence of events.

Computers systematically and precisely directed primary feedwater pumps to shut down. Minutes later, even before the closest technician could react, the condensate pumps tripped off, which in turn caused the turbines to trip. For no apparent reason eight nuclear power plants across the nation ceased production.

Technicians scrambled back to their control panels, fingers danced across keyboards. For several frantic minutes they tried first to restart the feedwater pumps, and when that failed, they tried unsuccessfully to start the secondary pumps. The turbines could not be restarted. All they could do was shake their head in frustration and offer a sickening look at one another.

The Nuclear Energy Commission representatives were still on site at all eight facilities. They too had breathed a heavy sigh of relief when the silenced alarm first indicated nothing seriously wrong with the reactor or turbines. That changed instantaneously when the turbines tripped and the control room went deathly silent. Within minutes the NRC reps at all eight locations began initiating emergency notification procedures.

At NRC headquarters in Rockville, Maryland, the night duty officer in the Emergency Operations Center had dosed off, feet propped up on the console. He nearly fell out of his swivel chair when the EOC console lit up with incoming calls on eight emergency lines. He input the information from each site into the computer, and then launched a command that sent an emergency call to his boss, the deputy director of operations.

~~~~~~~~

NCTC
Liberty Crossing
McLean, Virginia

AJ gazed down on the operations center. She was alone in the conference room, but the floor below was a beehive of activity. Occasionally the director of operations would look up at her through the plate glass and offer a hopeful smile before turning back to the bank of analysts and technicians busily tracking the wave of destruction sweeping across the United States. Areas thought to be impervious to terrorism, based on some outdated theory that defined the terrorist psyche as being focused on government facilities and financial institutions in large population centers, were now being attacked. Soft targets were defenseless against a well coordinated plan with superior numbers and firepower.

Her concentration was broken by the sound of the opening door, her boss entered the room.

"The president finally let you go?" She asked with a weary smile.

"Temporarily," Carter Manning shrugged. "He still has other obligations. The business of running a nation goes on."

Manning collapsed into a chair at the conference table with a huge sigh.

"Pretty bad over there, huh?"

"You have no idea, AJ. The press is relentless, finger pointing, making wild accusations. You'd never guess Downs is the most respected president since Reagan. The blame game on the Hill is even worse. The senate intelligence committee is demanding that Iran be turned into a smoking hole, while the opposition is trying to crucify him for failure to alert the general public sooner. Of course the media has picked that up and are running with it.

"So now we have wide-spread fear and panic, mixed in with a large dose of anger at the administration. Problem is they might be right. Maybe I gave President Downs bad advice, and now he's paying the price for my decision."

"*His* decision, Carter," AJ said emphatically. "And it was the correct decision. Once this is over and cooler heads prevail, they will look back and see his actions prevented a panic stampede, which could have paralyzed the nation."

"I hope you're right," Manning replied with a wan smile. He drew up his shoulders, hanging his head while reaching back with one hand to massage the stress-cramped muscles between his neck and shoulder.

"I am." She grinned. "But first we need to concentrate on defeating the immediate threat.

"That's for sure," Manning raised his head. "Where do we stand?"

AJ quickly brought him up to speed, pointing to the large flat screen opposite the table, which displayed a current situation status. The digital Sit/Stat board listed times, locations, types of recent attacks, resources applied to mitigate each attack, and the current status of each. A second screen displayed a list of federal assets available in reserve. These mainly consisted of hostage rescue teams from the FBI, Marine Force Recon, and Navy SEALS. Larger cities had their own HRT's, SWAT teams, and riot response units either already engaged or staged in reserve. Overall, assets on the reserve lists were diminishing at an alarming rate as new waves of attacks began to shake the nation.

"The president cleared the way for the use of more active duty military personnel to operate inside national borders." AJ continued. "We have special forces units from every branch gearing up. The list of locations provided by Clayton and Louis Rogers is a huge help. The terrorists are coordinated like a well choreographed plan, but at least we have a general idea where future attacks will occur."

Manning studied the screen while listening to AJ's briefing and leaned back in his chair. His composure returned.

"Very good," Manning said when she had finished. "What's going on with Matthew now and how can we help?"

"Matt is in the air as we speak. Relocating his CRT to Sioux Falls, South Dakota."

Manning nodded deep in thought. "Still think Hassam's headed for Idaho?"

"Yes, sir. An E-3 Sentry out of Nellis detected an upload signal originating near Sioux City, Iowa, several hours ago. Signature indicates high probability that it was message traffic from Rashad Hussain. Corresponded with the latest wave of attacks.

"Pretty much confirms Hassam is on a northwest track. Clayton has the UAV running surveillance north of Sioux City toward Sioux Falls. Meanwhile, Louis Rogers is trying to reestablish service operability with the COMSATS. Not much luck there as long as Hussain has his fingers on the computer. The AWACS bird will stay with Clayton until the satellites are back online."

The E-3 Sentry, an airborne warning and control aircraft, or AWACS, could help Clayton's Sea Avenger triangulate electronic signals from Rashad Hussain's motorhome. It was a game of patience, waiting for the terrorists to send another message.

"Matt requested aerial surveillance on Rashad's ranch near Clearwater, Idaho."

"Do we have available assets?" Her confident smile gave Manning his answer.

"The 9th Reconnaissance Wing at Beale Air Force Base, Marysville, California, operates the RQ-4 Global Hawk. It's a larger UAV, better capability than Birddog

One … don't tell Clayton I said that. Anyway, they have one available with your authorization. I signed for you," she added with a wry smile.

"You are getting pretty good at that," Manning said with sarcasm.

"Dated satellite photos show the Clearwater site is more formidable than a single CRT can handle."

"Don't underestimate what Matt can do with an armed Osprey," Manning grinned. "What about the computer equipment confiscated at the farm?"

"Junk! All fried. Louis says it's just network equipment. Says he needs the main server, which is with Rashad Hussain in the motorhome."

"*AJ!*" The operations director boomed over the audio speaker with an excited voice. "The NRC deputy for operations is on the horn. Says it's urgent!"

Forty-Four

The sun was below the horizon in a crystal clear sky. The blustery bitter wind cut like a knife. Matt was instantly chilled to the bone as he climbed out of the warm cockpit onto the concrete ramp at Sioux Falls Regional Airport.

Immediately after receiving word of the message intercept in Sioux City, Matt loaded the crisis response team into the Osprey and headed northwest. It was a pretty good bet Hassam was headed for I-90 before turning west.

From Whiteman to Sioux Falls was 370 miles; close to an hour and a half at max cruise. By the time they arrived, Hassam could be well to the west, but Matt figured he would be within striking distance when Clayton or a state trooper spotted the motorhome.

Lights flooded the parking ramp as he taxied his aircraft to the South Dakota Air National Guard facility located on the south side of the airport. Chase made a call while enroute and the commander of the 114th ANG

Fighter Wing, along with his deputy, stood ready to receive the crisis response team when the solid black Osprey rolled in.

"Colonel Jack Salmons, gentlemen." The commander greeted Matt and Chase with a firm handshake and ready smile. "This is the deputy wing commander, Lt. Colonel Hank Godfrey." The two officers were dressed identically in air force flight suits and leather aviator jackets. Salmons was a short man, barrel chest, red hair and matching mustache. Matt guessed him to be mid forties. Godfrey was medium height, slender, with short dark hair. He was a little younger than his boss.

Matt made introductions as his team deplaned. "Thanks for the hospitality on such short notice, Colonel."

"Not a problem. Made some inquiries on you guys before you arrived. I was quickly told to button my lip. That tells me you people are dealing with the terrorist situation, so you have carte blanche on this base. Understood?"

"Thank you, sir!"

"Let's get out of this cold night air and get some coffee in your people." Colonel Salmons grabbed Matt's elbow and steered him toward a large hangar just beyond the Osprey. Two airmen ran out to secure the aircraft under the gruff direction of Master Chief Walter Roberts.

"You folks hungry?"

"These are Marines, Colonel. They're always hungry."

Inside the cavernous building they found two long tables set end-to-end, adorned with white tablecloths, and loaded with steam tables and baskets of rolls and fresh fruit. China plates, silverware and napkins were on the end. Airmen in white aprons and hats stood ready to serve. A separate table carried a coffee maker, stacks of mugs and a water pitcher with glasses. A short distance away were several more tables with chairs to accommodate the hungry warriors. The food smelled great.

The ANG Base was typical of any air force facility except for not having residence quarters. Approximately 1000 men and women provided every function from aircraft and facilities maintenance, administrative, medical, personnel services, and security, all in support of the twenty mission-ready F-16 Fighting Falcons and their pilots. It was obvious Col. Jack Salmons had brought in a few of his people to roll out the red carpet and make the CRT welcome.

"Your people can stow their gear here in the hangar," Col. Salmons told Matt as he grabbed a quick cup of coffee and a chair across from him. The deputy commander was seated at the end of the table, laughing at something Chase was saying.

"Don't know how long you folks plan to stay, so I'm having cots and blankets brought in. There are restroom facilities with showers through those doors at the end of the hangar." Colonel Salmons pointed. "Separate ladies facilities, ma'am," he added, looking at Georgia.

"I doubt we'll be that long, colonel," Matt said, wiping his mouth with a napkin. "But thanks again for your hospitality. This is much more than we expected."

"Well, it's not often we have the opportunity to show off," Salmons smiled and glanced at his watch. "I hate to rush you, Matt, but when you are finished we need to head over to base ops. I've been told you can expect a video conference in … fifteen minutes."

~~~~~~~~

When forewarned of the special needs requirements for the crisis response team, Colonel Salmons directed that the base operations building be made available. A bank of computer terminals was arranged around a small conference table with six comfortable black leather swivel chairs set in the center of the room. A flat screen monitor located on one wall was prepared for the secure video link and a second large screen was on the opposite wall. A telephone was at each workstation. A low credenza near the head of the table held a coffee maker chugging out a fresh brew and a couple pitchers of water. A short hallway behind the conference table led to several offices and restrooms.

"Hope this will do," Salmons said almost apologetically when they entered the small block building. Chase, Georgia, and Butch followed Matt.

"Thank you, sir, this will be fine." Matt smiled.

Colonel Salmons gave Matt his cell number. "Make yourselves at home. Call me if there is anything you need."

Georgia Shayne walked around the room, stopped to admire a wall filled with plaques containing unit commendations. "Nice guy," she said. "Runs a tight ship."

"And not the least bit put out that he wasn't invited to sit in on the video link," Butch Larson added. "Smart man."

"Uh, huh." Matt mused. He poured himself a cup of coffee, settled into a chair, and closed his eyes while he waited.

~~~~~~~

"Beaver Valley, near Pittsburg; Peach Bottom, Pennsylvania; Nine Mile Point, New York; Browns Ferry Unit Two, Alabama; Calloway, Missouri; Diablo Canyon Units One *and* Two, California; Cooper, Nebraska; and Wolf Creek, Kansas ..." Clayton was on the video screen providing Matt and the others with an update on the affected nuclear power plants while they waited for AJ and Manning to join in.

Georgia pulled up a colored map of the United States on the large wall screen and placed an electronic red dot on each location as Clayton read them off.

"Only eight?" Chase asked.

"No," Louis Rogers stood behind Clayton on the screen. "The same identified signal was also sent to Comanche Peak in Texas. For some unknown reason the malware failed."

"Is it possible other sites may be targeted later, different code?" This came from Butch Larson.

"Well, there's always that possibility," Clayton cut Rogers off. "However, we think it's unlikely."

"Why?" Carter Manning popped up on the screen, AJ was beside him.

"For one thing, they have to know we are capable of intercepting their signals. To minimize transmissions they probably activated everything they intended in one shot—"

"Also," Rogers jumped in, "they would want to get all affected power plants activated simultaneously to prevent us from having time to respond and/or evacuate."

"These eight sites are scattered all over the country," Georgia observed. "Any idea why these particular ones?"

Matt moved over to the wall map during the dialog. He ran a hand through his close-cropped dark hair and traced a finger across the red dots. "Part of the terrorist's strategy," he said, pointing to the plant sites located in rural areas. "Turning our crop and livestock producing areas into a virtual desert."

"That may be part of it, Matt," Clayton responded. His face was stern. Anger flashed in his eyes. "We've discovered a logical explanation as well. Nuclear power plants constitute part of the national power grid. National Compliance Standards, established by the Nuclear Regulatory Commission, mandate that all nuclear plants share scheduling procedures for daily production. To facilitate the mandate, production schedules are integrated automatically through software programs.

"To maintain cyber security, the NRC requires a biennial replacement of all production software. The NRC bids out the replacement projects, most recent of which was nearly two years ago. Three vendors were selected. All one hundred and forty nuclear plants within the four NRC regions were allowed to choose between those three vendors.

"You will remember that emergency alarms tripped at twenty-eight nuclear plants. All twenty-eight chose the same vendor to replace production scheduling software. This includes the eight nuclear sites presently in distress.

"Here's where it gets interesting, guys." Clayton allowed a wry smile. "The vendor for those twenty-eight sites subcontracted their formatting software to NetDesign & DataSolutions, L.L.C."

"Holy Cow!" Chase exclamained, bolting upright in his chair. "Is that legal?"

"Sure," Clayton answered. "Done all the time."

"You call that cyber security?"

"Well, in retrospect I suppose not. But keep in mind that up until a few days ago NetDesign pretty much flew under the radar. Each vendor was required to provide a list of their subcontractors. The subs were vetted by the NRC, as were the vendors. Obviously this included background checks conducted by the FBI, but if there is no record of violations this is usually perfunctory—"

"Shoot-fire-and-save-on-matches! Our national security apparatus is a sieve!"

"C'mon, guys, we can point fingers later," Manning interrupted gruffly. "Tell us what we're dealing with, Clayton."

Clayton Downs was silent for a moment, staring back at the faces in the video screen before starting. When he did, his face clouded over. He knew he was delivering a devastating blow.

"People, a reactor meltdown is the end game for Operation Firestorm!"

A chill fell over the video link participants. Clayton outlined the situation as simply as possible. He was no expert on nuclear reactors, but he knew enough to understand what Rashad Hussain had designed and how he went about making it happen. It was brilliant, really. Years in the making. Clayton hated to admit it, but he felt a vestige of professional respect for his enemy.

He explained how Rashad inserted a virus into a single line in the formatting software. From there it was simply a matter of initiating commands, which ironically were activated by specific actions taken by control room technicians. Every time a technician initiated a procedural countermeasure to correct a detected problem within the reactor it would be countered by another of Rashad's hidden commands, which in turn exacerbated the original problem.

When plant personnel attempted to open valves to the auxiliary feedwater pumps the virus transmitted a bogus signal to the control console indicating a successful operation, when in fact the valves remained closed. Sealed from outside interference.

Heat continued to increase inside the primary loop, creating a sudden rise in pressure. The automatic relief valve diverted reactor coolant out of the primary loop in order to relieve the pressure, which is a safety function of the reactor. However, once the relief valve popped opened, Rashad's virus blocked the valve from closing again after the pressure abated, thus depriving the reactor of coolant water. At the same time the virus had overridden the automatic emergency cooling system, preventing it from engaging.

Even with the turbines shutdown, the reactor core continued to produce heat. With the absence of reactor coolant the water remaining inside the reactor containment was converting to superheated steam. A meltdown of the reactor core was in the making. Eventually a severe water hammer or hydrogen explosion would breach the reactor containment walls and tons of radioactive particles would be carried into the atmosphere by contaminated steam.

"*Dear Lord*!" Exclaimed AJ. "What are the chances of a nuclear chain reaction?"

"No chance," Clayton responded. "At each site control rods were inserted into the core to prevent a chain reaction."

"How long before the meltdown," Matt asked.

"It's already started."

"Okay, but how long before the containment walls fail and bad stuff hits the air?"

Clayton shrugged. "Only a guess, but I would imagine several hours, maybe. There's already been a minor breech at Diablo Canyon, Unit One." Clayton switched the video feed to show the nuclear power station at Diablo Canyon, California. A wispy white cloud escaped from a tall rounded structure. "The steam seeping from the containment dome on the left is highly contaminated. Luckily, on-shore breezes are light and there isn't anything downwind but foothills and brush for twenty miles—"

"An ecological disaster," Georgia whispered softly.

"It's going to get a whole lot worse, folks," Clayton said somberly.

"Clayton, there's gotta be a way to stop this," Matt said matter-of-factly. "How can we help?"

"We need Rashad's computer. More to the point we've identified a cryptic hardware accelerator operating through his computer. Hussain named the device *Rostam*. We *need* that device, guys! Louis traced the virus throughout the infected software, but he can't halt its progress without going in through Rashad's signature ... AJ, I know it will be a catastrophic nightmare, but you need to check the current and forecasted winds at each site. Start a forced evacuation, downwind first."

"On it!" She nodded.

Forty-Five

Regional Airport
Sioux Falls
South Dakota

One mile northeast of the Air National Guard Base Ops building, Ahmad Hassam stormed out of the general aviation terminal toward a waiting Cessna Citation jet.

"Are all of your passengers forced to wait this long?" Hassam derided the hapless pilot all the way from the terminal door to the jet's airstair. "It is a wonder you have managed to stay in business. Do you have any idea how long I have been waiting?"

"No, sir," the pilot muttered demurely. He was afraid to speak his mind. He knew who this passenger was, but was more afraid of the man walking several paces behind. The giant could easily snap his neck.

"I will tell you how long, you imbecile." Hassam shoved the pilot out of his way and climbed the airstair ahead of him. The pilot shrunk back, letting Ali go next. "I have been here over two hours," Hassam continued. His voice boomed louder once inside. "That is unacceptable. It is I who set you up in business. I have paid all of your expenses. I have allowed you to operate as you please for years." Hassam paused and glanced into the cockpit. The copilot, in the right seat, stared in disbelief at the outburst. Ali, squeezed through the narrow cabin door, hunched over due to the low ceiling, glared at him. The copilot quickly turned back to his preflight checklist. "And the very moment I need you THIS IS HOW I AM REWARDED?" Hassam screamed as the pilot entered the cabin.

"I am very sorry, *'ya qâd*! We just came from a long char—"

"ENOUGH! I do not want excuses. Get this airplane in the air. *Now*!"

Mohammad Hejazi had been in the United States for five years. He had been recruited by the Islamic Republic of Iran Air Force during his final year at Shahid Sattari University of Aeronautical Engineering. It was his outstanding record throughout flight training that landed him an audience of Major General Imad Abu Mughniyeh.

Less than two years later Hejazi was in the United States, listed in the FAA Pilot Certification data bank with commercial, single and multi-engine, and instrument ratings, along with an impressive list of type-ratings allowing him to fly a large variety of aircraft. The first-class airman's medical certificate in his pocket was also forged and slipped into the FAA data files—updated every six months by the handy work of Rashad Hussain.

With his impressive credentials, Hejazi landed a few jobs with various air charter companies, which provided him plenty of firsthand practical knowledge of the federal air transportation system and procedures at many U.S. airports. Once sufficient knowledge and credibility had been obtained, Hussain—under the direction of Ahmad Hassam—set Hejazi up with his own aviation business.

In the course of time, Mid-Plains Air Charter became a successful and legitimate air transport company with three aircraft operating throughout the United States. No one seemed to pay attention to the fact that several flights each week carried passengers of Middle Eastern descent. Nor did anyone give a second thought to the numerous freight runs made by the company's Cessna 208 Caravan.

Hassam's organization kept Mohammad Hejazi extremely busy.

"*As-Syf,* I just want to point out—"

"I SAID ENOUGH!" Hassam was inches from the pilot's face, his foul breath made Hejazi wince and shrink back. "One more word and I will cut out your tongue. Now fly this airplane."

"But sir," Hejazi cowered. "I must know where you wish to go?"

"Texas!" Hejazi saw the fiery hatred in Hassam's eyes, the fearsome sneer across his lips. "South Texas!"

Hejazi turned abruptly, pulled in the airstair, and locked the door. His face was red with anger when he dropped into the pilot seat. He roughly yanked his headset from the control yoke. The copilot looked over at him and spoke softly through the intercom.

"If I were you, boss, I'd tell that ungrateful lout to get his butt off my airplane."

Hejazi shook his head in disgust. "Someday, my young friend, I will tell you why that is not such a good idea."

~~~~~~~

Interstate 90
West of Sioux Falls, South Dakota

Hakeem Larijani followed the beam from his headlights, staring into the never ending white line, hypnotized by the straight-as-an-arrow highway. He blinked against the glare from vehicles on the opposite side of the divided highway. He hated driving; he hated driving this monstrosity of a motorhome even more; and he especially hated driving the huge albatross in the dark. The lines on the interstate were mesmerizing and the lack of sleep over the past several days took its toll. His eyelids closed, his head sagged. The big rig drifted until tires hit the shoulder rumble strip and the whole right side of the motorhome shook. Thumping echoed through the coach. Larijani jerked awake.

"Hakeem, what is it?" Hussain shouted from his seat at the small desk. He checked the computer screen for evidence of a threat. He wore a smug look— quite satisfied with the knowledge that he had outsmarted the combined technical genius of the United States—right up to the moment that the motorhome started rattling like it was coming apart, swerving hard to the left as Larijani jerked it back into the center of the highway.

"Never mind!" Larijani shouted, angry with himself and angry at Hussain for catching him lose control of the beastly vehicle. His eyes were wide with fear, he gasped for breath. His sweaty palms on the steering wheel made it difficult to get back in the center of his lane. Sweat streaked down his face and he searched the panel for the A/C control.

They had traveled eighty-five miles since dropping Hassam off at the airport in Sioux Falls. Eighty-five miles of wrestling this big pig down the highway. A sign indicated a rest area a few miles ahead. It would be a good place to stop and collect his wits, calm down. Maybe sleep until dawn. Surely the road would not be so scary in the daylight.

Larijani overcorrected and swerved again, this time to the left and went into the rumble strip adjacent to the median. He jerked the wheel hard right off the bumps. The top-heavy vehicle rocked back and forth as it careened down the highway, spilling loose items to the floor.

"HAKEEM!" Hussain screamed, holding tight to the arms of his desk chair.

Larijani ignored the whining computer geek as he finally gained control of the motorhome. He slowed to 50 miles per hour and let out a huge sigh. It was going to be a long way to Clearwater, Idaho. Just then, blue and red lights flashed in the side mirror approaching at a high rate of speed.

~~~~~~~~~

State Trooper Doug Huston eased his gray Dodge Charger to a stop on the west bound on-ramp at Exit 310 and switched off the headlights. He had mixed emotions about overtime. He and Barbara needed the extra dough for sure. They were buying their first home and finances would be tight for a few years. It also meant their two young children would be changing schools, which added to the stress. On the other hand, being home at night was comforting for his wife. Barbara hated it when he worked nights. The highways were not safe anymore. Especially with terrorists wreaking havoc across the country.

That is what brought Doug out tonight, after his regular ten hour shift. The nationwide BOLO for the black and silver Allegro had taken a sudden focus on South Dakota. Darkness grounded their aerial surveillance fleet, which necessitated bringing in as many off-duty troopers as there were patrol cars.

West-bound traffic was light, the six-year veteran trooper noted. He would have preferred having a partner in light of the circumstances: four suspects, considered armed and dangerous. But they were stretched thinly across the state and two-man units were being assembled farther to the west. Standing orders were to observe and report, keep the vehicle in sight at all times, but *Do-Not-Approach!*

From what he had heard through office scuttlebutt, there was some hotshot antiterrorist unit close by. Once notified, they would swoop in and steal all the glory, just like the feds always did. So how the heck was he to know which motorhome carried the suspects? There were dozens of black and silver Allegros with beige trim. In the dark it was hard to tell without getting really close. Besides, it was not as if he didn't know how to make a traffic stop on highly suspicious vehicles. He had made dozens.

Huston reclined his seat a few notches and scooched around until he was comfortable on the fabric upholstery. He turned the radio down just enough to monitor traffic stops from troopers in his division. He kept one eye on west bound traffic and one on his mobile data processor. Potential sightings of the motorhome were coming in from law enforcement officers as far west as Kadoka, north to Mobridge, and south to Wagner. He chuckled; it was like last summer's Big Foot sightings. Nearly every camper in the state was positive they saw the huge hairy creature crashing through the woods.

Huston retrieved his thermos from the passenger seat. He was pouring a cup of coffee when the motorhome passed, weaving from lane to lane like a drunk driver.

He pulled his seat upright, put the Charger in gear, flipped on the emergency flashers, and mashed down on the gas. The powerful cruiser rocketed down the ramp onto the interstate. He reached for the microphone and transmitted to the regional command center that he was in pursuit of a reckless driver, west bound near Exit 310.

Huston was determined to make the traffic stop. Terrorists evading detection would not go weaving down the highway at 20 miles under the speed limit. They would not be that obvious. No, this was probably some retired senior citizen with more money than brains, falling asleep at the wheel … or drunk on his butt.

The motorhome dutifully moved to the side of the highway and Huston pulled in behind. He transmitted the Missouri license plate information back to command and stepped out of his car. He approached the driver's side slowly, one hand on his Glock .40 cal.

~~~~~~~

"Hakeem what have you done? You have brought the police down on us." Hussain hurried forward and grabbed the nine-millimeter Makarov pistol from the glove box.

"Put that away, you fool!" Larijani hissed. "It is only one trooper. Let's see what he wants before you go bringing the entire force down on us."

Hussain shrugged and slipped the handgun under his waistband in the small of his back. He moved closer to the driver's side to get a good look at the officer. "If he reaches for his radio or his gun, I will kill him."

Larijani rolled his eyes at the computer expert and opened the driver's window. A chilly blast of air spilled in as the trooper approached. He noticed the trooper had one hand on his gun, but it was still holstered. They had been trained on the procedures of the western law enforcement officers.

"Good evening sir," the Trooper said. "Is everything alright?" The trooper's eyes darted from Larijani to Hussain and back to the driver.

"Yes, of course officer." Larijani noticed the suspicious look, but knew that was to be expected.

"Couldn't help but notice the erratic driving, sir. Are you sure everything is okay?"

"Yes, sir," Larijani attempted a light chuckle. "First time driving a motorhome. Seems I have much to learn, officer."

The trooper was silent. He studied the two men for a few seconds as if trying to make up his mind about something. Then he smiled for the first time, setting Larijani's mind at ease.

"Okay. These things can be intimidating. Try to keep it in the center of your lane and keep your speed down until you get the hang of it."

"Thank you officer for the good advice. I will be more careful, sir."

The trooper retreated to his cruiser and Hussain plopped down in the front passenger seat. "*I will be more careful, sir,*" he mimicked sarcastically. "That was uncalled for. Your sloppy driving nearly destroyed our entire operation."

"Relax, Rashad. The trooper did his job and now he is moving on, none the wiser."

~~~~~~~~~~

Trooper Doug Huston waited until the motorhome eased back into traffic. Routine procedure, under the circumstances, would have been to ask the driver to step out of the motorhome and administer a breathalyzer test, or some form of field sobriety test. But one look at the two men left no doubt that he needed to extract himself from a very dangerous mistake. He had made contact with the wanted suspects, and by God's Grace he was still alive.

He reached for the microphone and realized he was trembling uncontrollably. His voice quivered from excitement as he began to talk.

"Command Center, Unit 42 … I have … suspects under surveillance …West bound … I-90, Exit 310 … Repeat, I have …"

Forty-Six

114th Fighter Wing
Air National Guard
Regional Airport
Sioux Falls
South Dakota

"Got 'em!" Clayton shouted over the comm-set.

Matt was reclined, his boots on the table, arms folded across his chest, half dozing. The others were crashed out as well. Long hours and fatigue had won a temporary battle over consciousness. When Clayton blasted over the radio Matt's feet hit the ground, instantly alert.

"Highway patrol has them under observation at a roadside rest area, about 30 miles west of Mitchell." Clayton was monitoring several local agencies including the highway patrol. He relayed Trooper Huston's radio message the instant it came across the net and turned Birddog One toward the reported position.

"Copy, Birddog, how far is that from us?" Matt tried pulling up the area map on the computer, gave up and motioned Georgia to the keyboard. Chase and Butch were on their feet and moving. Energy charged the air inside the small base operations building like a burst of static electricity.

"Ninety-six miles, give or take ... I'm seventeen minutes out!"

Georgia zoomed in on the location and gave Matt a thumbs up.

"Got it, Birddog! Tell the highway patrol to stay back, observe from a distance. We have to assume the target has sensitive surveillance detection equipment."

"Roger that. The highway patrol's already scrambled their helicopter. I ordered them to stand-down by presidential directive!"

"Are they complying?"

"Uh ... don't think so!"

"Okay, thanks, Birddog One! We'll handle it. We are wheels up in fifteen. Keep us posted!" Matt turned to the others. "Butch, get Colonel Salmons on the horn. We need him over here, pronto! Chase, get the team saddled up and the Osprey ready to fly ...!"

"Hot diggity-dog!" Chase yelled, charging out the door.

"Georgia, get on the horn to the highway patrol. Order 'em to stay out of the target area."

"On it!" She had already picked up the phone.

"Tell 'em thanks for keepin' the target under surveillance. We'll get back to 'em if we need further assistance."

Matt felt the adrenalin flowing throughout the room. They were closing in on Ahmad Hassam and none too soon. Before dozing off earlier, he watched the endless reports of new attacks streaming across the TV screen. From Florida to California, dozens of suicide bombers brazenly walked into shopping malls, movie theaters, amusement parks ... even police stations. Hundreds of innocent civilians had been killed or injured, many maimed for life. The carnage seemed endless. There seemed to be no way to prevent the senseless slaughter of innocent citizens.

There had been violent clashes between terrorist brigades and HRT units and local SWAT. The outcome in most encounters ended in favor of the good guys, but not always. The feds and local law enforcement were bloodied far too often.

Occasionally, a few good reports trickled in. In California, based on a tip provided by NCTC through Clayton and Louis, a Navy SEAL team tangled with a large group of Hassam's warriors assembling at a storage facility within a large industrial complex where hazardous chemicals were manufactured and stored. When the brutal assault ended all fifteen terrorists had been terminated, one SEAL was hospitalized with serious gunshot wounds.

"Matt, we copy your traffic," AJ's voice was on the comm-set. *"Take them alive, Matt. We need the intel. Urgently!"*

"Roger that!" Matt was aware of what he had to do, he just didn't like it.

"It's in your hands, Matt. Godspeed!" She signed off. She knew they did not need her interference, or that of Carter Manning. It was up to Matt and his people.

~~~~~~~

Colonel Salmons burst through the door, eyes wide, still dressed in his flight suit.

He glanced around the room at the beehive of activity. "How can I help?" he quietly asked.

"You been briefed on the situation?" Matt replied.

"Pretty much."

"Good. We need an immediate departure from the ramp. Westbound."

"You got it," the colonel said to an empty room. Matt was already out the door with his team leading the way.

Fifty yards away the Osprey spooled up, its huge 38-foot prop/rotors turned slowly.

Sioux Falls Regional Airport served multiple users. Besides being home to the ANG 114th Fighter Wing, six different airlines scheduled more than three dozen daily arrivals and departures. The airport was also home to hundreds of general aviation aircraft. Air national guard flights took direction from traffic controllers in the tower just like all others. Air traffic right-of-way rules applied to all.

The wing commander immediately called the control tower. "This is Colonel Salmons, 114th Fighter Wing. Requesting immediate departure from the south ramp for an MV-22 Osprey ... I don't care, this is an emer—Look, Larry, this is big. Matter of national security. I'm not asking here, pal ... Hold all air traffic for an immediate departure ... Yes, Westbound, low level. Thanks."

~~~~~~~~~

Rest Area
14 Miles West of Exit 310
Interstate 90
South Dakota

"I am warning you, Hakeem, we must continue. If we are discovered the consequences from Hassam will be far worse than that of the infidels."

Larijani rubbed his bloodshot eyes. His body trembled. He looked up, slowly shaking his head.

"And I am warning you, Rashad," he said with more steel than he felt. "I am in command now. If I continue to drive in darkness, I will get us both killed. That risk is far greater to our operation than the slim possibility of being discovered. We will rest here and continue on at daylight."

Rashad Hussain glared at Larijani for several long seconds; his cheeks reddened from rage welling up deep inside. Finally, he turned back to his computer and stared into the screen. At least Larijani had sense enough to pull around behind the main building where they would be hidden amongst the big trucks. With the generator running and satellite antennas deployed, he had both computers online.

Overcoming his anger, Hussain first set security around the motorhome. A video camera on a short mast would pick up anyone approaching within 50 feet in any direction and sound an alarm. Probably it would be one of several truckers close by, but at least he would know to take a quick look. The audio system could pick up a highway patrol cruiser, or any other vehicle entering the rest area, or approaching helicopters from half a mile away.

With security measures in place, Rashad checked the progress of the virus burrowing deep inside control room computers at the nuclear power plants. He smiled; malware at each site was within seconds of each other. A cataclysmic nuclear meltdown would occur in eight locations simultaneously—*Eight?* His fingers danced across the keyboard. *Rostam* had infected nine power plants. *Where was ... Ah, there you are*! He mumbled to himself. He was keenly disappointed that the virus at Comanche Peak in Texas had failed to launch. Even so, it was a great relief that eight others were functioning properly, spreading their destructive force in systematic sequence.

Hussain glanced at the timer inset on the lower right hand corner of the screen. *Four hours, twenty eight minutes, and seventeen seconds!* He chuckled excitedly, just as Larijani exited the bathroom.

Hassam's second in command gave the computer geek a questioning look, shrugged his shoulders and padded down the hallway to the master bedroom. He would take *as-Syf*'s comfortable bed tonight—and every night until they reach the ranch at Clearwater.

Forty-Seven

Rest Area
14 Miles West of Exit 310
Interstate 90
South Dakota

The Osprey's 38 foot prop/rotors turned 333 rpm at cruise, making it relatively silent, undetectable from less than a mile away and comfortably quiet inside the cockpit. A warm glow bathed the cabin, reflecting off Matt's and Chase's flight helmets. The five screens on the instrument panel displayed flight and aircraft data with muted amber, green and red lights. It was pitch black outside, the air was cold and smooth.

"We have a problem!" Clayton's distraught voice flooded Matt's earbud.

They were five minutes from the rest area with Matt at the controls. He didn't like the tension in Clayton's voice. He knew the Sea Avenger was maintaining a tight surveillance orbit above the target motorhome.

"What's up, Birddog?"

"Only two occupants."

"Copy two occupants ... Could the others be inside the rest area facilities? Maybe patrolling outside?"

"Negative, Quarterback. Got eyes on them for ... thirty-one minutes. No sign of others." The UAV sensors detected the video and audio security system emitting from the motorhome and Clayton passed that information along to Matt.

Matt glanced at Chase. Concern filled his eyes in the dimly lit cockpit. This was disappointing news. Where had the other two gotten off? Who were they and what were they doing now? Matt had an uneasy feeling, but he chased it from his mind. They had an assignment and there was not time to second guess the situation until that assignment was complete.

"Four minutes out, Birddog. Keep checking for sentries."

~~~~~~~~

Chase identified a large, relatively flat open field one mile east of the rest area and highlighted it on the GPS. It was perfect for their LZ, well out of detection range from even the best mobile security system. With his right hand, Matt gently pulled back the thrust lever and reduced power while thumbing the knurled wheel aft to rotate the nacelles into helicopter mode. Ten feet from the ground, he made another power adjustment and the big tilt-rotor gently kissed the earth on all three landing gear.

"Show off," Chase glanced over and grinned.

"Eat your heart out, dude!"

They quickly ran through the shutdown checklist and Matt spun out of his seat, grabbed his M4A1 from the seat back as he stepped into the cabin. He had worn his thigh-mount holster during the short trip from Sioux Falls Regional. He slammed a 30-round magazine in the assault rifle and pulled the charging lever as he followed the others down the rear ramp.

He dropped to short dry grass and firm ground—spring rains were running late for this part of South Dakota. Between cattle and the antelope, grass was nothing more than stubble. Matt knelt and motioned the CRT members to gather around. They formed a circle around him and checked their weapons.

"LT, we'll divide into the same groups we used at the farm. My group makes the assault, you take the perimeter."

"Roger that," Lt. Wally Beemer responded.

"Everyone stay alert. Birddog says there are only two tangos inside. That means there are two more around here someplace. There are infrared targets in the parking lot, but they're most likely civilians.

"Remember, we take these guys alive, people. At all costs!" They nodded in unison.

~~~~~~~

Rashad Hussain leaned forward and checked the timer again: *Three hours, fifty-two minutes, twenty-nine seconds!* Everything optimal at all eight locations. He smiled again and then glanced at the video security screen. The IR camera showed a ghostly green image of a large man moving close to the darkened motorhome. Hussain bolted from his chair and grabbed his pistol from the desk. The only light in the room was from the two computer screens.

He crept to the side window between the passenger seat and entry door and parted the blinds with the barrel of the Makarov. He clicked the safety off.

It was a truck driver returning from the restroom. He walked past the motorhome and then climbed up in the sleeper of the big rig three spaces away. Hussain lowered the pistol, slipped the safety on, and retreated to his chair. He stared into the security monitor. *Nothing! Larijani may get a decent night's sleep, but I will not,* he groused.

~~~~~~~~~

"One in front, sitting at a table or desk, the other is at the rear, lying down." The infrared sensor on Avenger painted two yellow human forms inside the motorhome. It also picked up a few people, one with a dog, scattered along a trail that wound through the grounds. Two other images appeared to be returning toward semi-trucks in the rear lot.

"Any of them suspicious," Matt whispered into his comm-set. He crouched behind the front bumper of a big rig less than fifty feet from the motorhome. His team appeared as black shapes in the night, their faces darkened with camo-paint, in a loose semi-circle around him. They were well concealed from the motorhome's video security. The trees rustled in a light breeze punctuated by the distant howl of speeding cars on the highway, and a big rig's whining tires. The night air seemed to close in.

Matt cinched the M4A1 assault rifle tight to his chest, from a pouch on his tactical vest he produced a silencer. He threaded the device into his M9 Beretta and chambered a round, leaving the safety off.

"Negative, Quarterback, all civilians. No sign of combatants."

"Copy! … Overwatch?"

"I got nuthin!" EZ responded. Matt had directed the sniper—along with his spotter Watchdog Nine, Corporal Cody Allen—to find a good position to observe the motorhome and surrounding area. They had convinced a sleepy trucker that the top of his semi-trailer was perfect for their mission.

Matt was disappointed. He had hoped the two missing terrorists would be lurking in the woods or inside the rest facility, but Beemer's men had cleared both areas. He pushed the thought away and prepared to move.

"Okay, Watchdog units, move into position," Matt whispered to his team to surround the target

"*Seven!*"

"*Four!*"

"*Ten!*"

"*Eleven!*"

Matt gave the Watchdogs three minutes to get into position, then motioned Butch to close in. The fully loaded Remington 870 Tactical Shotgun carried at port arms looked like a toy popgun in the big Marine's hands. Chase and Georgia followed, covering the rear.

"Alright Birddog, do your thing!" Matt said softly and waited two seconds.

"*Done*!" Came the response. Clayton had assured Matt that the Sea Avenger electronics suite could jam the security system, at least a minute or two before the Iranian computer genius could jump to another frequency. The problem with jamming was that it produced white noise on the security screen. If the terrorist was actively monitoring the system, he would be instantly alerted and have time to destroy his laptop or at least the external device that Clayton had instructed Matt to find.

Matt was betting the whole operation on Clayton's ability to shut down the security surveillance long enough to breach the motorhome's door.

He jumped to his feet and dashed toward the motorhome. Butch breathed down his neck, one step behind. The ground seemed to shake with each pounding step the big Marine made. Matt feared the terrorists would surely hear or feel the rumbling, or even hear the pounding in his chest.

Matt pointed the silenced Beretta downward as he sprinted across the parking lot, gaining speed with every step. Two paces from the motorhome he stopped. Butch Larson stepped in front, simultaneously pointed his shotgun barrel four inches from the door, aimed between the latch and metal door jamb, and pulled the trigger.

The blast roared through the park, ripping the calm night air, and plainly heard at the eastbound rest area on the opposite side of the interstate. The Military M1030 breaching round, which Butch had loaded in the shotgun, instantly shattered the door lock and blew the door open several inches.

Ratcheting a plain buckshot round into the 12 gauge, Butch stepped aside and Matt bolted through the door, his Beretta held shoulder high, trained on Rashad Hussain's forehead. The terrorist was out of his chair, reaching for the Makarov pistol on the desktop.

"Don't even think about it," Matt commanded as he advanced into the room. His finger tightened on the trigger.

Butch followed on Matt's heels and turned toward the rear of the motorhome just in time to catch Larijani stumbling down the hallway, wearing loose fitting pajamas, his eyes were half closed in sleep, confusion written on his face.

"On the floor. NOW!" Butch yelled. He stepped toward the small man who was already on his knees, trembling in fear. "I mean *all* the way down, raghead!" The big Marine kicked Larijani in the chest with enough force to send him skidding three feet down the hallway floor on his back. Butch stood over Larijani and shoved the shotgun in the man's face.

Matt kept his pistol trained on Hussain; the terrorist's eyes went wide with fear when Butch kicked his cohort across the floor. His eyes darted back and forth between Matt and Butch as if trying to make a decision.

Without warning, Hussain turned and raced to the desk. He ripped the *Rostam* device from the laptop and spun back toward Matt. A wild-eyed sneer crossed his face as he held the device high above his head. He would not let these infidels take the device. It was not likely they could stop *Mylh-A'sifh,* but he could not take that chance. He would smash his master creation on the floor, stomp it into tiny pieces before they could steal it from him.

"Don't," Matt yelled. "Hand it over!" He suspected the small device was the thing Clayton warned him about, the key to whatever Clayton and Louis needed.

Rashad flashed a maniacal smile and raised his arm higher. Matt adjusted his aim to the left and pulled the trigger.

Pfffft! The silenced round sliced through Hussain's bicep, splattering the wall and curtained window in a spray of blood and gore. The terrorist let out a deafening scream and dropped to his knees. The *Rostam* device tumbled through the air end-over-end.

Matt lunged forward, going down on one knee, arm extended, and caught the device inches from the floor as he slid face first into the wounded terrorist.

Huddled on the floor in a growing pool of blood, Hussain clutched his wounded arm to his side. He screamed, sobbed, and wet himself as he mumbled a prayer in his native tongue and cursed Matt in the same breath.

Matt regained his feet and called Clayton on the comm-set. Chase and Georgia pushed into the motorhome, quickly assessed the situation, and holstered their weapons. Chase trussed Larijani with flex cuffs while Butch Larson held the little man down with the shotgun planted in his chest.

Georgia circled Matt and the growing bloody mess on the floor to study the image on the computer screen.

"*Describe it to me,*" Clayton breathlessly ordered.

"Well, it's a gray plastic case, 'bout the size of a cigarette pack. Got a wire hanging out 'bout a foot and a half long." Matt flipped the device over, checking to see if any writing or marking was present.

"That's probably it, Matt. Bring the laptop too."

Georgia made a frantic gesture and pointed at the blood splattered computer screen, a look of horror filled her face.

"Might not be enough time, Clayton," Matt said in desperation. "Countdown clock on the laptop says three hours, twenty-one minutes."

"Then you'd better knock on it, cowboy!"

Matt clinched his teeth and stared into Georgia's eyes. They both knew time was about to run out. There was little hope of averting a catastrophic disaster, but he had to try.

"Master Chief Roberts," Matt spoke into his comm. "Bring the Osprey, plenty of room in the rear parking lot. Break. All Watchdog units, assemble in the parking lot. We're outta here!"

"What are you thinking, Matt?" AJ was on the comm-set. Her usual steady voice quivered. The NCTC Ops Center had been monitoring the assault on the motorhome. Holding their collective breath while waiting to hear some good news for a change.

"AJ, patch me through to Colonel Salmons at the 114th Fighter Wing, Sioux Falls."

Forty-Eight

Rest Area
14 Miles West of Exit 310
Interstate 90
South Dakota

Matt's face twisted in rage. He knelt close to Hussain, ground his knee into the terrorist's wounded arm, and shoved the silenced muzzle of his M9 Beretta in the man's face.

"I'm gonna ask you only one time. Where is Hassam?"

Hussain's face was a mask of terror. He was a tech warrior for the jihad, not a *shaheed*. He was not prepared to give his life for the cause. He had much to live for. More that needed done. He screamed as Matt increased the pressure on his wounded arm and began to babble as he begged for mercy.

Larijani, still face down on the floor, hands tied behind his back, shouted in Farsi. "*Khâthaï, traitor!*"

Hussain stiffened and clamped his mouth closed.

Matt turned toward Larson. Fury danced in his eyes. "Shut his mouth, Butch!" Butch dropped the butt of the shotgun on Larijani's head, knocking the little man unconscious.

"You had your chance, raghead," Matt turned back to Hussain. The terrorist's eyes went wide in fear as Matt lowered the pistol.

Pffft! The nine-millimeter hollow point shattered Hussain's left kneecap and the terrorist screamed in agony.

"Matt! That's enough!" Georgia cautioned.

Matt ignored her. The thumping sound of the giant prop-rotors approached. He roughly pushed the muzzle into Hussain's right eye. "Where is Hassam?" His voice was softer now, but the steely resolve grew stronger.

"I … I do not know … I swear … He and Ali got off … airport in Sioux Falls." Hussain pulled his shattered knee to his chest in agony and rolled into the fetal position. Tears flooded his face.

Matt stood, holstered his weapon, and snatched up the laptop and hardware accelerator. He stormed out the door.

~~~~~~~

114th Fighter Wing
Air National Guard
Regional Airport
Sioux Falls

The 114th Fighter Wing's aircraft inventory included a pair of two-seat, D model F-16 Falcons. Matt called Colonel Salmons from the I-90 rest area to verify both D's were fueled and ready. The colonel raised an eyebrow when Matt called again twelve minutes later, requesting one of the F-16D's spooled up and cleared for an immediate flight to Whiteman Air Force Base soon as the Osprey landed.

"Dark Horse One, Sioux Falls Tower, you are cleared straight in for landing at Alpha November Golf. Traffic at ten o'clock, three miles, inbound Sioux Falls. No factor!"

"Cleared straight to ANG ramp, Copy traffic, Dark Horse One." Chase acknowledged the clearance from Sioux Falls tower and then pulled the landing checklist up on the right side MFD. He glanced at Matt.

"If you don't lighten up on that control stick you're gonna break it."

Matt turned, saw Chase's concerned expression, and grinned. He let out a big sigh, released his grip on the stick, and flexed his fingers several times.

"It shows, eh?"

"A little bit! It's gonna be okay, ya know? AJ will find out if Hassam flew out of Sioux Falls, and where to. When she does, we'll track the dumbass down and stomp a mud hole in 'im."

"I know where he's headin', Chase. And he's got a pretty good head start."

~~~~~~

With the laptop tucked under one arm and the *Rostam* device in his breast pocket, Matt took Georgia by the arm and practically dragged her out the Osprey's side door. She had not uttered a word since the incident at the rest area. They raced the short distance across the ramp to Colonel Jack Salmons and the aircraft crew chief close to the waiting F-16D. The high pitch whine of the F110 GE turbofan drowned out the Osprey as the big tilt-rotor spooled down. The twin canopies of the jet fighter were raised and a boarding ladder was in place.

"Afterburner all the way, Colonel," Matt shouted over the whine of the engine. "Time's critical."

Col. Salmon nodded and turned to Georgia. "This should fit, Special Agent Shayne. Go ahead and step into it." He held out a green G suit. "I wish there was time to brief you on the F-16 cockpit procedures," he yelled in her ear. "Suffice to say, don't touch anything unless the pilot tells you to. Understand?" An inflatable bladder in the G suit was essential equipment for keeping blood in the upper torso during high-speed maneuvering. As soon as they had the suit cinched up properly, the crew chief handed Georgia a white flight helmet with attached oxygen mask and helped her put it on.

Once Salmons had Georgia strapped into the rear cockpit he gave a quick lesson on emergency procedures. Matt then ran up the boarding ladder to hand her the laptop and *Rostam* device.

"Tell Clayton and Louis to work their magic." He glanced at his watch. "Two hours, fifty-six minutes!"

Georgia stared into his eyes. "Matt, about what happened back there. I understand why you did it … Guess I would have done the same thing." She smiled and gave him a thumbs up.

The F-16 taxied out less than six minutes after the Osprey had landed. Two minutes later the fighter jet thundered down the runway. Matt followed the bright yellow afterburner flame until it disappeared into the night, and then whispered a prayer. *Please Lord, let there be time.*

"Amen!" Col. Salmons overheard Matt's prayer. "They're gonna break a few rules, but they'll be on the ground at Whiteman in twenty-five minutes."

"Thanks, Colonel."

"You inquired about *both* of my D models?"

"Yes, sir. I might need one to go after Ahmad Hassam. With your permission, of course."

"Not a problem, young man. Let's get inside, get your people rested. Then you and I will see what's next." Colonel Salmons put an arm on Matt's shoulder and led him toward base ops. "The folks at NCTC recruited my wing intelligence officer for some follow up snooping here in Sioux Falls. He's waiting inside."

~~~~~~~

"That was a great job at the rest area, Matt," AJ's dark eyes were red from exhaustion, but her jaw was set, determined to push on until the current situation was resolved. "The president sends his appreciation."

Matt stared back at the screen. From the picture frames and paneled walls he knew she was still in the ops center conference room—probably never left. She appeared to be alone. The screen was split. The other half showed the equally weary face of Lt. Cmdr. Clayton Downs. Gathered around the table with Matt were Col. Salmons, Chase, Butch Larson, and Capt. Nick Graves, the wing intelligence officer.

Matt nodded at AJ. "Team effort. Couldn't get any intel out of Larijani or Hussain. Georgia is enroute to Whiteman with the laptop and *Rostam* thingy. It's up to you now, Clayton."

~~~~~~~

In silence, Clayton offered a wan smile and understanding nod. They all faced grim circumstances with consequences too dire for words. He turned to his sensor operator in the crew seat on his right.

"Your aircraft, Maggie. Bring her home." Clayton arose from the pilot seat.

"Aye, aye, sir. My aircraft!" CPO Maggie Williams answered. She moved over to the vacated seat and took control of Birddog One.

"Louis," Clayton said as he headed out the door of the advanced ground control station. "Let's get out there and meet the F-16."

~~~~~~~

"Where's Hassam?" Matt asked after a brief silence.

"Thanks to assistance from Captain Graves here is what we know so far," AJ answered glancing at her notes. Matt gave the young wing intelligence officer an appreciative nod.

"Approximately four hours ago, Hassam and a large man whom we assume to be Ali, entered the general aviation terminal at Sioux Falls Regional. The receptionist/dispatcher noted Hassam appeared nervous and agitated, apparently concerning a long delay.

"Two hours later, Hassam and his bodyguard boarded a Citation operated by Mid-Plains Air Charter. Don't know much about the company right now, but the FBI has launched an in-depth investigation. The dispatcher at GA was not aware of the flight destination, but FAA is tracking the aircraft southbound. Uh, presently … they just passed over Oklahoma City."

Matt and Chase exchanged glances.

"Don't know where they're going, Matt," AJ added, "but DEA and Customs are picking up unusual border activity with the Arellano cartel near Nuevo Laredo."

"I know where he's headed," Matt said, shaking his head. With desperation in his voice he turned to the wing commander. "Colonel, I need to get to south Texas. Fast!" *Dear God, please don't let it be too late.*

"I'm coming too, Matt." Chase was already on his feet.

"Sorry, Cuz, no room on this flight." Matt answered with a pained expression.

Forty-Nine

Brooks County Airport
Falfurrias, Texas

The gleaming white Cessna Citation touched down on the 6000 foot runway at Brooks County and taxied up to the small terminal/FBO office. Before Mohammad Hejazi could bring the jet to a full stop, the copilot was out of his seat and opened the door to lower the airstair. The sooner they could get the fierce-looking terrorist and his huge bodyguard off of their airplane the better. He bounded down the stairs into the chilly dark morning to offer a reluctant hand to the offensive customer. From the cabin lights he saw the man glaring at him as he took the stairs.

"Tell Hejazi to wait here until he hears from me." Hassam continued past the copilot, dismissing him without another word.

"But—"

"Do as you are told!" Ali said sharply from the top of the stairs. The whole aircraft shook with each step as the giant descended. He shoved the copilot out of his way. Hassam and his protective servant disappeared into the shadows, leaving the young, sandy-haired copilot staring after them with mouth agape.

The small, wood-framed building was illuminated by a single, pole mounted security light. The rear door facing the parking ramp was locked. A sign in the window advised office hours and a phone number for after-hours service.

"Find us a vehicle," Hassam commanded his bodyguard.

Ali nodded silently, stepped off the wooden porch and disappeared around the side of the building. Hassam had chosen this particular airport partly because it was small— there would not be many people around even in the light of day—and the runway was long enough to handle the jet. More importantly, it was close to his destination. He chose not to fly directly into Edinburg in case the airport was under surveillance.

Hassam looked back at the Citation; saw that Hejazi had joined his copilot at the foot of the airstair. They seemed to be in a perplexed, animated discussion. The master terrorist smiled. He moved to the front of the building. A few minutes later Ali returned with the hot-wired airport courtesy car, coughing and chugging like it was running on seven cylinders. The well used Ford Crown Vic smoked like a diesel truck, but at least it would take them three miles into town where they could lift a better ride from a sales lot. It wasn't like they would need it for long. If all went according to plan, Hassam would have abandoned it before the dealership opened their doors.

Traffic was light when they pulled onto Highway 281. The headlights reflected occasional glimpses of barbed wire, mesquite trees, and longhorns. Hassam shifted in his seat and sneered out at the barren scenery from the window of their stolen car. Only 58 miles and revenge would be his.

~~~~~~~

40,000 Feet Above
San Antonio, Texas

"San Antonio's coming up on the horizon," the pilot's voice reverberated in the earphones of Matt's flight helmet. He squirmed in the rear seat of the F-16D, stretching for room that was not there. He was almost thankful he had missed out on his dream to fly fighters in the Marine Corps. *Almost,* he smiled.

It seemed like a century ago, but the disappointment at being assigned to helicopter training at Pensacola had come as a staggering blow. In retrospect, however, he would not trade his rotary wing combat time with Marine Force Recon for a million bucks.

Even so, the thrill to now fly one of the premier fighter aircraft in the U.S. Air Force was incredible. The pilot had given him the controls for a brief time during their three hour flight. The amazing responsiveness of the jet would have been an absolute joy; an experience he would never forget, if it were not for the dark cloud of fear and worry that permeated his every thought.

Matt checked his watch. It had been twenty-three minutes since Clayton's last call. The interrogation team at Sioux Falls had been unsuccessful in obtaining Rashad Hussain's password—*they ain't using the correct "persuasive" technique,* Matt told himself—but Louis Rogers had done his homework studying the Iranian computer genius's background and had cracked the password dilemma after a couple dozen attempts. The *Rostam* code was "a bit more … adventurous," Clayton had said with alacrity. Once inside the hardware accelerator, the two computer gurus traced the worm that had spiraled its way throughout the software controlling the eight nuclear reactors.

Forcing Clayton to slow down and speak in layman terms had taken the usual delay, but Matt finally understood it was good news, so far! There was still a major software cleanup within the power plant systems, and they weren't completely out of the woods. There were serious contamination leaks from three of the plants. There would be environmental issues within a five mile radius at all three, possibly for the next decade. In time, there could even be a few thousand radiation poisoning casualties.

All things considered, it could have been a lot worse. Thank you God!

Matt stared out at the pink glow on the eastern horizon. It was a cloudless sky, smooth as glass. Perfect flying weather at 40,000 feet. He brushed back a moment of guilt, recalling the look of disappointment on his cousin's face when told he could not come along. *No, that was a look of betrayal*! Matt mused. It was small consolation, but at least the Osprey was following somewhere behind. If there was going to be a state-wide manhunt to keep Hassam from slipping across the border into Mexico, Manning agreed to allow Chase and the rest of the CRT to join the hunt.

It was Matt's responsibility to keep the team together, keep them on mission. But yet when the threat came too close to home, he was the first one to bail on them. Sure, he knew Manning and AJ understood, but—

"Gonna be tight on gas when we get there," the pilot's voice brought Matt out of his funk. "Sure glad you offered to top us off."

"Uh, I believe the offer was for enough fuel to get you to Kirkland." Matt glanced again at his watch and sighed.

~~~~~~~

South Texas International Airport
Edinburg, Texas

The sun was perched on the horizon when Maria Connors drove through the security gate at South Texas International. It was her normal practice to arrive at the office early to get the coffee on and everything open before the daily routine began. What was not normal about this morning was that her teenage daughter came with her. School was out for spring break and Carmen had decided to tag along with her mom. It was the second time this week and it made Maria smile—a fourteen year old getting up before daylight to go to work with her mother! *Amazing!*

But Carmen had been behaving out of character since learning that the McWain's would have a guest staying for the summer. Another teenage girl, Katalina Cortez. She would work for Uncle Matt and Uncle Chase around the airport and from what her mother had said, Katalina must come from a rich family. Her grandfather was buying a new high performance plane for Kat to learn competition aerobatics from Uncle Matt.

Carmen had it all figured out. Kat could stay with her and her mom at the ranch. Carmen's grandma was the main housekeeper for the McWain's and lived rent-free in a modern ranch-style home large enough to accommodate Carmen and her mom. Carmen's bedroom had its own bath and was certainly big enough for two teenage girls.

And that was the reason the teenager had asked to accompany her mom. Carmen was given free reign of the offices when the guys were away. Both Matt and Chase allowed her full use of their computers. So it had been pretty much nonstop Facebook, Twitter and email between two giggly teenage girls from the moment Carmen learned of Kat's visit.

Carmen Connors was blessed with the same features as her mother and grandmother: shiny, straight black hair cascading below the shoulders and bangs to her eyebrows. She had fine bronze skin, large dark mischievous eyes, a perfect smile, and bubbly personality. Petite like her grandmother, she stood barely five feet four, maybe a hundred pounds wringing wet, but already showed signs of a developing young woman. She had no physical features from her father—an army ranger still listed MIA from the first gulf war—but everyone said she had his impulsive disposition and big heart.

Maria pulled the car into her reserved space near the front of the Rio Grande Flying Service office where she was blasted with the raucous sounds of a hundred Boat-Tail Grackles competing for space in a large mesquite tree.

She paused and studied the open door of the large hangar a short distance across the parking lot. *Funny*, she thought when she saw the King Air still inside. *Scott and Sarah should have left an hour ago. Wonder where they are?* Scott and Sarah Adams were Rio Grande Flying Service relief pilots. The husband and wife team were on furlough from Delta Airlines and were gracious for any flights Matt and Chase could throw their way.

Maria turned back toward the front door, then paused again. The airport security guard's empty vehicle was parked against the chain link gate leading to the tie-down ramp; the front door was wide open, engine running. *Where on earth is Ignacio?* From Maria's vantage point she could not see the security guard slumped over, his brains splattered across the seat.

A sense of unease crept into her subconscious. Maria shook her head, closed her car door and followed Carmen, who was already bounding up the walkway. *What's going on around here today?* She stopped to look around while digging in her purse for the door key.

She nudged her daughter out of the way to unlock the door, but was surprised to find it already open. Carmen playfully bumped hips and giggled, vying for position to enter first. Without responding to her daughter's playfulness, Maria stepped over the threshold of the plate glass door.

Just then the air was split by the deafening roar of a jet screaming low over the runway on a high-speed pass. The windows in the building rattled and the ground shook.

"Wow!" Carmen shouted as she jumped from under the protected entryway to see the jet fighter arching into a tight climbing turn. "Who was that?" Her eyes danced with excitement.

The powerful roar of the aircraft drifted into the sunrise and the vibration was replaced with a familiar voice on the Common Traffic Advisory Frequency, CTAF.

"*South Texas Unicom, Lobo One Niner! Field advisory, over.*"

Maria's heels clicked across the ceramic tile floor as she rushed to answer the radio. She passed a four-place settee of black leather chairs surrounding a glass coffee table laden with a stack of aviation magazines, rounded the furniture toward the reception counter ... and stopped dead in her tracks. She brought a fist to her mouth to stifle a scream and automatically turned to pull her daughter to her breast and shield her from the grisly horror.

A blood smear stretched six feet across the pale green tile, terminating at the feet of a body mostly concealed behind the reception counter. Maria guided Carmen back to the leather chairs and ordered her to sit.

"Mom?" The girl's eyes went wide from fear when she saw her mother trembling and tears rolling down her cheeks. Carmen started to rise.

"I said wait," Maria commanded, placing a firm hand on her daughter's shoulder.

She moved back to the blood trail, tiptoeing as quietly as possible. She did not want to alert anyone who might still be in the building. Maria approached the desk, glancing around for something she might use for a weapon. *Just in case!*

She held her breath, her heart pounded. She leaned around the counter and shrieked. Pilot Scott Adams laid face down, half of his head blown off. Three bullet holes in his torso testified that he had probably dragged himself toward a telephone to summon help, before his murderer finished the job with a headshot.

Carmen rushed to her mother. The girl screamed and threw herself into Maria's embrace as she gazed down at the bloody carnage. It was more horror than she could ever imagine. "Oh momma," she sobbed, "who would do such a horrible thing?" She gagged.

"I … I don't know, baby girl." She held Carmen in a tight grip while moving around the counter to the phone. she took a deep breath and steadied her voice when the 9-1-1 operator came on.

Maria hung up the phone and then guided Carmen toward the pilot briefing room located down a short dim hallway. It was deathly quiet. Light filtered in through a glass panel in the door at the end of the hallway leading to a large aircraft maintenance hangar attached to the offices, and from a large plate glass window halfway down the hallway, which overlooked the flight planning room. The doorway into the room was just beyond the window.

Maria paused, her back to the wall, holding Carmen close to her side as she leaned forward to look through the window … and barely managed to stifle another scream. The girl peeked under her mother's arm and pierced the quiet air with a scream loud enough for both of them … the bile that had been building in her throat finally spilled all over the tiled floor.

Sarah Adams' headless body was bound to the straight back wooden chair with rope, her arms crossed tightly across her chest. Her white uniform shirt was soaked with blood, one of the *First Officer* epaulets had been ripped away. Blood splattered the table and an open aeronautical chart. Her head lay under the desk and out of the girl's sight. The bodiless face was a mask of terror, eyes wide with unspeakable terror, her mouth contorted in an unvoiced scream.

Maria hugged her sobbing daughter tightly and steered her down the hall away from the carnage. They moved quietly, their closeness a comfort to one another. The hallway was suddenly filled with the raucous chatter of the black Grackles and Maria knew the front door had been opened, her breath caught in her throat. She pushed Carmen against the wall and edged toward the end of the narrow hallway and the telephone. *If I could just …*

Footsteps of soft-soled boots whispered across the tile. Maria was near the end of the hallway, the reception desk was close, her back was tight against the wall and Carmen's hand crushed her own. She silently signaled a warning with a flash of her dark eyes. *BE QUIET AS A GHOST,* her expression screamed.

She inched toward the opening, the phone only a few paces away. *I can make it, maybe dial 9-1-1 before he reaches us. No, run for the hangar*! She turned … a hand grabbed her shoulder!

"Maria? Oh my God, are you alright?" Matt's eyes were wide; his face contorted in a mixture of fury and disbelief. He gripped the Beretta in his right hand, pointed to the floor. He pulled Maria to his chest. She flung herself into his arms and Carmen joined the protective embrace. Mother and daughter sobbed uncontrollably.

"Matt!" Maria cried, her voice muffled against his chest.

"Oh, Uncle Matt, I am so scared," Carmen's ferocious grip was not going to let go. They remained in the tight, comforting embrace for several long minutes until the sobbing subsided. Gently, Matt pushed them back, a hand on each of their shoulders; he looked down into large sad eyes and tried to speak, but rage overwhelmed him.

"Matt … Sarah …," Maria's voice cracked. She pointed weakly toward the hallway.

Matt slowly stepped away from mother and daughter and moved to the hallway window. He was not prepared for the grisly scene. *The sadistic jackass took the time to tie Sarah to a chair? He posed her for … me!* This was clearly a message from Hassam. He was saying *I have come for you, and everyone of yours!*

He turned to Maria. "Where's Uncle Billy?" he asked in a broken voice.

Fifty

Double M Ranch
The McWain Home
12 Miles West of
Edinburg, Texas

Felix Aguilar stood and stretched. He pulled the binoculars to his eyes and gazed down on the main road leading to the McWain ranch. He observed each of the four ambush sites where he had assigned his men, then resumed his seat on the large boulder.

Aguilar had earned his position as chief of security through years of faithful service to the McWains. He had grown up on the ranch, had worked for Elijah McWain III, Matt and Chase's grandfather, from the time he could sit a saddle. The hard outdoor life made him look older than his fifty-three years. His rough face was a network of laugh-lines and his tough bronze skin testified to years of toil in the hot Texas sun. His tall, lean frame was stooped, his legs bowed, but he was as strong today as if he were thirty years younger. His wavy hair was mostly gray, in need of a trim, much like his bushy mustache.

The McWain's Double M Ranch was the fourth largest in Texas, 523,000 non-contiguous acres of grassland, rocky mesas, cattle range, and oil wells. The largest parcel ran west to where the Rio Grande came down out of Starr County and south to the Mexican border. The smallest of three family-owned oil refineries was ten miles north of the main house, along with nearly half of their oil wells.

Aguilar sat on a knoll 300 yards from the sprawling three-story ranch house in the center of a 10-acre valley, surrounded by a scattering of smaller residential dwellings, stables, and storage barns. A grove of ancient cottonwood and mesquite trees intermingled with the buildings, concealing parts of the complex.

Aguilar's view of the main road was unobstructed from the ranch house complex, all the way to the entry gate off Farm Road 490, a major east-west route out of Edinburg. He had positioned four of his men at the gate, each with walkie-talkies. Between the gate and the main house were established ambush sites; two men in pickups at each, concealed in a thick copse of cottonwoods.

An urgent call from Uncle Billy had galvanized Felix Aguilar into action. He pulled in half of the twenty-man security force from the oil fields to guard the McWain home and residential complex. With Travis and Cory McWain away on business, Aguilar considered the protection of the McWain Empire his personal responsibility.

The security chief hiked his right ankle over his left knee and laid the black synthetic Winchester 300 Mag across his lap. He was good with the high-powered rifle, could tag coyotes at 500 yards on a dead run all day long.

The sun on his back warmed his old bones. A perfect spring morning. Aguilar smiled; satisfied with the life he had made for himself and Anita. His children and grandchildren all worked for the McWain's, too.

He smiled again and reached for his coffee thermos nestled in the rocks, and began to pour.

A massive arm encircled his neck, squeezed and jerked, snapping it in an instant. Aguilar died without making a sound

~~~~~~

Ahmad Hassam crouched behind the rock outcropping, Ali at his side. He pulled the binoculars from the dead security chief's body and surveyed the complex of buildings below, zeroing in on the large ranch house.

Hassam sneered. "It will make a glorious funeral pyre, right Ali?"

"Yes *yâ sayyid!"*

He gazed toward the entry gate, easily picking out several of the ambush sites.

He smiled inwardly. Premonition? Sixth sense? Something warned him that the path from the entry gate to the McWain home would be fraught with danger. He and Ali had stopped two miles from the gate and ditched their stolen car on a dirt road off County 490 that was marked by a dozen mail boxes tacked to a single weathered board nailed to a couple posts. They crossed the county highway on foot, slipped under the barbed wire fence, and followed a narrow drainage to the rocky knoll.

Hassam laid the binoculars down and picked up the Winchester. He sighted-in the ranch house and the big expanse of front lawn and then laid the cross-hairs of the Leupold scope on the front door.

He held the cross-hairs on the target for several seconds before easing his finger off the trigger. He swung the rifle to his left, using the high-powered scope to find an unguarded route to the ranch house. Satisfied that he had discovered a path covered by only one inattentive guard. Hassam propped the rifle against a boulder, and nodded for Ali to follow. Time was short. He could feel the presence of Matthew McWain bearing down. He would be ready.

~~~~~~~~

South Texas International Airport
Edinburg, Texas

Matt bolted out the door and sprinted across the parking ramp, pistol in hand, followed by the scolding cacophony of Boat-Tailed Grackles. The ANG pilot stood on a stepladder refueling his F-16D. The pilot closed the nozzle, jumped off the ladder, pulled his own pistol from his flight vest, and chased after Matt.

"Uncle Billy!" Matt shouted as he charged through the hangar past the twin-engine King Air in front of the open doors. "Uncle B—" Matt stopped short, his breath taken away. There, on the painted concrete floor directly behind the King Air, lay Uncle Billy, motionless. His shock of white hair was covered with blood and a growing pool encircled his head.

Matt dashed forward, sliding the last two feet on his knees. He dropped his pistol and cradled Uncle Billy's head in his lap, rocking back and forth, tears filled his eyes. With pistol still drawn, the F-16 pilot guardedly cleared the hangar.

"Uncle Billy, I am so sorry," Matt whispered, ignoring the blood soaking his flight suit.

"Uhhhh," Uncle Billy groaned. His eyes fluttered and he struggled in Matt's arms.

Matt yelled for the pilot to bring the first aid kit hanging above the workbench.

Blood oozed from a deep gash on the side of Uncle Billy's head. The old man clutched his ribs and groaned sharply as Matt helped him to sit up. Bracing his uncle against one knee, Matt did a quick survey for other wounds.

"Ohhhh!" Billy grimaced when Matt probed his ribcage. "That danged ... big galoot! ... Kicked ... like a ... mule!" Billy's breathing was ragged and he clutched his chest with folded arms, grimacing as he blinked back the pain. "Quit pushing ... on me ... you dimwit!"

"What happened?" Matt asked as he cinched the dressing tight to stop the bleeding.

"Mean lookin'... son of a ... camel jockey... shot me in ... the head ... after this giant SOB... knocked me ... to the ground ... and stomped on me!"

Matt glanced up at the F-16 pilot. "Get the tow-tractor and pull the King Air outside. Then I need your help getting the helicopter out."

"On it!" The pilot ran for the tractor parked on the other side of the large twin-engine. It appeared Uncle Billy may have been getting ready to tow the King Air out when he was jumped by Hassam.

Matt propped Uncle Billy in his sitting position and reached for the tow-bar lying on the floor several feet away. That's when he noticed that one end of the bar had been damaged by a bullet. Hassam's aim for Uncle Billy's head had been deflected by the bar, hence only a grazing wound.

"You are lucky to be alive, Uncle Billy," Matt said, showing him the damaged tow-bar.

"Just wait 'til I get my hands on that freakin' raghead," Uncle Billy mumbled, touching the bandage on his head.

The ANG pilot towed the King Air out on the ramp, then returned to help Matt pull the red, white, and blue Jet Ranger 206B-L4 helicopter out of the hangar. It was a newer version of the McWain Enterprises helicopter that Matt and Chase "borrowed" shortly after their first solos in a Cessna 172 over at McAllen International. The two youngsters brazenly told Uncle Billy, after he had caught them red-handed climbing out the rotorcraft, their eyes wide in fear—both from narrowly escaping death in their fathers' helicopter and from getting caught doing it— "Shoot fire, if you can fly one aircraft, you can fly 'em all!"

Matt checked on Uncle Billy again and found him struggling to his feet.

"You goin' after … that raggedy-headed pile … of camel dung?" Uncle Billy said on wobbly knees. His face was ashen, his body trembled. He coughed and blood spilled from his mouth.

"I am, Uncle Billy, but you need to lie back on the floor. Help will be here any minute." Sirens wailed in the distance.

"Nope! Goin' … with you … Help me up boy."

Matt shook his head. "You need to be in the hospital, Uncle Billy. I can do this without you."

"You junior-size … pissant … I'm goin'! … Now get me up … help me … into that chopper."

"You stubborn old coot." Matt grimaced at the ANG pilot as the two hoisted Uncle Billy up on his feet. The man stifled a cry and clutched his ribs tighter, but he was determined to make it out to the Jet Ranger.

"I'm going, too!" The ANG pilot proclaimed.

"Thanks man." Matt said with a mixture of sadness, trepidation, and anger boiling up inside.

~~~~~~~

"AJ, he's here! I'm at South Texas International. He killed two of my people and left. Pretty sure he is headin' for the Double M."

"Copy that, Matt. How can we help?"

"Close off the border so he can't escape again." Matt advanced the thrust lever on the Rolls-Royce turbo shaft engine and pulled on the collective. The Jet Ranger lifted gently off the ground. Matt continued to climb as they sped west down county highway 490.

"I'll take care of it," Georgia Shayne said. She was in base ops at Whiteman after delivering the precious cargo to Clayton. She now wished she was with the CRT team—or more importantly, with Matt McWain. *"We'll also set up surveillance at McAllen Miller International and the bus depot."*

"Thanks, Georgi. Break ... Dark Horse One, are you copying this?"

"Copied, Matt ... Who did he kill?" Chase's voice trembled.

"He got Scott and Sarah, Chase. Probably the security guard too. How far out are you?"

"Forty-eight minutes." Chase was pushing the Osprey hard as he dared. Master Chief Roberts sat in the copilot seat, puffed up like a bandy rooster.

"Okay, head straight for the ranch ... If I don't make it, you have to finish the job for me."

"Roger that! Leave me some of that raghead, y'all hear?

Fifty-One

Double M Ranch
The McWain Home

A lone sentry stood close to the side door at the ranch house, one foot on the ground, the other propped on the bench of a covered picnic table. An AR-15 assault rifle lay across his bended knee, a pouch of 30-round mags lay on the table. He wore Wrangler jeans, cowboy boots and a white tee-shirt. His wavy black hair was trimmed short and glistened from too much grease. He wore ear plugs attached to an IPod and tapped his foot to the beat of the music and scanned the front lawn through dark sunglasses.

The boyish features of the twenty-four year old Hispanic guard made him appear much younger. Hassam guessed he was not old enough to shave, certainly not old enough to have ever killed a man. A fact that would make his reaction time fatally slow.

Hassam and Ali slipped up from behind using trees as cover, slow and silent. The guard did not hear Hassam pull the large Persian sword from the scabbard lashed to Ali's back.

With the gripped sword in both hands, Hassam took a cautious look around the area before advancing the final three steps. The sword scythed through the air under Hassam's powerful swing. A shocked expression remained on the young man's face as his head tumbled across the lawn. A fountain of blood shot up from the stump on his shoulders; his lifeless body crumpled to the ground.

Hassam wiped the blade on the guard's clothes and returned it to its scabbard. He pulled the Makarov pistol from his shoulder holster and threaded the silencer in place. The two men slipped through the open side door into a wide, darkened utility porch containing a washer and dryer, three-foot shower stall, cabinets on each wall, and a long coat rack.

Another door separated the utility porch from a spacious, modern kitchen filled with stainless steel tables and cabinets; an assortment of pots and pans hung above the tables. Along one wall was a large commercial gas range with a hood coming down from the ceiling. A window over the kitchen sink overlooked the backyard and on the far wall were stainless steel doors to a pair of walk-in freezers.

Through an open door next to the freezers, Hassam saw a large walk-in pantry, its shelves stocked with gallon cans and large sacks of nonperishable foods. Surely the kitchen was capable of feeding an army. His anger flushed at the sight of yet another example of opulence from these infidels. People in his villages starved while these people ate like royalty.

Hassam spun around as a set of double interior doors swung open and a large Hispanic woman came through. She wore a white apron and was loudly humming a gospel tune. The grand smile on her face vanished and she stopped dead in her tracks, a scream caught in her throat.

Pffft! Pffft! Hassam double tapped the cook in the forehead. Blood and brains sprayed the white double doors. Her body dropped to the parquet floor like a sack of flour. The muffled shots echoed throughout the kitchen, but the suppressor contained the sound in the room.

Hassam stepped over the body and through the double doors into a huge dining room with a table longer than anything he had ever seen. Two dozen chairs lined the table and a glass chandelier the size of his stolen car hung above the center. Voices came from the room beyond.

~~~~~~~

The Air National Guard pilot sat in front with Matt; Uncle Billy sprawled across the rear seat. He held his arms tightly across his chest, clutching his ribs for relief. His face was a contorted mask of determination, rage, and pain. His McWain green eyes were dull. Matt twisted in his seat and offered a thin smile and a nod. "Doin' okay?"

Uncle Billy had managed to pull the headset over his ears. He offered a weak nod as if talking took too much effort. Finally he mumbled, "A good ... pilot ... would be there ... already." Foamy blood at his mouth told Matt the internal bleeding was bad.

"Quarterback, I have Texas Rangers and county sheriff units inbound to the ranch," Georgia Shayne's voice came through Matt's flight helmet. *"ETA front gate, ten minutes."*

"Copy that, Georgi. Thanks! Tell 'em to proceed to the ranch house ... Better give EMS a call." Matt closed his eyes when a horrible image flashed through his mind. "Have them respond an ambulance ... or two."

"Taken care of, Matt. How close are you?"

"Three minutes out."

"Matt! President Downs is with us on the net." AJ came on. Her trembling voice was comforting.

"Hello, sir," Matt said quietly as he gazed out at the familiar terrain below.

"Matt, I've been given your situation." The president sounded strained. *"I want you to know your family is in our prayers. There is nothing we can do to get help to you in time, but I have faith you will prevail. Godspeed, son!"*

"Thank you, sir!" He could not see the president nod his head or the grim look on his face.

~~~~~~~

Hassam walked into the great room , gun in hand, with all the confidence of someone who belonged there. His back was straight, shoulders squared, chin up in a display of arrogance. Ali stood at his side. The *whump-whump* sound of a helicopter could be heard in the distance.

The room was larger than most homes he had been in. Sunlight poured in from massive tall windows on two sides of the room, reflecting off light pastel walls. Wood trim matched the light oak floor largely covered with original Indian braided rugs.

The ceiling was at least 18 feet and numerous hangings artfully covered the walls. A large fireplace filled the wall next to where Hassam entered. A hand carved oak mantel spanned its width, above it hung a three foot portrait of Elijah J. McWain, adventurer, soldier, founder of the McWain Empire; Matt's great-great-great grandfather. On the other side of the entrance a grand staircase spiraled to the upper floors.

On the far wall a giant bookcase contained a collection of works by many famous early authors, as well as family journals passed down through the generations.

An open, oak-framed door next to the bookshelves led to a spacious office where the family patriarchs held occasional meetings and where all of the ranch business was conducted. A full-time receptionist held down the fort when Cory McWain—Chase's father— was away.

On the opposite side of the bookshelves an entryway led to the front foyer. The room was elegantly appointed with elegant furniture, including an antique hand-carved mahogany coffee table, a gift from Señor Samuel Cortez. Two dark hallways led from the great room to different areas in the house.

Three people were in the great room when Hassam and Ali entered. All three had their backs to the terrorists, all three were women. Two standing, one seated on an antique sofa near the center of the room. The elegant, tall slender woman in her 60's with long flowing blond hair streaked with gray appeared to Hassam to be the lady of the house as she seemed to be providing direction to the woman standing next to her.

The second woman was about the same age, a full head shorter and stocky. She had a radiant smile and her long salt and pepper hair was rolled in a bun. She was not dressed as elegantly. She was Maria's mother, the head housekeeper at the Double M. She was, in fact, receiving last minute direction from Matthew's mother, Eleanor Millicent McWain.

The regal woman on the couch reading a magazine and giving only cursory attention to the conversation was Chase's mother, Madeline Alice McWain. She was a year younger than Eleanor, though she looked ten years younger. Her close cut Auburn hair shined and her freckled face was without a single wrinkle. She was a petite woman who had raised three sons well over six feet. She didn't laugh much, but when she did it was a golden sound.

She was the first to see Hassam and the giant Ali enter from the dining room. A gasp escaped her lips and alerted the other women. Startled they turned. Maria's mother screamed when Hassam brandished the Makarov.

"You will not move," Hassam ordered with an evil sneer.

The receptionist entered at a run from her office. She stopped short at the sight, recovered quickly, then turned to run. Hassam leveled his pistol and fired. The nine millimeter round caught the woman in the right ear and knocked her sideways into the bookshelves. She fell to the floor.

All three women screamed. Madeline McWain jumped to her feet, clinched fists on her hips in defiance.

"How dare you—"

Pfffft! The round slammed into Madeline's leg just above the knee, shattering her femur. She crumpled to the floor in agony. Hassam did not want to kill the McWain women, yet. *Matthew McWain will watch them die.* The sound of the helicopter grew closer. *He is almost here. The fun is about to begin.*

"SILENCE!" Hassam yelled so loudly that the two women jumped back. Madeline writhed on the floor, crying, clutching her shattered leg to her chest. Hassam moved swiftly across the room. He spun Eleanor McWain around, held her tightly from behind, and pinned her arms against her sides. At the same time, Ali had seized Maria's mother, lifting her off the floor in a one-arm vise-like grip so tight she could hardly breathe.

"Just a few minutes longer, infidel woman," Hassam hissed in Eleanor's ear. His breath made her nauseous. She squirmed against his arms and dug her heels into his shins. He tightened his grasp until her breath rushed out and she stopped fighting.

Fifty-Two

Double M Ranch
The McWain Home

Matt set the Jet Ranger down on the helipad on the west side of the house. "You've got the back," he commanded the ANG pilot.

"Roger that!" The pilot leaped from the helicopter and dashed across the lawn toward the backdoor.

Matt twisted in his seat. "Uncle Billy, I want y—" He stared into cold, unseeing eyes. Matt gasped, his vision clouded, tears spilled down his cheeks. *Please God, no!* He pounded on the seatback and screamed in rage. Cold, calculating vengeance raced through his veins as he took a final glance at Uncle Billy's lifeless body. He drew in a deep breath and bolted out the door.

Matt ran hard as he could toward the front of the house, his Beretta pulled and ready. Seconds ticked away in his head, pushing him onward, faster, fearing what he would find inside. On approach to the farm at max cruise he had scanned the area for any sign that Hassam was there.

Everything appeared normal, but even so, alarm bells rang in his head. His sixth sense told him he was too late.

Texas Rangers, deputies ... even Chase with the entire CRT were all too far out.

It's all up to me, he realized. This was something he had carried in his heart and mind for more than six months. Ever since he came face to face with Ahmad Hassam in that burning warehouse in Guatemala, Matt somehow knew this moment would come, and he was ready.

He took the front porch steps two at a time and approached the tall, solid oak, double entry doors. Matt held the Beretta ready and pushed down on the door lever. He eased the door open with his foot, both hands gripping the pistol, muzzle down. He moved silently across the marble floor of the large anteroom and paused next to the entry into the great room, his back against the wall. Muffled cries from a woman sent a chill up his spine. His grip on the Beretta tightened, he took a deep breath and stepped into the entry, feet spread, his pistol aimed at a sight far more horrifying than his worst nightmare. He gasped.

Thirty feet away, standing behind a two-piece leather sofa, Ahmad Hassam shielded himself with Matt's mother. One hand covered her mouth and forced her head back at a severe angle. In his other hand he held a Karambit-style knife, the shiny curved blade pressed firmly against Eleanor's throat.

Eight feet to Hassam's right, Ali held Maria's mother in a bone crushing one-armed grasp. She hung limp in his grip appearing unconscious. With his free hand the huge bodyguard aimed a pistol at the center of Matt's chest. The small gun looked like a toy in the massive hand. His maniacal grin sent a shiver up Matt's spine.

On the floor several feet in front of the sofa, Chase's mother lay motionless in a growing pool of blood. Her chest rose and fell with shallow breaths, she was alive. The ranch secretary lying on the floor to his left was not so lucky.

Matt's blood boiled with rage. His eyes narrowed with a hatred more intense than he had ever felt in his life. He forced himself to calm. A mistake would cost the lives of people he dearly loved. He had brought this horror into their lives and it was up to him to resolve it without any more harm to them.

"It's me you want, Hassam. Turn them loose. We can settle this, one-on-one." Matt's eyes darted to Ali and then back to Hassam. He kept the bead of the front sight centered on Hassam's right eye. He was ninety percent sure he could put a round in Hassam's head, but he wasn't gambling his mother's life on the other ten. Her eyes were wide in fear as she stared back. Her head shook ever so slightly in Hassam's powerful grip, signaling him to not negotiate.

"Oh, yes, we are going to settle this," Hassam sneered. "But first you get to see them die. The only choice you have is whether they die swiftly … or I let Ali tear them apart, limb from limb." The madman's laughter roared.

"They've done nothing to you, Hassam. Please! I will lay my gun down if you let them go. You can do anything you want to me." Matt took a step forward.

"YOU DO NOT DICTATE TERMS, INFIDEL!" Hassam's voice boomed, reverberating off the walls. He pulled Eleanor's chin higher and pressed the curved ten inch double-edged blade to her skin. A rivulet of blood trickled down her throat, he muffled her scream with fingers so powerful they bruised her lips.

Matt knew time had run out. His finger tightened on the trigger and he uttered a silent prayer that his bullet would find its mark and that he would be able to turn and shoot the huge bodyguard before he crushed the life out of Maria's mother. He had practiced this kind of shooting scenario plenty of times, and he was almost always successful. Almost.

His pressure on the trigger increased … Then he caught a movement in the corner of his eye. A figure came from the shadows of the hallway behind Hassam. He eased up on the trigger, but kept his focus on the master terrorist.

"You don't have to do this, Hassam," Matt's voice was softer. He needed to calm the terrorists, keep their attention locked on him. His eyes were riveted on Hassam, fighting the urge not to look at whoever had entered the room. Any eye movement would telegraph an alarm to Hassam.

"Oh yes, American swine, I must do this. Everyone in this house will die before I am finished. You will be last." The person from the shadows moved closer.

Matt took another step forward. "An army of cops is only minutes away. If you leave now you might make it out of here … I'll fly you across the border myself, if you just let go of the women."

"Groveling becomes you, infidel," Hassam grunted a satanical laugh. "On your knees and beg."

"But—"

"NOW, OR I CUT YOUR MOTHER'S THROAT!"

The lone figure behind Hassam and Ali became clear, it was Grandma McWain. A tiny, frail woman of five feet, long gray hair to her waist, eye glasses thick as coke bottles. At eighty-three she was as full of fire and vinegar as she was when she married grandpa sixty-four years ago. She held a double-barrel 12 gauge. Matt had no doubt she would defend her family and home with every fiber of her being.

BOOM! The single deafening blast reverberated off the walls. Windows rattled and the floor shook. Ali staggered forward as a full load of buckshot caught him square in the back. An ordinary man would have been cut nearly in half, but the huge bodyguard was as thick as a tree trunk.

Ali grimaced and bellowed like a wounded bull. He dropped Maria's mother to the floor in a heap, turned, and took two steps toward Grandma McWain.

BOOM! The second blast rang out as she pumped the remaining barrel into the giant's midsection.

Ali stumbled back, bent at the waist. Then, unbelievably, he stood erect, looming over grandma like a giant grizzly. He staggered toward the defenseless woman, his arms outstretched as if to engulf her in a crushing bear hug.

Grandma McWain retreated several steps, took the shotgun by the barrel and raised it over her head like a ball bat. She stood defiantly against the giant, still advancing after receiving two fatal blows.

Ali was less than four feet from grandma when another figure appeared from the shadows of the hallway.

The Air National Guard pilot stepped into the room, his face was a mask of defiance. He brandished his Beretta service weapon with both hands, stepped between Grandma McWain and the enormous bodyguard, and blasted eight hollow-point rounds point blank, into Ali's chest. The huge man reeled with every hit and finally froze in his path, hovering as the gunshots echoed throughout the room. Like a huge oak tree, the bodyguard toppled forward, slowly at first, then gaining speed with rushing momentum.

The pilot attempted to step out of the way, but his feet tangled in a braided rug. The rug slid across the polished hardwood floor, dumping the pilot into grandma. Both fell to the floor. The fatally wounded bodyguard crashed on top of them in a twisted pile of humanity.

Through the melee, Matt failed to keep eye contact with Hassam, but now his attention was riveted on the master terrorist.

"Offer still goes, Hassam. Put the knife down, let my mother go, and I will kick your ass all over this house."

Hassam's dark eyes flashed fury and Matt found that taunting the egotistical terrorist worked better than begging.

"Or, I could slice her throat before killing you," the terrorist countered with an evil smile.

"Wouldn't work, Hassam." Matt moved forward another step. "I'll blow your freakin' head off before her body hits the ground. Then you know what I'm gonna do?"

He took another step. "I'm gonna sew your stinkin' carcass up in a pigs hide. Guaranteed to keep you from makin' it into your mythical paradise, you stupid sand rat."

With that Hassam roared in fury, forcefully casting Eleanor McWain to the side. She stumbled, clutched her throat, lost her footing, and fell to the floor in a heap. A quick glance confirmed she was alive.

Hassam made a show of removing the Makarov from his waistband. He placed the weapon on the table by the sofa and advanced menacingly toward Matt. His face was taunt, his lips thin in a vengeful smirk. He was going to enjoy gutting this troublesome infidel.

Fifty-Three

Double M Ranch

Matt laid his pistol on a lamp table and circled to his left, drawing Hassam away from his mother and Aunt Madeline. He pulled his matt-black Ka-Bar combat knife.

From the time he was seven years old, Matt had scuffled with the Hispanic boys on the ranch. For the most part it was all in fun, though sometimes tempers flared and a little blood was shed as the boys taught him to knife fight with realistic looking knives carved from a cottonwood and sharpened as best as they could. The game continued for years, Matt earned dozens of splinters and an accidental inch-deep stab wound in the gut, but he learned the art of street fighting well. *Hassam is probably better with a knife, but I'll show him how it's done, Texas style.*

The two men circled, looking for an opening to exploit their adversary's weak spot. They were boxed in by the grouping of sofas, chairs, and tables, but they were so intent on killing one another that the close confines offered no obstacle.

Hassam glared at Matt, taunting with a wicked, haunting grin. "I will enjoy spilling your guts on the floor and washing my hands in your blood."

"Fish or cut bait, raghead." Matt goaded the master terrorist, hoping to force the first move … and then he wished he had not.

Hassam feinted right, then slashed forward with blinding speed. Matt ducked and raised his left arm reflexively. The curved blade sliced his arm deeply between the hand and elbow. Matt grimaced with the searing pain.

Just as quickly, Hassam parried slicing from the opposite direction. The glistening blade missed Matt's face by less than an inch; he dropped to his knees. With Matt on the floor in front him, Hassam pulled his arms into a fighting stance and lashed out with his right foot. The kick slammed into Matt's head with enough force to drive him crashing backward onto the coffee table, smashing the antique into a dozen pieces.

Matt tried to shake off the blow as blood spilled into his eyes from a gash on his forehead. He back-pedaled away from a blurred image of the charging terrorist. Hassam raised the knife above his head, preparing to fall on Matt and deliver the death blow. Matt rolled away from the plunging blade and shakily scrambled to his feet. His left hand was numb, blood dripped all over his grandmother's favorite antique rug, and his head rang from Hassam's kick. A sick feeling filled the pit of his stomach. *If I let this joker win, people I love the most are gonna die!* The thought rekindled a surge of energy, driving him toward Hassam.

The terrorist saw renewed determination in Matt's eyes. Again he feinted to the right before lunging into the battle. But this time Matt was ready. He charged forward, dropped to one hip, and slid across the polished floor as if sliding into second base. His legs came up, catching

Hassam in a scissors lock. Matt twisted and rolled, throwing the terrorist off balance, slamming him face first onto the floor.

Matt rolled away and struggled to his feet. A burning sensation raked across his leg as Hassam lashed wildly and sliced through Matt's right calf. Warm blood splashed on Hassam's hand as the curved, razor-sharp blade cut deep into Matt's muscle.

Matt collapsed, his heart pounded, and he gasped for breath. The room grew fuzzy. A voice in the back of his mind screamed for him to get up. Matt dragged himself to his knees, the room spun, he collapsed, and rolled over on his back.

Hassam pulled in a deep victorious breath of air through his open mouth and relished the taste of his own blood spilling from his shattered nose. He shook his head, rushed forward, raised a foot high in the air, and brought it crashing down on Matt's chest.

Matt saw the assault coming, tightened his abdominal muscles, and turned just as Hassam's boot crashed into his ribs. He grunted and the air rushed from his lungs. It felt like someone had dropped an anvil on his chest. He opened his eyes to see Hassam rushing for a second attack, this time a well-aimed kick toward his head. Matt, nearly blinded from pain, pulled his elbows tight against his chest and rolled away from the brutal assault.

The terrorist planted his left foot and kicked with all he had. Matt attempted to roll clear and Hassam adjusted his aim in mid-stride. On the blood slick floor Hassam's planted foot slipped out from under him halfway through the kick. His heel clipped Matt's head as both feet flew up in the air. He crashed heavily on his back driving the air, from his lungs.

Both men lay on the floor, gasping for air, struggling to rise, fighting against searing pain. Both knew that failure to rise would mean death.

Matt gritted his teeth and rolled to his knees, his right leg was numb and he felt his strength ebb. *Please dear God, give me strength to save my family. Please Jesus!* He struggled to his feet, teetering back and forth, bent over at the waist, hands on his knees. Tears rolled down his face with each painful, ragged breath.

Matt slowly raised his head to face his enemy. Hassam was on his knees, struggling to stand, hatred spewed from dark eyes … Matt felt a new surge of adrenalin fueled by grit and determination. He lunged toward Hassam, momentarily surprised at the speed in which the terrorist responded with a backhanded knife swing.

Matt pushed off with his good leg, leaping above Hassam's arching blade in a full pirouette, and delivered a solid kick to the side of Hassam's head. The terrorist's jaw shattered. Hassam was driven across the floor two complete rolls before landing in a heap.

Hassam was dazed, staring back at Matt with glazed, disbelieving eyes. The terrorist was furious with himself for underestimating his opponent. He tried to shake off the blow before his enemy could charge again.

Matt landed squarely on both feet in a crouched position, out of breath, his chest on fire, legs wobbly. His left arm hung limp at his side, blood soaked the leg of his cargo pants and trickled down his head into his left eye. He realized he was nearly finished, exhausted. Only adrenalin kept him on his feet and that was rapidly dissipating. He could not withstand another onslaught from Hassam.

Matt flipped the Marine Corps Ka-Bar, catching the seven-inch blade between his thumb and knuckle of his index finger. He focused on the center of Hassam's chest, cocked his arm and threw the knife hard as he could, like pegging a baseball down to second base. End-over-end, the knife sailed straight and true.

Hassam, watched through half-focused, dazed eyes, but Matt moved with a blur. There was no time to escape the twirling object. The blade buried to the hilt, right where Matt had aimed.

Hassam grunted at the impact, stared down at the handle of Ka-Bar protruding from his chest, then back at Matt. His eyes closed and he rolled onto his back. Still and silent.

"Hey! Get this … stinking pile … of camel dung … off us!" The pilot's weak voice, strained from labored breathing, barely penetrated Matt's consciousness.

Matt dragged himself over to the pile of humanity lying on the floor. The pilot was mashed beneath the massive bodyguard and Grandma McWain's legs were pinned beneath the pilot. Neither was able to budge the dead hulk.

Matt knelt near his grandmother's head and gazed into her beautiful green eyes. Her face was pale, but she wore a welcoming smile.

"Hey there, Annie Oakley! You saved our lives," Matt said softly. He leaned forward and kissed her on the forehead.

"Uh, you wanna get … this tank … off me … I … can't breathe," the pilot gasped.

Matt could barely see the pilot's head beneath the hulking terrorist. He scooted around on the floor and put his feet on the wall. With his good hand, he grabbed the sword scabbard still strapped to Ali's back. He pushed with his good leg while pulling on the sword scabbard, straining with what little strength remained. He rolled the dead weight a few inches until he could see the pilot's eyes … Eyes that were wide, staring over Matt's shoulder, telegraphing fear.

Matt whirled around to see Hassam on his feet, staggering toward them. His left hand was on the Ka-Bar protruding from his chest. His right held the Makarov pistol, shakily pointed at Matt's head. His face was twisted in fury and hatred. Frothing blood oozed from his mouth. Even in death the master terrorist remained defiant.

Hassam raised his gun. Suddenly the air was shattered by twin echoing reports ... and Hassam's chest exploded in a pink cloud. The pistol fell from his grasp; he toppled forward, his face bounced on the hardwood floor with a bone-breaking thud.

Matt gazed across the room to see his mother, feet spread wide, his Beretta held in her outstretched two-handed grasp. Her face was pale. The front of her dress was stained with her own blood.

The familiar thrumming of the Osprey grew louder as it screamed in on approach. Matt's earbud came alive. Familiar voices were shouting ... then everything went black.

Epilogue

South Texas International Airport
Edinburg, Texas

Matt grimaced as he tried to prop his wounded leg on the desktop. His tight chest bandage did not allow much mobility and the pain brought tears to his eyes when he moved. He leaned back and let his mind drift and then swiveled his desk chair a few inches so he could gaze out on the flight line. It was a perfect spring day, cloudless skies, calm wind.

Weekend pilots worked the pattern, touching down to almost perfect landings, then taxiing back to takeoff and do it all over again. Saturday morning, and the locals were out for a little weekend relaxation. Watching them was a great catharsis for a sidelined flyer.

Absently, he folded his arms across his chest and grimaced again. Pain shot up his shoulder and took his breath away. He ignored the two powerful pain pills lying on the desk and took a long pull from the bottle of water Carmen had set beside the pills. The young girl did a good job playing nurse—if not a bit smothering.

Matt heard footsteps on the carpeted stairway and wished he had closed and locked his office door. He attempted an impatient sigh, but it hurt too bad.

"Knock, knock, anybody home?"

Matt glanced over his shoulder at the familiar voice. It was a painful stretch on his busted ribs, but when he saw his two visitors, he was not about to show any discomfort. He quickly covered the pain pills with a sheet of paper and offered a genuine Texas smile.

"Matthew McWain, what on earth do you think you're doing?" AJ stormed across the room wagging her finger. She was the perfect elixir for his aching body, a beautiful vision for tired eyes in tight black jeans tucked into red cowboy boots and a white long-sleeve silk blouse. Her long black pony tail bounced as she walked and her soft dark eyes belied the scorn in her voice. On her heels Georgia Shayne, perky as usual, smiled at AJ's rant.

AJ stood in front of Matt, feet spread, fists on her hips, glaring down as if she were a teacher correcting a misbehaving little boy.

"Cowboy boots?" He asked with a broad grin.

"When in Texas … Don't go changing the subject with me, mister." AJ's grin eroded her stern behavior. "Matt, it's only been two days, why did you leave the hospital?"

"Ever try restin' at a hospital? Ain't possible! Got all I need right here." Matt failed to admit that between Carmen bugging him every fifteen minutes and his mother calling several times a day it was nearly impossible to rest anywhere.

Georgia moved to AJ's side, arms folded across her chest, her smile friendlier than AJ's. Her black jeans matched AJ's and a bright yellow top complimented her brown eyes. She absently pushed her blond hair back behind her ears. "Think we ought to run his butt back to the hospital, AJ?" She asked jokingly.

"Serve him right," AJ responded.

"Okay, okay, cut the clowning. Manning didn't send you screwballs all the way down here just to harangue this poor defenseless aviator."

AJ was silent for a moment, her eyes began to water. She bent down and hugged Matt's neck. "Oh Matt, you had us worried, you big lug." She squeezed tighter until he yelped. "Sorry, sorry!" She stepped back.

"It's okay, I could get used to that." Matt drew in the sweet, faint fragrance of lilacs. He loved the way she smelled.

AJ smiled, then her eyes darkened in a frown. "Matt, we're sorry for your loss. We know Uncle Billy was very special to you."

"Thanks," Matt looked away for a moment, blinked his eyes, then turned back.

"So, how bad is it out there?"

AJ sat down in the upholstered chair across from Matt, reached out and placed a hand on his knee; Georgia pulled a chair to Matt's desk, plugged a thumb drive into his laptop, and began typing. He eyed her curiously, then turned back to AJ.

"President Downs and Carter figured you would be climbing the walls wondering what was going on, so they sent us on a little recon mission. You know how it works." AJ smiled.

Matt was more than ready to be briefed on the current situation. During his day and a half stay at the hospital he had been mostly sedated and with his family clustered around his bedside, he was unable to make sense of TV news. He quickly became bored with the same repetitive reporting after arriving at his office, so the TV was off and the earbud was piled on his desk. He knew Aunt Madeline and Maria's mother were making a full recovery at the hospital. His mother and grandma McWain had put their grief behind them and were busy restoring routine at the ranch.

He nodded for AJ to continue.

"Clayton and Louis discovered Rashad Hussain's little malware bugs had been planted in a number of military satellites and defense computers, in addition to the damage he's done to the nuclear power stations. The good news is they have isolated the virus and have assembled a joint team of analysts from Defense Intelligence, National Security Agency, and Nuclear Regulatory Commission to patch things back together."

Georgia rotated the computer monitor toward Matt and AJ. The screen displayed the familiar logo of the Office of Naval Intelligence. "This is a secure link," she said softly. A moment later Lt. Cmdr. Clayton Downs came in sharp and clear.

"Hey Quarterback! No offense, but you look worse than I feel," Clayton smiled.

"You haven't looked in mirror lately, pardner!" Clayton's eyes were bloodshot, sunken with dark circles underneath. Worry lines and exhaustion etched his pasty gray face.

Clayton ignored the remark, and cut straight to the point. "Pretty sure we have *Firestorm* contained. Radiation contamination is not as bad as initially predicted. Coolant pumps were re-engaged before meltdown at five of the affected nuclear plants. Diablo Canyon, Unit One, suffered the largest breach. The NEC estimates twenty-seven square miles inland from the coast may be affected. Mostly rugged, inaccessible foothills; no causalities expected there. Cleanup efforts are gearing up as we speak.

"Not so lucky at the Cooper plant in Nebraska and Nine Mile Point in New York.

"Spill releases were smaller in scope, but it's likely there will be some radiation poisoning, people and livestock. No estimates on numbers yet, could be significant.

"EPA suggests significant ground contamination at both locations, clean-up could take years, but everyone agrees it could have been much worse." Clayton leaned back, rubbed his face with both hands, and pulled in a large breath.

"Clayton, what about military software?" AJ asked.

"Dodged a bullet there, AJ. Rashad went after COMSATS over the continental U.S. Their initial objective was to blind our surveillance here at home so that their command and control would go undetected. We've not discovered a virus extending outside our borders, or in hardware beyond space platforms."

Matt shook his head and asked "What about the ground war?"

"Rashad's singing like a bird," Clayton grinned. "He was astounded we were able to figure out his password—"

"What's this *we* junk?" Louis Rogers yelled from beyond the screen.

"*Louis* figured out! Once Rashad realized we had shut him down, he started spilling his guts and begging for mercy. Gave up locations of safe houses and ammo caches. FBI has neutralized several caches and over a hundred suicide vests. Plenty more to go, but a good start.

"Larijani's playing the loyal jihadist all the way. Not saying a word. Feds hauled him away yesterday. Rashad's provided good intel on the next phase of their operation, including rendezvous points, so we get to keep him a while longer to glean every last bit of intel.

"You cut off the head of the snake, Matt." Clayton smiled again. "Now they are disorganized and disjointed. Suicide attacks are sporadic as if they are waiting for direction. I'm sending you a list on operations we have planned for the next few days.

"Your CRT is in Georgia, Linebacker has command until you return. Early this morning, Chase flew the team into the piney woods of Madison County. Local white supremacists, militia types discovered a large terrorist safe house and tried to take them on."

"The homegrown whackos are getting' into it just as we suspected," Matt commented.

The National Counterterrorism Center led an ongoing effort to track domestic terrorist groups and keep them under surveillance. Intelligence analysts had long predicted that a major catalyst could ignite them into a unified anti-government offensive.

"You got it, Matt. Except they bumped up against the wrong enemy and got themselves chewed up really bad. Ragheads escaped into dense woods pretty much unscathed. Your people are tracking them down as we speak."

Matt leaned back, frustrated and disappointed. He gripped the armrests so tightly that his knuckles whitened. He felt as if he had let his team down by not being with them. If it were humanly possible, he would rise up out of this cussed chair and march out the door.

AJ sensed Matt's emotion. She leaned forward and touched his arm. "They know, Matt. You would be there if you could. Just remember, we need you to heal as soon as possible. There will still be plenty of action when you are able to fight. We'll be digging out remnants of terrorist cells for a year or more."

It went unsaid, but all three were very aware that an even greater panic would soon grip the U.S. As the terrorist cells learned of their situation, they would go to ground. It could take days or weeks, maybe months, but they would reorganize, develop new plans ... and hit again.

Being sporadic and unpredictable worked to their benefit. Time was now on their side. No one could know or least suspect where or when the next attack would occur; when they might encounter a lone suicide bomber while shopping at the local mall or enjoying a family night out at the movies; or attacked by roving bands while exiting a sporting event, or worshipping in the safe haven of their own church.

~~~~~~~

Situation Room
White House,
Washington, DC

"Alright gentlemen, let's get down to business." President Harlan Downs glanced around the long table and stared into the exhausted faces of his crisis management team. Nearly all had worked nine straight days with minimal rest. Yet they pushed on, knowing that troops in the field working under extremely dangerous odds were putting in more hours than they were.

The large wall-mounted screen had gone blank after viewing Clayton's briefing. The president was relieved to see Matthew McWain was on the mend. His emotional state would be the next hurdle and the president was concerned. But for now there were more important things to worry about.

"Alex and Carter have assured us that the Islamic terrorist attack has been contained."

"Almost—"

"I know, I know, Alex!" The president waved dismissively. "You've couched it well, but suffice to say we now have the upper hand. So let's focus our attention on Iran."

They all nodded agreement, even Secretary of State Zachary Ringhold, which was a pleasant surprise to President Downs. Ringhold's dissenting views over military action were almost legendary. But the plain and simple fact was Iran had invaded the United States, forcing the U.S. into war. SecState had been lied to by the Iranian foreign minister and was seething with anger, as were they all.

"Admiral Turner," the president continued, his jaw firm as he looked to the end of the table. "You go first. Where do we stand?"

The four-star sat ramrod straight and cleared his throat. "Mr. President, we have one attack submarine on station in the Persian Gulf, two in the Gulf of Oman. There are four dozen Tomahawk cruise missiles between them targeting Iranian missile bases in *Shiraz, Bushehr, and Behbahan*. Intel has confirmed these sites are arsenals for chemical and biological warheads.

We're ninety percent certain the six nuclear warheads delivered to Iran from Russia are now at *Bushehr* ready to upload on Shahab 3 medium range ballistic missiles." This brought a collective gasp from the room. Everyone knew this could mean Israel was the target for nuclear annihilation.

"The USS *Abraham Lincoln* carrier strike group will be steaming into the Persian Gulf in three days with an aegis cruiser, two missile destroyers, and two frigates. Their mission is to take out the naval base at *Sartol,* the missile patrol boat base at *Bandar Ganaveh,* neutralize costal SAM and anti-aircraft batteries, and provide a combat air patrol for the strike group.

"The *Eisenhower* carrier strike group will be in the Gulf of Oman one week from today. They will be targeting *Bandar Abbas* naval base, *Semnan* missile base, the missile production facility at *Esfahan*, along with other air bases and fuel farms. Simultaneously, Air force B-2 Stealth Bombers will take out all of Iran's command and control bunkers.

"Operation *Wildfire* commences at 0130 local time, six days from now." The similarity in titles with the terrorist operation was not lost on the president.

"Six days?" President Downs asked. "Not any sooner?"

Congress was clamoring for action. The senate Committee on Intelligence knew Iran was behind the terrorist invasion and strongly urged the president to petition congress for a war declaration on the rogue nation. But President Downs had requested congress to hold off making a declaration until the initial strike package was in the air in order to give the pilots an element of surprise and increased survivability. Another six days would be asking an awful lot of patience from a legislative body whose constituents were demanding retribution. *Now!*

"Mr. President," Admiral Turner responded, "we do not want our actions to telegraph our intentions to the Iranians. Presently—"

"Presently, Mr. President," Alex Strayhorn, Director of National Intelligence interrupted, shooting the admiral a glance before turning to the president, "Iran does not suspect we know they sponsored this despicable act of war on the United States. If we can maintain that posture, the element of surprise is on our side."

"Exactly!" Admiral Turner resumed. "The *Eisenhower* Strike Group needs to appear as if they are merely coming onto station to relieve *Lincoln.* Won't fool the Iranians completely, but it might cause a moment of doubt. Perhaps long enough to launch the strike package."

President Downs nodded silently, then shifted his gaze to SecState. "Zach, where do we stand with our coalition partners? Are we in this thing alone?"

"Not at all, Mr. President. Our allies were appalled over the attacks. Some are bracing for similar attacks. Once they saw our evidence against Iran, they support a declaration of war and are compelled to join the fight. The UK, France, Canada, and Germany are making preparations as we speak. Of course, it will be several weeks before they mobilize assets into the area. The Saudis are reluctant, as always, but have agreed to allow us unlimited combat flights from their bases. I think later on we can count on their air force for combat patrols."

"That is good news." The president allowed himself a brief smile. "What about the Israelis?"

"Vindicated would be a good description. They want to lead the charge," Secretary Ringhold grinned. "Had to hold them back to wait for us."

Admiral Turner cleared his throat. "Mr. President, we are coordinating our attack with the Israeli Command Staff."

"How so?"

"Sir, they have demanded the lead on eliminating Iran's nuclear weapons program. We fully recognize the pressure the Israelis feel to rid themselves of the threat of annihilation and agree that this element of the attack belongs to them."

President Downs nodded agreement. No one had been fooled by Iran's ambiguous delays and blatant refusals to dismantle their nuclear weapon production facilities. He motioned Admiral Turner to continue.

"We'll provide them with combat air support from our carriers and U.S. Air Force squadrons out of Saudi, Kuwait, and Bahrain. The Israelis will be going in on the heels of one hundred and eighty-five Tomahawk missiles and B-2 strikes.

"It's a massive surgical strike, Mr. President. Designed to disable nearly all of Iran's military capability, while minimizing collateral damage, per your instruction."

The president was silent for a moment. He swiveled his chair to gaze at the large wall screen. The Situation Room was linked to the Joint Tactical Information Distribution System—JTIDS. The real-time image now on the screen was from the aegis cruiser USS *Bunker Hill* via satellite download.

The expanded overview of the Persian Gulf region not only included locations of all civilian and military ships and aircraft, but of the neighboring countries as well. President Downs allowed his mind to focus on the map of Iran. He stared at the image for nearly a full minute before turning back to the table.

His soft voice was hard as steel. "Gentlemen, it's time for payback."

From the Author:

Though I have previously acknowledged those whom I have been blessed by making this work possible, it is you, the reader that I want to thank most of all. You have taken time from your busy life to read this story, and hopefully, you have enjoyed the experience as much as I have in creating it. Without you, there would be no one to tell a beginning author to keep writing or stick to his day job. Without you, the telling of stories would be pointless and our imaginations would continue to build up inside us until we explode! I thank you for your time. If you liked it and wouldn't mind taking just a few more minutes, I would hope you would consider going online to the retailer where you purchased this book and leave a brief review. Reader reviews are the best way of telling a new author they're on the right track. I appreciate your positive reinforcement as I start to work my on next book. Thank you for your consideration.

Sincerely,
Carl A. Sparks